THE EXILE

SOLOMON CHURCH
BOOK 1

MORGAN GREENE

MERCURY BOOKS

Copyright © 2025 by Morgan Greene
All rights reserved.

No part of this book may be reproduced in any form or by any electronic or mechanical means, including information storage and retrieval systems, without written permission from the author, except for the use of brief quotations in a book review.

Book Cover Design by EbookLaunch.com

ALSO BY MORGAN GREENE

Solomon Church
The Exile
The Fury

Jamie Johansson
Bare Skin
Fresh Meat
Idle Hands
Angel Maker
Rising Tide
Old Blood
Death Chorus
Quiet Wolf
Ice Queen
Black Heart
The Last Light Of Day
The Mark Of The Dead
The Hiss Of The Snake

ALSO BY MORGAN GREENE

The Devil In The Dark
The First Snow Of Winter

Standalone Titles
Savage Ridge
A Place Called Hope
The Blood We Share
The Trade

THE EXILE

ONE

PRESENT DAY

Fire.

To live in fire is a sinful thing.

But we are not the good guys, after all, are we, Solomon?

The waves crashed against the stony shore, a din of white noise to drown out the shrill cries of the gulls wheeling overhead. On the dock, the bells on the trawlers rang gently, the water, rich with fish blood, slapping against the algae-covered stone.

The Southern Lass had just pulled in from her latest voyage. It was early, and she'd sailed through the night. Her crew disembarked, weary and heavy-footed, rubber waders squeaking.

Solomon Church looked up from his position behind the sturdy wooden table he'd built on the cobbled promenade, the blade of his knife pressed against the frayed line of fishing net he was rebuilding. He watched the men trudge towards him, heading for The Gallows, the only pub in Benalder. The place didn't need more than one; there were only about three hundred people living there.

The Southern Lass fished Atlantic Cod mostly, but crab, too. They'd keep another few hours in the coolers while the boys soused themselves. The captain was a different story, though. He stepped onto the dock last, heading for Church with a tired gait. He was in his sixties now, a strong man with a bristling grey moustache and deep-set eyes, the years of fishing the brutal North Sea catching up with him.

He was dragging a broken net behind him and wasted no time in tossing it at Church's feet.

Church tilted his head and looked down at it, scratching roughly at his unkempt, sandy-coloured beard.

'Needs fixin',' the captain growled. His name was Neville.

Church surveyed the thing with keen eyes. 'Looks like someone took a hacksaw to it.'

'Not far off,' Neville replied gruffly. 'Snagged a Porbeagle. Nearly took Pete's fecking arm off before we cut the thing loose.'

Church measured him. 'You don't seem too pleased that Pete kept his arm.'

'We lost three cod.' The reply was simple, curt.

Church sat back in his chair, pulling the knife through the net sharply. 'Last I heard, your license was for line-caught.'

'What are you, Defra?' Neville growled.

Church remained quiet.

'Just fix the fucking net. It's what you do, isn't it, John McCallister?' He all but spat the name. As though he thought he was privy to some secret.

He wasn't. He didn't know half of it. He knew exactly nothing, in fact.

Church turned the knife over in his hands before pressing the tip into the table until it stood upright. He pushed his chair back and stood, towering over Neville.

His hands were callused and strong, but aching all the same. On these cold mornings, it took a while for the sun to warm them through. He wrung them, massaging his knuckles as he stared down at the captain.

The man held fast for a few seconds, and then flinched, looking away. 'You do well not to cause trouble here,' Neville muttered under his breath. 'I know a man who's running from something when I see one.' He looked up at Church, eyes hard in pale light. 'Fix the fucking thing or don't. But don't pretend like you're something you're not.' He turned and began walking towards the pub and his men. 'And you ought to do a better job of hiding that ink if you want no one to see it. We're fishermen, John, not feckin' idiots.'

Church's hands stopped turning, his right moving to his left forearm, to the cuff of his long sleeve that was pushed above the wrists. He pulled the fabric down, covering the exposed tip of the dagger showing beneath it.

Neville reached the pub steps and climbed them tiredly, hunched forward, the picture of a man who'd been up all night.

Church stood there a few moments more, still in the morning air with nothing but the gentle clap of the waves against the dock wall and the gulls overhead to pierce the silence.

The morning sun climbed higher, burning away the thin fog that clung to the grassy dunes.

From his spot on the dock, Church had a clear view of the horseshoe-shaped harbour, the multi-coloured houses that lined its tiered streets. Benalder wrapped around the hill out towards the small headland where a lighthouse that had to be no more than thirty feet high perched. It was dark now, but would light up come nightfall, swinging lazily in circles, throwing shadows across the living room of his cottage as he lay awake, counting the revolutions.

The sound of a child's scream echoed and his head whipped around, his eyes homing on the source.

A young boy and girl ran in circles on the beach a hundred yards away. Church watched the boy, no older than eight or nine, chasing the girl with what looked like a strand of kelp. She shrieked, the terror in her voice making the back of his neck light up with gooseflesh. He became aware of his heartbeat, thumping hard and slow against the inside of his ribcage. And all at once, the weak autumn sun became a brutal ball of yellow fire, beating down with unrelenting force.

Church blinked and the ocean of slate before him became a wall of trees. The cobbled dock was orange dust.

His hands changed, his right suddenly around the stippled grip of his C8 Carbine, wrist crooked, index finger pressed against the muzzle in low ready position. The strap around his neck kept the rifle high on his chest with the stock against his shoulder. His left hand was under the barrel against the angled foregrip, the weapon tilted downwards and to the left so he could see clearly over the optic, giving him an unobstructed view of the area. It was a neutral position, not antagonistic, but close enough to the firing position that he could put a bullet into anything he wanted in less than half a second if it came to it.

Church watched as children laughed and howled, playing soccer with a red rubber ball in the distance. They ran barefoot, unphased by the forty-degree heat or the stench of cobalt and dynamite, the choking fog of dust that drifted through the air.

A hand appeared in front of his face, the fingernails dirty, poking from fingerless gloves with a Kevlar knuckle guard. They snapped twice in quick succession and Church looked up at the man they belonged to.

Captain Owen Cole was staring at him with that signature unhappy expression of his. He had a strong brow and heavy eyebrows, close-shaven dark hair, and a pointed chin.

'Hey—where are you?' he asked.

'Here,' Church answered, filling his lungs and resuming his line of sight to the compound gates.

'Stay frosty,' Cole commanded the men around him. 'I don't want this going sideways on us.'

Church swallowed, his mouth dry. A bead of sweat ran from under his helmet and down his temple, the heat of the African sun near unbearable on his back.

A heavy clap sounded and his rifle snapped to attention. But as he looked down, there was nothing in his hands. The orange dust was gone, the trees melted to slow-moving ocean, Benalder spread out in front of him once more.

He sucked in a breath like he'd been holding his for minutes.

'Sorry, John,' the man at his table said. 'Didn't mean to startle you.' The man was tall and edging up on seventy. He had long white hair sticking from under his flat cap. His name was Jules and he had a little skiff that he used to fish for crabs off the shore.

There was a broken, still-dipping pot on Church's table, but he'd not even heard Jules walk up.

'It's fine,' Church replied quickly, flexing his hands. They were tight, like he'd been clenching them.

'You looked miles away,' Jules said brightly. 'Something on your mind?'

Church just shook his head and pulled the pot towards him. It was barely holding together. They often got that way, smashed on rocks as they moved around the seabed with the current. Or if something hungry tried to get at what was inside. An easy fix, thankfully. One that would require his focus. One that would occupy his mind.

He lifted and turned it, surveying the damage. Something rattled inside, light and metallic.

Some silt dropped out onto the table.

Church shook the pot gently and an old pair of battered dog tags fell from between the soaked wooden slats, landing with a gentle plink. He reached out with a trembling hand and picked them up, weighing them in his palm.

In an instant, he was back there once more. The Kijani Delta. The DRC. The unrelenting sun. The gates ahead. The children playing in the distance, their laughter and shouts a flash of innocence in hell.

The shockwave came before the sound.

It hit Church in the side and punched the air from his lungs, threatening to burst his eardrums. He stumbled, along with the rest of the squad, and turned, throwing his hand up to protect himself from the blast. It roared through the jungle, sending a swarm of birds skywards, so loud it made his teeth vibrate in his skull.

Dust blasted through the trees in an orange tsunami, swallowing the football field and the children in a single, lightning-fast wave, their laughter extinguished in an instant.

'John?'

A hand touched Church's arm and he stood from his chair so quickly that he knocked it backwards, sending it clattering to the ground.

When he blinked, he had Jules' frail wrist in his grasp, bent at an awkward angle, his other hand curled into a fist, ready to lash out and destroy the old man in front of him.

Jules' face was one of horror and pain.

Church felt a flood of nausea, of sudden shame.

He lowered his hand, releasing Jules and stepping backwards. He stumbled over the upended chair, almost tripping, his mouth dry, the taste of blood and dust choking him.

'John...?' was all he heard, the voice shaking and frightened. But he didn't reply.

He just ran.

When he got to his cottage, he was breathless. A kilometre sprint. His heart pumped raggedly as he pushed through the unlocked door, throwing it closed behind him, and all but staggered to the upright post that supported the roof of the meagre building.

He collapsed against it, resting his sweat-slicked head against his forearm.

Church forced himself to breathe, chest tight, eyes screwed shut, and counted. Box breathed. Just like they taught him. Steady yourself. Feel yourself. Control yourself.

His heart began to slow and he opened his eyes, staring down in the gloom at his still-clenched left fist, the sharp corners of the dog tag digging into the flesh of his palm.

He turned it upwards, willing his fingers to uncurl.

But when they did, the only thing staring back at him was the silt in the lines of his hand and a rusted bottle cap.

His mouth formed a quivering smile, wry as it was.

Slowly, he turned his hand over, letting the cap fall to the weathered floorboards.

It bounced, then disappeared between them, swallowed by the darkness of the crawl space below.

He stood upright, eyes lifting to the photograph hanging just above eye-level on the post. There were sixteen of them in that troop. All clad in their ops gear, camo, rifles resting in the crooks of their elbows. Some were grinning, others were serious. There was nothing happy about that day. They'd taken it in Helmand Province. Now, it was just another faded memory of a life Church was doing all he could to forget.

He still knew all their names, though. Always would. Murphy. Foster. Reed. Mitchell. Norton. Boyd... and Cole, their captain, of course. In the middle. He was the one with the shit-eating grin. Toughest son of a bitch Church had ever known. Coldest, too.

Anger rose in him as quickly as it always did when he stared at the photo too long. His right arm wound up and then lashed out.

The cottage shuddered, then settled, and when Church pulled his hand back, the indent of his knuckles remained in the wooden post. Imprinted there from repeated blows. Same spot. Every time.

He looked at it for a moment, knowing he'd lived this moment a thousand times over the last ten years, but unable to recall any single one of them clearly.

Church rattled off another box breath and looked at the photo. 'Murphy. Foster. Reed. Mitchell. Norton. Boyd… Cole.' The last one stuck in his teeth.

He swallowed the bile rising in his throat and turned, walking back across the room, the trick floorboards halfway to the door creaking as he stepped on them. He barely thought about what was hidden beneath, but never forgot.

Church never forgot anything.

He pulled the door wide then, blinded by the high sun, and started down the overgrown path, down onto the dunes, down onto the stony shore.

There he stopped, staring out into the unforgiving sea. It roiled, dark and endless. Cold and terrible.

His hands went to the hem of his woollen sweater and dragged it upwards over his scarred body.

He let it fall to the ground next to him, and with his eyes fixed on the ocean, pulled off his boots.

Church let the cold wind numb his skin. He let the sharp stones dig into his feet.

He shed his trousers next, peeling away layers until he was fully exposed.

He stood there like that for a second or two more, letting the fear creep in. Letting the weight of the water and the earth settle on his shoulders.

The first step was always the hardest, but after that, he picked up speed, running faster and faster and faster until he cried out, the frigid water crashing around his knees, drowning out his voice.

He charged forward until the waves fought back, and then he raked in a final breath, closed his eyes, and plunged beneath the surface.

TWO

TEN YEARS AGO

LAND CRUISERS. It was always Toyota Land Cruisers.

He'd sat in the back of dozens of the things, jostling and bouncing down roads that weren't really roads in countries that didn't really feel like countries. Places where law, and order, and society seemed to have fallen by the wayside, replaced by bullet holes and blackened craters, by dictators and death. Though maybe he just had a one-sided view of things. They didn't really call on the SAS unless things had gone utterly to shit.

But of all the places he'd been, he thought he liked the DRC the least. The Middle East was hot, but Jesus, he'd never experienced heat like this. It was thick and choking, the air wet in his lungs. He'd been damp for days now, since the moment he'd stepped off the plane.

And now here they were, chugging through the

jungle towards a town called Maroua, which just so happened to sit next to one of the richest cobalt deposits in the whole damn country. And where there was cobalt, there was money, and in a place like this, where there was money, there was someone willing to do whatever it took to exploit it.

General Kwame Zawadi was like any self-appointed dictator. Brutal and charming. But his mines outside Maroua were hauling more cobalt out of the earth than the next ten combined, and there were even rumblings of lithium deposits discovered nearby, too. Which sort of half explained why Church was staring at the back of Sir Walter Blackthorn's balding head.

Blackthorn was a business magnate-entrepreneur-philanthropist and was being pegged for a political run sometime in the future. For now, he was pouring money into renewables and battery tech, set for the big shift to EV that everyone was talking about. And for batteries, you need cobalt and lithium. It was true that Her Majesty's forces didn't take interest in private business matters, but talks of Zawadi's war crimes had been flying around for a while, and seeing as Zawadi was only interested in selling to the highest bidder—China, if the UK didn't up their offer—that made the powers that be very nervous. It was—what did Cole call it?—a confluence of factors that let us ram the barrels of our C8s right up Zawadi's shit-crusted arsehole.

Church smirked to himself thinking about it.

He'd been part of missions to oust dictators before.

This wasn't new. But posing as a private security force accompanying Sir Walter Blackthorn deep into enemy territory to buy a king's ransom in slave-mined mineral, right into the den of a guy that had surrounded himself with an army of killers—that was new.

'Two clicks,' Cole called from the driver's seat of the Land Cruiser, turning his head to announce to the vehicle.

He was up front, with Murphy next to him.

Church was behind Blackthorn, who was parked in the second row next to Boyd. And sitting next to him was Anastasia Fletcher, Blackthorn's assistant, riding in the third row. Back of the bus. Church glanced down at her hands in her lap, kneading at her thighs. She was in a pair of olive-green cargo pants, a white shirt with the sleeves rolled up. Her dark hair was loosely pinned back, and her sharp, pale features were flushed with the heat of the jungle.

Church's hands were draped steadily over the stock of his rifle, muzzle in the thin and worn carpet between his boots.

He watched Fletcher continue to dry her palms as best she could, but her jigging knee told him it wasn't just the heat making her sweat.

He closed his eyes and rested his head against the seatback, listening to his heart beat slowly. 'Just breathe,' he said quietly, so only she would hear.

'Pardon?' she replied, her southern English accent pretty clear even over the rattle and squeak of the SUV.

'Just breathe,' he repeated. 'You need to be calm around Zawadi's guys, or they'll eat you alive.'

'I'm perfectly fine.' The words were barbed. 'Why don't you just focus on your job and let me do mine.' She tutted to herself, looking at his rifle. 'And try not to shoot anyone while you're at it.'

Church opened one eye, watching her turn and look out the window. 'You'll be glad I've got it if it comes to it.'

She scoffed this time.

Not a fan of guns, Church gathered. That'd change quickly if shit hit the fan, though. There wasn't anything worse in the world than being shot at and not being able to shoot back.

Still, he wasn't looking for a fight. Their mandate here was pretty clear—gather intel, gather evidence of Zawadi's crimes, report back. Wait for the green light. Take Zawadi out. Quiet and clean. And make sure Blackthorn wasn't caught in the crossfire.

There was no mention of Fletcher, however.

Though he thought telling her that wouldn't ease her nerves, so he just closed his eye again and waited for them to arrive.

The Land Cruiser rolled to a halt at Zawadi's gate, the whole car rocking before it settled. They were six in total, the SUV riding low on its heavy springs, laden with bodies and luggage. Church leaned forward to get a look at the situation, the solid steel gate in front of them an impenetrable barrier. No way to see what, or who, was on the other side. He couldn't help but feel like they were sitting extremely pretty if someone wanted to ambush them here.

Walls stretched away on either side, twelve feet tall and solid concrete, with razor-wire spun along the top. Standard fare for a dictator's stronghold.

A single CCTV camera was positioned on the post next to the gate, staring down at their vehicle.

Blackthorn shifted uncomfortably in his seat. Church could see the pulse doing double-time in his neck, a sheen of sweat forming above the collar of his linen shirt.

Fletcher's breath had audibly quickened next to him.

He had to admit, this was always the worst part. Because if he was going to take someone out, this is when he'd do it. While they were stopped. Sitting ducks, as it were. Just roll that gate open. Firing squad. Bang. They'd all be mincemeat before they could even get the vehicle into reverse.

Church set his jaw, moving his right hand to the grip of his rifle.

Fletcher watched him, eyes widening slightly.

He didn't look at her, didn't dare take his own eyes off the gate.

It lurched a little and then began sliding sideways. Church settled into the chair, tensing, ready to throw himself down behind the seats in front if he needed to.

But it wasn't gunfire that greeted them.

Two men stood there. They were tall, one bald and

the other with short black hair. They were wearing military fatigues and brightly coloured shirts. One had what looked like a Hawaiian button-up hanging open, and the other was in a red vest. At least the AK-47s in their hands matched.

Two of Zawadi's men. They stared out at the Land Cruiser for a moment or two and then stepped aside, waving them through.

Cole put the Land Cruiser into gear and eased forward slowly. The two men watched them come, and Church stared back, locking eyes with red vest man as they rolled past, deeper into the lion's den.

On the way in, they'd chugged past a host of run-down villages, no more than tin shacks and hand-sawn lumber to hold them up. Even Maroua itself, though a town of nearly fifty thousand, was still poverty-stricken, the roads unpaved, the electrical system a mess of wires and offshoots crisscrossing above the streets.

And yet, General Kwame Zawadi's compound was the picture of opulence and wealth.

Inside the gate, the road changed to stone chips. Lining it was perfectly a manicured lawn. A grossly large stone fountain bloomed from the grass, spitting crystal-clear water into the air while outside the gates, there probably wasn't a toilet that flushed for a hundred miles in any direction.

The driveway led to an open space in front of the white stone mansion. A row of cars was parked there—a Ferrari, a McLaren, a pair of Porsches, one 911 and the other a big hulking SUV. And a Mercedes G-Wagon that was splattered with mud. A two-hundred-grand runaround for any excursions outside the compound. Hell, the Ferrari and McLaren must have come in on the back of trucks. There's no way they'd be able to drive the roads. So what good were they other than just a way to spend his money?

Church didn't stare too long. There was a lot to take in. The building was huge, all glass and sharp angles. A brutish, brutalist construction for a brutal brute of a man.

And speaking of which… As they approached the cars and came to a halt, the man himself appeared on his terrace above them like an emperor come to survey his kingdom.

He spread his arms wide, and though he was safe inside his walls, and acting a king, he was still dressed in full military gear. Full combat uniform with jungle camo, chest adorned with medals, star-studded epaulets jutting from his shoulders, and a black beret denoting his rank. As though he'd let anyone forget.

He stood there above Church and the others, waiting for them to disembark so he could presumably welcome them fully.

Blackthorn reached for the door handle, keen not to keep the General waiting, but Boyd's hand shot out and grabbed his other arm, stilling him.

Boyd was a big guy with a square head. He wasn't much for words, but his face said plenty—don't fuck with me.

Blackthorn didn't.

Cole spoke calmly, his smile visible to Church in the rear-view. 'Okay, so we're clear: we're private security working for Blackthorn. Stonewall—that's the company's name. Everyone got it?'

Silence meant confirmation.

'Our exfil word is "dandelion". Say that, and we're out in under two mikes. Everyone ready?'

More silence.

'Alright. Blackthorn, your lead.'

'It's *Sir* Blackthorn,' Blackthorn reminded him, his voice as tough as a man like him could muster. A man whose body was the consistency of a piece of white bread.

'Apologies, Sir Blackthorn,' Cole said, meeting his eye in the mirror. 'You go. We'll stay.'

Walter Blackthorn's mouth opened, but no sound came out. He glanced out of the window at the group of armed soldiers forming up outside the Land Cruiser, then back at Cole.

'That's what I thought,' Cole said, turning his head now. 'We're not here to babysit you. So don't get shot, and don't fuck up my mission.'

Blackthorn swallowed and straightened, electing not to answer.

'What a charmer,' Anastasia Fletcher muttered under her breath.

Church restrained a smile. Cole was not a "people person," but he could blow the eye out of a field mouse at a hundred yards with his C8, would take a bullet for any of the men in his troop, and would sling a sixteen-stone man across his shoulders without a thought and march twenty-five clicks through the Kuhi Baba mountains to an evac chopper even if it meant crushing two vertebrae in his spine. And Church knew he could because he'd seen him do the last two first-hand. The first was a claim Cole made himself, but Church had seen him shoot, and he didn't doubt it.

Blackthorn seemed a little more tentative to exit now, but he knew better than to keep a man like Zawadi waiting, so after a moment, he opened the door and stepped from the vehicle and into the African sun. He took a pair of Ray-Bans from his top pocket and slipped them on as everyone else got out.

They were in neutral grey tac gear; ballistic vests, cargo pants, peaked caps, and sunglasses. No forces insignia except for what was inked on their skin. But any private security firm worth their salt were ex-forces. They'd have no problem selling that.

Church exited a moment after Blackthorn, covering his back while Murphy got out of the front seat, wiry and weathered, his short mousy hair sticking up at odd angles like he'd just pulled his head from a pillow, and protected him from the front.

Zawadi wasted no time in leaning on his balcony rail and yelling down. He grinned widely, waving them up. 'Mister Blackthorn!' he called. 'So good of you to come. Welcome, welcome!'

Cole rounded the back of the SUV, escorting Fletcher to the group, and pulled up just behind Church.

'Doesn't he know it's *Sir* Blackthorn? Maybe Walter should correct him,' he whispered.

Church smiled just a little.

Fletcher turned from her position in front of them and fired them both an icy glance.

Cole couldn't have given less of a shit.

He surveyed the guys at their flanks. The "soldiers." Armed but unseasoned. Half of them were visibly drunk, the other half visibly untrained.

If it came to it, they could probably be dispensed with. But even untrained soldiers got a lucky shot off now and then. And it had to be ten-to-one odds here. Thirty or forty guys milling around inside and out, protecting their feared leader.

'General Zawadi,' Blackthorn called back, 'We appreciate your hospitality. You must excuse my security here. Inside your walls, I'm sure there is absolute safety, but outside…'

'Yes, yes,' the general boomed dismissively. 'Maroua is a dangerous place. But now is not the time to discuss such matters. You have travelled a long way, and you must be thirsty. Come, come,' he said, beckoning them towards the stairs, 'we have prepared a feast for you.'

'Well, you're never too wealthy to turn down a free dinner,' Blackthorn laughed, clapping his hands. He was seemingly at ease now that he felt in good company with someone equally as deluded of their own importance.

Church thought they both must be doing a shit-load

of yoga to be capable of being that far up their own arses. But he said nothing. Instead, he just followed, walking with the group as they mounted the stairs towards Zawadi's mansion, the awaiting feast, and whatever bloody truths all this wealth was hiding.

Because one thing was certain. In a place like this, for one man to live this well…

A lot of people had to die.

THREE

PRESENT DAY

He swam until his lungs burned, the freezing waters and pulling currents enough to cleanse the dust from his skin and the heat from his back.

His head broke the surface, and he raked in a sharp breath, his feet finding the stone of the sea floor, the waves spitting him from the ocean and back onto the beach.

He staggered, tired and panting, from the water and regained himself, shivering in the wind.

Church walked slowly, drained of his energy and his anger, towards his clothes, and gathered them up, making the long trek back towards his cottage. He could have brought a towel, a blanket, something, but the air on his bare skin brought a good kind of pain. The kind he deserved, the kind he needed to keep him straight.

Life shouldn't be good, it shouldn't be easy. Not for a man like him. He didn't deserve that.

He'd spent too many years trudging through hot places in body armour, carrying packs and weapons. It was good to be cold. Good to be away from those places. Where the ghosts still lingered.

Benalder was almost far enough away that they couldn't find him.

The warmth of his cottage embraced him. It was one room except for the little bathroom at the back. A simple kitchenette, a wood-fired stove and small sofa, a bed at the back. A desk with a bookcase over it. He didn't need more. Didn't want more.

The wood-fired stove was always burning now, his only source of heat as the summer wound into winter. He approached, picking up a few pieces of split log and tossing them in, blowing on the embers to ignite them.

His fingers tingled as he held them to the growing flames, the droplets of seawater on his skin evaporating as he put them to the heat.

He rose then, flicking on the water-heater attached to the burner. It would take about thirty minutes to heat enough for a decent shower.

Until then, he could only wait.

He went to the desk and opened his laptop, tapping the keyboard. The screen came to life, and he logged in. He didn't expect any mail or contact. After all, only three people in the world knew he was alive, let alone what his email was. But just in case… You could never be too careful, and though he did all he could to shut the outside world out for good, if someone did find out he was still walking around... Well, they wouldn't be happy about it.

There was a little notification icon next to his news app, and he clicked it. New for search term "Walter Blackthorn."

Church pulled the chair out and sat, the wood tough against his naked bottom. But he didn't notice, his eyes already scanning the news article.

Sir Walter Blackthorn strikes new deal on mining rights in the Kijani Delta, DRC: Workers promised better working conditions and improved pay.

Church's lip turned down. 'You've got to be kidding me,' he muttered, clicking the link to expand the article. He read quickly. Blackthorn had made a successful run for MP in the last few years. A self-funded campaign that made almost no dent in his bottom line. But why would it, when he had a chokehold on the richest lithium and cobalt deposits in the Kijani Delta? He'd been working children to death for close to the last decade in those mines, and now he was being heralded as some benevolent fuck for improving working conditions there?

Gearing up for a run at Downing Street, no doubt.

Being in bed with China and having a fat Californian tech mogul's cock in your mouth didn't seem to matter to voters these days. That was one of his main platforms —improved foreign relations. Church tsked. No surprise considering Blackthorn was the main channel for their EV dreams, and they could stay clean, not touching the DRC directly. What they gave in return beyond money, Church didn't know, but Blackthorn was far from stupid. He always got his pound of flesh. And if he became Prime Minister… Hell. Church couldn't fathom. But a fucking orangutan in a wig would be better.

His mouth began to salivate then; the urge to drink, to drink it all away, seized him.

He swallowed the saliva filling his mouth.

Once, twice.

Breathe.

No good.

He got up, knowing there was nothing in the house. He'd been down that road, several times. It never led anywhere good.

Instead, he headed for the bathroom and the shower —the hot water be damned.

The desire to drink had died away somewhat, but the cold water had done little to warm him or his mood.

He dressed quickly, thankful that the room was small and the fire large. He crossed to the laptop, ready to shut it and while away the rest of his life in ignorance. But before he could, he noticed something else.

New email.

His hand hovered above the keys.

He was on no social media platforms, was signed up to no newsletters. He didn't have his name on any bills or bank accounts. His job was cash in hand, and the electricity for the place was paid for by the landlord. He was a digital spectre. So unless this was a mistaken address—it had happened before—it could only mean one thing.

He clicked the message, opening and reading.

Dear John,

It was wonderful to catch up. It has been too long. Thank you for your tip about the banana peels in the flower beds, it worked great—the roses are in full bloom.

Yours,
  Agnes

Only one word came out of Church's mouth. 'Fuck.'

He hung his head for a moment, drawing a slow breath. And then he looked up, reading the message again. *The roses are in full bloom.*

The Blackthorn article couldn't have been a coincidence. And there was no mistaking who this email was from or what it meant.

Church steeled himself and pushed back from the table, wasting no time as he walked across the room to the same trick floorboards he stepped over every day.

But this time, he paused and knelt down, digging his nails into the gap between the boards. He pulled, and it came up without any fuss. He didn't bother with the second board, instead reaching down into the darkness, laying his hand on the duffel bag lying there on the dirt below.

He hauled it up, sending the second unsecured board spinning, and dumped it in front of his knees.

Church remained there, dirtied hands on the thighs of his jeans, staring at the bag, willing it to just dissolve into nothing. Maybe this was a dream? Just a bad dream. And he'd wake up in his bed at any moment. Or maybe he was still in the ocean, drowning, and this was his greatest fear materialising before his eyes. The death throes of an oxygen-starved mind.

No, he didn't suppose he was that lucky.

And there was no time to waste.

The roses were in full bloom, after all.

He unzipped the thing roughly and pulled the seams apart, the contents clean and well-packed, just how he'd left them a year ago when he arrived in Benalder. He wasn't so careless as to stay in the same place for too long. That would breed familiarity, curiosity, questions from the people there. A year or so in each place was enough.

He'd been careful.

It seemed like he was the only one.

Church pulled the sat-phone out first and made sure that the USB stick was still taped to the back. It was.

For a moment, he hoped that would be enough. But he knew it wouldn't.

He pulled the ballistic vest out next, laying it on the floor next to him, and then reached for the zip-locked sandwich bag that had been underneath it. The familiar smell of grease and steel was almost pleasant. A smell that he'd both missed and hoped never to smell again. But now wasn't the time to lament.

He pulled the Glock 17 semi-automatic pistol free of the bag and ejected the magazine. Still loaded. He pressed on the round at the top of the magazine with his thumb, making sure it bounced correctly, that the spring was still good.

He pulled the slide back a few times on the weapon then. Good action. Crisp.

As it should be. He'd cleaned them before they'd gone in. And did so every time he moved.

The gun would shoot.

But he prayed it wouldn't come to that.

Still, he slipped it into the back of his jeans, dropped the hem of his shirt over it, and closed the bag, putting it back in the hole. He replaced the boards, picked up the ballistic vest and sat-phone, and stood.

He took one last look around, wondering if he'd ever see the place again. And then he grabbed his keys off the hook on the side of the post in the middle of the room, took a final glance at the picture hanging in front of him, raised his middle finger to it, and headed out the door and into the gathering darkness.

Church didn't really have anything in the world that he took pride in or cared about other than his Land Rover Defender 110. He'd picked it up as a rusted heap of junk in his second year of exile and spent nearly four years restoring it. Slowly, carefully, to eat up his time. He did everything he could and more to the vehicle. Until it was perfect. And it still didn't take long enough.

Though it meant getting behind the wheel was never a chore. Not until tonight, at least.

He wasn't sure he'd ever wanted to make a drive less in his life.

Church threw the ballistic vest onto the passenger seat and, checking his surroundings—empty, because, who was he kidding, this was Benalder after sundown. The only thing moving out here was sheep—he pulled his Glock from his waistband and slotted it into the holster he'd affixed to the side of the driver's seat. Easily within reach while driving, but hidden from view of anyone looking in the windows.

He flexed his hands around the wheel a few times, drew a slow breath, steadying his heart, which he told himself was only racing because he'd been kneeling for a while before he got up and he'd moved to the Defender too quickly. But he knew that was a lie.

So instead, he just ignored it, cranked the key in the ignition, and began trundling over the uneven, sandy grass behind the cottage and up towards the road some three hundred yards away.

When he reached it, it was worse. The tarmac was smooth, which meant that the rattle and squeak of the cab was no more. And his heart was louder than ever.

The drive to the nearest town was an hour. There were closer villages, but none that had an internet café. Weirdly, they were pretty uncommon these days. Once they all died out, he wasn't sure what he'd do. But that was a bridge to cross when the time came. He hoped he wouldn't be running for the rest of his life.

The streets were quiet when he arrived, pulling in on a side street about twenty metres down from the place. There was space right outside, but also a CCTV camera over the door, and he didn't need his Defender or its fake plate getting documented if he could help it.

Church slipped from the car with unusual nimbleness for a man of his stature and skirted the wall. He'd grabbed the hooded jacket he kept in the truck and thrown it on, hood up to hide his face from the other camera in the street—they really were everywhere these days—and slipped beneath the one above the door, heading inside.

He could feel the weight of the sat-phone in his pocket as he headed to the counter. It was four pounds for an hour. He'd only need five minutes. But he put a fiver down anyway and told the eighteen-year-old behind the counter that his internet was down at home due to a billing dispute with BT and he just needed to hop on Skype with his sister in Australia real quick.

The lie was unnecessary, but it did the trick, making the kid's eyes glaze over by the third word. He'd not remember Church if asked about him later. But a big guy like that coming in and saying nothing? That was out of the ordinary. Memorable.

Church proceeded to computer number six, having asked for it so he could be at least a few seats from the forty-year-old man playing Minecraft on computer number one.

It came to life as he approached, the little timer in the corner beginning its countdown.

Church settled into the chair and glanced at Minecraft man. He had headphones on, a pretty fierce double chin, and glasses like jam jars. His attention was on the game.

The kid behind the counter was scrolling Instagram or something. It didn't matter to Church, so long as he was occupied.

No time to waste.

Church pulled the sat-phone out and then took out a pair of headphones from the other pocket, along with a USB cable. He peeled the flash drive from the back of the phone and inserted it into the computer. While the program started running, he plugged the headphones into the phone and inserted one of the buds into his ear, leaving the other free to the room.

The program on the USB installed itself and opened a window. It was a basic encryption re-router that, once connected to the phone, would allow him to make a call via the internet. It would be impossible to trace, even if someone was looking for them, which, if the roses were in full bloom, might well be the case.

Church slotted the cable into the phone and the computer and waited for them to connect. Then, he dialled the only number he had saved.

It crackled a little as the program loaded the VPN and re-routed the call through a dozen countries. And then it rang.

Almost immediately, it was picked up.

'Church.' There was relief in his voice.

'Mitch,' Church replied, speaking quietly, one eye on jam jars. 'What's wrong?'

There was silence for a moment. Something had to be wrong. That was the only reason they had for reaching out to each other. That's what they agreed. Total silence unless one knew of imminent danger to the other.

'It's Foster,' Mitchell said. 'He's... he's gone. Fucked.'

Church was quiet for a moment. Foster was a good man, a brother in arms. One of the only ones to get out of Maroua alive. Mitch was the other. It was just the three of them.

Harry 'Mitch' Mitchell had always been level-headed, pragmatic. He was a planner, not a risk-taker. He always had to be in control, in the driver's seat. So if something had him worried, then Church knew it was serious.

'How?' was Church's reply.

'He… he reached out. A few days ago. Asked about Blackthorn.'

Church listened carefully.

'You know he's running for PM, right?'

'Mmm.'

'Foster… he wanted to do something about it. Wouldn't let it lie.'

Church let out a little breath, preparing himself for what came next. 'What did he do, Mitch?'

There was quiet for a moment, and then Mitch said the words that Church hoped he'd never hear again.

'It's Maroua, Church. He… he went back.'

FOUR

TEN YEARS AGO

They walked up the steps towards Zawadi's mansion, Blackthorn leading with Cole and Murphy at his flanks. The royally knighted prick kept his eyes forward while Cole and Murph eyed Zawadi's guards standing sentry at the top with their hands around the AKs.

Boyd and Church brought up the rear, shielding Fletcher and watching their flanks.

The mansion was elevated, seemingly standing on ten feet of solid concrete. But Church was under no illusions that the base was anything other than a blast-proof bunker. Zawadi stood on heads to get where he was, and when wealth came to a place like Maroua, there were those who were always hungry to take the crown. When it came to defending the place, he wanted a hole he could crawl into. And no doubt he'd scuttle straight there when the bullets started flying.

Church made a note of that. And to look for anything resembling a reinforced door leading to a stairwell. When they came for Zawadi, they'd need to know the layout of the place inside and out.

As they climbed, he became aware of Fletcher's ragged breathing, her hands clenched at her sides. Seemed like she was nervous, after all. But who wouldn't be?

Surrounded by guys with guns, wearing no Kevlar? It wasn't surprising.

Ahead, Blackthorn reached the top of the staircase and entered Zawadi's house. The outside was whitewashed and plain. Quickly constructed by builders with little experience building anything this big or ostentatious. It was basically a big white cube of poured concrete. But Church knew inside would be different.

And he was right.

They stepped through the huge wooden doors, antique and solid, and into the main foyer. It was grand, with a chintzy chandelier hanging overhead, terrible abstract artwork on the walls, and a huge rug guiding people through an archway guarded by two white marble statuettes. Beyond, there was another large room whose only purpose was to display Zawadi's wealth and bad taste in interior decoration and art.

Here, a large staircase led to the upper floors. From the gallery landing, a group of women peered down. They were young, slim, and heavily made-up. They looked utterly miserable. But if you were strapped in a place like this and your only purpose was to sexually service a dictator that enslaved and exploited your friends and family, you would be too. Still, it had to be better than being in the mine. Didn't it?

Church pulled his eyes from the women and homed in on Zawadi himself, who was now walking in from the terrace he'd greeted them from. In the time it'd taken for them to come inside, he'd lit a fat cigar. No doubt he'd brag to Blackthorn where it was from.

'Mister Blackthorn,' Zawadi called. He extended a hand, accompanying it with a jolly smile. 'Thank you for coming.'

'My pleasure, General,' Blackthorn beamed. You could practically see the shit between his teeth. 'And, I hope you don't mind me saying, but it's Sir Blackthorn. I didn't meet the Queen for nothing!' he laughed. He was the only one.

Cole restrained a smirk, glancing back at Church.

'Of course, of course, Sir,' Zawadi said, adopting a playful bow. 'You're good enough to address me by my correct station, the least I can do is the same. As you imagine, we don't get many "Sirs" in Maroua.' Zawadi laughed now, long and loud. His voice was deep and bellowing, filling his concrete palace. He pulled the cigar from his mouth then and looked at it. 'Cuban— hand-rolled and flown in especially. Could a humble soldier tempt Sir Blackthorn?'

Right on cue. Church let out a soft sigh. And the self-professed humility to go with it? This guy was the whole package.

'You can do more than tempt me! But only if there's

some decent Scotch for seconds.' Blackthorn laughed again.

Jesus, these guys were funny—a couple of true-blue comedians. Church just hoped there wasn't a mirror around, or they might have to give Blackthorn and his new buddy Zawadi a few minutes alone to pleasure themselves.

After more back-clapping and circle-jerking, Blackthorn was handed a cigar and promptly began sucking on it like it was Zawadi's tit. And then they headed through the room and another set of doors into the dining area. More chandeliers. An oversized table to sit twenty with just three places set at the far end. Shock.

Zawadi went to the head and Blackthorn sat at his right, with Fletcher reluctantly taking the seat on his left.

The general seemed to notice her then. A woman in his presence. Fletcher's features were fine if not sullen at that moment. She was wearing no makeup, her hair scraped back to limit her femininity and draw as little attention to herself as possible. Even her shirt was buttoned up tighter than Blackthorn's. She had an athletic build and was doing what she could to hide her pale skin, but despite all that, his eyes still licked her up and down. Slowly, and without mercy.

She seemed to suppress a shudder but didn't look at Zawadi. Instead, she kept her eyes on the shining silver plate in front of her.

There was no food yet, but with a clap of his hands, a fleet of women in half-open white shirts appeared and threw down mountains of food. At the centre of it looked to be the leg of a roasted pig, along with both British and local offerings, including lots of prettily arranged fruit.

Church's mouth began to salivate, but he knew that there was no chance of any of it coming their way.

And as though reading his mind, Zawadi, elbows on the table and cigar between his teeth, looked up at their troop with unveiled disgust. 'I didn't spend two hundred thousand British pounds decorating this room just to sit and stare at your security team, Sir Blackthorn.'

Blackthorn paled a few shades, feeling the money teat being dragged from his lips.

He turned to Church and the others, lined up at the foot of the table, and shooed them away with his hands. 'Make yourselves scarce. We don't want to look at you.'

Cole's lips twisted into a wry smile, but he didn't bite back. Instead, he just gave a slow salute. 'Yes, Sir,' he said dryly before motioning the others to split up.

Standing in the background was hardly new territory, so they slipped into the spaces between statues lining the walls.

Church took up a position behind Fletcher, keen to overhear whatever Zawadi was going to say, and it seemed Cole was of the same mind, standing opposite him, behind Blackthorn.

And there they stood while everyone stuffed their faces and drank, the air thick with cigar smoke and hot air. And not the kind that was blowing in through the windows.

The conversation circled lazily as both men told tales of their various conquests, business and otherwise. After nearly an hour of it, Fletcher pushed her chair back, having just picked at her food, and excused herself.

Cole lifted his chin at Church to go with her.

How he'd been saddled with being her guardian, he wasn't sure. It had been luck that had him sitting next to her in the Land Cruiser, and now he was stuck with her, it seemed.

Though Church knew it wasn't to protect her. It was to protect the mission. Stop her doing something to jeopardise it, stop her getting into trouble.

Still, the conversation seemed to show no sign of heading in the direction that Cole or Church needed it to, and there was little hope of sneaking off for a recce while they were dining. So at least this would give Church a chance to see some of the house.

And Fletcher probably did need a chaperone. The men under Zawadi's command were the meanest, sickest fucks in Maroua. They had to be to work for a guy like him. So, a woman, walking alone through the house? Church doubted they'd think twice about it.

He followed Fletcher out of the dining room and through another archway into a corridor.

As he reached it, he saw one of Zawadi's men, a mid-twenties guy, short, wearing a Juventus football club jersey with the arms cut off. His arms were sinewed and wrapped around the tarnished body of an AK. But cleaned and oiled or not, those things were workhorses, and Church had no doubt it would fire without issue or much encouragement.

The guard was already walking towards Fletcher by the time Church appeared and seemed to pay him no mind.

'Hey, woman,' the guard called, his English rough.

Fletcher slowed with a sigh.

'Where you going?'

'Bathroom. That alright?' Fletcher asked, her voice barbed.

The guy grinned with gapped teeth.

'You want some help?'

Church didn't need to see Fletcher's face to know her expression.

'No,' she said flatly. 'Now, if you please.' But as she opened the door, his hand shot out, slapping against the wood, shunting it closed.

Fletcher pulled back a step, realising how close the guy was, and how quickly he'd gotten there. And perhaps how alone she was and how very far from England.

She only managed a step backwards, though, before she bumped into Church's chest.

He felt her body freeze up and heard the sharp intake of air, thinking the worst: there were two of them.

She whipped around, and seeing Church, looked at the ground and took the opportunity to zip around him and back towards the dining room. She'd hold it, it seemed.

The guy with his hand on the door let it slide down

the wood, leaving a smear on the polished surface. Church could smell the booze coming off him, could see the glaze in his eyes, the slow, laboured rise and fall of his shoulders.

This guy was used to being drunk and lecherous, no doubt. Probably the reason Zawadi's girls looked so unhappy. Though Church doubted they were 'available' to the likes of this guy.

He sized Church up, and despite seeing that the man in front of him was probably eight inches taller than he was, still decided to try his luck.

Unfortunate choice. More unfortunate that Church was on his best behaviour. Can't go pissing off the General you came to assassinate on the first day.

And yet, turning his back wasn't really an option.

Church drew in a slow breath as the man walked towards him, one eye slowly closing.

He leaned sideways, looking around Church, presumably at Anastasia Fletcher's bottom as she made her way back to the dining room, and then back at Church. 'That your woman?' he asked, voice practically slurring.

Church had his right hand around the grip of his C8, hanging off his neck. His other was holding loosely onto the barrel. 'She's not yours,' he said easily.

The guy's grin widened. 'We see, huh?'

'Suppose we will.' Often, when Church felt threatened, his brain sort of fizzed—adrenaline dumping into his veins, ready to react. He wasn't getting that now.

He lifted his chin towards the door that the guy had

been guarding, the one next to the bathroom. The kind that looked heavy. The kind with a keypad lock. Perhaps the kind that led to a reinforced basement. 'What's in there?'

The guy turned slowly, looked at it, then chuckled. 'Nothing that concerns you, *big man.*' He spat the last words, as though Church's stature was a sore spot for him.

Clearly, it was a sore spot for Zawadi's man—the Juventus fan wearing what looked like a boy's medium.

Church just let a slow smile spread across his face. 'We'll see, huh?' he said, parroting his own words back to him.

The guy didn't find that funny, and his grin began to fade. 'What you want here, hmm? You want to start something?'

Church sighed. 'Not today. But if it comes to it, come find me, hmm?'

The grin returned. 'I will. And then I find your woman.'

Church looked back at the door with the keypad. 'Run along now, before I tell Daddy you abandoned your post to harass his guests. He might not find it as funny as you do.'

The guard tried to hold his smile, but the threat of Zawadi's wrath was enough to shake him. Which told Church a lot—about these soldiers, their loyalties, and the man himself.

The General.

No sooner had the guy turned away than Church was already striding back towards the dining room.

He slowed a little, not seeing Fletcher through the doorway and back at the table. Another bathroom? No, she wouldn't make that mistake again.

He saw her then, her slim figure outlined through the flowing chiffon drapes in front of the open terrace doors, billowing softly as a breeze blew in across Zawadi's papal terrace. She was hunched over the rail, staring out at the jungle beyond the compound walls. At Maroua, rippling in the distance through the afternoon heat haze. And at the mine.

He could hear it as he stepped out onto the terrace with her. The clunk and roar of machinery, the call of distant voices. The yellowed ridge of exposed stone just visible through the treetops. A mountain of quarried earth. And a column of orange dust drifting into the cloudless sky.

Church didn't need to clear his throat to announce his arrival. Fletcher spoke even as he stepped into the sun, knowing it was him without turning around.

'It's going to be like this, isn't it?' she asked, her voice tired. 'Never another moment to myself. Never a moment to…'

'Let your guard down?' He stopped a few steps behind her, surveying the grounds, the number of guards, their paths and movements. Their capabilities. 'No. Not until you're on a plane home with your belt buckled.'

Fletcher scoffed a little. 'You're just going to be

following me around from now on, then? Every time I need the bathroom? Every time I want to be alone? There's going to be no escaping you, is there?'

'This is a dangerous place.'

She shook her head now. 'No. Fucking. Shit.'

'It's not about limiting your liberties,' Church answered. He'd been close protection before. He knew the reaction. But that didn't mean he wasn't bored by it. 'It's about keeping you safe.'

'Of course it is.'

'You knew what this place was when you agreed to come,' Church said.

'I did.'

'So why did you come? Blackthorn twist your arm?'

She glanced up at him coldly. 'That's *Sir* Blackthorn.'

'Right.' He measured her for a moment, wondering if she was serious in that reminder, or if that was some sort of snipe at her employer. She didn't seem the type to want to subjugate herself—or subject herself, for that matter—to a guy like him.

'No, he didn't twist my arm,' Fletcher said then, pushing up from the rail, pausing for just a moment to meet Church's dark, slate-grey eyes.

'So what then?'

She stared at him. 'I asked to come.'

And then she stepped past him and headed back towards the dining room.

He watched her go for a second and then followed her.

By the time they got back to the feast, Blackthorn and Zawadi were on their feet, standing in front of the huge window at the far end of the room. They were shaking hands.

Church slowed next to Cole, watching the scene. 'What's going on?'

Cole drew a slow breath, his keen eyes weighing the two men at the window. 'They made a deal,' he said, his voice lowered.

'A good one?'

'Not for the people who live here,' Cole said. 'Come on, we're heading out. Going to be a long day tomorrow. Blackthorn just asked for a full tour of the mining op.'

'Sounds fun.'

'No doubt.' He looked at Fletcher then, who'd sat back in her chair, seemingly disinterested in the man whose title she'd just defended. 'Any trouble with her?'

Church's eyes narrowed a little as he watched her. His mouth opened to answer, but then he stopped. Because honestly, he didn't know what to make of the woman, her allegiances, or her intentions.

FIVE

PRESENT DAY

Church sat there in silence, all the possibilities running through his head at once.

'He went back?' he whispered. He had no doubt that he'd heard right, but he had to check. Had to make sure that he hadn't just had an aneurysm, that he'd heard right. 'Why the fuck would he do that?'

Church knew why. He knew exactly why. He'd lain awake a thousand nights thinking about it himself. Imagining, planning. Every detail. Every moment. Every trigger pull.

'When he found out Blackthorn was going for PM, he became obsessed. He showed up at my house, Sol,' Mitch said. 'At my fucking *house*. Blind drunk. On a tear. Asking me to go back, begging. Saying we needed to get in there, that Zawadi would have everything we needed to make sure Blackthorn never saw the light of day again, let alone made it into office. He was talking about righting wrongs and… Fuck.'

'What is it?' Church asked, scanning the room, suddenly on high alert.

'I turned him away,' Mitch said bitterly. 'I told him to go home, to forget about it. There's nothing we could do. We're dead men. He was better off leaving it lie. But…'

'He couldn't.' Church let out a sobering breath. He'd been there. The drink. The darkness. The stranglehold of guilt that coiled around your throat in the night, that woke you up, drenched you in a cold sweat, playing all the worst moments of your life on repeat behind your eyes in the darkness.

The DRC followed him everywhere. He could still taste the dust if he thought about it. Still see the faces of those kids, picture their bodies caked in dirt and cobalt. He shook his head, trying to get the pictures out.

'He called me five days ago, said he was going. Gave me one last chance to go with him, do the right thing.' Mitch's voice was strained. 'I refused, but I've been tracking his phone, watching him the whole way.'

Church waited for the hammer to fall.

'He made it there. All the way to Maroua, Zawadi's compound. He did it right. Made laps at night, did his recon. And then he went inside, quick and quiet, an hour before dawn. But…'

'He never made it out.'

'All of a sudden he just stopped. And then a few minutes later, the signal went dead. Which means…'

'Foster is dead,' Church muttered. 'Caught and killed.'

'Hope so,' Mitch added, practically spitting it.

Church drew a difficult breath. He knew exactly what Mitch meant. If he'd been caught out there, death was by far the best fate he could hope for. To be taken alive, inside Zawadi's compound? He couldn't imagine the pain, the suffering they'd put him through just for the hell of it. They'd take fingers, toes, testicles, just to watch him squirm.

He'd seen the things people could do for their own amusement. He'd been boots on the ground in Iraq, Afghanistan, had seen what the Taliban did to the interpreters, the sympathisers they found. What they did to their wives, their children.

He'd seen people strung up in the street for sport, like piñatas. He'd come across bodies nailed to walls and eviscerated. He'd seen bodies so badly beaten and maimed he wasn't sure at first they were even human.

But inflicting pain for their own pleasure wasn't exclusive to the Middle East. No, he'd been in Sierra Leone, Somalia, Kenya. People knew how to be evil everywhere. And a lone gunman assaulting Zawadi's compound?

Church had met those men, dealt with those men. He knew that the best thing Foster could hope for was to bleed out before they could save him.

Church never thought it'd come to it, but in that moment, he hoped more than anything else that his friend, his brother, was dead.

'We have to consider the possibility, though…' Mitch began slowly, tentatively, 'that he's not. That he's still alive. That they managed to capture him. And that if they did—'

'Foster wouldn't break,' Church said.

'Sol…'

'He wouldn't,' Church insisted, keeping his voice as even as possible.

Mitch was silent for a moment. 'Are you saying that because you really believe it? Or because you know what happens if you're wrong?'

Church shifted in his chair, his heart beating harder. God, he hated Mitch for being so fucking right all the time. The thought of what would happen if Foster did break was terrifying.

Not just because he could tell them that both Church and Mitchell were still alive—no, Church cared little for his own life. But the reality of it was that if the truth came out, then it would make its way to Blackthorn, and he'd stop at nothing to ensure that they never breathed a word of what they knew to anyone ever again.

He wouldn't come for them, though. Not directly. He'd force them into the light the only way cowards knew how.

'It's time, Church,' Mitchell said. 'It's time to go to them.'

'Not unless I know I have to,' Church replied, the words barely making it past his lips. 'They think I'm dead.'

'You have to,' Mitch said. 'Before he gets to them.'

Church watched his hands curl into fists on the desktop, feeling the blood rush in them.

'What do I say?'

'It won't matter what you say,' Mitch replied gravely. 'If you're too late to say it.'

SIX

TEN YEARS AGO

The entire country was a sweatbox.

Africa in the summer was the hottest place Church had ever been. He'd worked across the north of the continent, but it was a dry heat. This was something else entirely.

The hotel they were posted up at was passable. They'd booked the entire place out and paid extra for the staff to all take the week off. No one to see them come and go, no one to notice their patterns or ask questions, no one in their rooms when they weren't there. Necessary for an op like this. It hadn't taken much to persuade the owner. He was glad for the extra money, and for the time away, too.

There was one street in Maroua that was paved. There were a couple of shops, a run-down bar and restaurant, and their hotel. It was the only one in town, and it didn't even have a star rating. The rooms were spartan but good enough. So long as they didn't have bed bugs and the toilets flushed, it was more than anyone on the team was used to.

Church and Cole had done a sweep to make sure the rooms were clean before Blackthorn and Fletcher went in, both of them unabashedly aghast at the standard of living. He hid a smile as Fletcher gasped when her door opened. Church had slept in way worse places.

These rooms even had AC, loud and asthmatic as it was. But it was a double-edged sword. The unit rattled all night long, drowning him in cool, Legionnaires-laced air, which, while not wholly pleasant, made him forget what it was like outside.

So stepping from the room and into the heat was like plunging into a hot bath, even though it was barely eight in the morning.

They crammed into the Land Cruiser in the same formation as before, heading for Zawadi's mine and their VIP tour of the place. Cole and Murphy were up front, Boyd was in the middle row next to Blackthorn, and Fletcher was in the back with Church.

This time, they were rolling in force, though, with a second Land Cruiser running vanguard. It hammered through the jungle ahead of them, Mitchell driving, Foster next to him. Reed and Norton in the middle row, with their kit all in the back.

Eight was a good number. Strong and fast. All of them experienced, battle-hardened. From the outside, they were just a few, but Church knew together they were formidable—could take out a force ten times their size. Force multiplication. That's what they called it.

They'd been bigger, smaller. Had run full squadron ops and singleton missions. But when he was shoulder to shoulder with the guys, he felt better.

Still, there was something wrong about this place. Everywhere they went there was always a sense of creeping death following them. But he couldn't quite put his finger on this one. Like the whole place was holding its breath, ready for the rug pull.

Church could feel the sweat running down his neck and under his collar. He was in a long-sleeve compression shirt, but his ballistic vest was heavy and quickly soaking up all the moisture pouring from his skin.

The vehicle jostled on the rutted road, and Fletcher bounced to his right, closing her eyes suddenly, brow furrowing as though in pain.

Church looked over at her, noting the flushed cheeks, the long, steadied breath, the little tremble of her lips.

'Make sure you drink plenty of water today,' he said, quiet enough that no one else would hear. He lifted the steel bottle he'd brought from between his heels and offered it to her. 'You sweat more than you think.'

'Excuse me?' Fletcher replied, barbed as ever.

Church leaned in a little closer, pushing the bottle into her lap. 'The hangover's going to get worse, not better. Dehydration and vodka is a bad mix.'

'I'm not…' she began before trailing off. They hit another bump, and no doubt a bolt of pain shot through her head. She took the bottle roughly and drank from it before offering it back.

Church held his hand up. 'You need it more than I do.' He eyed her as she took another draught. 'Want to talk about why you decided to raid the minibar last night?'

'Isn't it obvious?' she scoffed under her breath.

Church stuck out his bottom lip and looked forward. 'It is,' he replied. 'But regret's not a good reason to make bad decisions. Trust me.'

She looked like she wanted to say something snarky but elected not to. Instead, it felt like a glimmer of honesty showed through.

'I was just having a bad day.'

He thought of the man that had confronted her at Zawadi's house. Then, of what she said. That she wanted to come. She'd not elaborated, and Church hadn't, couldn't have, pried further.

'I get it,' he said. 'But you've got to be sharp out here. We've got our mandate,' he said, knowing he shouldn't say more. 'And it's mission first, Blackthorn second.' He turned his head to look at her, dropping to a whisper. 'But it doesn't say anything about you.'

He stared at her until that sunk in.

Her lips twisted downward at the corners. 'So you're just going to leave me on the side of the road if it comes to it.' She tsked and shook her head. 'Good to know.'

'I won't do that if I can help it,' he said slowly. 'But you need to know where you are on the totem pole. You need to do everything you can to help yourself out here.

And getting shit-faced on night one because one of Zawadi's guys looked at you funny isn't the right call.'

'You don't know anything,' she muttered, turning to look out of the window.

'Maybe not,' Church replied. 'But I've seen hasty decision-making cost lives. More than you could imagine.'

She kept her eyes out of the window, but he knew she was listening.

'Be smarter,' he warned her. 'There'll be no second chances out here.'

They drove on in silence, rattling and bouncing their way through the trees until they gave way to ruthlessly hacked stumps. The din and roar of the jungle was replaced by the clank and rumble of heavy machinery, the call of birds supplanted by the shouts of men. And the thick, wet jungle air became a sudden haze of yellow dust.

The convoy rolled to a stop at the gate to the mining operation. Ahead, Church could see that a hillside had been strip-mined. Hundreds of locals swarmed across it wearing shorts and T-shirts. Men, women, kids, too. They were passing buckets of rocks along lines, digging at faces with pickaxes, sorting and separating material with their bare hands while Zawadi's men stood by with their automatic rifles, drinking from their hip flasks while their neighbours slaved away under their boot heels.

A blockade had been set up on the road, the whole place ringed by a battered chain-link fence. It didn't look unclimbable, but it wasn't designed to keep the workers trapped inside. It was meant to allow bullets through it, and to make sure that the workers could see anyone trying to escape getting shot in the back. It was so they could see their bodies cooking in the sun. That's why the trees had been hacked down fifty metres back from the fence.

Church wondered how many tried anyway. And how many bodies had been dragged into the treeline or buried in shallow graves since Zawadi announced they were coming for the tour. Ten, fifty? Maroua had ten thousand people. How many of them would die here before he was stopped?

Cole shifted in his chair up front, unholstering his pistol and holding it to the side of his chair. Church couldn't see it, but he knew the movement well enough, could tell Cole had done it by the way he'd moved.

Church reached down and clicked the safety latch off his own holster, and Fletcher tensed next to him.

Two of Zawadi's men walked around the swinging arm barrier and the concrete blocks that formed the gateposts, and split up. One went to Mitch's window in the front vehicle, and the other took a lap of the convoy, hands on his AK, eyes checking the Land Cruisers over. What he was looking for, Church didn't think he even knew.

He was just throwing his weight around, trying to intimidate. It's what these guys did. They ruled and policed and got their way through fear. They were terrorists by the most black-and-white definition of the word.

Church would have happily put them down right here like the dogs they were, liberated the miners without losing a second's sleep. But all that would do was start a war they weren't ready to fight yet. And tomorrow, when Zawadi's army had rolled over them like a storm of shit, the mine would re-open, and everyone would go back to work.

No, for all the crimes being committed here too, Church could only stand by and watch. Live to fight another day. Live long enough to cut the head from the snake when the time came.

The first soldier seemed to like what Mitch was saying and turned away to raise the barrier just as the second soldier reached the rear window and locked eyes with Church. He stood motionless as the car pulled forward, neither of them flinching.

Church saw it then—that these men, untrained and unseasoned as they were, had been selected for one reason and one reason only: they liked to hurt people, and they liked to kill people.

African child soldiers were the stuff of legend now. Warlords taking kids and plying them with alcohol, drugs, women—indoctrinating them before putting guns in their hands and making them into killers. Forcing them to shoot and rape to desensitise them to it.

That took time. Years. But to find the ones who liked that anyway? That took desire. The desire to create an army that gave no quarter, no mercy.

These men, Zawadi's men, were dangerous. Not because of their skill, but because their desire to fight, to pull the trigger, was greater than their desire not to.

They were looking for an excuse.

Church had seen it in their eyes.

The two Land Cruisers pulled in a circle in front of the metal sheet-clad building at the centre of the mine. A single-storey structure where Zawadi's men played cards and sheltered from the sun while the workers killed themselves outside.

Behind it, a huge mechanical rock crusher clanged away. A long belt fed rocks up to the hammer, which broke them down, filtering them through a series of screens into a huge bucket below. Once processed, the crushed rock was being hauled to the other side of the mine, where it was dumped out and hand-sorted.

Cobalt itself couldn't be mined directly. So what they were extracting from the ground here was copper ore. That's what the workers at the far side of the mine were sifting for. They had baskets on their hips and were digging, barehanded and barefoot, through the mountain of sandy rock, looking for chunks of copper. They'd put them in their baskets and then head over to a waiting truck, where more workers would dump their finds into a huge tub, ready for transport to a refinery somewhere.

Church had read that more than seventy per cent of the world's cobalt was mined in the DRC. And that despite regulations prohibiting what they called "artisanal mining"—code for slave mining—they still operated all across the country.

He had to try hard to hide his disgust as he scanned back across the mine, down the line of men and women passing breeze-block-sized chunks of stone along to the start of the crusher's belt.

And at the far end, a fleet of miners dug away at the stone with pickaxes as Zawadi's men, rifles on their backs, drove dump trucks and small plant machines in circles, pulling the felled rock away so the miners could get at the fresh face.

They could easily use the machines to dig, but tired workers were obedient workers, and easier wasn't what they were aiming for. Crushed spirits were.

Blackthorn was visibly sweating as he looked around, though Church wasn't sure if it was nerves or just the heat. Fletcher was shaking, though Church wasn't sure if that was nerves or the hangover, either.

Cole and Murphy disembarked first and cast around, assessing the situation. Zawadi was nowhere to be seen, though that wasn't surprising. He'd no doubt have plenty of people wanting his scalp, and the crown that came with it. Church bet he rarely ventured beyond the safety of his walls. No, they'd have to hit him at home when the time came.

For now, they'd be dealing with an appointed lieutenant, Church guessed.

Blackthorn waited diligently in the car until Cole was satisfied and opened the door for him. Church wondered if he'd had a word with the knight of the realm after yesterday, given him the lay of the land, as it were.

Blackthorn seemed to have found a new respect for the leader of his security team, even giving Cole a little nod as he disembarked.

Boyd climbed out the other side, and then Church and Fletcher both pushed the seats forward and clambered into the sun. Even through his sunglasses, Church's eyes ached in the brilliance.

It took a few seconds to adjust, but then he was there, head on a swivel. They were sidearms only today. That meant no rifles. Just pistols. Cole said it played better, that they were less threatening, and less likely to cause any kind of issue. They were Zawadi's guests now, and they needed to play that role.

Church didn't like it, but ten of them with just sidearms would have no problem rolling over this place.

Cole let out a low whistle and beckoned Church and the others over before the fun started.

'Boyd, you and me are on Blackthorn. Church, you're on Fletcher,' he ordered.

Church nodded back. Anastasia Fletcher folded her arms unhappily.

'Murph, you stay with the truck. Mitch, you and Foster hold here. Reed, Norton, scout the perimeter. Keep it tight, keep it cool. Got it?'

Everyone nodded back—a well-oiled machine.

Church was reading between the lines, as they all were. Mitch, Foster, and Murphy were to take care of the vehicles and be ready for a quick exfil. The others were to spread out, keep an eye on what Church and Cole couldn't from the middle of this place, look for any signs that things weren't above board, and analyse the layout and set-up. Where an attack would come from, where defensible positions would be. Just in case.

They never dealt in absolutes—shit could *always* go wrong. And it paid to be prepared.

Just as he finished talking, the door to the site office opened and a guy in his forties strode out. He was in camo trousers and heavy combat boots. He had a tank top on, heavy gold chains hanging from his neck, and a Tec-9 slung from his shoulder. He was wearing a beret on his head, same as Zawadi had been, and his wide, toothy grin told Church this was the guy.

This was Zawadi's lieutenant.

'Welcome, welcome,' he called out, holding his hands wide. 'The General told me you were coming to visit our humble operation.'

He swept his hand to his stomach and gave a low bow. He stood upright then and homed in on Blackthorn, walking forward with his hand extended.

Blackthorn stayed where he was, as though not wanting to interact with the man. He'd been chummy with Zawadi the day before. Did he think this man was beneath him somehow?

Cole nudged him with his elbow, and he seemed to get the picture then, shaking the lieutenant's hand.

'Sir Walter Blackthorn,' he introduced himself. 'Pleasure to be here.'

He forced a smile, but Church couldn't help but feel like it was lopsided.

'My name is Katenda,' the man with the gold chains

said, putting his hand on his chest. 'I must say, Mister Blackthorn, you have brought a lot of men with you.'

He glanced at the troop of soldiers around him. 'It is almost as if you do not trust the General. Is that the case?'

Blackthorn blushed violently.

Cole spoke now, knowing exactly what Katenda was doing.

'Sir Blackthorn doesn't get to decide how many of us are with him. He's here as an envoy from the British Government, and we're being paid to ensure that he comes home unscathed, and that relations between Her Majesty and the DRC are in a better state when we leave than when we arrived. I see you've got a good handle on the language, but do tell me if the meaning of the idiom *better safe than sorry is lost on you.*

'Or, if you want it in simpler terms: it's not that we don't trust the General. It's that we don't trust *anyone*. In fact,' Cole said, stepping between them so he was looking Katenda in the eye, 'we get paid not to. Trust is earned, my friend. You want ours? Earn it.'

He stared Katenda down, not allowing the man to gain an inch of leverage on the situation.

Church watched, impressed as always with Cole's ability to be frightening as hell.

Katenda held firm for a moment, and then seemed to remember that he didn't have the authority to piss without Zawadi's say-so, let alone antagonise his guests just because that's the kind of prick he was.

So he balked, stepped back, laughed, and then swept his hand across the mine.

'Of course,' he said. 'Then allow me to earn it—for the General, for the Congo, and for myself.

'You will see,' he went on, returning to Cole and waggling a finger playfully at him, Tec-9 swinging at his hip. 'Katenda is a man of honour. You can trust him.'

'Uh-huh,' Cole said, narrowing his eyes in the harsh sun. 'I guess we'll see.'

SEVEN

PRESENT DAY

Church drove through the night.

A day hadn't gone by where he hadn't thought of his sister.

Nanna was two years older than Church and wasn't actually called Nanna. Hannah was just hard to say, but the nickname had always stuck. They'd been as close as two siblings could have been, and to go to his death without getting to say goodbye to her... It had been awful for him.

For her—to really think her brother was dead, killed in action. It had torn her apart.

The first year or so, he'd kept tabs on her, made sure she and her kids were all right. She was the only family he had left, and his AFC—Armed Forces Compensation—payment had gone to her, which at least had covered his funeral, allowed them to say goodbye in the way they wanted.

Going to your own funeral was surreal.

Watching your family cry for you was torture.

He'd wanted to leap out then and hold them, tell them it was all a mistake. But he knew that his death was the only thing keeping them safe.

The first year was the most difficult. A lot of tears on her part. A lot of drinking on Church's.

But it had eased, slowly.

And once he knew she was going to be okay, that the kids would be okay, he began drifting away.

Nanna had come to accept it, come to live with the difficult truth that he was gone.

But now, to go back, after all this time—to tell her that he had allowed her to believe he was dead? That he never reached out, never told her the truth. That he'd made her carry his life for ten fucking years?

He had no idea how she'd react, but it wouldn't be good.

Nanna was the one who taught him to be hard. Who gave him the strength and resilience he needed to survive his childhood—the qualities that made him so damn effective in the forces.

He wasn't sure she wouldn't murder him then and there when he showed her he was alive.

She'd definitely take a swing at him.

And he fucking deserved it.

God, what was he going to say when he saw her?

He knew where she lived—had always kept track of that.

As Church passed under the sign signifying the end of the M1 was fast approaching, his fingers began to tingle.

He'd gone into Middle Eastern war zones, the sound of gunfire and ordnance incessant overhead, without even breaking a sweat.

He'd run singleton night ops in Eastern Europe, going toe-to-toe with guerrilla militants that executed children for fun, his heart rate barely breaking sixty beats a minute.

But this?

Nanna?

This was as nervous as he'd ever been.

He wound towards the centre of the city, heading for Highbury.

She'd done well for herself.

Nanna was always smart and was smart enough to pursue a career in finance while he'd thrown himself into the army.

The biggest stumbling of her life was marrying a soft-cock called Keith.

He was a soggy mollusc of a man who'd managed to father two children with Nanna before he'd had his first affair.

He'd been Nanna's manager when they'd got together, and it didn't take a genius to figure out what'd happen next.

History usually liked to repeat itself, and Keith wasn't immune to that pull.

When Church found out, he wanted to choke him.

Not just a little.

To death.

He wanted to watch the light go out behind his eyes.

But Nanna had no one else, no family outside of Keith and her girls.

And he had promised to change.

Their life was good—house on Highbury Terrace overlooking the park—and being the come-from-money snivelling prick he was, their prenup was iron-clad.

Which meant that even if Church had killed him—and he'd planned the whole thing—it was likely that Nanna wouldn't have got anything, the house going back to his parents, the ones who owned it.

She'd be out on her ear. And she was smart enough to know that.

So she stayed.

She forgave.

She went to couples' counselling.

And they got through it.

Except Keith didn't get through anything.

He just got better at hiding his affairs. And Nanna got better at looking the other way, at developing a thick skin, at not caring. She was being as tough as she'd showed him how to be.

Church had wanted nothing more than to see her, to speak to her. To tell her she deserved more. And if he'd been able to, he'd have helped her get out of there.

But he'd not been there.

At all.

For anything.

The girls were fifteen and thirteen now. Almost all grown up. And he'd missed it all. Too much of their lives when they were little. And all of their lives when they weren't.

He rattled out a long breath, going over all the things he was going to say, all the things he could say, and all the things he shouldn't.

Dawn was breaking, and though he'd been up for almost twenty-four hours straight, he was dialled in.

Laser-focused.

Because beyond all of the emotional difficulty this was going to cost, there were greater forces at play.

And the reason he was coming out of the shadows now wasn't to right some old wrong.

It was to protect them.

Because Blackthorn would be coming for them if he knew Church was alive.

Hell, he might have been there already.

He'd take the girls, hold them, use them against Church.

And he was not going to let that happen.

Blackthorn was a parasite.

And Church would not let him hurt his family to get his way.

He was too used to that, too used to operating with impunity.

But if he hurt Nanna, if he hurt the girls, it would be the last thing he ever did.

The anger began to stir in Church, his grip on the steering wheel ratcheting tighter as he turned off Holloway Road and onto Fieldway Crescent.

Just a few hundred metres from Highbury Terrace and number twenty.

Nanna's house.

He pulled left, slowing down, the engine of the Defender dwindling to a slow chug as he eased forward.

Driving right up to the front door would be stupid.

Because there was another option, too.

That Blackthorn wouldn't snatch Nanna.

That he'd put people outside to wait there to see if he showed up.

That he'd leave Nanna, bait on the hook, waiting for the big fish to come in, mouth open.

Well, Church might have been a shark, but he wasn't about to choke down anything that Blackthorn was hanging out for him, especially not his limp little worm.

Church parked up, light trickling into the sky over the trees of the park, and scanned the area.

Highbury Terrace was a series of brown-brick townhouses with big Georgian windows. Three-storey homes with cellars and steps to the front doors.

It was a beautiful street. Quiet, right opposite the park. A great place to raise children.

But a difficult place to stay out of sight if you were there working an op.

He pulled the Glock from the side of the seat and

pushed it under the hem of his canvas jacket, slipping from the cab of the truck.

Church hadn't prepared for combat, but there wasn't a pair of shoes he owned that weren't good for door-kicking and running at the same time.

He glanced around and then slipped up his hood to cover his face, pushing the Glock into the front of his jeans and pulling the hem of his knitted sweater over it.

Among the line of Mercedes and other executive cars parked along the kerb, only two stuck out—the only two that matched.

A pair of black Range Rovers.

One parked right outside Nanna's house, the other about fifty yards back, on the opposite side of the road, keeping eyes on the first.

Their lights were off, but the curl of steam and smoke from the exhausts betrayed them as running.

Church was too late.

They were already here, and that made his life that much harder.

He exhaled and steadied himself, hoping there was a way through this without bloodshed.

The last thing he needed was to drop multiple bodies in the centre of London.

If he thought Blackthorn was gunning for him now…

Church crossed the road and circled behind the Range Rover.

He hoped if they were still here, that meant he wasn't too late.

If they were both staking the place out, then one wouldn't be parked outside.

His brain laid it out for him, as it often did as he approached situations like this.

The one in front of the house was there to collect Nanna and her family.

Likely one in the driver's seat and one in the house at that moment, getting them ready to be taken somewhere 'safe'.

Somewhere that would draw Church into a kill box.

He couldn't let that happen.

Had to move fast.

These guys would be trained, whoever they were. Private contractors, no doubt. Ex-military, likely. Maybe government payroll.

Hard to say.

Either way, killing them was a last resort.

One thing he could rely on, though, was that the doors would be open.

They'd keep them like that, ready to leap out at a moment's notice.

And that played to his advantage.

Slow is smooth and smooth is fast.

He repeated it in his head as he continued his approach, stepping up onto the grassy verge at the side of the street and between the trees there.

A path ran between the trees and the playing fields, far enough from the side of the car that it'd put Church in their blind spot.

He just hoped they were dog-tired from being up all

night and focused more on the house in front of them than what was behind.

Though he'd be a fool to think this was easy.

He'd only get one attempt at this, and if he had to fire his weapon, it'd be game over.

Everyone in a mile radius would know where he was, and a net would close so fast and tight he'd be dead before the sun even came up fully.

Putting that thought out of his mind, he tapped into the muscle memory he'd embedded across his career, allowing the cold focus of a special forces soldier to descend over him.

He was almost level with the driver's door now.

He pulled the Glock out and racked the slide, chambering a round.

For a brief moment, he paused, looking around.

No witnesses.

No other assets in play.

No other choice.

Two bodies in the vehicle, both in the front seat.

He mapped it in his mind.

Then executed.

Three long strides put him at the door.

He crossed his hands and pulled it open with his left, swinging it wide before the driver could even clock the flash in the wing mirror.

Church didn't even register the features, just the widening eyes as the pistol came up, twisted, and then he drove the butt of the grip into the man's temple.

Before the woman in the passenger seat could even

get her hand into her blazer, the muzzle of Church's Glock was against her cheek, hard enough that she winced against the bite of the steel.

'Don't,' Church whispered.

The driver was already lolled forward, unconscious, held up by Church's arm pressed against his collarbones.

He did a quick assessment.

The two of them didn't look ex-military close protection.

Which meant that Blackthorn was utilising the PaDP, the Parliamentary and Diplomatic Protection Service—the UK's equivalent to the Secret Service.

Even more of a reason not to pull the trigger.

They were in black suits, wearing earpieces.

'You say a fucking word,' Church muttered, low enough the mic wouldn't pick it up, 'and you'll have a new hole to breathe out of.'

He reached forward and grabbed the earpiece, pulling it from her ear.

She winced again at Church's touch, no doubt in her mind as to who he was or what he was capable of.

Church had no doubt that Blackthorn had painted a severe picture of him and his 'conspirators' Mitchell and Foster.

Lies or not, his reputation was giving him an advantage.

He tugged at the wire until it popped out of the transmitter affixed to her belt, and dragged it free.

He kept the gun in her cheek and did the same to the driver.

'Weapon,' he ordered the woman then.

She was in her forties, well-built, with short, dark hair.

'By the fingertips, toss it in the back seat. Slow.'

She obliged.

Church risked a look up at number twenty.

Still no movement.

No one running towards their car. Yet.

He was still in the clear.

He looked back at the woman as she gently pulled her service pistol free of the rib holster, thumb and forefinger on the grip, and dropped it behind the centre console.

'Phone.'

She did the same thing, visibly shaking.

'You're carrying restraints.'

Not even a question.

A little nod.

'Where?'

'Inside pocket,' she muttered, voice strained.

It was natural for humans to feel shame, to feel pity when they were scaring someone.

When they were in a situation like this.

The army trained that out of you.

At that moment, Church was a machine.

The world was ones and zeros.

He saw nothing but the outcome, and a series of moves to create it.

Life became chess, and the knight never pitied the pawn during a take.

The consequences of that, of hesitation, of not pressing the advantage, was often death.

And Church had no desire to not take this to checkmate in as few moves as possible.

With his left hand, he felt inside the jacket of the driver and pulled out a looped pair of cable ties.

Ones meant for him, no doubt.

'Hands on the steering wheel.'

He pulled back gently and she moved with him until she was sprawled across the centre console.

She didn't need telling twice and laced one hand through the wheel so Church could fasten her there.

He zipped the ties tight and she hissed a little.

It fell on deaf ears.

Once she was secure, he relieved the driver of his phone and weapon too, pushing the pistol into his belt and tossing the phone into the back.

He found the woman's restraints then and jammed the driver's hand through the same gap in the wheel, securing them awkwardly so they were both locked in.

'The driver here your friend?' Church asked the woman, now standing in the open door to the Range Rover, acutely aware that more than a cursory look over at this vehicle from the one in front of Nanna's house would result in all hell breaking loose.

'Partner,' she replied bitterly. 'Six years.'

'Right, well, if you have any desire or inclination to try to ring this horn or get the attention of anyone else before I've done what I need to do, I'm going to come over here and execute him in front of you.

Then I'm going to put a bullet in your spine to make sure you live a long life, thinking about how you got him killed while you shit into a bag, parked in front of a window in your wheelchair.

And it won't be a nice window, because the government does not have your best interests at heart.

Trust me.

What's your name?'

'Sarah,' she squeezed out, looking up at Church.

'Blackthorn is a fucking cancer,' Church said, no waver in his voice.

'He's using my sister and her family to try and lure me into a trap so he can kill me.

All because I know what he did to get where he is.

That's who you're working for.

Don't get your partner killed for him.

It's not worth it.

Sit here, still, quiet, and this will be over soon, and you can just go on with your life, unhurt, and knowing you made the smartest decision of your life.

Do we have an understanding?'

She didn't even think about it.

Just nodded.

'That's good, Sarah.

And I trust you'll relay the same message to your partner?

It's the difference between you two getting a pint

when this day is over, or you calling his wife to tell her that he's dead and it's your fault.'

Another nod.

'I'm closing the door now.

Don't let me down.'

He kept his eyes on hers for as long as he could and then closed the door to the Range Rover, stepping down off the kerb, making a beeline for number twenty.

He hoped that Sarah knew he wasn't bluffing.

He'd been out of the game for ten years, but he could still feel it.

Everything he'd honed and built of himself over his career, like a caged animal ripping at the cage door to get out.

Sarah had seen that behind his eyes.

And that pint at the pub with her partner today would taste better than any she'd ever drunk.

And because of that, he approached the second Range Rover in silence.

'Good choice,' he growled to himself, breathing deeply, readying himself for a second go-around.

But before he got there, right in the middle of the street, the door to number twenty opened and Nanna stepped out onto the porch.

Church froze, staring up at her.

He'd not seen her in person since his funeral.

She looked older.

Tired.

But still his sister.

His heart beat harder, a lump forming in his throat.

She paused and turned back to the doorway, picking up a suitcase and guiding her youngest, Mia, the thirteen-year-old, through the door.

She'd gotten so big.

She looked like a woman now.

Beautiful, like her mother, thankfully.

She looked sullen, oversized headphones on, staring down at her phone.

Nanna leaned in and kissed her on the head, her face fear-stricken.

A shadow loomed behind her.

A tall man in a black suit, ushering Nanna's eldest daughter, Lowri, outside too.

Church was rooted to the spot, transfixed on them.

So much so that he almost didn't see the driver's door to the Range Rover open.

A man stepped out—mid-fifties, bald head.

His feet hit the ground, and he froze, clocking Church.

Church looked back at him.

They both remained still, the bald guy's eyes flitting to the Glock in Church's hand.

Church shook his head, urging him not to.

But he did anyway.

The guy's hand plunged into his jacket, and Church kicked forward.

He took one bound and pushed off his left leg, launching himself forward, knee impacting the man right in the middle of his torso before the gun even came free.

All the air left his body, and he was launched backwards into the side of the SUV.

He hit it hard, the whole car rocking, his right hand flopping through the air, pistol in it, eyes bulging.

Church threw a tight right hook into his ribs, stunning him, and grabbed for the gun, wrestling it free.

The officer swung back, elbow up over Church's shoulder, into the side of his face.

The pain was instant, blinding, but momentary.

Church ripped the gun free, pulling the guy's arm down over his shoulder as he turned his back on him, feeling his feet lift off the ground as he threw him.

Church took a big step and pulled down—hard.

The shoulder throw was one of the fundamental techniques in Judo, and in the forces they taught a mix of martial arts: elements of Judo, Jiu-Jitsu, kickboxing, grappling and striking techniques.

Church called on that knowledge now, flipping the officer over his shoulder, watching him tumble through the air and land square on his back with a loud thud and a quiet squeak.

He was dazed but still capable, but there was no time to choke him out.

He needed him incapacitated—and fast.

The other officer at the door was already calling out for him.

But before he could draw breath and answer, Church lifted his heel and stomped down on his solar plexus, stunning it.

He wouldn't be able to breathe for a minute, let alone answer.

'Shane?' the officer at the door called.

'Shane, what's happening? Shit.'

Footsteps on the concrete.

'Stay here,' he ordered Nanna.

'What's happening?' she asked, her voice all at once familiar.

Warmth washed over Church at the sound of it, his resolve strengthening as he stepped around the back of the car—not looking at her, not able to.

He needed to focus.

Needed to end this.

And fast.

He charged into the open and whistled.

The second officer froze at the front wing and looked back at him, rooted to the spot.

His hand moved for his weapon, but he was far too slow, and Church was already running, arm cocked back.

His fist catapulted forwards like the head of a sledgehammer, and Church felt bone crack under it.

Nose.

Cheek.

Eye socket.

Something was broken.

The officer left the ground and sailed backwards, heels catching on the pavement, sending him sprawling to the floor, where he lay still.

Church would have liked to have checked his pulse, made sure he wasn't dead, but there was no time now.

'Solomon?'

Church stopped in his tracks, looked up at the sound of his name.

Nanna was standing on the top step, Mia under one arm, Lowri under the other, clutching them both as tightly as she could, her fists scrunched into the fabric of their jackets, her mouth open.

'Nanna,' he said, staring back.

She tried to speak, but no sound came out.

She just blinked, shaking her head.

'I know,' Church said, taking a step forward, stretching out his hand.

She recoiled. 'No, you're…'

'I know,' Church said, harder now. 'But we don't have time.'

He turned his hand over, offering it to her.

'We have to go. Right now. I'll tell you everything, I promise. But we have to get out of here.'

He pleaded with her.

'Please. You have to trust me.'

She looked at his hand, the morning air still around them, light just beginning to bleed through the tops of the trees opposite the house.

Church swallowed the burning lump in the back of his throat, willing her to move.

Willing her to trust him.

But she just stood there, clutching her children, staring down at a ghost in utter disbelief.

EIGHT

TEN YEARS AGO

BLACKTHORN DISAPPEARED into the site office following Katenda, Cole, and Boyd at his back. The door opened and snapped shut, and then they were alone in the sun.

Church was wearing a black cap—the preferred colour of private security—and he was regretting it. Sweat was beading on his temples and running down into his beard. Even the crooks of his elbows were sweating, his hands loosely around his rifle.

He could feel the dryness in his throat and wanted nothing more than to be out of the sun, but if Fletcher wasn't moving, neither was he. She had her eyes fixed on the door to the site office as though she could see through it, see what was going on behind, what Blackthorn was saying. But she couldn't, despite her desire to.

Church had to wonder if Blackthorn was keeping her in the dark, and if so… why? She was his assistant, and surely she should be there at every turn to *assist* him.

She muttered something under her breath that Church didn't quite hear but was sure was profanity, and then she turned on her heel and strode in the opposite direction.

Mitch shot Church a questioning glance, and he shrugged back, jogging to catch up with her. Even in the split second she was alone, it seemed like all of Katenda's men identified that fact. Like wolves following the newborn at the back of the herd, waiting for it to fall.

Church followed Fletcher in silence as she headed back up the dusty track towards the gate, veering off halfway and heading towards the line of miners passing rock towards the conveyor belt. She squinted in the dust and shielded her face from the sun with her hand as she got closer.

The guards nearby seemed to stiffen. Church clocked four of them. Two on the upper levels of the mine's excavated wall, looking down at them as they approached, as well as one standing up by the gate, and another who was to their right, making a slow lap of the place but now course-correcting to head straight for them.

Church kept his hands loose but mentally mapped where they were just in case. Fletcher was only going one place—right for the workers. She intended to talk to them, and that was something that Church doubted Zawadi's men would be interested in letting happen.

As she got closer to the line of workers, she scanned

up and down it as though identifying a specific person, and then suddenly quickened her pace, casting a quick look at the guards. Judging how much time she'd have.

Church stayed in lockstep with her, tempted to grab her and drag her back, but the last thing he wanted was to cause a scene.

Fletcher knelt and touched the back of a middle-aged man. He was hunched forward, his T-shirt faded and filthy, his ribs showing through it. He flinched as she made contact and looked over his shoulder, fear in his eyes.

'*Excusez-moi,*' she said quickly, keeping her voice low. '*Tu parles français?*'

French was the official language of the DRC, spoken predominantly in the capital and in built-up areas, but this far out, it wasn't common. Their mission brief had included this information—that the preferred local language here was Swahili.

But Fletcher didn't know that, and Church wasn't about to tell her. He wanted the conversation to end here. Now. Before the guard walking towards them arrived.

The man stared at Fletcher over his shoulder, not understanding. The woman next to him, trying to hand him a large stone, was now looking at her, too. Not only was Fletcher talking to someone she shouldn't have been, but she was also disrupting the workflow, and the ripple was already travelling quickly down the line.

Church tightened his grip on his rifle and scanned

for Zawadi's men once more, placing them in his periphery.

Fletcher didn't give up, though, and quickly switched tack. *'Lingála?'* she asked, quickening the pace. Another local language. The man stared back.

'Kiswahili?' she tried now.

Bingo.

The man's brow crumpled, and he risked a little nod.

'Jambo, jambo,' Fletcher said, nodding back and grinning.

"Jambo" was a friendly greeting—"hello" in Swahili. But where was she going with this?

She wasted no time in digging a piece of paper out of her pocket and unfolding it.

The guard coming up on them was picking up his pace, the two men above on the wall now standing right above them, staring down.

Church looked back at Fletcher, saw the paper she'd unfurled had a couple of handwritten lines on it. French on top, and what he guessed was Lingala or Swahili below.

She'd come prepared.

'Je, uko hapa bila hiari yako?' she asked in a stunted accent.

Church didn't know what the hell it meant, but he guessed nothing good.

The man just blinked at her. Either he didn't understand, or he was just dumbfounded by the question.

'Je, uko hapa bila hiari yako?' she asked again, faster now, stumbling over the words.

The guard was just ten feet away, almost running towards them.

'*Je, umeletwa hapa kwa lazima?*' Fletcher managed, a constant slur of noise as she tried desperately to read the words she'd written down.

But the worker couldn't answer before he spotted the guard and twisted away from Fletcher so fast that she jolted a little.

The guard reached out then, his long arm glistening with sweat in the sun, his sleeveless military shirt doing little to conceal the criss-cross of scars across the skin. He was going for the paper in Fletcher's hand, and Church knew that if he got it, it wasn't going to help things.

He stepped forward and dipped his shoulder, connecting with the guard mid-stride and almost throwing him off his feet.

In the same movement, he seized Fletcher by the arm and twisted it outwards, pulling the paper roughly from her grip and stuffing it into his ballistic vest.

He barely registered the indignation on her face before a sudden, blinding pain above his right eye made the world blink dark for a second.

Church stumbled, clutching at his head reflexively, and almost lost his footing, regaining himself a moment later. He pulled his hand away and saw blood on his fingers, his eyes tracing back to the guard he'd shouldered. The man's AK-47 was raised, the butt held aloft from where it had just struck him. He had a shock of black hair, dark eyes yellowed around the irises, and a mean snarl that told Church he'd got off lightly.

But that didn't mean he'd let it slide.

He righted himself and strode forward, the man lifting his rifle again as though he was going to hit Church a second time.

Church invited it, not lifting his hands or making a move to attack.

The guard lunged, ready to teach him a lesson for his insolence, and Church reacted. The guy was slow, untrained, used to hitting people who didn't hit back.

Church swerved the strike and hooked his leg behind the guard's heels, grabbing a fistful of his shirt and shoving him so violently that his body went fully horizontal before he slammed into the ground.

He let out a sharp grunt and tried to speak as Church ripped the rifle from his hands and tossed it away into the dirt. But he fell silent the second he found himself staring up into the black maw of Church's carbine.

A chorus of metallic clacking echoed around him, and Church looked up to see the two men on the wall with their guns raised, pointed in his direction. The guard at the gate had run over too and was readied to shoot.

Fletcher was five feet away and had gone white.

Church surveyed the men around him carefully, not taking his eyes off them.

'Fletcher,' he said calmly.

She swallowed and stared at him, not saying a word.

'Go and get in the car. Don't run. Don't look at anyone. Keep your hands in plain view. Do it now.'

She moved—almost too suddenly—then caught herself and walked quickly past Church, eyes on the ground.

Only when he heard the door of the Land Cruiser open and shut did he step away from Zawadi's man and begin backing towards the cars. He kept his rifle low but ready to pop up if needed, and halfway there, he heard the footsteps of the others joining him.

They'd seen what had happened and were walking over—a simple show of force that evened the odds.

Church clocked Mitch and Murphy at his sides now, and all three of them traced their way back to the vehicles. By the time they got there, Foster was already leading Boyd, Cole, and Blackthorn out of the site office, much to Katenda's displeasure. He followed, complaining that they were leaving in the middle of negotiations. But it didn't matter—this place was now a powder keg, and they were lucky it hadn't blown already.

Blackthorn was squawking, demanding to know what had happened as he was bundled into the car.

Foster climbed into the back with Fletcher while Boyd got in next to Blackthorn.

Cole locked eyes with Church and snapped his fingers, pointing towards the lead car.

Church understood. It meant drive. It meant tell me what the fuck just happened.

Church obliged, got in, and, wordlessly, they swung in a circle and bolted for the exit.

The trail car, housing Mitch and Murphy, slowed for Reed and Norton to climb in, and then they hammered it out through the gates after Church and the lead car.

They sat in silence, not relaxing or saying a word until they were almost a mile from the mine.

Cole was scowling, checking the wing mirror, hunched forward in the passenger seat.

He sat up then and looked at Church. 'What the fuck happened back there?'

Church risked a glance in the rear-view, hunting for Fletcher's eyes, but she had them firmly fixed on her lap, head bowed.

He could feel the blood pulsing in his temple, the hot trickle of blood running down the side of his head.

'Fletcher,' he said then, and she looked up at him. 'One of them tried to grab Fletcher,' Church went on. 'I stopped him.'

'This could do with a stitch,' Norton said, bent over Church in the lobby of the hotel. He had an open medical kit next to him and was dressing Church's new head wound. 'Won't heal right otherwise.'

'Do it,' Church grunted, staring into space. He didn't much like being poked with needles, especially when the injury wasn't his fault.

'Going to leave a scar either way. You straight?'

Norton asked, pulling back and holding up three fingers, waving them around. 'How many fingers?'

'The same number I'm going to jam up your arse if you don't hurry up,' Church replied.

'You're fine,' Norton laughed. 'This'll just take a sec,' he promised, digging for a needle and thread. 'It'll leave a nice scar, though.'

'Add it to the collection,' Church said, closing his eyes.

'Stop,' came Cole's voice then. 'Stitches can wait.'

He appeared from the stairs to the upper floor, the lobby split into two halves—a simple space with a few chairs and a table, and a little bar-restaurant on the other side. The stairs were opposite the door and cut the building in two.

He strode towards Church and stopped in front of him, hands on his hips. 'I need to speak to Sol.'

Norton put the needle down and walked away, and Cole seemed to want to wait until he was out of earshot before he spoke.

'You ready to tell me what really happened at the mine today?'

He'd come from upstairs, which meant he'd probably talked to Fletcher. Probably talked to everyone about what happened.

Did he fold and tell Cole exactly what had gone down? He had no loyalties to this woman, and she'd acted rashly, risked her own life and his. And for what? Church didn't know. Yet.

And the way Cole was looking at him, he suddenly

felt like it wasn't only Fletcher who wasn't giving him the full picture.

'I told you,' Church replied, deciding that a middle ground was the best approach. The truth, but not the whole truth. 'Fletcher took a walk, I followed. She tried to speak to one of the workers and one of Zawadi's guys made a grab for her. I intervened.'

Cole narrowed his eyes, pointed to Church's head. 'And that?'

'I tried to get Fletcher out of there, and he clocked me with his fucking rifle,' Church growled, trying to emphasise how unhappy he was about it.

'You let one of Zawadi's guys tag you?' Cole raised an eyebrow.

'I had my back to him.'

'Why the fuck did you turn your back on a hostile?' He phrased it like this was an interrogation.

'I was protecting Fletcher,' Church replied.

'Fletcher's not the mission.'

Church stiffened in the chair a little, wanting to bite back, to tell Cole he was just following orders. His orders. But he didn't want to invite more questions.

'Understood,' he said. 'Next time I'll just let her get attacked.'

He couldn't help but add the last part and regretted it instantly.

Cole glowered down at him. 'We got a problem, Church?'

Church looked up at his captain. 'No, sir,' he answered curtly.

'You don't like how I run my ops?'

'No, sir.'

'I put you on Fletcher because I trusted you to be able to watch her. To keep her in check without jeopardising my fucking mission. Was I wrong?'

'No, sir.'

'Is it too much for you?'

'No, *sir.*' Church was all but gritting his teeth now. He'd been with Cole for years, and as much as he respected him, the guy could still be an unabashed prick.

'So get your fucking act together. She steps out of line again, you put a stop to it. Right?'

'Right.'

Cole stared at him for a second more and then nodded. 'Good. Now get Norton back in here to fix your fucking head, and then get it down for a few hours. I just got word we've got live sat-coverage on Zawadi's compound for the next twelve hours. We're green-lit for phase two.'

He looked at Church for a second longer as though trying to see inside his head, and then turned away, heading for the front door. He stepped through it and into the African sun, pulled a pair of sunglasses from his pocket, and then disappeared from view.

Church waited to make sure he wasn't coming back, then got up and headed for the stairs.

He climbed quickly, his head throbbing, and ignored the pain.

When he got to the fourth floor, he turned right, stopping at Fletcher's door.

He knocked without hesitation, a hard rap that was an order to answer, not a polite request.

A few seconds later, it opened a few inches, hitting the security chain. Anastasia Fletcher stared out through the gap at him, her eyes red and bloodshot. She'd been crying.

'What?' she asked, still sniffling a little. She began tearing up as she spoke, holding them back as best she could. It was clear he wasn't the first to endure an interrogation.

'You alright?' Church asked, leaning a little closer.

'Am I alright?' she practically spat. 'What do you think?'

He cleared his throat, looking down through the gap at her hands clasped in front of her. He could see the red marks on her wrist from where he'd grabbed her at the mine. She quickly hid them behind her back.

'Your wrist,' he started, 'I'm sorry, I—'

'Save it,' she replied, cutting him off. 'And don't bother coming back. If there's one thing I'm not looking for out here, it's a friend.'

And with that, she shut the door in his face and left Church alone in the corridor with just his throbbing head for company.

NINE

PRESENT DAY

Her hands fell from the heads of her children, and she stepped forward, inspecting every line and wrinkle of his face, as though looking for something to tell her it wasn't true. They were both older, both different, but unmistakable to each other. Siblings like them shared a bond that was unbreakable—the kind where they'd kill and die for one another without a second thought.

That's what Solomon had done. He'd died for her. And yet, here he was, right before her.

Nanna came down the steps one at a time, unsteady on her feet, towards her brother.

'Nanna—'

He didn't get to say another word before a right hook came out of nowhere, hitting him square in the jaw.

The punch rocked him, and he staggered backwards,

holding his face. When he looked up, the look of shock had gone, replaced with one of fury. The kind he used to see in his father's face. The kind he locked deep inside himself and never let out.

'You bastard,' she spat, hands locked in fists at her sides. 'You goddamn bastard.'

Church righted himself and looked up at the girls, the pair of them staring down at him in fear. There was no recognition there. They'd been so young when he'd died, they didn't know who he was.

His eyes came back to Nanna, a knot of shame in the pit of his stomach so tight it hurt worse than any of the bullets or blades he'd taken over the years. 'I know,' he said, lowering his head. 'I know I have no right to ask anything right now, but…' He looked up at her. 'You have to trust me. There's no time to explain, but these people'—he gestured to the cars, the downed men—'they're not here to protect you. They're here to lure me into the open so they can kill me.'

Nanna narrowed her eyes. 'Why?' she snapped.

'Because of what I know. Because of what they did. Because of what *he* did. I don't know what they told you Blackthorn said this is about, but it's a lie. It's all a lie.'

Her jaw quivered as she weighed it, the anger in her clouding her mind, her judgment. She'd have believed him before. But now… they were strangers, and the man she'd trusted most in the world had lied to her in the most painful way possible.

'If you don't come with me, they'll send more

people for you. And then they're going to hurt you, hurt the girls, if I don't do what they want.' He drew a slow breath, looking up at them. 'And I can't have that.' He locked eyes with his sister again. 'You're coming with me.'

She held firm as the first sounds of sirens began to rise in the distance. The back of his neck began to prickle. A quiet groan reached him from the other side of the Range Rover—the bald officer coming around. Was he the one who'd called it in?

Nanna lifted her head, as though testing the air, listening to the wail of the police's battle cry.

She sighed then and turned to her daughters. 'Girls,' she said, beckoning them forward. 'Come here.'

They held firm. 'Who's that?' Lowri asked.

'That's your uncle,' Nanna said. 'Solomon.'

'Isn't he…'

'Dead?' She looked at Church. 'He's supposed to be.'

That hurt more than the punch.

'But we don't have time right now. Come on, we're going with him. Now. Bring your bags.'

The sharpness in her voice, the fierceness, took him back to his childhood. He thought that Hannah Church was just about the only person in the world he was frightened of.

She was tall, a long head of dark curls bouncing off her shoulders. She held herself with the kind of poise and confidence that made everyone else want to stoop in her presence. Which made it all the more soul-destroying to see what Keith had done to her. What he'd *made* of her.

But the girls knew who she was as well as Church did, and came without any more protest or question. They stepped down off the porch, eyeing Church, and walked between them.

'We're going to have a *long* talk about this,' Nanna said, voice low and hard.

'It's a long drive,' Church replied. 'And you deserve the whole story.'

'You're damn right.' She nodded. 'Where are we going?'

He pointed down the street.

'Just look for the Defender, I assume?'

He cracked the smallest smile.

'Some things never change. Not even in death, it seems,' she said with a little scoff, shaking her head and taking off after the girls.

A new voice echoed from the hallway of the house then. 'Hannah? Where are my—'

But Keith's words died in his throat as he saw the scene. The officer on the ground. Hannah and the girls walking away. Church standing in the middle of it.

'Solomon,' he all but gasped. 'What…'

Nanna paused and looked back at her husband, his close-set eyes behind thick-framed designer glasses, his weak chin lined with stubble that he no doubt thought made him look more masculine. The disdain in her face was clear.

Then she looked at Church.

They exchanged a few silent words, and then she looked back at her husband with the kind of satisfaction that told Church she was happy to never see him again.

And then she kept walking, the girls going with her.

Old enough to know who he was, and what he'd done.

It hurt Church even more to know he was the difference in that. That him not being here had forced her to carry on with this charade. With this man.

'Hannah?' he asked, voice cracking. 'Where are you going?'

Church knew time was short, but he didn't have the strength to resist. 'Alright, Keith?' he asked, stepping up onto the porch.

The man paled and moved backwards, shoulders rounding in submission. 'Solomon,' he said, laughing nervously. 'I, uh…'

'Thought I was dead,' Church replied. 'Yeah. But I hope that's not why you cheated on my sister. Though I understand if it was.'

The colour drained from his face.

'Because, you know if I was alive that I'd have pulled your cock off with a pipe wrench the second I found out. Right?'

He swallowed, looking up at Church, and he wondered if Keith might actually piss himself.

'I'm a little short on time at the moment,' Church went on. 'But you can bet that I'm coming back, and we're going to have a proper conversation about this.' He clapped Keith on the shoulder, and the man's legs all but buckled. Church thought he could audibly hear his testicles shrivelling in his pants. 'You wronged my sister,' he said, turning towards the door. 'And there's a price to pay for that.'

He fired a cold glance back at Keith. 'Men always pay for their sins, Keith. Eventually.'

And then he turned his back on the sorry excuse for a man and followed his sister down the street.

'What'd you say to him?' Nanna asked as Church caught up, the sirens louder, closer.

Church hurried their pace. 'Nothing I'm sure you haven't wanted to.'

She offered him the smallest smile but resisted the urge to touch him, as though doing so might make him disappear again.

They reached the Defender, and Church loaded it quickly. The girls got in without a word, and Nanna did the same. Church was glad that even after all this time, she still trusted him. Trusted him enough to ignore the orders of police officers. Trusted him enough to go with him despite what he'd just done. The violence he'd just exhibited.

He fired the engine and drove away from the scene quickly, skipping the main drags, the hour still early enough that he could guide the truck through the side streets with little resistance.

He made it about a mile, the sirens still echoing from all directions, before he pulled over and went to the boot door. He opened it quickly and pushed the bags forward, lifting up the floor panel and reaching into the gap there. He pushed aside the Benelli M4 Super 90 semi-automatic shotgun and the L119A1 CQB Carbine, a 5.56 with a ten-inch barrel ideal for room-clearing and close-quarters engagements—and storage in a spare-wheel bay—and reached for the magnetic number plates bundled together with a rubber band.

He pulled two fresh ones out—front and back, currently registered to the same year, model, and colour Land Rover Defender that made its home on the Cornwall coast—and swooped around the vehicle, switching the current plates. No doubt the Met were scouring CCTV and working their NPR tech overtime to try and pin him down. This wouldn't give him much of a head start, but if they could clear the city, they'd have a much better chance of making their destination.

Church tossed the old plates into the gutter and hopped back into the driver's seat, getting the hammer down.

Defenders weren't known for their speed, but when you have as much time on your hands as Church did, there was plenty of time for tinkering and upgrading, and the engine swap he'd done for something with more *umph* was definitely coming in handy now. It really was amazing how much you could learn when you didn't have a phone or internet access.

They streaked through the city, catching only glimpses of flashing blue lights in the rearview as they scarpered across their path, heading in the wrong direction. And before long, the high-rises disappeared, and fields took their place.

The girls were in the back seats playing with their phones, and Church knew the next piece of news wouldn't be welcome.

He glanced over at Nanna, who was looking out of the window aimlessly, the dreary dawn-riddled sky turning from black to grey as the sun fought its way through the clouds.

'You okay?' Church asked, regretting it as soon as he saw her face.

She just shook her head at him like it was the stupidest question in the world. Once she'd thought her way through the mess in her head, she'd speak. She'd ask her questions. And Church would answer. Nanna was as smart as anyone he'd ever met, and he was her little brother, after all. Which meant when she talked, he listened. Not the other way around.

Except the next thing from his mouth was non-negotiable.

'You need to get rid of your phones,' Church said. 'All three of you. Factory wipe them and toss them out the window.'

Nanna stared at him but didn't question it. He wouldn't ask if it wasn't necessary. And he wouldn't be back from the dead if it wasn't life and death.

'Fine, but you're taking the brunt of it,' she said, sucking air through her teeth and turning to the back seat. 'Girls,' Nanna said, holding her hand out. 'Phones.'

'What? Why?' they both answered in unison, folding them into their chests.

'You want to tackle that?' Nanna asked Church.

'Depends if you want me to give them the truth or not.'

Nanna sighed. 'Chicken.' She pursed her lips for a second, wondering how to sugar-coat: *because the prime minister-to-be will use them to track us and will come and murder your uncle, and possibly us too, if we're in the way. And that supersedes the discomfort of you not being able to access TikTok every second of every hour of every day.*

She cleared her throat then. 'It's not safe. Your uncle's mixed up in some stuff, and they can use your phones to track us.'

'We'll turn them off,' Mia said quickly. 'I need my phone.'

'Nanna…' Church insisted.

She gritted her teeth. 'Girls. Phone. Now. No arguments.'

Slowly, they handed them over, knowing arguing with Nanna was like arguing with a brick wall. Or maybe it was the fact they'd just seen her slug Church in the face like Mike Tyson in his prime. Either way, Nanna got them and factory-reset them, along with her own.

'You're sure all this is necessary?' She was hesitating. The trust wasn't there yet.

Church didn't want to keep telling her. Didn't want to keep threatening the lives of her daughters to make her understand.

'It is,' he said instead, with as much gravity as he could.

'Fine. Then it's on you,' she said, shoving the phones into his lap. 'God knows they're going to hate me enough for blowing up our family. I don't want to be the one who threw their phones out the window, too.'

Church thought on that as he wound down the window, slinging the phones out one by one, the girls watching them go, eyes glued to the glass like Church was throwing away their only lifeline from a sinking ship.

'He blew up your family a long time ago,' Church said. 'You held onto it far longer than he deserved.'

She harrumphed to herself in the passenger seat, looking down at her empty hands. 'I'm sure that's how it's going to read in the divorce papers. He's going to rake me over the coals. His parents, too.'

'So you've decided then? You're leaving him?'

She closed her eyes, lowering her voice. 'I left him a long time ago,' she muttered. 'I just never moved out.'

Church looked at the road ahead, hunting for their exit. It was coming up fast. 'I threatened to pull his cock off with a pipe wrench,' he said. 'But if you'd prefer, I could just kill him.'

She scoffed. 'There's always that option.'

'I'm serious,' Church said, looking over. 'When I found out what he did, I planned everything. Almost did it, too.'

'You knew? You were watching me?' Her voice trembled a little.

Church smiled, turning his hand over so that his palm faced the sky. 'Always.'

She took it. 'Why didn't you ever reach out?'

'I wanted to. Every day,' he said. 'But it would have put you in danger. Would have taken everything from you.'

She squeezed his hand. 'Like it is now?'

'No—not like it is now,' Church said, taking back his hand and steering them off the main road and down a dark country lane. 'I'm not going to let it.'

TEN

TEN YEARS AGO

NO ONE COULD EVER ACCUSE Solomon Church of not being a good soldier.

He returned to his room after Fletcher slammed the door in his face and drew the curtains, doing as he was told: getting his head down. The pain began to recede slowly as he caught up on some sleep, but when there was a knock at his door, he pulled his head out of the pillow quickly and ripped off the scab that had formed over the cut.

He hissed at the pain and touched his fingers to the fresh blood, grumbling a few swear words under his breath as he got up and padded over to the door. The room was dark and hot, and his body was sheened with sweat. He stretched out his shoulders and cracked his knuckles—he'd been clenching his fists in his sleep again—and answered the door.

Mitch was standing there, a strange expression on his face. Frustration, mostly, but a little bit of angst, too. He was breathing a little hard, his brow shining like he'd practically run up the stairs. Maybe he had.

He pushed into the room before Church could say anything.

'Close the door,' he said.

Church checked the corridor and then did so, walking towards Mitch, keen to keep their voices low. If he was here, that meant he'd done what Church had asked.

'Well?' Church folded his arms, heart beating a little harder as he waited for the answer.

Mitch chewed the inside of his cheek for a second and then dug in his pocket, pulling out the piece of paper Church had taken off Fletcher. He held it up, drawing a deep breath. 'It's not good.'

'Not good *how?*' Church asked.

'I think we can assume that she's not telling us everything.' He held out the paper to Church, and he took it, unfolding and reading it.

He saw the same three sentences as he had at the mine. French, Lingala, Swahili. But this time, there was an English translation at the bottom.

ARE YOU HERE WITHOUT YOUR CONSENT? ARE YOU HERE BY FORCE?

'That's the Swahili translation,' Mitch said. 'I found a doctor in town who did it for me.'

Church looked up at him.

'Don't worry, I was careful,' Mitch reassured him.

'And the French, the Lingala?'

'French is the same. A little different wording, but the same questions,' Mitch said. 'I don't know about the Lingala, but I'd bet we'd be three for three.' He came forward a little, his brow creasing. 'Why did she have this? She must have gone to some trouble to get these translations done, right? To have them written down, just waiting for an opportunity to ask miners here? You think she grew a conscience when she arrived, or…'

Church crumpled the paper in his fist. 'Or she came here with an ulterior motive.' He looked over at the door, angry at himself for not seeing through her sooner. And angry at her for being so damn blatant about her duplicity.

Before he could move towards it to confront Fletcher, there was another knock. This time, a hard pounding with the heel of a fist. Church and Mitch froze.

Reflexively, Church pushed the paper into his pocket and glanced at Mitch. He nodded and made himself comfortable, sitting in the chair across from the bed.

Church opened the door to find Murphy standing there.

He was shorter than Church, wiry, with weathered features that made him look like he'd been left in the sun too long. He looked at Church first, then leaned around him to look at Mitch.

'Interrupted a romantic moment, did I?' he asked dryly.

'Don't be jealous, Murph, there's plenty of me to go around,' Church replied easily, offering as much of a smile as he ever did for the man.

He let out a little *humph* of amusement. 'Get your shit together. Cole says it's time to go. Zawadi's on the move. We're out the door in two.' He leaned around Church now. 'You hear that, Mitch?'

'Loud and clear,' he replied, legs crossed.

'Good. Saves me repeating myself.' He looked up at Church again, eyes narrowing just slightly as though he was trying to read his mind. 'Solomon.'

'Murphy.'

The man turned away and walked slowly towards the stairs, as though waiting for the door to close before he left.

Church didn't give him more reason to be suspicious and left it open. 'Thanks for checking in,' Church announced to Mitch. 'My head's fine,' he said, loud enough for Murphy to hear.

Mitch got up wordlessly and laid a hand on Church's shoulder. They'd talk later.

He exited the room and headed for his own while Church pulled on a shirt and grabbed his bag. He picked up his rifle last, weighing it in his hand for a moment before he slung it over his shoulder. He rarely considered whether he was on the right side of things or not, but now, here, he couldn't help but feel like more was going on than he knew. That there were strings being pulled behind the scenes, moving him like a puppet, without his consent or knowledge. And he didn't like that.

For now, though, he had other things to focus on. The mission was still very much in motion, and one wrong step could jeopardise not only his life but that of his team, and who knew how many others.

He put those thoughts out of his mind and zeroed in on the mission, finding his focus as he headed down to the lobby.

The guys were already there: Reed, Murphy, Boyd, Norton, Foster… Mitch would arrive in a second. But where was Cole?

Reed spoke before Church could ask. 'We're on the clock here, so we'll catch Mitch up on the road. We've got word that Zawadi's on the move, so we're going into his compound to install surveillance. We need to gather rock-solid intel if we want the green light to take him out.' He glanced around the men, and Church couldn't help but wonder why the hell he was doing the pre-mission and not Cole.

'We're splitting into two teams. First team is going to go to the main gate and make noise—ask about Zawadi, demand to know what the hell happened at the mine this morning. Cole's going to take the lead on that, draw as much attention as possible. Team two is going to slip in the back, quietly, and get inside the house. If we can't get inside, we pull back and reassess. Do not engage,' he emphasised. 'If they shoot first, shoot back, but otherwise…'

'Do not engage,' everyone replied.

'Good.' He nodded to the guys as Mitch appeared from the stairs. 'Murph, Boyd, you're with me and Cole at the gate. Norton, Foster, Mitch, Church' — he seemed to look directly at Church as he said his name — 'you're going inside.'

Church thought he saw just the faintest flicker of a smile on Reed's face, but he didn't know what it meant. Hell, he might have even imagined it.

Still, he felt his blood rise just a little as Reed made a whipping motion with his finger to signal they were moving.

His feet went on autopilot, the seven of them forming up into their teams wordlessly. Church and Mitch headed for the front seats of the second Land Cruiser parked at the kerb outside the hotel, and though Mitch was speaking to Church, asking him for the details of what they were doing, he didn't even register the words.

He couldn't take his eyes off Reed and Murphy, talking to each other in low voices as they approached their vehicle, casting glances in Church's direction. When they spotted him watching them, they broke off and climbed in.

Church spotted Cole then and slowed before he reached the car, holding up to watch him come through the doors. But just as he reached them, he stopped and turned back. Church could see his back through the glass, and he could see Blackthorn, too. He was following Cole, arguing with him. He was gesturing, keeping his voice low but speaking harshly. Cole stood his ground, then put a finger in Blackthorn's chest and quickly sliced the air with his hand as though to cut the conversation there.

Blackthorn visibly puffed, clenching his fists at his sides as though he wasn't liking what he was hearing.

Cole backed through the door, keeping his eyes on Blackthorn until he was outside, and then turned to the cars.

He stopped abruptly when he saw Church standing there but said nothing.

'What was that about?' Church asked, coming forward and lifting his chin towards the hotel. Blackthorn had already disappeared.

Cole looked back at Church, taking his time to answer as though deciding what to say. 'Just Blackthorn being a prick,' he opted for. 'Trying to throw his weight around.'

Church measured his captain, his friend, and saw something there he wasn't sure he liked. 'And did you let him?'

A coldness seemed to take control of Cole, and he clenched his jaw, his nostrils flaring a little. 'We're short on time,' he growled. 'Just get in the fucking car.'

ELEVEN

PRESENT DAY

THEY WOUND NORTH, sticking to the backroads, avoiding the cameras that Blackthorn's Met would no doubt be scouring. He was living poison, able to sink his fangs into anyone and anything he wanted. He wanted Zawadi in the DRC, he got him. He wanted China and California lining up for his cobalt, he got them. He wanted a career in politics, he got it. And now, with that power at his fingertips, there wasn't an office in the land that was safe. The Met, the PaDP, politicians, business people, journalists. All of them within his reach, and all of them no doubt feeling his poison.

The worst thing of all was how many liked it. How many wanted to give up their honour for a little something extra. For more money, more influence, for a favour.

Or maybe they were smarter than they were weak.

Church wouldn't bend or break for Blackthorn, but he had his training, guns, the capabilities to resist and to fight back. Others weren't so lucky. They knew that if they didn't go willingly into his embrace, if they didn't take the carrot, they'd face the stick. Blackthorn would get them, with gifts or with a gun to their head. People were afraid of losing what they'd worked their whole lives for, and Blackthorn was not above using that.

These days, a tweet, a Facebook post, a message in private to friends. Something you did when you were sixteen. Something you said at a Christmas party ten years ago. All these things were enough to do it these days.

But most people had more skeletons than that. And with the network Blackthorn had working for him, it wasn't hard to find them.

Church pulled onto a rough, unpaved lane and slowed for a steel bar across the road—the kind you find on forestry tracks. He left the engine running and climbed out, looking down the length of the road in either direction in case they were followed.

It looked clear, and they needed to get out of sight. He approached the bar, keeping his ears pricked for any hint they weren't alone, but as he reached under the lockbox for the heavy padlock there, the only sound he could hear was the idle of the Defender and the birds in the trees around him.

He stooped and entered the right code into the combination lock and then swung the bar out.

Church drove through and closed the gate behind

him. Nanna looked drawn, tired already despite it not being even midday yet. The girls were sleeping in the back. Early start for them. What time had the PaDP arrived? Four, five in the morning?

Luckily, it was a Saturday. There'd be no questions of whether they were going back to school for another day or two. Hopefully, there'd be no questions about going back to their lives at all for a few days. Church was banking on them being old enough to understand the kind of stakes they were playing for, but eventually, they'd start to demand some kind of resolution.

Nanna would need to be the one tackling that, though. She could do so with grace, with some tact. Neither was his strong suit. He could do the truth, he could do blunt. Anything else…

He thought of that, how long this would take, and how it was liable to play out at all. How bloody it was going to get. And whether there'd be a 'normal' on the other side. Blackthorn had thrown the first punch, and he'd thrown it low, way below the belt. He'd gone after Church's family, and he had to know what that would bring.

But taking someone like Blackthorn down wasn't easy, and if he did it wrong, it'd put him at the top of every wanted list in the country. Something he was keen to avoid. It was hard enough to hide when the world thought you were dead. He didn't think he could slink off to the Scottish coast to avoid a nationwide manhunt.

So many things rushed through his head as they jostled down the uneven track. It curved gently, and he did his best to avoid the potholes, but it was still rough enough to wake the girls, to prompt questions of, 'Where are we?' and 'Where are we going?'

Church answered neither, and Nanna didn't know to speak either.

But as they broke from the trees into a wide-open, sloped field, she saw the little stone farmhouse, and another ghost.

'Jesus,' she said, shaking her head as he lifted a hand in welcome, lowering the HK417 battle rifle he was holding. 'Mitch is alive, too? The others as well?'

His troop had been like family to him. And over the years, Nanna had come to know them all well. When they'd put him in the ground, he'd been one of four empty caskets. Alongside Mitch, Foster, and Norton.

'No,' Church replied. 'Norton died in the Congo. And Foster…' He brought the truck to a stop in front of the house and Mitch. 'He got out. But we don't know if he's dead. Not yet, at least.'

Nanna seemed to read the unsteadiness in his statement and didn't pry further.

Church got out, turning his attention to Mitch. He hadn't seen him in a decade, and he was looking older. Church was feeling it, but there was still some colour in his hair, still some bulk to his shoulders. Mitch had leaned out, lost the strength he'd carried. His hair had gone from blonde to silver, and his face was lined. He was a little older than Church and looked it. But, despite all that, his bright blue eyes still shone, warm and soft, like they always had.

'Mitch,' Church said, embracing his brother.

Mitch returned it, squeezing tightly, the pressure enough to tell Church how he was taking Foster's disappearance. How much guilt he was carrying over it. 'It's good to see you,' he said, releasing him and turning his attention to Nanna. 'Hannah,' he said, hugging her then. 'You look good.'

'You too,' she lied, hugging him back.

'I'm sorry you're caught up in all this,' he said apologetically.

She waved him off, as though it were all fine, but Church could read the anger in her, could feel it coming off her in waves. Later, when they were alone, she'd let him have it.

'My goodness,' he said then—Mitch was a man of faith, always had been. Never took the Lord's name in vain—'These can't be your girls?' He looked at Lowri and Mia as they climbed out of the Defender.

They stared back at him, then at the gun hanging from his grasp, their eyes widening, the reality of their situation sinking in a little deeper with each passing second.

'They are,' Nanna said, smiling at them, a sudden sadness in her eyes. 'Fifteen and thirteen now.'

'Wow.' He put his hands on his hips, his eyes gravitating towards Church, his stiff posture and folded arms signalling that they could all catch up later. That right now, he needed to know what the fuck was going on.

Mitch obliged, turning back to Nanna. 'Why don't

you take them inside? There's some food out if you're hungry—I guessed you'd be.'

Nanna took one last look at Church, reminding him that they weren't done, and then beckoned her daughters towards the farmhouse. They went in silence, unnerved by it all.

Church couldn't blame them.

He and Mitch waited until the door was closed before they spoke, Mitch pulling the rifle back into his grip, eyes scanning the perimeter of his property.

Church followed his gaze, noticing now the trees he'd cut down around the property, the way the undergrowth was trimmed short at the treeline, minimising cover for anyone approaching. In front of his house, he'd built a stone wall, too. It hemmed in the forecourt and was thick enough to stop any bullet from any gun.

He had been here for years, not moving around, unlike Church. But he'd not gone soft, not gotten slow. The place was fortified, ready for a fight. One had never come, but when it did, Mitch would be ready.

'Any word from Foster?' Church asked, knowing the answer.

'No, nothing. His phone hasn't come back on, either.' He watched Church. 'You meet any resistance getting Hannah and the girls out?'

'Resistance?' Church folded his arms. 'That's one way to put it. Four PaDP guys were pulling her into protective custody when I got there. Was very nearly too late.'

'But you weren't, and that's what matters,' Mitch

replied brightly. He did have an annoying habit of always seeing the silver lining. 'You kill them?'

'No,' Church said.

'That makes a change. Just trying to assess the situation.'

'Trying to see what trouble I've brought to your door, more like.'

Mitch curled a smile. 'I like my door. And I like it untroubled.'

'I don't think there's much chance of it staying that way,' Church said uneasily. 'If there was any doubt that we were still alive, there isn't now, and Blackthorn is going to want to end this, and fast. He'll be coming for us hard.'

'But he'll keep Foster alive,' Mitch replied. 'Make sure he's got everything out of him. It won't be a quick death for him.'

'You want to go and get him.' Church's jaw flexed. 'Blackthorn will be banking on that.'

'Maybe,' Mitch said. 'But it's Paul. We can't just abandon him.'

Church all but ground his teeth. No, they couldn't leave him to that fate. But they also couldn't barrel in there headless.

'First, we clean up our mess here,' Church said. 'Then we can talk about Foster. He know where you are?'

Mitch shook his head. 'Same as you. I never told him anything. We're safe. They're safe.'

Church was thankful for that. Mitch had only let him

know where he was going that morning. He was smart. Smarter than Foster had been.

'That's good. But I'm guessing you know where Foster was set up?'

He nodded.

'Then that's where I'm going. I'll scrub the place, make sure there's nothing that could lead them back to us, and see if I can find out what drove Foster to go back there.' Church shook his head at the thought of it. 'All he had to do was keep his head down.'

'It was eating him. What we did there. What we didn't do. And seeing Blackthorn making a run at Downing Street… It put him over the edge. You can't blame him.'

Church looked up at Mitch's house, thinking of Nanna and the girls. Whose lives had been irreparably altered now.

'I can blame him,' Church said. 'But I don't. I get it. But I still need to be sure that we're safe here. And if he was planning an incursion, Paul would have done his homework. We're going to need his intel if we've got any hope of getting him back.'

He looked Mitch up and down, wondering how capable he still was of getting this done. Doubting that it was enough.

'I should get going,' he said. 'Before they start splashing my face all over the news.'

'You've been up all night.' Mitch put his hand on Church's shoulder and squeezed. 'Come in, eat, rest a little. And talk to Hannah. She looked like she had a bone to pick.'

'Not just one,' Church replied.

Mitch laughed, and it warmed him. 'Who are you more afraid of, her or Blackthorn?'

Church smirked, shaking his head as Mitch guided him towards the front door.

'Come on, Mitch,' he said. 'Do you even need to ask?'

TWELVE

TEN YEARS AGO

THE PLAN TO infiltrate Zawadi's house and plant surveillance went off without a hitch.

It looked like Zawadi had rolled out in force—taking most of his men with him for protection—and the compound was sparsely manned.

Mitch parked up a half-mile from the walls on Cole's command, and they hoofed it through the jungle to a blind spot on the walls.

Cole gave the signal when they were approaching the gate, and when he made a fuss loud enough to draw the attention of the remaining guards, Church and Norton slipped over the wall while Foster and Mitch hung back to give them cover.

They were in and out in a few minutes and got a bug into Zawadi's office before pulling out. They could hear music coming from the upper floor and didn't risk it. Church slowed as he passed the electronically locked door once more—the one that he and Fletcher had asked about—and wondered. It looked like the entrance to a vault, but what exactly was it protecting?

Norton dragged him out before he could think too long on it, and they were back over the wall before anyone knew they were there.

By the time they made it back to the truck, Cole and the others had already left, headed back to the hotel. And as they climbed in, Church couldn't help but think that Cole was rushing back to continue his conversation with Blackthorn.

He said nothing on the ride, just stared out at the slowly darkening sky, watching the jungle roll past, the column of orange dust rising into the air in the distance above the mine. He licked his lips slowly, trying to piece it all together, the slow and painful throb in his temple keeping him focused.

The sun was down by the time they reached the hotel. But inside, none of the others were around. No one in the bar. They climbed to their rooms, keeping an ear open, but heard nothing. Foster and Norton peeled off, and Mitch stayed with Church until after they'd gone.

'You want to pick up where we left off earlier?' he all but whispered.

Church thought on that. 'No,' he said. 'I want to get some rest, my head's killing me. Let's pick it up tomorrow.' He put his hand on his friend's shoulder and squeezed, reassuring him everything was fine.

Mitch measured Church and then nodded. 'Alright. Call if you need anything.'

'Will do.'

Mitch headed to his room, and Church watched him go, digging into the pocket of his cargo pants after he heard Mitch's door close. He pulled out another little surveillance rig, like the one they'd planted in Zawadi's house. A battery-powered microphone and radio transmitter, and the receiver to listen in. As he walked, he matched up the frequencies, making sure they wouldn't interfere with what they were getting from Zawadi's.

Church reached Fletcher's door and stared at it. Should he just knock? Just ask her outright? No, she'd lie. Deny. Evade. She was smart. So he needed to be smarter.

With a little sigh, he stuck the bug on the outside of her doorframe and pushed the earpiece affixed to the receiver into his ear.

He lingered a moment longer, weighing up when he should go to Cole, what he should tell him, and then walked back to his own room, letting himself in, listening to the gentle static of silence coming through the receiver—hoping that it'd stay that way until dawn.

But knowing it wouldn't.

And at one in the morning, he was proven right.

He started suddenly, the sound in his ear loud in his sleep. He was in the chair Mitch had been in, arms folded, feet up on the corner of the bed, sleeping in his clothes and boots. Something he was all too accustomed to.

Church blinked and sat up, a little stiff, and pulled his legs to the floor, rubbing his eyes and regaining his senses. There was a creak and then a clap in his ear, and he knew that Fletcher was on the move. Out of her room.

He checked his watch and saw the time, frowning as he did. He'd hoped he'd be proved wrong.

Church eased himself to his feet and looked at his rifle, freshly cleaned on the bed, right next to his pistol, the smell of gun grease still thick in the air, and decided against it.

He didn't need them. Not for this.

Church headed for the door and slipped into the corridor. The staircase was right in the centre of the building with no door to it. It doubled back on itself upwards, and Fletcher was on the floor above. Church could already hear her coming down the stairs as he waited outside his door, keeping it open not to alert her to his presence.

She was trying to stay quiet but was moving quickly. The way someone did when they didn't want to get caught, but also didn't want to hang around. When he heard her on his floor, he leaned right, trying to catch a glimpse, and saw her in dark clothing, a rucksack over her shoulder.

What was she up to?

When she was a full floor below, Church closed the door gently and went after her. But unlike Fletcher, he'd been trained to move silently and had no trouble keeping pace without her knowing a thing.

He hovered at the bottom of the stairs and watched her exit the building, look left and right, and then set off quickly, pulling up a headscarf to cover her hair, clutching at the hem of her coat over her hip.

She was carrying a weapon. A pistol in a holster on her belt. And she was nervous about it.

And she should have been. She was out, alone at night in a strange place with no discernible police presence, she stuck out like a sore thumb, and she didn't speak the language. Anyone hanging around the streets of Maroua at this time wasn't likely to be your reputable sort. And there was no nightlife here to speak of, nothing worth pursuing at this time, anyway.

So what was her goal?

Before Church even started after her, he had a pretty good idea of it.

He stepped onto the street, grimacing at the oppressive, choking heat, and with sweat already beading in all the wrong places, he followed Fletcher.

She kept a fast pace, but his legs were longer, and he reeled her in to the distance he knew he could catch her at a run in seconds if he needed to.

She made no effort to check behind her as she moved, and Church couldn't help but think how ill-suited she was to this world. How much danger she was putting herself in. And by the way she was moving, hunched forward and hurried, she knew that. So what was so important for her to risk her life like this?

A car rattled by, an old, decrepit Mercedes in burgundy, its shocks blown out so it was basically scraping on the ground. It bounced forward on the springs, laden with guys, and Church hoped that it'd just drive right by. But in the dim glow of the streetlights on this main stretch of road in Maroua, it was clear that Fletcher was a woman. She was slim, she was wearing khaki cargo pants that didn't disguise her figure well enough. And because of that, the brake lights flared.

Church slowed for just a second and reached to his thigh instinctively. No pistol. Shit. He'd specifically left it at the hotel not to intimidate Fletcher, but now he was regretting that.

His mind did the calculation. Twenty metres to her. Less than four seconds at a sprint.

He swallowed and started walking, faster now.

The car slowed, and he tensed to run.

It pulled up alongside her, and a man hung out the window, calling to her.

Fletcher glanced at him and quickened her pace. He held out a hand to grab at her, and the driver eased them closer to the kerb. She stepped away, and the man called out, smacking his lips, beckoning her.

She didn't look at him. Kept walking.

But Church knew that wouldn't help. Wouldn't work. And he knew what came next.

The car accelerated suddenly and swerved onto the kerb, boxing her in against the building.

Church was already running.

The guy in the passenger seat opened the door and stood up, towering over her.

The man in the rear seat did the same thing.

Fletcher clutched at her hip, scrabbling at the hem of her jacket to get it back, to get her pistol out, staring up at them.

One reached out, and she slapped his hand away.

There was a moment of stillness, and then their grins shifted, falling away. This wasn't funny anymore. And Fletcher knew it.

But it was too late to run.

The man from the back seat stepped to her left to surround her.

The one from the passenger seat lunged.

But then Church was there, sweeping around Fletcher. She inhaled sharply, gasping in shock as Church lifted a heel and threw it into the passenger door. It shunted closed, clanging into the man's legs, clamping them against the frame hard enough that Church was surprised his tibias didn't just shatter.

He called out loudly, and the man from the back seat made some sort of effort to attack. But it was haphazard and brutish. Church parried the well-telegraphed swing and drove his fist into the man's solar plexus, winding him and then shoving the guy off the kerb so hard he landed almost in the middle of the street, flat on his back, gasping for air.

The first guy tried his luck now but barely wound up before Church slung a hard uppercut into his gut, the man doubling up over his fist. He pulled it back and threw his knee upwards instead, right into the guy's cheek. He hadn't intended to do it so hard, but there was something in him in that moment. He knew exactly what they would have done to Fletcher. He'd been all over the world, seen what guys like this did to women when they thought no one was looking, when they thought they could get away with it.

Well, they couldn't. Not this time. And though obliterating this man's orbital bone with his knee wasn't going to bring any justice to the others, Church would sleep soundly that night thinking about the sound of it breaking.

He slumped forward onto the concrete pavement without another sound, unconscious, and lay there in a heap.

Before the remaining two men could get out of the car, Church had liberated Fletcher's pistol from its holster and had it jammed through the open door, trained on the driver's head. The man froze and lifted his hand slowly from the door handle, raising them next to his head.

Church backed away, keeping the gun levelled, and took Fletcher by the wrist, gripping tightly. She didn't struggle, knew that even if she did, she'd have no chance of getting away from him.

They walked backwards together until they were clear of the car, and then Church turned her around and marched her forward, deciding that putting the muzzle into the small of her back wasn't necessary for her to get the picture. They moved in silence, Church keeping the pistol in his grasp but at his side, Fletcher steaming as she walked, her shoulders tight and low.

When they were almost to the hotel, Church slowed.

'Alright, far enough,' he said.

She stopped but didn't turn around, her hands now locked in fists at her sides.

'Backpack,' Church ordered.

She hesitated and then shrugged it off slowly, turning and holding it by the cargo loop in front of her. He didn't think he'd ever seen someone look at another person with as much contempt as she was looking at him with.

'Open it.'

'You going to shoot me if I don't?' she asked glibly, looking down at the pistol in his hand.

'Do you understand what just happened back there?' Church asked. 'What *would* have happened if I didn't?'

She looked away, scowling. 'That's why I had the gun.'

'And you would have been too slow to use it,' he replied. 'I was under the impression that you were smart and just not telling me the whole story—now I'm considering the possibility you're just fucking stupid.'

He was trying for a reaction, and he got one. She looked up at him, fire in her eyes, indignant at that.

'Open the fucking backpack,' Church said again.

She reached down and flapped it open, letting Church peer inside by the light of the streetlamp overhead. He could see a camera case for a DSLR, a lens bag for a telephoto, a pair of binoculars.

'Didn't know you were such an avid birdwatcher,' Church said.

'It's not for birds,' she snarled.

'I know,' Church replied. 'You want to tell me what it *is* for?'

'Looks like you already know.'

'I need to hear you say it.'

'Why?'

'Because I need to before I decide what to do about it.'

'You going to *tell on me?*'

'Depends if you lose the attitude,' Church said coolly, lifting the pistol and pushing it into his waistband as a show of peace. 'You're looking at me like you don't know if you can trust me.'

'I don't.'

'Tonight's the third time I've saved your life.'

'It's the third time you've stopped me from getting what I want,' she retorted.

'Your story.'

She averted her eyes.

'Say it. Who you really are. Because you're clearly not a personal assistant. And if you are, you're the shittest one I've ever seen.'

She sneered. 'You want to hear me say it? Fine,' she said, huffing. 'I'm... not Blackthorn's assistant. Not really.'

'I'm shocked.'

'I'm a journalist.'

Church didn't even bother blinking.

'I've been tracking Blackthorn's businesses for nearly two years now, and I knew he was wrapped up in all manner of shady things but could never tie him to anything. When I saw that he was looking for a PA, I knew it would be a good chance to get closer to him, to find something real. Something actionable. And when I found out that he was getting the opportunity to come here to build his EV business, I knew it'd be my best chance to take him down. But…'

'You decided the best time to try and double-cross him was in broad daylight in front of a hundred people,' Church finished for her.

'I was going to say, *but you kept stopping me.*'

Church folded his arms. 'Hence trying to sneak out in the middle of the night.'

'How did you know I was sneaking out anyway?'

Church sighed. 'Because I'm actually good at my job. And what the hell were you hoping to take photographs of anyway, in the middle of the night?'

She swallowed and tightened her grip on her bag. 'I… don't know. Honestly, I just… I just need something. Anything. To show for this trip. Blackthorn doesn't tell me anything. I think he suspects who I really am, or what I'm really doing… I think this is my last job. After we get back, he's going to sack me. I know it.'

'I don't blame him,' Church said, thinking on it all.

'What are you going to do?' she asked.

Church stared at the ground. He knew what he should do. He should call Cole, hold Fletcher until he arrived, and then confine her to her room until the mission was done. He should tell Cole the truth, inform Blackthorn—a friend of the crown and the country on this mission—of her duplicity, and ensure that she didn't do anything to further jeopardise the mission.

And yet... He couldn't get the image of Cole and Blackthorn arguing out of his head. Of the way Murphy had seemed so suspicious of what Mitch was doing in his room. Of how, all of a sudden, there seemed to be a line dividing their team. Cole, Murphy, Boyd, and Reed on one side. Church, Mitch, Norton, and Foster on the other.

'You're hesitating,' Fletcher said, almost tentative. Almost expectant. 'You know I just want to help these people, right? Want to save them from what's already happening here. And from something even worse.'

'Blackthorn.'

'He's not a good man. He exploits and hurts for profit. And this place is no different. What he sees here is opportunity. To line his pockets at the expense of these people. And he's already calculating and scheming and getting his hooks in wherever he can to make it happen. I don't know exactly what's going on with you guys and him—but I know you're not private security here on a diplomatic mission.'

Church looked up at her.

'My guess is military, special forces? You're here for Zawadi, aren't you? To stop him. For good.'

Church stayed quiet. He *had* to stay quiet.

'The thing is, you're working for Blackthorn.'

'We're not working for Blackthorn,' Church said with a little bite.

She smiled at him, almost sadly. With pity, even. 'You are,' she said. 'You just don't know it.'

THIRTEEN

PRESENT DAY

CHURCH WANTED to wait for nightfall, but there was no way he could endure another eight hours with Nanna.

He hadn't seen her in a decade, and yet he already needed to get away; her words were cutting too deep, too close to the bone. She needed time to process, and he needed time to shove the guilt and shame he was feeling back down into the steel trap he'd built for it.

He stepped from Mitch's house with just a few hours of sleep under his belt and headed for the Defender. Mitch stepped out behind him and called his name.

'Sol,' he said, 'you know you can't take that thing. You'll be spotted before you hit the main road. I got something a little more low-profile under a sheet out back. If you're determined to go in the light, at least take that.'

'I'd run there right now if I had to,' Church grumbled, looking back up at the house, keeping his voice low enough to make sure Nanna wouldn't overhear.

Mitch chuckled a little at that. 'Yeah, families, huh. Who'd have them?'

Church stared back at him and felt just a little more guilt. Mitch was never married, never had kids; both his parents were dead, and as far as he knew, he had no siblings. He was the definition of a loner, shut away out here on this farm—no neighbours, nobody for company. Church couldn't imagine how he hadn't gone insane, but it did explain why he was so glad to be hosting.

'Thanks for this,' Church said, 'for looking after them.'

'Of course. You're my brother.'

That was all the explanation he needed to give. Church held out a hand, and Mitch took it, pulling him in for an embrace.

'Car's unlocked, keys are on the dashboard.'

'In case of a quick escape?' Church asked.

'In case of a quick escape,' Mitch grinned.

Church, armed with Foster's address (which was dangerously close to the city), headed to the back of his Defender to stock up. He lifted the floor of the boot and pulled out a case, withdrawing a suppressor and thigh holster for his Glock, along with a concussion grenade and a smoky. He hoped he wouldn't need them, but he wanted to be prepared just in case. If they had Foster, and they knew Church was alive, then there was a good chance they had his address too. Hell, he was probably too late already, but if they were watching the place, Church might need to get creative—and he didn't want to get caught unarmed.

As he screwed the suppressor into the muzzle of his pistol, he thought about the common misconception that a suppressor—often wrongly referred to as a silencer—didn't actually lower the decibel output of a gun all that much. A good suppressor would only bring the noise level down from around 160 decibels to around 125 decibels. Still extremely loud, but what it did do was limit reverberation and echo, making it more difficult to know where a shot was coming from by sound. It also severely limited the muzzle blast and flash, meaning you could use one at night without advertising your location or showing up on thermal imaging.

Again, Church hoped it wouldn't come to that—that he wouldn't be scurrying through the streets of London on foot with just a pistol when the sun did go down, fighting for his life. But in case he was, he wanted every advantage he could get.

As he walked back towards Mitch, he couldn't help but ask:

'Why the fuck was Foster living so close to the city?'

Mitch shook his head gently. 'He was obsessed with taking Blackthorn apart and wanted to be as close to him as possible—I think to remind himself of it all.'

Church said: 'I'm surprised he didn't blow up the Houses of Parliament.'

Mitch sucked air through his teeth. 'I don't think he

was far off.' He took on a sombreness then. 'He wasn't right, Sol. When I spoke to him, he was changed, paranoid, like he was losing his mind. When you get in there, be careful—he thought Blackthorn was coming for him. Who knows what kind of welcome wagon he rolled out for them.'

'I should keep my eyes peeled for tiger pits, then,' Church almost joked.

But Mitch wasn't laughing. 'Just watch your back,' he said. 'I'm sorry I can't go with you.'

'It's okay. You're the only person in the world I trust with Nanna and the girls right now, and if anybody but me comes up to that gate—'

'Don't worry,' Mitch said. 'I've got a welcome wagon of my own.'

Mitch went back inside, and Church uncovered the Volvo estate that Mitch was hiding. The model year was 1996, and Church knew the engines in these things were good for 300,000 miles—and that Mitch, like him, took care of his possessions.

Church slid in behind the wheel, his Glock strapped to the side of his right thigh. He crawled away from Mitch's stronghold; there was a sat nav wired into the console, and Church paused just before the steel gate to type in the address.

Church frowned at just how close it was to where he'd come from that morning. Foster would have had to be crazy to want to set up inside city limits—in the most surveilled city in the world. With half a million public and registered cameras in use, and tens if not hundreds of thousands of private cameras operating, it was the most difficult place you could choose to put yourself. The wilds of the Scottish coast or the rural interior of England were much easier to get lost in.

Church thought of Foster as he drove. He was a big guy, short-haired, with a flat, crooked nose that'd been broken ten times over. He was a brawler, a fighter through and through. He was the guy who was always hoping they'd run into trouble on a patrol or a march, that they'd get sucked into an engagement—that a job wouldn't be quick and quiet. A firefight was his idea of a good night out. But stupid, he wasn't. So if he'd decided London was where he should be, then maybe Mitch was right. Maybe Foster was losing his mind.

He cruised with the mid-afternoon traffic, sitting back in the chair to make the cameras' life more difficult. Church trusted Mitch had been careful with the registration and insurance, that it was all in order and untraceable. Still, he never let his guard down, keeping his eyes sharp all the way—checking side streets and alleyways for any plainclothes cars on patrol. If he spotted anything amiss, he'd just keep going, would leave Foster's well alone, and head back to Nanna to figure out their next move. Likely leaving the country. But maybe, just maybe, Foster had held out long enough not to give his address away. Church didn't know what he'd have had to endure, but he could imagine. There wasn't much he hadn't seen in his years.

What he wasn't seeing was any police presence. No marked cars, no sirens, no blockades. After that morning, he'd half expected the city to be in lockdown—but Blackthorn had a lot to lose, and Church doubted he wanted to explain the minutiae of what was going on to anyone he didn't have to. He was keeping this under wraps, and Church wasn't complaining.

He eased up on Foster's hideout: a rundown former brick-built factory that had been converted into apartments. It looked all but abandoned, tucked down a long side street that ended at train tracks.

Church looked along the street, assessing it, before he drove past and parked around the corner. Foster had chosen well. There was no back entrance to the building, and only one way in, from one direction. Mitch said his apartment was on the top floor—that Foster had given him the details in case he didn't make it back, so he could go in and torch the place. Metaphorically. Or perhaps literally, considering Foster's status.

Church glanced around the deserted street and reached down, unstrapping the holster from around his thigh. It was secured to his belt at the top and could be flipped up, hidden under his jacket as he walked. The last thing he needed was some bystander calling 999 because they'd seen a man with a gun trotting through London.

He exited the vehicle, moving quickly, keenly aware of the feel of his ballistic vest against his chest—of all the high windows around him—and of the vest's inability to stop a 7.62x51mm NATO round, the standard calibre for most modern, urban-suited sniper rifles.

Church quickened his pace, making himself a

tougher target, and turned the corner, walking down the access lane to Foster's building. Mitch didn't have a key, but Church didn't need one. Foster had put a combination lock on the door and given Mitch the code.

There was a twelve-foot brick wall at the end of the road, stopping anyone from jumping or climbing onto the tracks, making the lane a dead end. The phrase didn't sit well with Church, but he understood why Foster had chosen it: a defensible position that would force incoming opposition into a perfect kill box. Church fully expected to find a rifle set up at a window, ever ready for it. That's what he'd do.

Church approached the door and let himself inside. There wasn't even a lock.

He stepped into the inner corridor, which led straight, then cut right along the back wall of the building. A sign reading '1 & 2' pointed along the corridor beside the corner. On the left-hand wall, a concrete staircase led to the second of four floors. Foster was in apartment eight.

Church opened the hem of his jacket, letting his pistol fall back into place. He clicked the latch together and started upwards, drawing it from its holster as he moved. Other people would use these stairs, so they wouldn't be laden with traps. Yet as he crested the first flight, he noticed the tiny camera in the top corner, the kind they used on ops when monitoring a location and waiting for a target. No doubt it was feeding back to a screen somewhere in Foster's apartment.

Church moved upwards quietly, listening for any

signs of life from the other flats. There was music on the first floor. The sound of a television echoed from the second. The third was silent.

He took the last flight of stairs carefully, checking each step. But, presumably, there was someone else living up here too, not just Foster.

Church reached the landing and pricked his ears, hearing nothing, then pressed forward, bringing the pistol up into both of his hands, holding it at low ready, leading with his right foot, half on, close to the wall.

He followed the corridor along, passing the door for apartment seven and continuing on to number eight. The corridor grew darker as he approached. There were no windows, and it looked like the light above Foster's door was broken. On purpose, Church thought—likely to obscure a tripwire. If Foster wasn't sure he was coming back, there was a good chance he'd have rigged this place up. And the last thing Church wanted was to get caught out with an IED. He'd successfully managed to avoid them his whole career; he wasn't about to lose a limb in a London apartment block.

Keeping his steps small, he stooped and edged forward, looking for any kind of device.

He leaned into the wall for stability and felt it bow. He pressed it and found plasterboard—stud wall. Made sense. The whole space would have been open originally, now partitioned.

'Smart,' Church muttered, searching for something else now. He'd been keeping his eyes peeled for an explosive device of some sort, but plasterboard meant nothing to a claymore or a block of plastic explosive. Having it positioned behind the wall—with just a line coming through the plasterboard—was more likely to catch intruders off guard.

He kept moving slowly, straining his eyes for a glimpse of what he guessed was low-gauge fishing line, and stopped an inch short of tripping it. Church's heart beat faster as he dragged his toe back from under it, then gingerly lifted his boot over, stepping clear of the line.

A long, rattling breath escaped his lips as he closed in on the door, knowing that if there was one, there'd be more. He dared not move as he typed in the code for the door and listened to the electronic bolt recede. Once it was unlocked, he twisted the handle and eased it open just a centimetre, dragging the three-and-a-half-inch folding hunting knife he always carried from his pocket. He opened it and pushed it through the gap, running it up from the bottom of the door until he found what he expected: another wire had been rigged, though Church doubted this one was tied to an explosive payload. That would risk setting off a chain reaction with the other charge. No, he guessed this one would be hooked to a good old-fashioned twelve-gauge packed with buckshot on a tripod six feet from the door—ready to fill whoever was unlucky enough to open it with steel ball bearings.

Church gently sawed at the line until it cut through, knowing the trigger pressure for a typical shotgun was around five to seven pounds—which meant he needed a light touch.

Once the line was severed, he eased the door wider,

cursing Foster for forcing him to waste so much time and wondering how the hell he'd managed to rig all this and still get out.

Putting that thought to the back of his mind, he stepped inside and let out a low whistle, closing the door behind him. 'Fucking hell,' he muttered, looking around.

He was dead-on about the shotgun. It was a Benelli M4, just like the one in his truck. Old habits died hard—it was the one they used in the service.

Church looked at it for just a moment, noting the line from the door rigged to a pair of pulleys angled back towards the handle. Simple but effective engineering that wouldn't pull the gun off course if someone threw the door open. Not that it'd matter from this range; it would make mincemeat out of anyone standing in front of it, the sawn-off barrel widening the spread of the shot.

Church's eyes roved wider then, homing in on the left-hand wall. He was standing in the living room, but where a television should have been mounted on the exposed brick, there was a huge mural of newspaper clippings, online articles, and surveillance photos.

Church approached, holstering his pistol, and looked over it all. Wire-transfer records, bank statements, redacted government documents, pictures of Blackthorn alone, Blackthorn meeting politicians and business people, dignitaries, even Zawadi. Lots of them, taken with a long lens from who knew how far away.

The wall was laid out chronologically, tracking

Blackthorn over the last three years or so. Meticulously. Fanatically. Foster wasn't just determined to bring Blackthorn down—he was obsessed with it. He was stalking him, hunting him, waiting for the moment to take him out. But he didn't just want to put a bullet in him; he wanted to tear his empire down first, to expose who he really was before ending him.

Church looked over to the window, to the unmistakable outline of a rifle set up on a bipod, angled towards the lane's entrance, just as he'd suspected. How many hours had Foster stood here, imagining pulling that trigger and watching Blackthorn fall?

Church caught something else out of the corner of his eye then—a photo of someone he hadn't seen or thought about in a long time. On a console table in front of Foster's wall of Blackthorn was a file, with a photograph of Anastasia Fletcher paperclipped to the cover.

Church walked towards it and picked it up. But before he could open the front page, a loud chime sounded from the other side of the room.

He slipped the file into the back of his jeans under his jacket and headed for the noise. A desk was set up next to a door leading to Foster's bedroom, a computer monitor on top.

Church tapped the keyboard and waited for the screen to light up, glancing to the right of it, seeing another photo there. The same one that hung on the pillar in his cottage at Benalder: a photo of their troop. Him, Mitch, Norton, Murphy, Reed, Boyd, Cole... The whole gang.

The screen came to life and Church's blood ran cold. Three of the men in that photo—Cole, Reed, Boyd—were coming up the stairs. And judging by their movements and the C8s pinned to their shoulders, they weren't planning a friendly visit.

FOURTEEN

TEN YEARS AGO

CHURCH WOKE up like he went to sleep. Thinking about Cole and Blackthorn.

He wasn't sure if he woke before the knock at the door or as it was happening. But either way, he was on his feet before the last rap and striding quickly towards it. Was it going to be Fletcher? Mitch? Murphy again?

He froze for a second, reaching out for it, unsure if he wanted to know what was beyond. *No, that's not you, Solomon.* He shook off the trepidation and pulled the handle, opening the door to reveal Cole.

He narrowed his eyes, inspecting Church like a trainer does a horse.

'Late night?' he asked, gaze fixed on the bags under Church's eyes.

'I'm not sleeping,' Church replied. 'The heat.'

'AC broken?' Cole leaned forward and peered up at the box in the corner of Church's room.

'Just noisy. Had to switch it off. Gets too hot and wakes me up. I get up to switch it on, it's too noisy to sleep. Rinse and repeat.' He shrugged, dismissing it as a *me* problem, and Cole stuck out his bottom lip.

They both knew full well that they'd slept in hotter, colder, louder, and way worse places. There was an art to it that they taught in SF, and Cole knew as well as Church that it was an excuse and nothing more. But he didn't call him on it.

'Looks like our trip to Zawadi's yesterday ruffled his feathers,' Cole went on, hooking his thumbs into his belt. 'Looks like he bought the reason for our little visit, and now he thinks that his trade deal with Blackthorn is in danger and wants him there for a feast to smooth the waters.' He narrowed his eyes at Church again. 'We're heading over there in an hour. Be ready.'

Church nodded, and Cole moved to turn away, pausing and turning back. 'You good, Sol?'

'Yeah, of course,' Church answered. Maybe a little too quickly.

'Sure? Nothing you want to tell me?'

Was he fishing, or did he know something? Church shook his head. 'I'm solid. Going to shower, get myself straight.' He hooked a thumb over his shoulder, and Cole licked his bottom lip, weighing it up.

'Alright then. Downstairs in sixty.'

'Wilco,' Church replied before closing the door. He

let out a little breath and flexed his hands. Not much made him nervous, but lying to Cole did.

And as he headed for the shower, he realised that he owed Fletcher exactly nothing—and the man he'd just lied to a whole lot. He'd been so concerned about Cole betraying his trust, he'd been blind to the truth of it: it was *him* that was betraying Cole's.

Church barely registered the next hour, going over and over the last few days in his head, looking for any and every crack in the narrative for some hint of which way to go on this.

They convened in the lobby, but there was no sign of Fletcher.

Church wondered but didn't ask, and they loaded into the trucks in their usual formation. At the last moment, Fletcher stepped out of the hotel and climbed in next to Church, keeping her eyes fixed out of the window. No intention of talking.

Church looked up and saw Cole staring at him in the rear-view from the front passenger seat. He gave him a little nod, and Cole turned his eyes to the road ahead, motioning for Reed to drive.

As they approached the compound gates, Church expected the usual, but this time they were waved through, expected. And as they came to the house, he realised that this wasn't a normal day. Vans were parked in front of the house, and young men and women in freshly pressed white shirts were ferrying food and drinks into the house on silver platters. Enough for a feast.

'What the fuck?' Cole muttered in the front as he waved Reed to drive around the fountain and stop facing the gate.

He did as instructed, and Church couldn't help but notice Blackthorn staring up at the place nervously. From Cole's message, Zawadi was looking to broker peace here, cement their supposed trade deal. But Blackthorn didn't seem his usual, puffed-up, cocky self.

Something was off.

Cole ordered them out of the vehicle, and the four in the front disembarked first, leaving Church and Fletcher to climb out as usual. When they were alone, Church reached out and touched her leg, trying to get her attention. She swatted his hand away without a word and stepped into the relentless sun.

Church climbed out his side and found Cole waiting for him.

'Fletcher,' he said, his voice low.

'What about her?'

'You're on her today. Like a fly on shit. Got it?'

Church tried to mask any physical reaction. 'Got it.'

'Don't let her out of your sight. She pisses, I want to know what colour it was.'

'I'll bring you a glass.'

Cole curled a little smile and lifted a loosely balled fist, knocking gently on Church's broad chest. 'I knew you were the right man for the job, Sol. I can always rely on you, can't I?'

He was really asking.

Church nodded firmly. 'You can.'

'Good.' He turned to the others. 'Rifles and packs stay in the car. Side-arms only. Keep it cool.' He glanced around, and everyone nodded. 'Reed, Boyd, you're with me. The rest of you stay with the vehicles. Be ready for quick exfil.'

Church was already aware of Fletcher at the edge of the pack, standing off like a pariah. She was doing little to shield herself from the suspicions that were clearly building around her. She said that Blackthorn was going to fire her when they got back. And it was clear that she wasn't involved enough in his businesses to have her story yet. He was keeping her at arm's length because he didn't trust her. And the chasm of space between them reinforced Church's summation of that.

He didn't have any more time to assess the dynamics before Zawadi's voice rose from his papal balcony.

'Sir Blackthorn!' he called, bowing over the concrete balustrade. He lifted a hand then—and Church was sure he thought that it was a gesture of magnanimity, of a gracious welcome. But Church couldn't help but think it looked far more dictatorial. 'Welcome, welcome!' Zawadi went on. 'Please, come inside out of this heat. I have much to show you.'

He disappeared from view, and Blackthorn looked at Cole, waiting for the go-ahead.

Cole gave him the signal, and Blackthorn shook off his nerves, literally shaking out his hands and exhaling. He assumed his usual pompousness like he was throwing on a coat and strode towards the front steps, waiting for the waiters and waitresses delivering the food to get out of his path.

They did so, keeping their heads down, and Cole, Reed, and Boyd all followed behind like ducks. Fletcher made no attempt to hide the roll of her eyes before she followed. Church fell into step with her and couldn't help himself.

'Can I count on you keeping your head down today?' he asked as they approached the stairs.

'I don't know what you're talking about,' she replied, taking the first step.

'You know exactly what I'm talking about. You try anything, and you put me in a tough position. One where I have to decide whether to lie or not to cover your arse,' he muttered back, shoulder to shoulder as they climbed.

'Well then,' she said, fixing a grin to her face as they got to the top and reached the front door, 'I guess you'll just have to decide what's more important, won't you? The lives of the people here, your moral duty'—she turned to him, the grin false and strange on her mouth—'or your job.'

Fletcher pulled her shoulders back and strode inside, taking a glass of champagne off a silver platter being offered to her. She threw it back in a single gulp and headed after Blackthorn and his entourage.

Church politely declined a glass from the waitress at the door and went after her. They headed through to the dining room once more, where the huge table had been laid with food. A suckling pig was in the centre, surrounded by beautiful arrangements of fruits and other expensive foods from around the world. It seemed like Zawadi had gone all out, unsure what Blackthorn liked and not risking it. There was fresh fish, fresh pasta, little roasted game birds, a beef wellington, a rack of lamb, a huge slab of beef, and even sushi. It was enough food to feed the dozen men in that room three times over. But there were only four places set.

Zawadi was smoking a cigar and holding a glass of scotch when they entered, talking in a low voice to his lieutenant from the mine, Katenda. Zawadi made a hushing motion with his hand and pointed, and Katenda turned, grinning, and bowed to Blackthorn as he entered. The man spread his arms wide and beckoned Zawadi into an embrace as though they were old friends.

'I'm sorry for all this mess,' Blackthorn said.

'No, no,' Zawadi replied, clapping Blackthorn on the back, sprinkling ash onto his polished marble floor. 'It is my fault—I take full responsibility for what happened at the mine. It was your right to inspect the place as you saw fit, and how my men reacted...' He put his hand on his chest now, the cigar gently curling blue smoke into the warm air. 'It is unacceptable.' His eyes floated to Church then, lingering on the bruise and cut on his temple. 'This is your man? The one who was struck?'

Blackthorn barely looked at Church. 'Never mind all that, it's what he's paid for,' Blackthorn laughed. 'In Britain, we call these *teething problems*. Expected with any new business venture. It's already forgotten,' Blackthorn gushed.

'Nevertheless,' Zawadi said apologetically. 'I have spoken at length to Katenda here, and he assures me that when you return to the mine, you will be treated with the respect and reverence that a man of your station deserves. He will ensure this.'

'I appreciate that,' Blackthorn said without a hint of humbleness.

Church resisted the urge to roll his eyes. He thought if everyone else left the room right now, they'd probably just jump straight to cradling each other's balls. Luckily, their audience seemed to dissuade them of that, and they settled for a lengthy, two-handed handshake instead.

Zawadi finally pulled away and clapped, and a fleet of waiters snapped to attention, ready to serve and possibly spoon-feed the guests.

Fletcher took her place next to Blackthorn without a word to anyone, and Church formed up around the edge of the room as they had done before. Now, though, through the open doors, he could see that Zawadi's men were lingering too. Closer than before, as though poised to intervene if necessary.

Church placed himself next to the door leading deeper into the house, a good distance from Fletcher but with a clear line of sight to her. He wanted to see her face, be able to read her expression for any hint of what she was thinking. She wouldn't be speaking during this celebratory dinner, but he'd still watch her, try to make sure she didn't do anything stupid. Though he knew that hope was likely misplaced.

One of the things that Church had become especially good at over the years was tuning out noise. Whether it was gunfire, car tyres, aeroplane propellers, or inane dinner conversation, he could comfortably make his mind go elsewhere and disconnect his ears from reality. And he was glad of that right now. The kind of sycophantic, ego-stroking conversation at this table would have been enough to drive him nuts. They feasted like pigs, gorging themselves on a fraction of the food before sitting back to drink.

Blackthorn suddenly erupted into laughter loud enough to shock Church back to the moment, and he dialled himself back into what was going on.

'—if you insist!' Blackthorn finished.

Zawadi lifted his hands and clapped once more. A line of women began filing into the room, their skin smooth and shining, their faces made up, their slender figures on full display in their short, figure-hugging dresses.

They took up the empty seats around the men and began draping themselves over them, sitting on laps and leaning over shoulders, rubbing chests and fondling ears seductively.

Blackthorn looked rather pleased with the outcome, but Fletcher, disgusted, pushed back from the table and dropped her napkin onto her plate, excusing herself from the dining-room-cum-brothel.

Church perked up and glanced over at Cole for the

silent confirmation that he should trail her. But Cole wasn't looking at him. He was fixed on Murphy, standing on the other side of the door from Fletcher.

When she breezed between them and into the hall, he lifted his chin at Murph, and he nodded, twisting to follow her out into the hall.

Church froze for a second, unsure what to do. Cole had asked him to keep an eye on her but had instructed Murphy to tail her now? If she did try something and got caught... Murphy wasn't liable to go easy on her. And if she broke down, divulging that Church knew who she really was...

Without meeting Cole's eye, Church ducked out of the room, past Zawadi's men, and in a few quick strides caught Murphy by the arm.

'Hey, I've got this,' Church said, watching Fletcher head further down the corridor.

'It's fine,' Murphy replied. 'You head back. You've babysat Fletcher long enough.' He smiled at Church, but it didn't feel quite right, not quite real. 'I'll watch her.'

Church's grip tightened a little. 'Seriously, it's fine. I'm used to it.'

They stared at each other, neither wanting to yield, and Church felt like he'd oversold it.

Murphy put his hands up then. 'Fine, you want her that bad, take her,' he said, chuckling. 'I don't blame you. She's sort of alright, if you like that whole *miserable bitch* thing.' He shrugged and gave Church a little faux salute before he headed back to the dining room.

Church thought about glancing over his shoulder,

but he knew Cole would be watching him. He pushed forward, knowing he'd likely sealed his own fate—and maybe Fletcher's too—and caught her up. The corridor was empty, with Zawadi's men clustered around the dining room.

Church hoped she was just headed for the bathroom like last time, but instead, she breezed straight past, aiming for the double doors on the right. Because of the shape of the house, they were out of sight of the dining room now, but despite that—and Church breaking into a run—Fletcher had gone into Zawadi's office before he got there. The same office he'd been in the day before with Mitch to plant their surveillance equipment.

He swore silently as he entered, easing the door closed as quietly as possible.

The room was big, with large windows facing out over the garden. The walls were lined with expensive art, and at the back of the room, a huge hardwood desk dominated the floor. Fletcher was already behind it, rifling through the drawers.

She looked up at Church, scowled, and then immediately went back to searching. This was dangerous, and she was clutching at straws, trying for anything to give her story some credibility. What did she even hope to find?

He closed the gap on her fast before she could say anything incriminating. The recording device behind the painting to the right of the desk would pick it up—there wasn't a shadow of a doubt about that.

'If you're here to try and—' she began, looking up at him again before he seized her.

Church clamped his hand over her mouth and had to take her by the waist so she didn't fall backwards. She began to mumble quickly from under his hand, trying to push him off, but he tightened his grip, the look in his eyes enough to still her. When he was sure she wasn't going to try and claw his eyes out, he leaned in and whispered in her ear, the words barely audible.

'The room is bugged,' he muttered. 'Don't say anything.'

Her brow crumpled, but he felt her nod under his grasp. Tentatively, he took his hand from her mouth, and she whispered back to him.

'How do you know the room is bugged?'

'Because I'm the one who bugged it,' he replied. 'Now, quietly, let's go.'

'I'm not leaving,' she practically hissed.

Church, hand still raised, threatened to silence her again.

'I'm not leaving,' she replied, lowering her voice once more. 'Not until I find something—'

She cut herself off suddenly, her eyes flying to the door.

Church's skin prickled, the hair on the back of his neck standing up like it did when he knew someone was watching him.

Without hesitating, with his still-raised hand, he cupped her face and made to kiss her.

She pushed him off and straightened her clothing, clearing her throat and gesturing to the door.

Church turned, as though it was the first hint he got that they weren't alone, and saw that one of Zawadi's men was standing in the doorway.

Church still had his hand around Fletcher's waist and held onto her tightly, hoping she'd get the idea that this was the ruse they were going with.

'Can we help you?' Church asked before the guy could speak.

'What are you doing in here?' the guard asked, stepping inside. They'd clearly been told to *dress up* for the formal occasion, so the guy was in military fatigues and black boots, a semi-clean T-shirt.

'What does it look like?' Church said back, his tone sharp enough to convey his displeasure at the interruption.

'This is General Zawadi's private office,' the guard said, coming forward. He was unarmed but made a grab for his hip as though he was armed, stiffening slightly when he realised he wasn't. 'No one should be in here.'

'Which is why we chose it,' Church sighed, releasing Fletcher and coming around the desk. 'We wanted some peace and quiet. If you know what I mean.'

The guard narrowed his eyes at Church and then leaned out to look at Fletcher, her eyes firmly fixed on the ground. 'In the General's office?'

Church shrugged. 'Better than his bed, isn't it?'

The man flexed his jaw, not liking Church's attitude.

But this was how it had to go now. If they apologised and ran out, that would be more suspicious. At least this story might sell to this guy, might get them off the hook with Zawadi, and who knew—maybe even convince Cole that the only collusion going on between him and Fletcher was the physical kind.

'Look, I don't want to get too graphic here, but you want to give us a few minutes?' Church asked him.

'I cannot leave you in here,' the guard said.

'I don't really give a shit if you stay and watch, but the lady might, so why don't you just pretend you didn't see us, hey? Or maybe I'll have to tell Zawadi that his men are causing more problems for Blackthorn.'

The guy flinched a little at that. Church wondered what had happened to the guard that struck him. Whether he was still working for Zawadi, or, hell, whether he was even still breathing.

'Just walk out that door. Don't say anything, and I won't either. And the whole world just keeps on turning. If you don't… You're going down,' Church said, stepping closer to the man and standing over him, 'and I'm going to tell Zawadi that you swung first. And that's going to be your word against mine. You want to find out what happens after, or just let me get on with what I came here to do?' Church asked him coolly, staring right into his eyes.

The guy swallowed, nostrils flaring, and broke first. He stepped away and headed for the door, pausing and looking back. 'Five minutes,' he said. 'Then I'm coming back.'

Church gave him a little nod, and the man disappeared. He let out a relieved sigh and turned back towards the desk, blinking in astonishment to see that Fletcher hadn't wasted a second before she'd started her search again.

'Are you fucking kidding me?' Church whispered, going back to her.

'You heard him, we've got five minutes,' Fletcher replied curtly. 'Now, are you going to just stand there like an idiot, or help me?'

Church looked over at the painting, the recorder. There was no way he could spin this. Cole would hear the whole thing, and he'd know Church was playing both sides. He watched Fletcher tearing through Zawadi's papers and knew she'd find nothing. But worse—she'd happily get him killed for her crusade. He had no loyalty to her, and no reason to protect her when she kept throwing his help back in his face.

He stepped forward.

'Good, you're finally growing a pair, then,' she practically scoffed, shaking her head at him as she continued to search.

'Sorry about this,' he said, knowing it was by far the cleanest and quickest way to get it done.

'Sorry about what?'

She looked up as he grabbed her, pulling her in and spinning her around in one swift motion, locking her into a chokehold, her chin in the crook of his elbow. He applied even pressure to the jugular veins on either side of her neck and held fast. She struggled for a few seconds, managing a few garbled words before she slipped smoothly into unconsciousness.

He hadn't touched her oesophagus, she was still breathing normally, but the blood supply had been cut off to her brain, and she fainted. It was coerced, but the mechanism was the same. He'd hold a few seconds longer and then release. She'd regain consciousness pretty quickly but would be groggy, and by the time she got her wits back, she'd already be in the car.

Church let her go and picked up her limp body, slinging her over his shoulder before he made for the door, knowing that if he was spotted, this would be hard to explain—but a damn sight easier than the alternative.

He was loyal to his unit, to Cole, to the mission.

Fletcher had tugged at his heartstrings briefly. But she'd overlooked one major aspect of the situation.

Church was a good soldier—but it didn't mean he was a good man.

FIFTEEN

PRESENT DAY

CHURCH WAS HOPING they might have just tripped Foster's gift and blown themselves all up, but it wasn't the case. It was clear that, as well as his address, whoever was torturing Foster in the DRC got him to spill the goods on his booby traps as well, and with surgical, militant precision, they disarmed the trap and moved towards the door.

Church stood at the desk, the photograph in his hands, listening to them move on the other side of the wall. He placed the photo down in the exact position from which he'd picked it up and stepped through into Foster's bedroom, easing the door shut behind him. Drawing his pistol from its holster, he held it ready in both hands, waiting for them to come into the apartment, and gave a quick glance around, looking for any kind of cover in case they decided to search the place in its totality.

He saw it then. The square hole cut through the wall leading into apartment seven, the one next door. That's how he'd got out. Foster had rented both apartments, likely under different names, to give himself a quick exit route if anybody tried to breach the door.

'Clever boy,' Church muttered under his breath, listening as Cole and the others cracked the front door and let themselves in.

Church cursed himself. He'd cut the line of the shotgun and not reaffixed it or even removed it. If they spotted that, they'd know somebody had been through, and he guessed by the silence they were sharing and the lack of movement that they'd seen the trail he'd left and had paused to make sure they were alone.

Church pressed his ear to the thin partition wall and listened, closing his eyes, trying to map their movements by sound. Alone. Their footsteps spread through the room and, once they'd checked behind the couch in the kitchen nook, he heard someone coming towards the bedroom.

He took one look at the door, realising it opened towards the wall, and moved across just as the handle began to turn. Pressing his back into the corner and lifting the gun so it hovered next to his head, the door swung around, forcing him to splay his toes so it wouldn't knock into them. Whoever was on the other side kept their hand on the knob, and Church could place them exactly. He was half-minded just to tilt his gun forward and pull the trigger—put a bullet through the side of their head. But he knew that whoever was unlucky enough to be standing there wasn't alone, and that still left pretty shitty odds for him coming out of this alive.

The man stepped forward, pulling his rifle to his shoulder, and walked into the room, heading for Foster's escape hole. Church tilted his head sideways, seeing around the door. They were in civvies—jeans, fleece, black watch cap. Church couldn't tell which it was from behind, but he guessed Boyd. He approached the hole and ducked through. It crossed Church's mind that he could go after him, get up behind him and stick his knife in his jugular. But any sound would send Cole and Reed running. If it was Cole moving through the hole, Church probably would have done it anyway. But he needed to get out of this, needed to temper himself.

He heard a sigh then on the other side of the door and ducked back behind it, leaning the other way to look through the thin gap at the frame. Cole was standing five feet away, at Foster's desk, staring down at the photograph Church had been looking at.

The man picked it up. He looked older, more weathered. Like the years had been unkind to him. His face was pockmarked, like some disease had ripped through him, his eyes ringed with dark circles. But despite that, Church knew he was still lethal.

He watched his old captain, moving his finger off the trigger and onto the side of the pistol so he didn't get any ideas.

Boyd came back then, footsteps approaching across the room quickly.

Church stilled, held his breath as the man stepped back into Foster's apartment, pulling the bedroom door behind him. It swung out enough that Church could slip from behind it, but he dared not move.

'Clear,' Boyd said, nodding to Cole.

Church watched them through the gap.

'No sign of anyone,' Boyd said. 'If anyone was here, they're long gone.'

Cole nodded slowly. 'Alright, clean this place out,' he said, his voice rasping, harsher than Church remembered. He gestured to Foster's wall. 'Take everything, make sure there's nothing left behind.'

Boyd nodded, hovering for a second before he gestured to the photograph. 'Getting sentimental all of a sudden?'

Cole stared back at him, cold as steel. 'No.' He dropped the photo and it cracked as it landed, a sharp line lancing through their troop. Cole started forward then, grinding his heel into the picture before he went to inspect Foster's investigation.

'And when you're done,' he said, putting his hands on his hips, surveying the wall, 'burn this place to the ground.'

Boyd chuckled, and Reed chimed in from across the room.

'Wilco,' Boyd said with a grin, stepping forward and tearing into Foster's wall.

Reed joined in, and Cole hung back, hooking his hands into the collar of his Kevlar vest, watching them.

Church stepped silently into Foster's bedroom, staring out at the three, and lined up his pistol. Could he take them all out before they turned? One, definitely. Two, maybe. All three? He had only his pistol and no cover, and these walls wouldn't stop their bullets.

He lined up Cole's head and let out a soft breath. *Do it. Do it,* he told himself.

But this was bigger than him, and bigger than the men in that room.

They needed to take Blackthorn down, and killing Cole right here wasn't going to do that.

He backed away slowly, covering them until the frame of the door obscured his view, and then slipped through Foster's escape hatch into the adjoining apartment. It was spartan, completely empty except for a rope that had been knotted through an eyelet bolted to the floor next to the window. Jesus, Foster really was preparing for all outcomes.

Church thought of his friend, of what they were probably doing to him right now. What they were pulling off—fingernails—or pulling out—teeth. What they were clamping on—jumper cables to testicles—or breaking—toes with a hammer—and promised himself he'd do all he could to help. To get him out. Or, if it was too late already... to avenge him.

Church unlatched the door carefully and checked the corridor was clear, then made a beeline for the stairs, descending at pace, wanting as much distance as possible between Cole and him. Not because he was afraid the man would catch up, but that if he lingered too long, he'd lose his nerve, go back, and take the shot. His own life be damned.

He stuck close to the wall of the building and hit the corner, spotting a blacked-out G-Wagon parked across the street. He could slash the tyres, slow them down, but he'd also be announcing his presence. And right now, he was a ghost. And that's how he planned to stay.

When he got behind the wheel of the Volvo, he drove off quickly, stopping only once he was more than a mile away, pulling into a residential street to catch his breath.

Church shifted in the chair and pulled the file from the back of his belt, laying it out on his lap.

Anastasia Fletcher stared up at him. The photograph looked to be one taken from a company website. It had that look about it—grey background, neutral smile. She looked older than when he'd seen her last in the DRC, more mature, thin lines showing around her mouth and at the corners of her eyes. But she was still the same woman. At least on the outside.

He turned the page and saw another photo of her paper-clipped to the top. This one wasn't downloaded, though. It was taken. Long lens, same as the ones of Blackthorn.

Church's eyes narrowed a little. Why was Foster following her? Was she still involved with Blackthorn? Questions raced through his head as he pulled the paper-clip free and began going through the pages in the file.

More pictures of Fletcher. Going in and out of buildings, in and out of her house, at lunch, running. Hell, Foster was practically stalking her.

Church didn't know how to feel as he flipped the pages, reaching the end of the photographs and getting into the paper trail instead. Foster had been invasive—likely found someone to do some digital hacking and slashing for him. There were plenty of redacted government documents on his wall. He wasn't worried about scruples. And Fletcher was also on his hitlist, it seemed. Her work history, her medical history, her bank accounts, phone records, her travel history. Hell, there was even a map printout of where she lived and the routes she took to and from work, timings that she was likely to hit key intercept points. Foster had treated this whole thing like an op. Start to finish.

But was his intention to hurt Fletcher?

Church's blood pressure flared as he thought of that, forcing himself not to jump to conclusions. He flipped back to her work history to check whether she was still involved in Blackthorn's businesses—though he couldn't imagine a world where she was.

He felt the blood recede in his ears seeing that she'd moved out of the UK almost right after the DRC and had been a foreign correspondent in the Middle East, then North Africa, and then Asia, hopping from Hong Kong to Seoul before settling in Japan. And then it looked like she took a job in the UK.

Strange. Her history had all the hallmarks of fleeing Blackthorn's reach in case he came for her. But to be back now, starting her job—lifestyle editor at a magazine, a step down from key foreign correspondent for a major news outlet—just two months before Blackthorn *officially* announced his run for PM?

That felt off. More than coincidence.

Church chewed his lip, thinking on that, and then flipped more pages until he found Fletcher's private emails. Foster had left most out but included a few key ones—ones sent to a private address, but one that no doubt belonged to someone with some clout. The messages weren't explicit themselves, but the meaning was clear.

Going after the big fish we always talked about. Will update you when I have something concrete.
- Fletch

The date was six days before the start of her new job in the city.

'Blackthorn,' Church muttered to himself. She never did get her story in the DRC. Never did nail him like she wanted to. But now she was going to try again. She'd bided her time, and like Church, his announcement of his intentions to run for PM had been enough to make her throw her life away and step back into the ring.

She still had an axe to grind. Foster knew it, and he'd been working up to reaching out to her.

Maybe he was going to when he got back from the

DRC. Mitch didn't seem to have a clear idea of what exactly he hoped to achieve there, just that he wanted to take Blackthorn down. Was he trying to find the smoking gun that Fletcher would need? Church didn't think he'd involved her already, but going to her with evidence she could use to finally bring him to his knees?

Foster needed Fletcher to make sure Blackthorn didn't die a hero struck down before he could make his mark on the world.

And now, Church needed the same thing.

'Fuck,' he muttered to himself, pulling out the map of Fletcher's movements and holding it up. He didn't know how she'd react to this, but he didn't really have another choice.

And by the time he got across the city, she'd be in the perfect position for intercept.

No time like the present, he thought as he put the file on the seat next to him, slotted the car into first, and took off, thinking as hard as he ever had about what the hell he was going to say to her.

SIXTEEN

TEN YEARS AGO

When Fletcher finally came around, she was sitting in the back seat of the Land Cruiser next to Church. His pistol was on his lap, finger on the trigger.

She looked at it, blinking slowly, and then glanced up at him. 'What did… Did you…?' She put her hand to her neck, remembering.

He turned his head and stared back at her. 'I did.'

'Why?' she asked.

'Because you were a danger to the mission, and this has gone far enough. And now it's over.'

Her lip quivered just a little, and then she resigned herself to silence and turned away, facing the window.

And that's how they stayed until, after an age, Cole led Blackthorn out of the house and towards the vehicles. He clocked Church in the back of the truck and gave him a questioning look.

Church nodded firmly to him, and he nodded back before they all loaded up.

Blackthorn blathered on about how gracious Zawadi was, and how stupid, drunk, and even more arrogant than usual.

Church tuned it out, closing his eyes now that they were trapped in the back and Fletcher couldn't escape. Waiting for the ride to be over. Waiting to be rid of her, once and for all. She'd be on a plane back to the UK before the sun set, and Church could get back to doing what he did best.

His fucking job.

They arrived at the hotel, and Blackthorn practically fell out of the vehicle, stumbling towards the door. Before Boyd could get out next to him, Fletcher stood in the back row and leaned across Church, shoving the seat forward and climbing over him to get out. She stood on his toes unapologetically and shoved her way past his knees, climbing down into the sun. She stormed towards the hotel and went inside, leaving the four soldiers in the car to watch her go.

Cole looked up at Church in the rearview. 'Give us a minute, would you, lads?'

Without being told who or why, Murphy and Boyd got out and headed inside, leaving the two of them alone.

Church massaged his chin and then wiped a sheen of sweat from his forehead with his fingers, watching the cloudy liquid bead on the end of his fingers and drip onto his leg. He let out a long sigh and met Cole's eyes in the mirror once more.

'You finally ready to tell me what's going on?' he asked.

Church was. 'Fletcher isn't a PA. She's a journalist.'

Cole didn't react. His poker face was good. 'She got anything that could hurt the mission?'

Church shook his head. 'She thinks she knows a lot, but she can't prove shit. She's got no evidence of anything. She's here to try and pin some shit on Blackthorn, but he's careful. It's a fishing expedition, and she's caught nothing.' Church felt like he needed to underscore that. 'She thinks Blackthorn's going to fire her when they get back, and we had a little chat in the car. She's done. And she knows it.'

'And what about you?'

'What about me?'

'How long have you known?'

Church didn't hesitate. He couldn't. 'I had a feeling, but I only found out today. I followed her out of the dining room and caught her snooping in Zawadi's office. One of Zawadi's guys showed up, but I convinced him to forget he saw us, then I made sure Fletcher didn't make any more waves.'

'How?'

'I choked her out and threw her over my shoulder. Put her in the car.'

Cole curled a little smile at that. 'You sure we're not vulnerable? I don't want this mission going tits-up on us because you weren't on the ball.'

'We're good,' Church assured him. 'But right now, we need to get Fletcher out of here. Call home, get a plane booked. They'll grab her and make her sign an NDA. She'll keep her mouth shut. She's smart enough to.'

Cole studied him for a few seconds and then nodded. 'Yeah, alright.'

He didn't seem convinced.

'We just need her out of the way, and then we can focus on the mission. On Zawadi.'

'Sounds like you found a little extra motivation all of a sudden.' It almost sounded accusatory. 'You wouldn't be the first guy to get sidetracked by a woman on mission.'

'I didn't,' Church insisted.

'Well, you've found your way now. I appreciate you telling me,' Cole said. 'You're a good soldier, Church. Always have been.' He kicked the door open and stepped down out of the truck, leaving Church alone to think about that.

He watched Cole enter the building, could see Murphy and Boyd inside waiting for him. He exchanged a few words with them, and he caught Murph glancing out at the Land Cruiser. Then, they broke and headed for the stairs together.

Church sat there, thinking about Cole, thinking about Fletcher.

He knew what he'd done was right.

But he also couldn't help but feel like it was the wrong choice, too.

He entered the hotel, thankful to be back in the meagre air conditioning, and went up to his room. There was no one around, and almost without thinking about it, he breezed past his floor and went up to Fletcher's, approaching her door. He slowed, quieting his footsteps, and paused at her frame, peeling the bug off her door-frame and heading down the corridor towards Blackthorn's door instead. He hesitated, knowing he should trust his captain, but then did it anyway, sliding the device in behind the frame of Blackthorn's door instead.

He didn't know what Cole was going to do—he'd said his piece: get Fletcher out of the country. And yet, the way he'd reacted, or hadn't... Church couldn't be sure what he was thinking. And that vision of him arguing with Blackthorn was still plaguing him. Fletcher's words: *you're working for Blackthorn. You just don't know it yet...* They were rattling around his mind.

He let out a soft breath and flexed his hands, willing the rush of blood to subside, hoping that, for once, he really would be wrong.

And with that weighing on him, he returned to his room to rest, knowing deep down it was likely to be a long night.

It was dark by the time someone went to Blackthorn's door.

Church was dozing with the earpiece in, and for the last six hours, there'd been no sound from Blackthorn's room. The man had clearly taken himself to bed, and even now, it wasn't him rousing. Footsteps came first, then the knock. Someone at his door.

Church sat upright and blinked himself clear, listening intently, instantly sharp.

He waited for Blackthorn to come and answer, and he did.

'What do you—' he began, gruff and groggy. But he didn't get to finish.

'Not out here,' a voice replied. Hushed. Hurried. Cole.

He pushed his way inside, and the door closed.

Church closed his eyes, straining to hear, but there was no sense of what they were saying. Just mumbled sounds coming through the wood.

He ground his teeth, wishing he'd put the bug somewhere better, knowing he couldn't have. What were they saying? Why now? Why in the dark?

The door opened again and then closed, hurried footsteps fading.

They hit his floor, and then there was a knock at his door, too.

He pulled the earpiece out and stuffed the wire down the side of the chair cushion, rising to answer the door.

Church opened it and feigned surprise. 'Cole.'

'Expecting someone else?' Cole asked, pushing inside.

'Not expecting anyone,' Church replied, closing the door behind him. 'What's up?'

'I just wanted to check in with you,' he said, circling the room slowly, as though looking for something or someone hidden. 'Tell you how much I appreciated your honesty earlier.'

'Don't mention it,' Church said tentatively, folding his arms as he watched his captain.

'But now I need you to do something for me.' His tone shifted, became cold suddenly, stopping to look at Church. 'Go get lost for a few hours.'

Church stared back, the pair of them like gunslingers in a stand-off. Church knew exactly what Cole was asking, what he was intending to do.

'Just take a walk, go for a drive, go for a drink. Go for ten drinks.' He stepped forward. 'I don't really care. I just need you gone.'

Church narrowed his eyes. 'Why?' It was barely a question.

'You know why.'

'No, I don't.'

Cole blew out a hard breath through his nose, the frustration palpable. 'You're going to make me say it?'

'I am.'

His jaw flexed, the vein in his temple bulging. 'Fletcher.'

'What about her?'

Cole came forward a little. 'You know what, Solomon. She's a danger to this mission.'

'That's bullshit, and you know it,' Church replied, all but squaring up with Cole. He had a few inches on him, but he was under no illusions that if it came to blows, he wouldn't have his hands full.

'This isn't me asking. This is an order. Get out of here.' Cole's tone was sharper now.

'With all due respect, Captain,' Church said. 'No.'

'No?'

'This is not the mission.'

Cole cracked a smile. The kind of sadistic smile that Church had only ever seen once or twice on his face. The kind that scared him. 'The mission is whatever I say it is.'

Church stood his ground, knowing he was the only thing standing between Fletcher and two bullets in the back of her skull.

'You going to make me tell you again?' Cole threatened.

'You can tell me a hundred times. I'm not letting you do this.'

'So that shit in the car, you *coming clean*, that was all an act? Where's your loyalty, Church?' Cole spat.

'Where's your *honour*, Captain?' Church bit back.

'This is a dirty fucking job. You know that as well as I do. Our hands get bloody so no one else's have to.' There wasn't a hint of a waver in his face. He believed that.

And Church thought, at one time or another, he probably did too. 'You're doing this for Queen and country? That's what you expect me to believe?' Church asked, quietening himself, reserving himself. 'You questioned my loyalty—tell me, where does yours lie?'

Cole's fists balled at his sides. 'The fuck did you just say to me?'

This was it. The tipping point. Church was backed into a corner, and the only way out was right through

Cole. 'I've seen you talking to Blackthorn, your little tiffs, your secret conversations.'

'Secret conversations?'

'You didn't just go to him to tell him what you're planning? Or maybe it was his plan, and you're just the errand boy doing Blackthorn's bidding. Which is it?'

Cole said nothing. He didn't know how, but he knew that Church *knew*. He didn't bother denying their meeting.

It didn't matter which was right, though. The reality was the same—Blackthorn wanted Fletcher dead, and Cole was happy to do his bidding.

'You said the mission is what you say it is—but you're not yourself, and you've forgotten something. We're here for Zawadi,' Church reminded him, lifting his fist and putting it on Cole's chest. 'And we don't work for Blackthorn. No matter what he's paying.'

SEVENTEEN

PRESENT DAY

When Church opened his eyes, he didn't know where he was.

His back was against a stone wall, his hands aching from being clenched so hard. He blinked a few times to focus his eyes and looked around. He wasn't where he last remembered, and the sun was going down. He squinted up into the darkening sky, a thick layer of cloud obscuring the fading sun.

He knew at once what had happened and squeezed his eyes shut until they hurt. He'd lost time. Something that he hadn't experienced since he'd stopped drinking. There'd been many days, many nights, that it had happened. That he'd blinked and woken up somewhere else, his mind whirling through a haze of memory indistinguishable from reality. Africa, Eastern Europe, the Middle East... His career, his missions, his life playing in an inescapable slideshow. But he'd got it under control, hadn't he? Sick of waking up with bloody knuckles and loose teeth, not knowing where he'd been or who he'd hurt.

He let out a sobering breath and wondered *why now?* But he knew the answer before he even finished the question. All this shit getting dredged up again. Seeing Cole. He was running on no sleep, too. And when was the last time he ate? Yesterday morning? He wasn't even hungry.

Church stared down at his shaking hands and curled them into fists, trying to figure out where the hell he was.

There was a carrier bag between his feet, and he stooped down, parting the handles. Inside were two phones. Smartphones, used ones. He pulled them out and unlocked them side by side. He couldn't remember buying them or where he'd got them, but he knew he had because that's what he'd planned to do.

He pushed back the hood of his coat, looking around for the Volvo, spotting it parked down the street. That was a relief, at least.

Church returned his attention to the phones and navigated to the contacts, seeing that both phones were completely blank except for one saved number in each —which he guessed was for the other phone. Prepaid SIM cards. As untraceable as it got on short notice.

One for him, one for Fletcher.

He pulled his hand up quickly, looking at his watch then, hoping he hadn't missed her while he'd been in whatever fugue state he was. He'd never have admitted it, but it frightened him. Not being there. Not being in control.

But he still had time. Foster's notes said that she'd be coming home around this time, and when he opened the map on one of the phones, he saw he was already on her street. This was the route she'd take, getting off at the tube stop a hundred yards to his right, walking in front of him, and then heading down the street towards his Volvo.

Despite not remembering planning any of this, he knew that he had done.

And right on cue, there she was.

Church stacked the phones in his hands and kept his head down, pretending to look at the screen as Anastasia Fletcher, in jeans and a roll-neck sweater, bag on her hip, strode with that same confident, world-burning stride she always did.

He watched her close in on the corner, and then, unhurriedly, reached down and picked up his carrier bag, crossing the street and falling into step behind her. He pulled up his hood once more, careful not to get too close too fast and spook her. By his estimation, he'd parked about thirty yards from her front door, which meant he had fifty yards to close the gap before he missed his window.

She was walking fast, but Church was taller. He didn't have to rush to make up the ground, lining up the plant just before the Volvo. With his hands still shaking, he made the final push, lifting the phone towards her bag as he moved diagonally towards the door of the car. The opening was snug, and he twisted the phone, slotting it down into the bag just as he reached the door of the car, keys already in his hand.

Fletcher felt the nudge and turned quickly to look at Church.

He was hunched forward, pushing the key into the ancient lock on the door of the Volvo.

Fletcher paused, watching him for just a moment, face obscured by his hood, and then backed away, deciding she must have imagined the sensation or that this man had just nudged her as he'd reached his car.

Church glanced up out of the corner of his eye as he opened the door, seeing Fletcher tighten her grip on her bag and make for her front door double-time.

He got in behind the wheel and cranked the ignition, pulling away casually and driving down the street as she got to her door.

In the wing mirror, she looked up at his receding taillights, and then she was gone.

Church pulled back into the first available space and checked the street for anyone that might be watching, holding up his watch to count the seconds.

She was staying in an apartment on the first floor. Ten seconds to climb the stairs. Ten more to get inside. Ten to put the bag down.

He didn't want to wait too long and already had the sister phone out. He dialled the number and held it to his ear, imagining her freezing as she heard the strange, alien ring coming from her bag, approaching cautiously and discovering the phone, thinking back to the nudge from the stranger, rushing to the window to see if someone was outside, and then... she answered.

There was silence on the line. She wasn't going to speak first.

Church respected her intelligence. And her caution.

'This is Solomon Church,' he said. 'Don't hang up.'

There was more silence on the line. Stunned silence, Church thought.

He only had one option. Truth. Trust. Fletcher was on the right side of things ten years ago, and he had to hope she was now, too.

'I know you're back in London to try and expose Blackthorn before he makes it to office. And I want to help.'

He waited for her to speak.

It took an age.

'Solomon Church is dead,' she said quietly.

'For a while, I wished that was the case too. But I'm not. And neither are Paul Foster or Frank Mitchell,' Church said. 'After you got out of the DRC, we were double-crossed by our own men, paid off by Blackthorn to keep the mines at Maroua open and supplying him with cobalt. They tried to kill us, and they thought they did. But we're alive, and now we're going to do what we should have done then.'

She considered that for a long time, still sceptical about who Church was and whether what he was saying was true. And there'd be only one way to fix that.

'Two days ago, Paul Foster went back to Maroua

and got captured,' Church said as he opened the door and climbed out. 'He was looking for evidence to take Blackthorn down. He'd mapped a timeline of Blackthorn's network and activities dating back twenty years,' Church went on as he started walking up the street. 'But he didn't have enough. Nothing concrete that he could go public with. That's why he went back.'

'So why are you calling me?' she asked, voice low, probing.

'Because Foster had a file on you too,' Church said, coming up on the dimly lit first-floor window of Anastasia Fletcher's building. He stood in the middle of the street, staring up at her silhouette, half-hidden behind the curtain, and peeled back his hood, showing her his face. 'And he thought you were the only one who could help.'

There was a little intake of breath as she saw him.

'Blackthorn is being hailed as a hero—the man who's going to fix this fucking country. Who's going to herald in a new, green era. An EV magnate with his fingers in all the right pies, a benevolent leader we can all get behind, we can all follow. We can all close our eyes and blindly trust because he's just a *good man*. But you and I know different, don't we? We've seen who he really is and what he's really like. We know what kind of man he is. And we might be the only ones.'

Church took a step forward, eyes fixed on Anastasia Fletcher's figure in the darkness. 'Foster might be dead already. And if not, he's being tortured within an inch of his life. He's given everything for this, and I'm going to as well. I know you're back because you're searching for a way to stop Blackthorn. And this is it.'

Fletcher remained still, not speaking.

'Are you there?' Church asked into the ether.

She swallowed gently, clearing her throat. 'What do you need me to do?'

'Pack a bag,' Church said. 'We're leaving. Right now.'

EIGHTEEN

TEN YEARS AGO

COLE LEFT with a grim smirk and a nod that told Church a stone had been cast. And it couldn't be retrieved.

'Sleep well, Sol,' he said, pausing at the door.

But as Cole left, Church knew he didn't mean it. In fact, he knew that Church wouldn't sleep at all.

And he was right.

No sooner had Cole walked out the door than Church grabbed a pillow off his bed along with his pistol and headed into the corridor. He climbed the stairs and headed to Fletcher's room. It was late now, too late to do anything. But tomorrow would be telling. Church needed to get Fletcher out of the DRC, and he needed to figure out how. Right now, though, he needed to make sure that she was alive when that time came.

He didn't bother knocking, knew that she wouldn't answer, and even if she did, she would refuse his help.

As such, he just eased himself down onto the carpet and tucked the pillow behind his shoulders, sitting back against the corner. He put his pistol in the back of his belt and folded his arms, staring into space, thinking about all the moves and missteps that had got him there. And whether this was some kind of cosmic justice for all the shit he'd done in his life.

With that in mind, he closed his eyes against the bright, stinging halogen lights overhead and slept.

It wasn't a good sleep, or a restful one. But when Fletcher's door opened, he was definitely not awake. The noise stirred him to action, and before she even made it across the threshold, he had his pistol in his hand and out in front of him.

She stopped, already dressed, and stared down at him. 'What the fuck are you doing?' she asked, surprised to see him.

Church smacked his lips, his mouth dry, and rolled to a knee awkwardly. He was stiff, his back in tatters. He levered himself to his feet, checking his watch, and saw it was barely six in the morning.

He clocked her then, bag on her shoulder and packed to the brim, boots laced, hair pinned back. She was ready to travel.

'Going somewhere?' he asked, barring her exit.

She rolled her eyes. 'They sent you to guard the door? Stop me from leaving?'

Church was getting a little sick of her attitude. 'No, actually,' he replied, unsure whether the truth was the right move, and whether she would even believe him if he told her. 'The opposite, in fact. We need to get you out of the country. Today.'

She tilted her head a little. 'You read my mind.' She let out a sigh. 'So if you'll excuse me.'

He didn't, and put his hand against the frame to stop her from going. She'd come in with a suitcase, and through the door, he could see that it was on the bed, open, and half her clothes were still inside. His brain did the maths. She'd discarded half her stuff so she could travel with just her rucksack. That meant she was going light.

'You booked a flight?'

'Not that it's any of your business, but yeah, I did. Now move—'

She tried to grab at his arm, but his hand was clamped around the frame.

If she was ditching her stuff, that meant she was in a hurry. Her hair was still wet, and Church could smell the soap on her skin. This was more than leaving in a hurry. This was a mad dash for the exit.

'What did you do?' Church asked.

'I don't know what you mean.'

He stared at her, and she could see in his eyes that it wasn't a polite request.

'Tell me what you did,' Church demanded. 'Because I'm guessing it's something stupid.'

'I don't have to tell you anything,' Fletcher replied.

'You do,' Church said. 'Because I sat out here all night to make sure you didn't get murdered in your fucking sleep. I'm doing everything in my power to make sure you walk out of this fucking country alive, and you seem hell-bent on making sure of the opposite—so I'll ask you once more: what did you do?'

She stewed on that for a second, searching for any hint of a lie in his face. And then she broke.

'I... I sent some pictures, some words, to an editor friend of mine, alright? They're running a story this morning, and by the time it went live, I wanted to be on a bus, very far from here. And very far from Blackthorn.'

Church's brow crumpled. 'What pictures? What words?'

She looked at him, blinking a little like the question was confusing. 'What do you mean?'

'Show me. Right now.'

She looked towards the stairs longingly, but she knew Church wouldn't relent. With a grumble, she went back into the room and set down her bag, fishing for her laptop. Church checked the corridor and went in after her, waiting impatiently for her to open her laptop.

She fired the thing up and then navigated to her emails.

'Who did you send this to?' Church asked as he hovered behind her.

'A friend at *The Guardian*,' she replied. 'There, happy?' She gestured to the screen and then stepped out of the way.

Church looked down, scanning the notes she'd sent over—the awful working conditions, suspected indentured servitude, the opulence of Zawadi's mansion, his exploitation of the locals, and Blackthorn's desire to get his fingers into it all.

Church felt his heart beating harder as he leaned in and clicked the attached file, a folder full of photographs. He opened it and stared, dumbfounded, at them.

'Where did you get these?' he asked.

'What do you mean?'

'Who sent you these photographs?'

'I don't…' she started, shaking her head. 'You did. Didn't you?'

Church stared back at her. 'What? Why would I have sent you photographs?'

'I thought…' She came forward now and moved him out of the way, opening another email. 'Look. Here.'

Church read. The message simply said:

I KNOW WHAT YOU'RE TRYING TO DO. THESE SHOULD HELP.

'You didn't send these? I thought you felt guilty and wanted to help, wanted to make amends, or…'

Church shook his head. 'It wasn't me.'

'So who was it?'

That was a question he knew the answer to but didn't want to say out loud. If he did, he knew it would become real, that everything would be set in motion. Events that there'd be no coming back from.

'Who sent them?' she insisted.

'Cole,' he replied. 'It was Cole.'

'The leader of your... *whatever?* Group? Gang? Team?'

Church nodded gravely.

'But why? And how did he know I needed them? And... I don't understand.'

Church did. Perfectly. 'I told him you were a journalist.'

'Why the fuck would you do that?' she hissed.

'Because that's the position you put me in. And I had a loyalty to my team, to my mission,' Church growled.

'Had? Past tense?' She lowered her head, looking to meet his eyes. 'You've got to tell me what the hell is going on. Right now.'

Church steadied himself, getting it straight in his head. 'These photographs,' he said, pointing at the computer. 'I've seen them before. Pictures of the mine, of Zawadi's house. All of them.'

'How?'

'Because we're the ones who took them. They're from our initial surveillance of Zawadi's operation.' He was already racking his brains for a way out of this. 'Last night, Cole came to me after he met with Blackthorn, told me to leave the hotel.'

'Why?'

'So he could kill you.'

Her mouth opened to reply, but no sound came out.

'But I made it abundantly clear I wasn't going to let that happen.'

'Which is why you were outside the door…'

'I'm not looking for a thank you,' Church continued gruffly. 'I just didn't want your life on my shoulders. There are enough of them there already.'

'So why would Cole send me these pictures? He's turning on Blackthorn?'

'The opposite,' Church said. 'He's smart. Smart enough to know that if he tried to kill you, I'd stop him, and he'd either have to kill me to get to you or risk me going to the SP. He'd be facing court martial, prison. The whole thing.'

'So why risk it? Why send me these?'

'He's not trying to help you,' Church said, closing the laptop and handing it to her. 'He's trying to get someone else to kill you for him.'

Fletcher paled.

'He sent you these photographs knowing you'd pass them along. Knowing you'd expose what Zawadi was doing. And when Zawadi found out…'

'Shit,' she croaked. 'Zawadi would try to kill me instead.'

'I'd bet that he got word to Zawadi the second he sent those pictures. Maybe before. He was banking on you passing them along, and then he was banking on you trying to get the fuck out of here. Zawadi's guys are going to be on every road, stopping every car looking for you.'

She looked over at the door, wobbled on her feet, and almost fell at the realisation that she'd signed her own death warrant. That if Church hadn't stopped her, she'd be getting on a bus headed right towards a firing squad.

Church thought he was going to want to berate her for being so naïve. But looking at her now, scared witless, facing her own doom… he just felt sorry for her. And he knew that if there was any hope of getting her out of here alive, it was squarely on him to make it happen.

She turned to him slowly, a hopeful look in her eye. She knew she had no right to ask for his help, but she had no other choice. 'What do I do?' she asked.

'You cross your fingers,' Church said, already heading for the door, 'and hope that it's not just me that's in your corner. Because if it is…' He glanced back at her. 'Well… just cross your fingers.'

NINETEEN

PRESENT DAY

CHURCH STIRRED before Mitch reached the bottom step.

He sat up on the folding cot in the darkness of the living room, the embers from their fire still glowing in the burner, and watched him descend quickly, already on alert.

He swung his legs from the cot and put his bare feet on the cold flagstones, blinking the sleep from his eyes. He catalogued the room instantly. The clock on the wall said 2:30 a.m. Fletcher was asleep on the couch opposite him, snoring softly. The smell of Mitch's beef stew still lingered in the air.

He'd been surprised how quickly, with a full belly, he'd dropped off, the exhaustion finally setting in after thirty-six hours on the go.

'What's wrong?' Church asked, reaching under the cot and pulling his boots out. He dragged his socks on and snatched his trousers off the radiator next to the cot, standing to meet Mitch.

He glanced over, heading for the kitchen, blue eyes wide in the darkness, just catching the glint of the coals. 'Perimeter alarm,' he said, not panicked, but tight.

Church froze for a second, mind working furiously. Had he been followed? No. He'd been meticulous. His eyes went to Fletcher then, lying on the couch. She was staring up at him silently.

He'd instructed her to leave her phone in her apartment, but she'd insisted on bringing her laptop to write the story. He'd told her under no circumstances was she to access the internet.

'What did you do?' Church asked.

She sat up slowly, the blanket around her shoulders.

Her lack of an answer was confirmation enough for Church.

'What did you do?' he asked again, stepping towards her.

She recoiled a little. 'I sent an email. Hotspotted the phone you gave me. It was from a private account, no one knows I have it. I was letting an editor know—'

'For fuck's sake,' Church growled, shaking his head, blood surging in his hands. 'I told you not to…' He cut himself off, knowing that scalding her wasn't going to help. 'You just killed everyone here,' he snapped then, unable to stop himself.

'Sol,' Mitch said then, at his shoulder, his voice soft enough to quell Church, to stop him from gutting Fletcher.

Church looked down at the rifle he was being offered. It was the HK417 that Mitch had been holding that morning—a semi-automatic battle rifle equipped with a telescopic sight.

'Armour-piercing rounds,' Mitch said.

He wouldn't say that unless he was expecting significant resistance. His words had been that there was a perimeter alarm. But what had he seen? Did he have cameras or just motion sensors?

Church accepted the weapon and met his friend's eye. 'What about Nanna, the girls?'

'You wake them, bring them to the kitchen.' Mitch looked at Fletcher then. 'Bring your bag. Come with me.' He extended a hand, but Fletcher stayed put, fear in her eyes. 'You can stay there if you want, but they'll kill you. I won't.'

Her eyes flitted to the crucifix around his neck and then went to Church.

'It's us or Blackthorn,' Church grunted. 'Your choice.'

She swallowed and nodded, steeling herself as she got up, coming to Mitch. For a moment she paused, head lowered, and spoke to Church. 'I'm sorry,' she said, 'I thought—'

'Save it,' Church replied, turning from her and heading for the stairs.

He slipped the sling of the weapon over his head and climbed towards the guest room.

By the time he opened the door, Nanna was already awake and getting the girls up. She looked at him as he entered, eyes wide. 'I heard Mitch get up. Is it bad?'

The girls were staring up at him from the single bed they were sharing, wide-eyed. He didn't know what to say. So he didn't say anything. A single, firm nod and an extended arm, beckoning them quickly.

Nanna pulled the girls to their feet and passed them their bags. It looked like she'd asked Mitch for backpacks and had transferred their essential belongings into them for this eventuality.

In any other circumstance, Church would have smiled, impressed. But tonight wasn't that night. He was just thankful that Nanna was like she was. Even though he was furious she'd been dragged into this.

Church beckoned them onto the landing and followed them downstairs, guiding Nanna into the kitchen, where Mitch was waiting with Fletcher.

'Everyone good?' he asked.

No one answered.

The kitchen was long and narrow with a solid flagstone floor. At one end, there was an old pantry, and Mitch headed for that now.

Church had seen inside it when Mitch had opened it earlier that night. Inside was a fridge, shelves full of spices and dried goods.

'Help me with this,' Mitch ordered him.

'I don't think they're all going to fit,' Church admitted, staring into the cupboard.

Mitch grumbled and took hold of the fridge. 'Come on, quick now.'

Church went and helped him drag the fridge into the kitchen, the little wheels jostling on the uneven stone. He saw it then—a steel hatch under the fridge.

'Cellar,' Church muttered.

'Inside, everyone, now,' Mitch said, herding the girls towards it.

Fletcher was first and dragged the thing open, staring down into the dark hole below. She turned to the rest of them, her expression one of distinct regret.

'Don't think,' Church told her. 'Just climb.'

Mitch came forward now. 'There's light, beds, food, water to last days. You'll be safe down there. I promise.'

The urgency in his voice was enough to get Fletcher moving.

'Mum, I don't want to go in there,' Mia, Nanna's youngest, said, clutching her arm.

'It'll only be a little while,' Nanna replied, looking at Church as though to ask if she was lying.

He couldn't give her the answer she wanted.

Mitch's phone dinged then, and he pulled it up, an alert from his security system displayed on the screen.

'They're almost here,' he said, quickening everyone's pace.

Nanna got the girls into the hatch and went after them, pausing for a second before Church could lower the hatch. She reached out and grabbed his hand, squeezing hard.

'Don't leave me,' she said, her eyes filling as she looked up at him. 'I only just got you back.'

Church was afraid he was going to crush her hand, he was holding it so hard. 'I'm not going anywhere.'

'Sol,' Mitch said.

He swallowed and let go, shutting her away but unable to get the last image of her frightened face from his mind.

They shoved the fridge back into place and closed the door then. Church kept his hand on the wood, wondering if any of this could have been prevented. If all of it could have.

But now was not the time to put his ghosts on trial.

Mitch was at the long cupboard door next to the sink then, the one that would normally hold an ironing board. Except Mitch kept his iron under the stairs.

He opened the cupboard and reached for the L115A3 bolt-action rifle, complete with an infrared scope, hanging there. He then took out a belt fitted with grenades and passed it to Church, before picking up an odd-looking weapon that Church hadn't seen in a long time.

'Remember how to use one of these?' Mitch asked as he handed him the M320 40mm grenade launcher.

Church held the thing up—it was about twelve inches in length, with an extendable shoulder stock. It was held like an MP7 sub-machinegun, with the rear and foregrips at each end of the short barrel, but instead of bullets, it fired grenades.

'Fallujah,' Church said. 'What a fucking mess that was,' he mumbled as he opened the action and slotted in one of the grenades. He held the weapon with the muzzle to the ground and slipped the grenade belt over his shoulder.

'One more thing,' Mitch said, handing Church a pair of night-vision goggles. 'We're going dark.'

'Roger that,' Church said, pulling them on and setting the goggles in their upright position.

Mitch stared at him for a moment, setting his own on his head. 'I can't say I've missed this.'

Church didn't reply to that. 'Let's just get it done.'

Mitch let out a long, rattling breath. He was out of shape, out of practice, and out of the mindset. He was scared to go out there. And Church should have been scared that he wasn't.

They headed for the door, and Mitch flipped open the fuse box next to it, killing the lights. The whole house plunged into darkness, and Church flicked down the NVGs, the whole world lighting up in a pale glow.

Outside, the air was cool and still. And though whoever was coming up Mitch's road was doing so without running lights, the sound of the engine was unmistakable.

'Take the corner of the wall,' Mitch said, pointing him right. 'They'll funnel to your right once they come in through the gate. Better cover. You'll have the angle, though.'

'What are you going to do?'

'I'm going to ram this right down their throat,' Mitch replied, holding up the rifle. 'See you on the other side, old friend.'

Church gave him a nod and watched him lumber off,

half-limping, the years of service more than catching up with him.

He moved to the side of the house to a small outbuilding that housed the well and water pump and clambered up onto the slanted roof, lying flat, aiming straight down the driveway and through the gate.

As Church headed for the stone wall, he thought of that entrance road. Two tall banks on each side. He didn't know how many were coming, but he guessed it would be in force. His mind did the calculations. It wasn't going to be the Met or Armed Response. No, they didn't do this kind of work, and to get them out in force in the dead of night? That's a lot of paperwork, a lot of plying of the right people. It'd take too long and be too loud for a PM in the making. It would be PMCs, he guessed. Blackthorn's personal payroll. Trained, armed to the teeth, very prejudicial. That way, he could shield them from the blowback if there was any, and they wouldn't ask too many questions about the task at hand. He'd seen Cole and Boyd and Reed in their tac gear, armed up. He expected they were at the head of whatever outfit was coming right now. But how many was enough to take them out?

He tried not to think about Fletcher's stupidity as he settled down behind the corner of the wall, choosing a thick spot with plenty of cover.

He laid the battle rifle, complete with a dual mag—two separate magazines attached to one another, each inverted for faster reloading. That was sixty shots. He hoped he wouldn't need either of them.

Church looked over to Mitch, some forty yards away or so. He gestured to his eyes with his right hand, rifle already in position, and then pointed to the gate. He was eyes on. They were here.

Church steadied himself and shouldered his own weapon, surveying the area. The gate to Mitch's farm was in line with the trees, and once they reached it, they'd be exposed, in the open. Mitch was correct that the shape of the land gave them natural cover if they peeled to their left, but they'd also be running right at Church. They'd come in quiet, he figured, on foot, without the vehicles. They'd try and sneak up on the house and—

Before he could complete that assumption, a column of yellow flame erupted from the gate, and Church screwed his eyes closed, the sudden brilliance in his goggles enough to blind him. 'Holy fuck!' he grunted, tearing them from his head as he turned away, his retinas seared.

There was a roar of engines then, and by the time Church managed to stop seeing stars, two black Toyota Land Cruisers barrelled through the gap, blowing apart what remained of Mitch's gate.

He opened fire, the call of the rifle accompanied by a dance of sparks off the roof of the lead truck.

So much for quick and quiet.

As Church shifted position, pulling the grenade launcher to attention, a group of men filtered in through the gate behind the SUVs and began spreading out.

They were lit only by the flames of the explosion now engulfing the trees at the flanks of the gateposts.

Church had to ignore them for now. Mitch wasn't equipped to deal with the trucks, and he was.

He made for the house, needing to take the vehicles head-on. From here, he'd have no chance of judging the travel time of the grenade.

The battle rifle swung from his shoulder as he charged forward into the courtyard in front of Mitch's house, the vehicles coming fast.

Church slowed and went to a knee, letting loose with the first grenade.

It leapt from the barrel with a satisfying *thwoop* and whistled through the air, landing just in front of the lead car.

The flash was instant, the sound and shockwave coming together. The grenade detonated on impact right in front of the passenger wheel and flipped the car. It arced upward and then slammed down onto its side, skidding on the gravel with an ear-splitting scrape. The trail car swerved to avoid it, veering off the path and towards the stone wall surrounding the courtyard.

The engine flared as it struck, riding up over the wall and hurling itself into the air in front of Church.

He dove sideways from its path, rolling out of danger as it landed heavily and then speared forward, its wheels finding traction once more, disappearing across the front of the house towards the slope on the far side.

Mitch's rifle called out in the darkness once more, a

bolt of fire lancing from the muzzle, closely followed by a scream rising up from near the gate.

He'd hit his mark this time.

Church got to his feet and checked his shoulder. No sign of the second vehicle, but the first was right in front of him, wheels spinning madly, engine pinned at the rev limiter.

He exhaled and regained himself, shouldering the battle rifle now, and swept around the nose of the Land Cruiser, peeking the corner before he put two shots through the windscreen into the passenger, and two into the driver.

They both fell still behind the cracked glass, the engine noise dwindling as the accelerator was released.

He didn't pause to consider the men he'd just killed. Instead, he kept moving around the Land Cruiser, watching as shadows flashed in the field below the house.

Mitch fired again, and one went down.

Church lined up the next one and fired three rounds, the kick of the rifle vicious, the bite of the bullets worse.

The shape twisted and fell, lying still.

'Good kill,' Mitch said from his perch above Church. 'Hostiles flanking right. Can't get them from here.'

Church turned and started moving the other way, rifle against his shoulder, eye down the optic.

'Repositioning,' Mitch said, already sliding off the roof and starting down the hill towards the gate. He moved left, towards the treeline, giving him a better line on the remaining men.

The Land Cruisers would seat seven each, which meant that outside of the two in the lead car and the three that were already down near the gate, that left up to nine men remaining.

Church kept that at the back of his mind as he made his way back to the corner of the wall, chasing the second vehicle.

As he neared his vantage point, he could see it down at the treeline ahead of him, driver and passenger door open. But where were the occupants?

He saw the flash of the muzzle first, heard the air unzip next to his left ear an instant later.

Church threw himself to the ground as gunfire erupted in a frantic chatter from the trees, and he crawled forward, firing back with little to no idea what he was aiming at.

The discarded goggles were just a few feet away, and as if reading his mind, the deafening boom of Mitch's long gun sang its death song, and the pinpricks of light in the trees dwindled from two to one.

Church scrabbled for the goggles and pushed them onto his head, waiting for his eyes to adjust as he lined up the rifle. He could see now, like a cat in the dark. Target straight ahead. Black tactical gear, helmet, body armour, what looked like SIG MCXs. Blackthorn wasn't skimping.

But Church had the high ground and a better shot.

He exhaled, squeezed the trigger. Blood arced

through the air before he even registered the shot, and the guy twisted to the floor.

Seven left.

Church scrambled to his feet as Mitch loosed another shot.

Six.

Where were the others? Church swung the rifle around, bracing it on the wall, and went hunting. He saw nothing, no one. No movement anywhere.

Mitch's gun was quiet, too.

Shit.

Church couldn't move from his position to advance —he'd be in the open.

But he couldn't stay here, either. Easy pickings for an enemy sniper.

He had to get to Mitch, had to regroup and figure out how many were left.

Church pushed himself to his feet and started running.

He got halfway past the house when his skin erupted in gooseflesh. He stopped dead and looked towards the gate just as he heard the pop-whistle of the ordnance.

It zoomed past him, no fire or smoke, and before it even hit the house, he knew what it was. AT4. Unguided, shoulder-fired anti-tank weapon.

Designed to punch through plated steel, it made light work of Mitch's stone home.

Church leapt forward, covering his head as the whole place erupted in fire, the explosion throwing him like a ragdoll. He felt heat, pain, then the cool rush of air, the hard embrace of the earth.

He landed, bounced, rolled, trying to find his feet, clutching hard at the gun.

It had come from the gate, an auxiliary force holding back in reserve.

Church's fists found grass, and he pushed himself to his knees, staring up at the farm. Flames licked the stone black, pouring from the burst windows. Smoke curled through the slates on the roof, and Church looked on in horror.

'Nanna—' he tried to scream, his cry snuffed out as another round ripped through the air, hitting true.

Stone blasted outwards from the wall, the entire front half of the house sagging and then collapsing in on itself. The roof bowed heavily, the wood groaning and wailing as it gave way, plunging into the burning inferno, sending a tornado of sparks and embers into the night.

Headlights at the gate now, the calls of men told to advance.

Church saw red. A bloody rage seized him in a chokehold, putting his feet underneath him, the rifle at his shoulder. He sighted the weapon and fired, stepping forward like a stalking tiger, finger rebounding off the stock as he put round after round into the men before him. He didn't see anything except cardboard cutouts. It was like a shoot house. Static targets locked in place, his sights leaping from one to the next to the next as he moved forward with deadly efficiency.

He didn't know how many rounds he'd fired or how many men took hits, but the second he felt the empty trigger click of a spent magazine, he twisted the rifle and ejected it, flipping it and slamming it back into place in a second flat.

Quick breath, snap the bolt back to chamber the first round, keep firing.

The sounds of falling stone and burning home cackled behind him as he made his way down the slope.

The hostiles were firing back. Cole. Reed. Boyd. Were they out there? Church didn't know. Kill them all. Every last one. Nanna. Mia. Lowri. Anastasia. They were dead, crushed under the rubble. Nanna. Mia. Lowri. Anastasia. Taken from him. Murdered. Murdered for Blackthorn. NannaMiaLowriAnastasia. The names played over and over in his head until the rifle ran dry.

He discarded it, and it swung on its sling. Before it even hit his hip, he was already ripping the pistol from its holster on his thigh, shooting before it was even fully up.

NannaMiaLowriAnastasiaNannaMiaLowriAnastasia. The names became a blur, rolling into one inside his head, his breathing ragged. He could taste blood.

He flinched, pain in his shoulder, and looked down —a gouge in his skin, a graze from a bullet. He didn't even know they were firing back.

Something hit him then, hard, taking him off his feet.

Church landed on his side and wrestled his way onto

his back, someone on top of him. He swung hard, his fist connecting with something solid before he saw blue eyes glinting above him, made out Mitch's face in the darkness, pinning him down.

'Sol!' he yelled. 'Come back.' He grabbed Church by the collar of his shirt and lifted him, shoving him down onto the ground to shake some sense into him.

Church gasped, drawing the first breath he had in what felt like minutes. 'Mitch,' he said, the sounds of gunfire and yelling making their way through the haze. 'They're—'

'We gotta move, Sol,' Mitch cut him off, dragging him to his feet now. 'Trees, now.'

Church's legs were numb, but Mitch wasn't asking. He hauled and then pushed him forward, the two of them keeping low, moving fast until they found the trees. Wood and bark splintered around them as bullets chased them into cover. But they didn't stop.

Church wanted to dig his heels in, end this. But Mitch kept running, holding a fistful of his shirt so he couldn't get away.

They ran and ran, blind in the forest, stumbling and sliding their way forward until they broke onto a rough double-track.

'This way,' Mitch said, pulling Church by the shirt still, sending him down the track to the left. He went without protest, running on autopilot now, breath ragged in his chest, blood pouring down his arm. But he couldn't feel it. Couldn't feel anything.

He'd practically checked out.

He could still see Nanna's face in that hatch.

Don't leave me, she said.

But that's exactly what he'd done.

TWENTY

TEN YEARS AGO

'You stay on me,' Church told her at the door. 'I fucking mean it, alright? Actually—take my shirt.'

'What?' Fletcher stared up at him, not understanding.

'My shirt. Grab a handful and hold on,' Church ordered.

'You're not serious,' she practically scoffed.

'I'm going to have two hands on my gun, and I'm not going to want to check over my shoulder to make sure you're there,' he said plainly. 'You take my shirt, and you don't let go until I tell you. You move when I move, you stop when I stop, and you stay behind me at all times. Got it?'

She paled. 'My God, you're serious.'

He didn't feel like that warranted an answer. 'Ready?'

She swallowed and reached out, taking a handful of fabric as he ordered. He could feel her shaking through the cotton.

'Just breathe.'

She nodded, but it didn't seem to help.

'We're moving,' he told her, opening the door and pressing forward. They'd already wasted time, and though he didn't think Cole would be waiting for them, Zawadi's men may well have been tipped off to the location of their hotel.

They swept down the corridor, Church leading with his pistol raised, and rounded the corner onto the stairs. They went down one floor and across to Mitch's room. Church knocked firmly but quietly, and it was the kind of knock that they all knew well—the kind that said not to hang around.

Mitch was there in seconds, bleary-eyed. 'Yeah?' he asked, spying Fletcher clutching at Church's back, at the gun, and immediately snapping to attention. 'What's going on?'

'Cole put Fletcher in a frame, sent Zawadi's men after her. We need an exfil, right now.'

He stared at Church, considering that, weighing it. Like Church, Mitch had a lot of loyalty to the cause—to Cole. But they'd been friends, brothers, since before they'd fallen in with their captain. Church trusted Mitch like no one else. And he hoped it went both ways.

'I'll get my kit,' he said, leaving the door open and diving into action.

Church turned and walked Fletcher through the

door, covering the corridor. It was still quiet—for now. 'You think you can get anyone else to help?' Church asked.

'Who do you have in mind?' Mitch asked, pulling on his ballistic vest and belt.

'I think there's a pretty clear divide,' Church admitted. 'Murphy, Reed, Boyd—they know which side their bread is buttered. I was thinking Foster, Norton?'

Mitch paused for a second. 'It's worth a try. I'll get them.'

'Great. I've got to get my shit. Lobby in two?'

'Wilco,' Mitch said, throwing his pack over his shoulder.

Church moved fast, dragging Fletcher along with him, and entered his room as Mitch went towards Foster's. 'Bed,' Church said to Fletcher, pointing for her to sit on the end.

She did as she was told, still pale, still shaking, the reality of it all setting in. Surrounded by Church and the team, protected by them, she'd gained a false sense of where she was—of her own safety. And now, with the world against her, it was becoming starkly apparent what this place was. And the odds of getting out of it alive.

Church moved methodically, pulling on his bulletproof vest, affixing his holster to his thigh, pushing extra ammunition and supplies into his pack—water, MREs, spare socks, anything else he could think of.

Fletcher watched him. 'You're packing heavy,' she whispered, barely able to get the words out.

'Don't know how long we'll be out there. Don't know where the evac point will be. Don't know anything. If we've got to hoof it through the jungle for a few days, you'll be glad I didn't pack light.'

Church didn't think her skin could go any whiter. 'I don't have anything…' she began, clutching her backpack to her hip.

'You'll be fine,' Church said, though he didn't know if he sold it. Because he honestly didn't know what was waiting for them. 'The important thing is that we go now, we go fast, and we hope that we can slip through the net before it closes.' He slung his pack on and tightened it, turning and gesturing to the strap above his hip.

She took the cue and grabbed onto it. Church steadied himself with a final breath and then plunged into the corridor once more, heading for the lobby.

There were footsteps on the stairs above them, and Church turned, shielding Fletcher and lifting his pistol.

'It's Mitch,' came a voice from above, followed by Mitch's face peeking around the corner.

Church lowered his weapon, and Mitch appeared fully, followed by a tired-looking Norton and an ever-stalwart Foster. Norton had a thick beard and was wearing his usual grin. 'Jesus, Sol, what shit have you got us into this time?' he asked, clapping Church on the shoulder as he passed. He shook his head and went down after Mitch.

Foster lingered for a second, as though looking for confirmation in Church's eyes that they were on the right side of things. Then he nodded and motioned

Church on, sandwiching Fletcher between them as he covered the rear.

Church felt better about their odds, but if it was Cole's intention to kill Fletcher, then he'd be a fool to think this would go smoothly.

They were into the lobby and out into the early morning heat without pause. The sun was low, scattering splinters of red light through the canopy across the road. The heat was palpable already, and as they bundled into one of the Land Cruisers—Mitch driving, Church shotgun, the two others in the back with Fletcher squeezed in the middle—his collar was already soaked with sweat.

Mitch cranked the engine and dug in the pocket of his cargo trousers, tossing a sat-phone over his shoulder to Norton. 'Call command, tell them to scramble an emergency exfil—military, civilian, doesn't matter. They should be on standby for our op.'

'What do I tell them?' Norton asked as they pulled away from the kerb.

Church knew what he meant—they couldn't really come clean about this. Cole would have been clever enough not to leave a trail. So if they told them the truth, it would be nothing more than a baseless accusation.

'Tell them we need a medical evac,' Church replied. 'God knows we might fucking need it.'

Norton let out a little sigh and dialled. 'Roger that.'

As they sped through the town, Church glanced up at the rear-view mirror, finding Fletcher staring wide-eyed at her knees. He could tell her some gentle words, something soothing. But it'd be as much of a lie as the ones coming out of Norton's mouth. This was a situation of her own creation. And right or wrong, in a place like this, morals meant nothing. There were only two things in Maroua that morning. Heat. And blood. And they'd both come out in force. Of that much, Church was sure.

They rattled forward with a quiet focus. Norton finished up the conversation and informed Church and Mitch that evac was being scrambled from Kananga—a twin-prop that was liable to be the best part of an hour before it touched down in Maroua.

They were little over twenty minutes from the airfield, which meant they'd have to hold that position for forty minutes. Though they didn't really have much choice.

The houses around them thinned, and they were once more into the jungle, bouncing along the rutted dirt track. Mitch had eased off the throttle—there was no point blowing out a shock, and they were in no rush now. So they trundled along, their eyes roving the treeline, the road ahead, the road behind, for what they knew was coming.

'Contact,' Mitch said after just a minute or two. 'Twelve o'clock.'

Church saw it too. A pair of rusted pick-up trucks were slung across the road, nose to nose, forming a loose 'V' shape to trap approaching cars.

'Eight hostiles,' Mitch muttered, leaning forward over the wheel.

Two guys were standing in the road already, hands raised, AK-47s in their grip, demanding that they stop.

'You want to blast through?' Mitch asked, measuring the distance.

Church assessed it. They were outmanned, and the second they accelerated, they'd be fired upon. They'd have trouble moving those trucks, their wheels likely to get caught in a rut in the road. They had more chance of wrecking their own vehicle than shunting those two out of the way cleanly. The speed they'd lose trying would make them easy targets, too.

'No,' Church said. 'We stop.' He didn't turn around, and he hoped they were far enough back that they wouldn't have seen their target yet. 'Fletcher,' Church said easily. 'Climb over the seat and lie down in the back, in the footwell.'

She didn't bother to ask if he was serious. It was pretty clear this wasn't a time for jokes.

Foster edged forward on the seat, seeing as he was taking up so much of the bench, and allowed Fletcher to manoeuvre herself backwards, flopping down into the back. Church felt like he could hear her heart hammering from the front seat.

'Keep it chilly,' he said as Mitch slowed to a stop. 'Weapons free on my go. Mitch, back up when the fun starts. You know the drill, boys.'

'Wilco.'

The brakes squealed, and Mitch brought the car to a

halt, depressing the clutch and pushing it into reverse, ready for Church's signal.

The two men in front of the pick-up trucks started their approach, and Church surveyed the others. Two guys in the driving seats of the pickups. Two in each bed. Eight total. All armed.

'Beds, then cabs,' Church muttered over his shoulder before rolling down the window for Zawadi's men.

They approached, splitting around the car, one coming to Church's window, the other to Mitch's. They were in army fatigues and boots, open camouflage shirts. They didn't look as green as some of the others Church had seen. These men were trained. Not special forces trained, but they'd seen action. They were seasoned enough. And the tension in the car reflected that.

The two men came to the windows simultaneously. One held up his rifle to show they meant business while the other leaned in Mitch's window to talk, looking around the interior before he spoke.

'Out of the car,' he said.

'Why?' Mitch asked.

'We're looking for someone.'

'Is it one of us four?' Mitch asked dryly, looking around at the faces in the vehicle.

'A woman.'

'Then you're out of luck. Now, if you please, we need to go.'

'Go where?' the man asked.

'I don't see how that's any of your business, really.'

The man scowled, his bloodshot eyes roving the men in the car more keenly now. He knew who he was looking at. That much was clear. He had instructions from Zawadi, and this was the vehicle he was waiting for. The people he was waiting for. Whether he'd been told to expect one man alone, a single soldier—Church —he wasn't sure. But either way, Church knew that they weren't talking their way through this roadblock. And if they didn't shoot first, they'd probably not get to shoot at all.

Church turned his head towards the man at his window. 'Psst,' he whispered.

The man narrowed his eyes and leaned in.

Church's hand moved quickly, ripping the pistol from the holster on his thigh and angling it upwards. He pulled the trigger, putting a bullet into the soft patch of flesh under the soldier's chin, covering his own face in a spray of blood as he did.

The soldier in Mitch's window tried to react, tried to lift his rifle, but wasn't quick enough.

Mitch remained still, pressed back against the seat as Church turned the pistol across the centre console and lifted it, firing as he did.

Muzzle flash filled the vehicle, and the bullet struck the soldier mid-chest. He staggered backwards, still lifting the rifle, and let loose with a stream of fire as he tumbled.

Mitch swore, the bullets peppering the side of the Land Cruiser, and dumped the clutch, flooring it.

The car lurched backwards in a cloud of dust, and Church put another bullet into the stumbling soldier through the windscreen.

Mitch swung the wheel around and sent them into a J-turn, stomping on the brake when the Land Cruiser was side-on to the roadblock.

Like they'd practised it a hundred times before, they even stopped—Norton already had his rifle out the window, and Foster was out of his door and standing on the wheel, rifle across the roof of the truck.

They fired through the dust before the soldiers even knew what was happening, and as Church kicked open his door and advanced on the pick-up trucks, the guys in the beds were already falling.

Church zeroed in on one of the drivers and put him down, turning the pistol on the other. He lifted his hands in surrender, but they weren't taking chances. He used to have to think about it, about disconnecting that human part of his brain from his trigger finger. Now it didn't even register. He was tagging cardboard cutouts at a shoot-house.

The guy sagged forward onto the wheel, the weight of his limp head sounding the horn for a second before he sagged sideways and slumped onto the seat.

And then there was silence.

Church remained still, listening for any hint that anyone was alive.

But they weren't. Trained or not, Church's men were well-oiled machines, and this was what they were built for. Killing was what they did best. And they'd put down all eight of Zawadi's guys in just a few seconds.

Church finally exhaled and lowered his pistol. 'Clear,' he called, glancing back at the Land Cruiser. 'Let's get these out of the way,' he said to Norton and Foster as they joined him on the road. 'Dump the bodies.'

Norton and Foster advanced past him to get to work, but Church's eyes were fixed on the Land Cruiser, on Fletcher's face peeking through the rear window. Suddenly, the back seat tilted forward, and she lurched into the sun, landing and falling to her hands and knees, emptying her stomach into the dirt.

Church watched her throw up and, for a brief moment, considered going over and helping her up.

But he had little sympathy. This was a mess of her own doing. She needed to see this.

She needed to live with the consequences of her actions.

Just like he did. Just like they all did. This was the reality of their world. Grim as it may be.

It took them a few minutes to clear the road, and then they bundled back into the truck and started driving, waiting for whatever came next. But things were quiet, the road empty. And when they arrived, the airfield was deserted.

They rolled in, wondering if there'd be another blockade, another contingent of Zawadi's men. But the only thing that awaited them was a long stretch of open dirt cut into the trees.

There was no terminal building, nothing resembling any kind of control tower. It was line of sight on approach and take-off, and if there was another plane in the way, it was on you to get the fuck out of there.

Mitch rolled them around to the far side of the runway and killed the engine.

Norton checked his watch, once more sandwiching Fletcher between him and Foster. She was still green, still shaking. 'They're about ten minutes out if they're on time.'

Fletcher grimaced and shook her head. 'I need to get out. I need air.'

'I don't think that's a good idea,' Norton said.

But she wasn't listening and didn't care. She reached across him for the handle and shoved the door open, scrambling across his lap to get out.

'Fucking hell,' Norton grunted as she kneed him in the crotch. He made to climb out after her, but Church was already out the door.

'I've got it,' he said, waving Norton off.

Fletcher was striding into the open, breathing hard, hands on her hips.

'You going to be sick again?' Church asked, coming up behind her.

'If I had anything left in my stomach,' she growled.

Church could have said a hundred things. Could have told her it was normal. Could have told her they had to do it. Could have told her that you got used to it. That the first was always the hardest. But he knew none of those things would help. So he said nothing instead.

They stood there, staring down the runway, the heat haze already shimmering over the red earth. The sky was cloudless above, blue tinged yellow as the sun made its steady climb to their right. Around them, the trees lining the runway marked the start of a dense and endless jungle alive with birds and animals. A truly wild frontier, one not meant for humans. And yet they were here, had carved out their place, their space, as they always did. Proved their resilience, their fierceness, their will to survive. Their will to dominate and destroy everywhere they went. Even here, in this place with its corruption and violence, the solution was more killing.

But Church? He was a man built for a place like this. For a life like this.

Anastasia Fletcher was not.

And it was good she was leaving.

A little black dot grew in the distant sky, the first hum of engine noise reaching them as the propellers on their evac churned the thick air.

'Where am I going?' Fletcher asked quietly, noticing it.

Church couldn't help but think that sounded like a bigger existential question than one about the plan.

'What you did here,' he said after a moment. 'It was the right thing. You tried to do something good, and you should be proud of that.'

'I almost got myself killed. And I did get those men killed.'

Again, Church could have told her what kind of men they were likely to have been. Tried to ease her conscience. But this was how things were. Death was death. It was never pretty. It was never good. And Fletcher needed to learn that. If this was the game she wanted to play, then she needed to know the stakes.

'We did what we had to,' Church said. 'And now you get to go home. Would you rather be dead?'

She swallowed but didn't answer. Though Church knew she wanted to say no. Of course, she wanted to say no.

'Get on the plane. It'll take you to Kinshasa. Go to the British Embassy. Get them to organise a flight home for you.'

'And then what?' She shook her head. 'What I did? Blackthorn will… He'll…'

'Maybe. Maybe not. But if you keep going after him, he'll have a reason to. If you don't…'

'If I don't, he just gets away with it.'

'You won't be the first to go after him, and you won't be the last,' Church reassured her. 'Let it go now, and live to fight another day.'

'Live to fight another day,' she muttered back.

'Or you can turn around and head back down that road,' Church offered, pointing to the track they'd used to get there. 'Confront Blackthorn, try to liberate the people in that mine, and die here in Maroua. They'll bury you in an unmarked, shallow grave, or maybe they'll just leave your body out in the sun to rot and get eaten by birds. Either way, no one will mourn you. No one will remember you or what you died for. You'll martyr yourself for nothing, and none of the people you died trying to stop will lose a second of sleep over you. They won't think about you. And they won't stop anything they're doing.'

She looked up at him, furious and silent.

'Get on the plane. Forget about Blackthorn and this place and us. Live your life. Have a life.'

The engine noise swelled, and the plane descended towards the earth.

Fletcher kept her gaze fixed on Church as it touched down, rumbled towards them, slowing and turning without cutting the engines.

It came to a halt, and the rear ramp began to lower, the propellers whipping up dust, blasting Church and Fletcher.

She shielded her eyes, and he just stood there in the wash.

'It's time to go,' he said.

She nodded, exhaling and steeling herself. She gave him one final look, her expression a mix of apprehension and fear, and then stepped forward, gaining confidence with each step.

She climbed the ramp and looked back, lifting a hand.

Church just watched her go, his mind already beyond this, already thinking about what came next. What Cole would do when he found out about this. That Church had gotten her out.

He tore his eyes away from her, thinking about his own words. How much he wanted to, in that moment, for the first time, he thought, get on the plane too. How much he wanted to fly away from this place, forget about this life, the pain, the death, the weight of it all.

He was unsteady for a moment and closed his eyes, exhausted and utterly spent.

The engines climbed in intensity over his shoulder, and the peppering of soil and sand on his face told him the plane was taking off. Fletcher was inside and headed home.

He kept his eyes shut, kept his back to it until the wind began to die and he knew the plane was headed down the runway.

When it took off, the noise dwindling to a distant din, he finally turned to watch it go, knowing if he'd done it any sooner, he might not have been able to stop himself from flagging it down. From getting on it with her.

Live to fight another day, he'd said, feeling deep down like he should take that advice.

That somehow, his whole life had led here, and that not getting on that plane had sealed his fate.

There wouldn't be another day.

This would be the day that Solomon Church died.

TWENTY-ONE

PRESENT DAY

The hints of dawn were creeping into the sky when they reached Mitch's stash car.

It was an old Nissan 4x4 under a camo tarp off to the side of the track, more than three miles from the farm. Church would have probably thought that it was one of several Mitch had planted in these woods, ready for a quick exfil—if he wasn't dead behind the eyes.

Mitch dragged the tarp back and glanced over at Church, standing stock-still, pistol still in his hand, arm soaked crimson with blood.

He tossed the sheet to the ground and felt under the wheel arch for the key, unlocking the tailgate, muttering under his breath as he did.

'Come here,' he ordered, still not wasting time.

Church stared blankly into space.

'Solomon,' Mitch said, clapping to grab his attention. 'Come here.'

Church stumbled over as Mitch pulled a heavy black flight case towards himself and unlocked it. He flipped it up, revealing more weapons, ammunition, spare clothes, and a first-aid kit. In the back of the vehicle, the seats were down, and it was filled with sleeping bags and tents, camping equipment, vacuum-sealed MREs—everything you'd need to disappear for a while.

'Arm,' Mitch said.

Church didn't even hear him.

Mitch grabbed him then, sinking his thumb into Church's upper arm, next to the graze.

Church hissed in pain, eyes flaring as he looked at his brother.

'They're not dead,' Mitch said, pulling Church closer and wrapping his arm with gauze from the first-aid kit. 'This is going to need stitches, but we don't have time right now.'

'What did you say?' Church asked, blinking at him, wondering if he'd imagined those words coming from his mouth.

Mitch pinned the gauze in place, blood already soaking through the bandage, and reached, with bloodied hands, into the flight case, pulling out a satellite phone and holding it up. 'They're not dead. Get in the truck, and I'll call them.'

He didn't wait for an answer before he slammed the boot closed and headed for the driver's door.

Church followed suit, holstering his pistol and

taking the rifle off his neck, wondering what kind of Houdini bullshit Mitch was talking about—trying to discern if he was lying just to get him to move.

He climbed into the cab, unsure if he was about to thank his brother for pulling off a miracle or break his fucking nose for saying that.

Mitch hunched over the phone, firing it up and punching in a number. It rang once, and then he handed it to Church. 'Keep it short and don't mention where they are. Better safe than sorry.' His blue eyes glimmered in the half-light, the forest all but dark around them.

Church's hand shook as he reached out for the device, and only when he heard Nanna's voice—tinny and small—coming from the receiver, did he snatch it from Mitch's hand.

'Nanna?' he asked desperately.

'Sol?' She sobbed fitfully. 'Oh my God, I thought— What— What happened? There was so much noise. Gunfire, explosions.'

Church ground his teeth, a tear threatening to fall. 'Blackthorn,' he growled. 'They levelled the house. I don't know how—'

Mitch reached over and grabbed the phone from him, hitting a button to put it on speaker. 'There's a computer in the corner that's hooked into the cameras around the farm. Boot it up and tell me what you see.'

'I...' Nanna began, sniffing back tears. 'Okay, hold on.'

There was pacing in the background, tapping as she tried to fire up the computer.

Mitch put his hand over the mouthpiece. 'The cellar is fortified. When I redid the house, I excavated it, lined it with steel and concrete twelve inches thick. The whole house could fall down on it, and it wouldn't break a sweat.' He nodded to Church to reassure him.

'The whole house *did* fall down on it,' Church said.

'And that's a good thing. The cellar's not on any plans, there's no record of it. And the only entrance is buried under the rubble. There's no way they're going to find it because they're not going to be looking. They're safe there, Sol. I promise.'

Church felt like saying that Mitch couldn't know that. But he was trying to help, and throwing it in his face wasn't the right move.

'Okay, I'm on,' Nanna said then. 'I see… Shit,' she muttered.

'What is it?' Church asked.

'They're everywhere. A… dozen men.'

Church's blood rose.

'They're cleaning up, loading bodies into SUVs, flipping one back onto its wheels… My God, what happened out there?'

Mitch jumped in again. 'Are they combing through the rubble of the house?'

'No. But it's still on fire, a big pile of rocks and wood and…' She lowered her voice so the girls wouldn't hear. 'Are we…'

'You are,' Mitch said. 'The cellar is reinforced, and

it's got its own air system rigged to a pipe that leads out into the woods. They have no idea they're right on top of you, and if you stay there, stay quiet, they'll leave.'

'And what if they don't leave?' Church asked. 'What if they *do* start sifting through that rubble?' He eyed his friend.

'Then they'll open the big red door and use the tunnel that leads to the old shepherd's cottage in the forest above the farm. It's two hundred metres, and there's a Land Rover there they can take,' Mitch said, hurrying the conversation along, acutely aware that if they were being followed, they were burning crucial seconds going in circles.

'You have been busy,' Church said.

'Ten years is a long time. And I knew this day would come, one way or another. And I haven't survived this long to die on my knees,' he replied, a flash of his old, formidable self showing through.

Church reached out, finally feeling the pain in his arm, and squeezed Mitch's shoulder. 'Thank you,' he said, turning back to the phone. 'Nanna, you hear that?'

'I did,' she said.

'Okay. You and the girls lay low. Keep an eye on the cameras. Let us know when Blackthorn's men are gone or if you need to bug out. I'm sorry—'

'Save it,' Nanna said. 'Just… Just get this done, okay? *Finished.* For good.'

Church could hear the conviction in her voice. It steeled him.

'Be safe, Sol.'

'Look after yourself, and—'

Mitch hung up before he could finish. 'We need to go,' he said. 'Happy reunions later, after we dispense with Blackthorn.' He started the engine and pulled onto the rutted, muddy track, driving as quickly as the car would allow.

Church repositioned himself in the seat, breathing through the swelling, throbbing pain in his arm. 'And how exactly do we do that? Dispense with Blackthorn?'

'Same way Foster tried to,' Mitch said, driving towards a brightening opening at the end of a tunnel of trees. 'By going back to where all this started.'

Church didn't like it, but he knew Mitch was right.

They had to go back to Maroua. Back to the DRC. They needed to find something tying it all to Blackthorn and bring that home. Church knew that if he were going it alone, he'd have no chance of getting there, let alone succeeding. But while he'd been drinking himself into oblivion, bouncing from one nothing town to the next, Mitch had been better. Smarter. He'd taken care of himself. The farm, the vehicles, the weapons. Church wondered how he'd got it all done, and on the flight to Africa, he was going to ask him.

For now, he was just glad that Mitch had people he could call on—people he'd told he was alive, people who knew what had happened and who would help when the time came. It turned out that despite Blackthorn being a shining beacon of hope for the uninitiated, those in the forces knew full well what men with that much money and power often did to get it. And that, under no circumstances, could they be trusted to do right by the people they governed.

Weird how billionaires always seemed out of touch with the plight of the common man. But it was the truth.

And though it wasn't often said aloud, behind closed doors there had always been rumours swirling about what really went down in the DRC. The fact that three surviving members of that mission had transitioned to the private sector to work for Blackthorn didn't exactly do anything to snuff those out. Accusing your brothers of turning on their own was tantamount to heresy in the forces, but a man's thoughts were his own. And any one man thinking that wasn't alone. So, when Mitch reached out over the years, there was no one unhappy to hear the news. And no one was surprised to hear the truth.

The words, *If you need anything, I'm there*, had rung in his ears over the years. And now, he did need something. And they were there for him. No questions.

Before the sun had set that night, they were sitting on the runway at Brize Norton, in the back of an Airbus A400M Atlas transport aircraft. It was headed to Somalia, where the British military was engaged in a training programme with the Somali National Army in Baidoa to help them fight Al-Shabaab, the militant terrorist organisation waging civil war in the country.

They were the only people on board, but vehicles and ordnance were being brought in, and they'd be on the tarmac before sun-up. From there, it was a twin-prop taking them into the DRC.

The Congo was still a hotspot of international interest, with the WHO and UNICEF working to stem outbreaks of Ebola and other diseases, bringing clean water and medical care to the country. But it was also rich in gold, diamonds, oil, and, of course, cobalt. Which meant it wasn't just of humanitarian concern, but of global economic concern too. And that added up to a lot of countries having boots on the ground in less-than-official capacities.

Old friends and old favours meant that a Land Cruiser was waiting for them at the airfield, courtesy of someone who definitely wasn't working for the CIA.

If there was one thing Church definitely didn't miss about the SAS, it was transfers like this. You got used to it, learned to sleep anywhere, any time. But you could never shake that sense of dread when you opened your eyes and realised you were in a different country, about to spill blood for a cause you didn't quite understand—and that it wasn't all just some dream.

He got up from the seat in the back of the empty twin-prop, deafened from the ride, his spine ground to dust from the turbulence, and stretched out.

Mitch was opposite, looking drawn—like he felt even worse than Church did.

They pulled their canvas duffels from the row behind, packed with combat gear that Mitch's contacts had liberated on their behalf, along with their weapons, and shouldered them, stepping down into the oppressive morning heat.

Church was bowled sideways by it. The hot wind. The sun, like someone holding a welding torch to the side of his face. He hadn't missed it, had done his best to forget it.

He blinked and wasn't sure if it was now or ten years ago. Their initial arrival had been much the same —the first breath thick and choking, the sun so bright it blinded him.

'It's okay,' Mitch said, catching him, guiding him back to his feet. 'Happens to me too.'

Church righted himself and pulled his arm free of Mitch's grasp. 'Sun's just bright,' he muttered, striding forward towards the only car on the tarmac.

It was an old, piece-of-shit rust bucket that looked like it barely ran. Probably didn't.

Mitch had always driven, and though Church was dying to get off the runway and this whole thing over with, he still climbed into the passenger seat on reflex.

He settled in, realising the wheel wasn't in front of him, and cursed silently.

'Old habits, huh?' Mitch asked, getting into the driver's seat.

'Just fucking drive,' Church replied, digging the pistol out of the duffel bag between his knees and ejecting the magazine.

Mitch pulled away as Church confirmed it was loaded and slotted it back into the grip, chambering a round.

'Expecting a fight already?' Mitch asked as they bumped down off the runway and onto the dirt road to town. 'Not even had breakfast yet.'

'In this place? Always,' Church said, keeping his eyes peeled.

They began passing people walking on the road. Locals turning to see who was arriving now. Another fresh import here to exploit them and ravage their land. Church barely registered their angry expressions, his eyes fixed on the column of yellow dust rising off to their left beyond the jungle.

The mine.

Still going. Still churning rocks all these years later.

How many had been buried beyond the fence now? How many had been left to rot in the sun?

They drove onwards, Church closing his eyes to it all but only seeing more in the darkness.

He breathed through whatever the hell this was, opening his eyes only when they slowed, the sounds of car horns and voices dragging him back to the present.

They were in town now, pulling down the main strip that was just as he remembered it. A wide slab of unpainted tarmac with rough concrete pavements, telephone poles replete with a million wires spidering out to a million buildings overhead. Street vendors with carts full of fruit. A throng of people walking, riding bikes, swerving on mopeds between traffic as cars, bumper to bumper, oozed through the melee of it all.

Church's attention drifted upwards as Mitch navigated forward with quiet confidence, his eyes settling on something he thought he'd never see again.

'Jesus,' he muttered, leaning forward in the chair to get a better look at the blackened building. 'It's still here.'

Mitch looked up, not mentioning the blasphemy, and took it in too.

They stared in silence at the burnt-out ruin, boarded up and abandoned—the town just growing around it like a piece of shrapnel not pulled from the muscle.

The traffic flowed past, and the sight dwindled in the rearview.

'What's the plan here?' Church asked then, almost afraid to hear the answer. He swallowed the bile rising in his throat and stared out of the dusty window at Maroua, a town firmly in the stranglehold of the West, whether they realised it or not.

'We pick up Foster's trail. Get into the mine. Find something linking it to Blackthorn.' Mitch drew a slow breath. 'And then…'

'And then we take that prick down.' Church looked at Mitch, a cold calm settling over him. 'Once and for all.'

TWENTY-TWO

TEN YEARS AGO

'Church.'

He turned to see Mitch standing by the Land Cruiser, holding up the sat-phone.

'It's Cole,' Mitch said.

Church's guts twinged a little.

'He needs us.'

He started towards Mitch. 'What do you mean?'

'He said Blackthorn's been summoned to Zawadi's compound. It's all hands. We're greenlit to take Zawadi out.'

'Did he mention—'

Mitch shook his head. 'No. He just said the mission takes priority over everything. He wasn't fucking around. We gotta go. Right now.'

Church swallowed the lump in his throat and went

forward. He had no way to know what was in Cole's mind. But he wasn't looking forward to seeing him. After their conversation in Church's room the night before, and what happened this morning... Their team was divided. Right down the middle. And if they were moving on Zawadi—if this was to be an all-out assault on the compound—then not knowing if your team had your back could mean the difference between life and death.

'Alright,' Church said, going around the truck and climbing into the passenger seat.

As Mitch wheeled them towards the exit road, Church looked out of the window at the tiny dot of a plane disappearing into the brightening sky. He turned away from it and watched the road instead.

He'd made his decision. And now he had to live with it.

They drove fast and made it back to the hotel without any stops. Cole was already loading up, bundling their gear—and Blackthorn—into their vehicle.

Reed, Murphy, and Boyd all cast glances at them as they approached but quickly looked away.

Cole waved them into the kerb.

Mitch cut the engine, and it seemed like no one wanted to be the first to get out.

This was Church's mess, though, and his responsibility to clean up. He got out and approached Cole.

'We grabbed your gear from your rooms,' Cole said

without hesitation. 'It's in the lobby. We're on the road in five. Norton, you're riding in the lead car, Reed's with you. He'll brief you on the road.'

Cole turned away and went back to packing.

Church looked over at Mitch, who didn't risk a shrug, but was communicating it anyway.

The mission was taking priority. That's what Cole had said on the phone. Church guessed he'd get chewed out after they were done.

And if they all died, well, it saved Cole the trouble.

Inside, Church found his duffel with his clothes and kit shoved inside, his rifle on top. He shouldered both and headed back towards the Land Cruiser, spying Blackthorn hanging out of the window, having a hushed conversation with Cole.

Church slowed to watch, but Reed was there suddenly, pushing him towards the car.

'We're out in less than two. Move it,' he ordered, all but marching Church along.

He seemed to have grown a spine in the last few days. Clearly empowered by something—maybe the taste of Cole's arsehole.

Either way, right now, Church wasn't looking to make waves.

Alongside the others, he loaded up.

Mitch was in the front, Reed next to him, and Church and Foster crammed into the back like two ogres squeezed into a clown car.

The doors snapped shut on the lead car, and it pulled

away quickly. Mitch punched it too, and Reed twisted in his seat to brief them.

'A news story went live this morning naming Zawadi as a dictator enslaving the local people here, and Blackthorn as a co-conspirator.'

He seemed to look at Church longer than he did Foster when he said that.

'They used our surveillance photos in the article—fuck knows how they got them.'

Did he really not know, or was he just playing dumb?

Was Cole keeping him in the dark on his dealings with Blackthorn?

Church didn't care to guess and didn't want to say anything either way.

Reed went on. 'Zawadi reached out as soon as he got wind and demanded Blackthorn come to his compound to give an explanation. We're playing dumb, obviously. We're taking Blackthorn in with the hope that it'll get us through the gate.

'The plan is to let Cole escort Blackthorn into a private meeting with Zawadi, and then take him out. Once he's down, we sweep the building, retrieve Cole and Blackthorn, and then make our exfil. Got that?'

Church and Foster both nodded, and Reed turned back to the road ahead.

As Church watched him, he couldn't help but wonder why he hadn't asked about Fletcher. Where she was, even. If they'd swept the hotel, they knew she was gone.

Reed looked calm, but from Church's position, he could see the quickened pulse in the side of his neck.

Was he nervous?

If he didn't ask about Fletcher, then he must have known something. Maybe everything.

But right now, they had to focus on the mission. Everything else could come later.

They thundered through town, the rumble and clank of the mine rising in the heat to their left, echoing through the trees. The noise and the dust drowned the town all day, every day. You couldn't forget how close it was. And even from Zawadi's gates, you could hear it.

They slowed for the approach, Mitch leaving enough room behind the lead car that they could back up quickly if they needed to.

Reed shifted a little in his chair as though preparing for something he knew was coming.

Church unholstered his pistol and gently pulled back the slide, making sure a round was chambered.

Ahead, the lead car stopped at the gate.

A pair of Zawadi's men started motioning them out of the vehicle. The first of the two stayed with the lead car, while the second came to their Land Cruiser and waved at them with his rifle to do the same.

Church eyed the guy while Reed reached for the door handle.

'Out of the car,' he said. 'Keep things relaxed 'til we're inside.'

Reluctantly, Church followed suit, the whole thing not sitting right with him.

These two guys looked green. Young and nervous.

Church expected them to be swarmed at the gate by Zawadi's men, the whole place on high alert after the story breaking. And yet, it was quiet. No noise coming from beyond the wall. Two inexperienced soldiers at the gate.

'Over there,' the gate guard ordered them, pointing to the open space of ground next to the cars.

Reed started walking without a word. It was Church who asked the question.

'Why?'

'We search the vehicles,' the soldier replied.

'Why?' Church repeated, keeping his hands by his sides.

The soldier blinked, not really understanding the question, or maybe he just didn't know what he was searching for.

Church turned his head to look at the open space, the wall of the compound on one side, the wall of trees on the other. Thick and shadowed.

The distant clank of the mine rumbled in the hot, thick air, but there was no wind. Everything was still.

Church didn't like this.

Reed had started walking, Mitch too. Foster was lingering to hear the answer to Church's question, and from the lead car, Cole and Blackthorn weren't moving to the other side of their vehicle either.

He remained planted, not moving even when the soldier came forward and pressed the muzzle of the rifle into Church's chest.

'Walk,' the man said.

But Church did no such thing. His eyes were fixed on Cole, who was also unmoving. And the guard who had covered the first car wasn't giving him or Blackthorn any grief. He was following their team into the open.

Church could feel the sweat beading under his jaw.

Cole was stalwart. Blackthorn was visibly nervous.

Slowly, Cole looked down, lifting his watch to check the time. As though waiting for something.

And Church knew something was wrong. Very wrong.

The guard jabbed Church in the chest again with his rifle, and he reacted quickly, driving his left hand up into the barrel with enough speed—and so suddenly— that by the time the guard reacted and pulled the trigger, the muzzle was already over his head.

The AK-47 let off a barrage of rounds into the sky, and everyone ducked.

Church stepped forward, ramming the body of the gun into the guard's face while Foster ripped his pistol from his holster and put two bullets into the first gate guard before he could home in on Church and fire.

He hit the ground with a dull thud as Church tore the rifle from the young soldier's hands and tossed it, lifting his right hand and the pistol in it, firing as he did.

The guard staggered backwards and convulsed with the impact before he collapsed to the floor.

Church's eyes swung around to Cole, who was still standing still, watch still raised.

He lifted his eyes to Church, unmoving, unfazed by the exchange—as though he knew he and Blackthorn were never in danger.

But before Church could ask, could even think, the shockwave hit him.

It tore through the trees, stripping leaves from the canopy, rocking the cars on their springs, and almost bowling them all off their feet.

Church stumbled and looked up, seeing the column of fire and smoke lancing skywards above the mine, hearing the explosion, seeing the tsunami of orange rust engulfing the jungle—surging towards them in an unstoppable wall.

'Everybody down!' he managed to roar before it hit, almost as hard as the shockwave itself.

It was like getting sandblasted.

Church threw his hands up to shield his eyes and staggered backwards in the gust, finding his feet a moment later.

He choked on the dust, opening his eyes to a thick red fog.

He couldn't see ten feet.

It was a thick, choking cloud, and all he could make out was Foster, braced against the Land Cruiser in front of him.

Church turned to look for Cole, for Blackthorn—but they were nowhere to be seen.

'Where's—' he started, coughing and hawking on the dirt, not able to get his words out.

From beyond the cars, the chatter of gunfire echoed,

dim bulbs of muzzle flash flickering through the miasma.

'Contact!' came the call of one of his guys. 'Fall back!'

The shots were from AKs—Church knew the sound as well as any.

A dozen, maybe more.

An ambush.

Set up that way.

Church settled down against the truck next to Foster, grinding his teeth, the crunch of sand between them reverberating through his skull.

The two gate guards getting them out of the vehicles, marching them into the open.

That's what it was about—getting them in a line. Executing them.

Cole had somehow arranged the blast at the mine. Had somehow set this all up.

With the express intention of getting them all killed?

Could Church really reckon with that?

Did he really believe that?

The AK-47s continued their song.

Someone called out in pain.

'I'm hit!' a voice echoed.

Pistols fired back. Everyone had their sidearms—their rifles in the vehicles.

That way, by design.

Church held firm, knowing rushing out into the fog was suicidal.

He couldn't see them.

Couldn't see his own guys.

Zawadi's men shouted their advance and made their way forward, the volume and intensity of their onslaught growing.

Boyd appeared suddenly, dragging Reed by the straps of his vest.

Reed was holding onto a wound on his flank, a little below his liver, as Boyd pulled him into cover and let go, kneeling down to assess the damage.

There were more shapes in the fog then, and Church lifted his pistol, watching as Cole and Blackthorn appeared—Blackthorn behind, shoved by the collar.

Church lined Cole up between the sights for a second and considered it.

Cole froze.

'Pull the trigger or get that the fuck out of my face,' he snarled, batting it away.

Church lowered the gun, watching his captain, wondering if he should have done as Cole said and pulled the trigger. He was wrestling with himself. Cole might be double-dealing, but condemning his team to death? No. Church couldn't believe that. Wouldn't.

'Ah, fuck,' Cole muttered, looking down at Reed. 'Boyd, get him up. Get him in the truck,' he ordered. 'We're taking Blackthorn. We're pulling back to the hotel.'

Mitch, Murphy, and Norton appeared then, sliding around the sides of the Land Cruiser—filthy and sweat-slick, all three of them panting.

Cole looked at the five remaining men. 'Foster,

Church, Norton, Mitch, Murph—it's now or never. We've got the green light to take Zawadi out. And we're finishing the mission.' He looked at each of them. 'You good?'

Church wanted to say no. To argue. To refuse. To call Cole out then and there. But he couldn't. Not now. Not in the middle of all this. He was a good soldier. A good soldier. And Cole was right—this was the job. This was what they signed on for.

He, like the others, nodded.

Get Zawadi.

That was all that mattered.

They would all die for that cause.

'Move,' Cole commanded, and they all jumped to it. Like a well-oiled machine, Church, Foster, and Mitch pulled their bags and rifles from the truck as Cole and Boyd heaved Reed into the back and loaded up.

Church checked his rifle and shouldered it, catching —out of the corner of his eye—Cole seizing Murphy by the chest and pulling him in. 'You know what to do,' Cole told him.

Murphy stared back, then nodded firmly.

Cole released him and climbed into the passenger seat, Boyd already behind the wheel.

As Boyd threw the vehicle into reverse and backed up, Cole kept Church's gaze through the windscreen. Cold and unflinching.

And then he was gone. Swallowed by the fog.

Leaving Church with Foster, Mitch, Norton, and Murphy, their mission clear:

Kill Zawadi.

At all costs.

And as they started forward, Church couldn't help but weigh those costs.

And for the first time in his life, he thought that might just be too much.

TWENTY-THREE

PRESENT DAY

THERE REALLY WAS no time to lose.

They geared up quickly, and while Church was strapping into his ballistic vest, Mitch came over, holding up his phone.

'Just had word from Nanna,' he said. 'Blackthorn's men have cleared out. They're safe.'

Church breathed a little sigh of relief but read more in Mitch's expression than just that. 'What is it?' he asked.

'You're not going to like it,' Mitch said.

A cold sensation ran up Church's back. He looked at his brother. 'Is it Nanna? The girls... are they okay?'

'Yes, yeah, yeah, they're fine,' Mitch said. 'But... well... they took your Defender.'

Church stopped dead in his tracks, blinking at his brother. 'They stole my fucking truck?'

Mitch hissed a little through his teeth. 'Yeah. Nanna said it was Cole, she recognised him on the cameras. It was parked round the back where you got the Volvo from, and apparently, she saw Cole take a liking to it. She said they broke the window and then hot-wired it. You really should have thought of installing some modern security along with that engine swap you did.'

Church growled under his breath. 'The places I lived before... people knew better than to rob me.'

Mitch shrugged. 'Just another reason to hunt them down when we get back.'

'Like I didn't have enough already,' Church said, snatching up the battle rifle he'd been cleaning and loading, then snapping back the mechanism.

They exited the safe house Mitch's contacts had arranged and hopped in the Land Cruiser. Though Church hated wasting more time, they had to wait for nightfall to execute something like this. Slipping in during the middle of the day wasn't going to be possible.

The mine had quietened now, the thump and bang of the rock crusher subdued for the night. And aside from a few guards, Church hoped security would be light on the ground. After all, who was stupid enough to try and rob Blackthorn?

They parked up about a mile from the mine, well off the main road, hidden from view by the trees, and got out. The moon was high and bright, making it easy to navigate without light or night vision, and they moved fast.

Church was in the vanguard with the battle rifle against his shoulder, while Mitch brought up the rear carrying an M4 carbine—another little gift from his contact who definitely wasn't in the CIA. They moved quickly but quietly in single file, keeping a straight heading for the mine, and before long they saw the first flicker of the searchlight on a brand-new guard tower that had been erected in the centre of it all.

They paused about twenty yards back from the clearing between the trees and the perimeter fence and took it in.

'Changed a little since we were here last,' Mitch muttered, looking around.

It had indeed. There'd been a single chain-link fence here ten years ago, one rock crusher, one site office, and a few tiers in a hillside where the strip mine was still in its infancy. Now, though, the mine was huge, wrapped around into a horseshoe shape easily twenty times bigger than before. The chain-link fence was topped with razor wire, and the site office was now a trio of long, warehouse-like buildings. Huge earth-movers were positioned around, and in the centre of it all was a massive conveyor belt feeding rock into a steel funnel above a maw of churning teeth that ground rock to pebbles. Church counted half a dozen dump trucks and, in the middle, the watchtower, complete with a roving searchlight.

Church reached into the pocket of his cargo trousers, pulled out a pair of compact binoculars, and spied the sole guard manning the light. 'Easy shot from here,' he said.

'Yeah, if you want to alert the whole place to our arrival,' Mitch retorted.

Church sighed and lowered the binoculars. 'It was just a suggestion.'

'Why don't we try to keep this quiet until we have to go loud? I can't see there being many guys here. I mean, what… what are they guarding? Rocks?'

Church didn't answer. He didn't have an answer. 'Let's make tracks,' he said. 'We'll circle the perimeter, look for a way in.'

Mitch seemed more amenable to that idea and followed as Church stuck to the trees, making a slow circle around the compound. Both of them were aware of the space of stumps between them and the fence—the killing field that Zawadi had cut all those years ago. It seemed like Blackthorn's men were keen to keep up traditions.

Church tried to put it out of his mind, zeroing in on their goal. They were here to collect intel—intel enough to link Blackthorn to this place, dead to rights, enough to force him into the light.

As they walked, Mitch was diligent, snapping photos on his phone of the whole thing: the guard tower, the mine, the buildings, the razor-wire fences, and, every now and then, a suspiciously human-shaped mound of earth. He lingered on each one to say a silent prayer, then moved on. There didn't seem to be any fresh bodies littered around, but then again, it didn't take many to prove a point, and just a few were more than enough to break the spirit of the workers.

Eventually, Church found what he was looking for. A tanker was parked behind one of the long buildings, supplying it with water, and from that building, a drainage ditch had been dug that ran out under the fence. Though it smelled like piss and shit, there was a two-foot gap that would make for easy ingress.

As they approached, Mitch didn't even need to be told what was going through Church's mind.

'I really thought we were done with all this,' he muttered, staring at the shit-filled pit.

'One last one,' Church said. 'For old times' sake.'

They moved towards it, skulking down into the ditch, trying not to think about what was squelching under their heels. Church passed his rifle and pack to Mitch, levering himself under, doing his best not to dip himself into the effluent. Mitch passed their gear through and followed suit while the searchlight swung around on the other side of the buildings to cover the courtyard between the mine and the warehouses.

With the size of those earth-movers and dump trucks, Church had to assume the buildings were filled to the brim with copper ore, ready for export—that they were producing more raw material than they could truck out easily. He'd seen greed ten years ago, but this was on another level, enough to make him sick to his back teeth… or maybe that was just the rancid stench of sun-baked human faeces.

He shouldered his pack and rifle, then motioned Mitch forward. Now that they were inside, there'd be no words. They'd fall into that old silent routine of hand signals, eye contact, reading each other's body language. An unspoken conversation made up of every slight gesture and step.

Church made a beeline for the back of the first building, crouching against the wall and checking for anything resembling a security camera. He saw nothing on this side. So far, so good. He signalled for Mitch to keep his eyes open, then went round the corner of the building, making his way towards the front, hidden in the shadow of the adjacent warehouse.

As he reached the far end, he slowed, the smell of cigarette smoke and the sound of voices reaching his ears. Slowly, he passed the rifle under his arm and pinned it there with his elbow, drawing his pistol from his thigh holster with his other hand.

They were dressed in black tactical gear with no insignia—no marks of where they were from or on whose authority. If they were spotted, they couldn't be easily identified. But getting spotted wasn't an option. Neither man had said it, but they both knew capture wasn't on the table, and if things went sideways, there was only one choice. And they would do it for each other without hesitation.

Without hesitation, Church gestured to Mitch to pull up his scarf to cover his face, hide his identity, and then peeked around the corner. There were two men standing under a white floodlight, smoking a cigarette, their backs turned. Both looked to be in their twenties or thirties. They were in cargo pants and boots, one wearing an old Manchester United jersey, the other a stained white tank top.

The searchlight was facing away, with the guard in the tower taking his time scanning the fences for weaknesses or intruders. They could take them. Clean. They were only a few yards away, backs turned, laughing as they smoked. They wouldn't know what hit them.

Church slowly holstered his gun and slipped his combat knife from the sheath at his hip, Mitch doing the same without needing to be told. Church motioned him forward, and they stood shoulder to shoulder, then moved in unison—a few quick strides and strike.

Left hands over their targets' mouths, pulling heads back. In films, slitting someone's throat was usually what people did, but it was inefficient and not guaranteed. You had to cut deep and wide, getting both arteries to have any chance of a good kill. But that would cause arterial spray, make everything slick, risk you losing your grip. You also had to sever the vocal cords to prevent a scream, and there was always the chance of getting your hand bitten. No—the cleaner option was to slip the blade under the right arm and drive it towards you, through the sternum, piercing the aorta. Massive blood loss, death in less than thirty seconds, the blood draining from the upper body so quickly that consciousness went with it, no time to call out. Then you could guide or drag the body away without fuss.

If you couldn't reach the sternum, you went up into

the armpit, twisting the blade into the axillary artery, attached to the brachial and subclavian. It was a major highway for blood, and severing it also cut major nerves, causing spasms and paralysis of the right arm. Either way, no chance of defence.

Church was approaching at an angle, so the sternum wasn't an option. He made the choice instinctively, placing his knife where it would do the job. They struck, and he and Mitch dragged their marks back into the shadows together, laying them against the wall of the warehouse, out of reach of the searchlight.

'Let's make this quick,' Mitch said, sounding disgusted by what they'd just done.

Church understood. This was a life they'd all left behind. Coming back to it now had a bitter taste, though Church found picturing Blackthorn's smug face helpful to ward off guilt creeping into the corners of his mind.

They moved around the corner and cracked open the warehouse door. Slipping inside, they found themselves in a long corridor with doors on the right-hand side. There were no cameras here, but Church doubted only three men would guard this entire place. Sooner or later, they were bound to stumble on quarters with more guards and, if they were lucky, an office with something useful.

'Room by room,' Church whispered, drawing his pistol—more effective for close quarters than the rifle, easier for crowd control than the knife. He peeked into the first room and found nothing but a store cupboard. The second was a break room, empty of people. The third was a bunk room; two men lay there, snoring soundly on cots in the dark.

Church contemplated ending them both quietly, but Mitch was wearing a reluctant look and shook his head, motioning for them to continue. No need to engage if it wasn't required; they could get in and out without those men ever knowing. Church eased the door closed, and they went on. Ten years ago, Mitch would've been right there with him. Had he gone soft or just become wiser?

The next room paid off. An office with a computer, filing cabinets, and a desk. A potential font of information. They didn't hang around. Church covered the cabinets, sifting through files for anything they could use. He found cargo manifests, logs of outputs from the mine, invoices for deliveries and exports. Nothing with Blackthorn's name on it.

Church rummaged in another few drawers, knowing in his gut that Blackthorn wouldn't be sloppy enough to have his name or signature in plain sight like this. Meanwhile, Mitch was already gutting the ancient desktop computer for hard drives, ready to examine them later for anything incriminating.

Once Mitch had prised out the drives, he slipped them into his pack. 'All right, let's get out of here,' Church whispered, already checking the door. The corridor was clear. He let out a little sigh of relief. So far, so good. They had what they needed, or at least a lead. Two more buildings might remain, but every minute spent here risked running into reinforcements.

The men outside would eventually be missed, and when that happened, it would get loud fast.

Mitch followed Church out into the corridor, then slowed, glancing down at the other doors, the ones they hadn't checked. Church could guess what he was thinking but gave him a hard look to let him know it was time to bug out. Yet Mitch seemed driven by something deeper, as though sensing something wasn't right. He signalled that it would only take a minute and doubled back to the next door along, pressing his ear against it.

He drew back sharply and beckoned Church forward.

Another bunk room? More guards mobilising? Church tightened his grip on the pistol, preparing to deal with whoever was inside.

Before Church reached him, though, Mitch opened the handle and stepped in, forcing Church to rush into the gap, pistol raised, covering the room for threats, searching for his first target.

But it wasn't armed men. It was the opposite.

The room was cavernous, the bare concrete floor lined with thin sleeping mats. The best part of a hundred people were in there. Men, women, children, all half-starved and exhausted, their clothes filthy and tattered, their bare feet orange with dirt and dust. The light spilling in from the corridor illuminated their frightened faces, eyes wide as they stared up at the two masked and armed men in the doorway. They cowered, lifting their hands as if to beg for mercy, pleading not to be shot in a language Church didn't understand. But it translated perfectly well. He'd heard it enough times from enough people.

Mitch reached out and shoved Church's pistol down, knowing exactly what they were looking at. This operation wasn't just ferrying in day labourers anymore. These workers lived here too. And not by choice. Many had their hands bound. Several had broken arms badly set, swollen faces bruised and cut. It was slavery. Forced labour. These people had been pulled from their homes in Maroua and other villages across the DRC and worked to death in this mine.

Mitch took a step forward, hands raised, about to speak words Church knew he couldn't utter. *You're all safe now.*

Church grabbed his brother by the collar of his flak vest, pulling him back and shaking his head.

'These people need our help,' Mitch hissed, full of the fire and fury of someone desperate to right a wrong. Perhaps a lifetime of them.

'I know,' Church said, pulling Mitch closer. *'I know.* But we can't. We'll start a war we're not equipped for, and we'll get these people killed before we get them out of here.'

'We can't just leave them...' Mitch whispered back.

'We have to,' Church said. 'We have to get out clean, see if we got what we came for. If we have, then we can come back and do what needs to be done. And we do it right.'

Mitch searched Church's face for any hint of a falter,

pleading silently for him to change his mind. Church hated how it sounded coming out of his mouth, but it was the truth. They had come for information, not liberation. That was their first priority. If they tried to free these people now, some might escape, but many would die. Word would spread fast of what had happened and who'd done it, and Blackthorn would shut the site down, scrubbing himself from the record. They'd lose all hope of ever tying him to Maroua. No, if they took these people out now, the whole mission would fail, and then, like the cockroach he was, Blackthorn's operation would just resume elsewhere. Another town sitting on a mountain of cobalt. He didn't care whose back it broke, so long as he satisfied his supply chain and kept himself flush.

But hanging around wasn't going to help Mitch's decision.

'Come on,' Church said, dragging him towards the door by the back of his vest. 'We live to fight another day.'

Mitch held firm.

'I promise,' Church added, sincerity burning in his eyes. 'We'll help them.'

Mitch stared for a moment, then relented, moving slowly, unsteadily on his feet. He cast one last look at the people on the ground, confused and scared, looking until Church eased the door closed and shut them away.

Mitch was silent as they headed back towards the front door, walking quickly, only slowing when they neared the room with the two sleeping guards. He stopped and looked back at Church, and Church stared back at him, questioning. And then there were no more questions.

Mitch slipped his knife from his sheath once more and plunged through the door without warning, forcing Church to go in blind after him.

Mitch lined up the man sleeping on the cot to the right of the bed and stuck his knife through his heart before he could even open his eyes. He drew a sharp intake of breath and made something resembling a shout of surprise before he fell silent, but it was enough to rouse the second man, and Church was only halfway to him by the time he tried to sit up.

Church leapt forward, knife drawn, and pinned him back to the bed, his forearm in his throat to stifle his cry for help. The man scrabbled at Church's head as he drove his knife between his ribs, deeply enough to reach his heart, and watched as the light went out behind his eyes. His arms fell to his sides, and he lay still.

Church let out a shaking exhale and drew the blade out, wiped it off on the thin mattress, standing up to find Mitch walking towards the door.

'A little warning would have been nice,' Church said.

'I didn't plan that,' Mitch practically spat. 'Wasn't even thinking about it until I reached the door.'

'I get it,' Church said. 'But we can't just leave them here now.'

'Let them bleed,' Mitch spat. 'It's the least they deserve.'

Church looked back at the two dead men, knowing that this was the opposite of what they had planned to do. That it would be far from a clean operation when these two bodies were discovered. But Mitch didn't seem to care and just headed for the door.

They stepped back out into the heat of the African night and headed around the building, stepping over the bodies of the two men who had been smoking, and made for the drainage channel once more. Church had intended to carry those bodies out, to hide them. Make it tough to know who'd been inside and what they'd been after. It seemed like Mitch had lost all interest in that now, though.

Mitch reached the fence first and dropped his pack, handing his kit off to Church as he slipped through, then pulled up the bottom of the fence for Church to clamber under. By the time he got to his feet, Mitch was already making his way back up the slope to the tree line, back towards the front of the compound. Church jogged to catch up and found him waiting in the trees, staring out at the man in the watchtower with a cold look in his eye.

'Rifle,' he said, holding his hand out to Church.

Church fastened his grip around the barrel, the weapon still slung under his arm. 'Why?'

Mitch looked up at him, a look of repugnance on his face. 'Why d'you think?'

Church shook his head. 'No. We're not waking the entire place up.'

'You saw what they did. You know what they deserve,' Mitch said coldly. 'All of them.'

'I do. And I know that right now we're outside the fence, and despite the four bodies we dropped, they don't know who was in there or why. Hopefully, it'll take them a day or two to put two and two together. By that time, we could have all the evidence we need on Blackthorn. It could be in that hard drive right now,' Church said, pointing at his rucksack. 'But if you take that shot, if they call for backup, there could be a hundred, two hundred, five hundred men here before we even make it back to the car. And if you go down, that hard drive goes down with you. Tomorrow we're buried in a pair of shallow graves right here, and everything just goes back to the way it is. We're out. We have what we need. Let's finish the mission.'

Mitch stared back at him, not saying a word, which was why they both jumped out of their skin when they heard someone else speak.

'He's right, you know,' came a woman's voice from the darkness behind them.

They both twisted, drawing their pistols and aiming into the shadow of the trees.

A woman stepped into the moonlight with her hands raised. She was slim, with long black hair drawn into a ponytail. She wore a white shirt and a ballistic vest, a pistol in a holster on her belt.

'Don't shoot,' she said. 'I come in peace.'

'Who are you?' Church asked, keeping her dead between the sights of his gun, finger light and ready on the trigger.

'I could ask you the same thing,' she said. And as

she finished, Church saw the moonlight glint off a dozen gun barrels. A fleet of armed men in military uniforms stepped up beside her, rifles at the ready, pinned on Church and Mitch.

'But that can wait. Right now, I just have one question,' she said, looking from Church to Mitch and back. 'Do you know a man named Walter Blackthorn?'

TWENTY-FOUR

TEN YEARS AGO

THE GUNFIRE WANED, and shouts to advance echoed towards them through the dust.

It had been set up as an ambush from the start. They'd drawn them all there with the express purpose of killing them—but how much of a hand did Cole have in it? What was the angle? He wanted Zawadi dead, didn't he? But then why try and get them killed, too?

It didn't make sense. Not yet. Not fully.

Mitch took Church by the arm and squeezed as Norton and Murphy pulled their gear from the lead car.

'You good?' he asked him. 'You with us?'

Church centred himself and nodded. 'Yeah, I'm here,' he said, squinting in the fog.

Murphy turned to them, throwing his bag over his shoulder. 'We go over the front gate, fight our way in,' he said.

Church stared at him and only saw Cole in his face, heard Cole's voice in his words.

'No,' he replied. 'That's suicide. We have no idea what's waiting for us, and we already know Zawadi's rolled out the welcome wagon. We could be running into a firing squad.'

'It's Cole's orders,' Murphy said firmly, his thin, weathered face caked with dirt, his beard orange with it.

Church crunched more grit between his teeth. 'Fuck Cole's orders,' he growled, growing more certain by the moment that the idea was to make sure they didn't get out of here alive. He was taking control of this operation, and if Murphy didn't like it, he could hop the front gate himself. But these men—Mitch, Foster, Norton—they were his brothers. And he wasn't marching them knowingly to their deaths.

'We go around back,' he said. 'There's a rear gate, and a back entrance into the house. It's closer to Zawadi's office, and cover is better. We force entry with shape charges if we need to. Breach formation. Good?'

He glanced around the men, and they waited for his go.

'Move. Double-time,' he ordered, getting up and leading the way.

They ran right, sticking close to the wall, leaving the Land Cruiser where it was, and skirted the compound. Church hoped that the majority of Zawadi's forces would be concentrated around the gate, waiting for them. Though he knew there'd be resistance. And plenty of it.

He was spitting dirt and choking on it in equal measure by the time they reached the corner and went left down towards the back of the compound. The wall was twelve feet high and slick, razor-wire topped. Unscalable. But the back gate was like the front gate—a solid slab of swinging steel, which meant hinges. Nothing a couple of charges couldn't deal with.

Church mapped it out in his head, and as they rounded the last corner, he called Norton to the front of the line and whispered over his shoulder.

'Charges. Four. Hinges. You know the drill.'

He slowed up, letting Norton pass, and motioned Mitch to his side.

'You and Foster cover the rear, make sure we're not snuck up on. Murph?'

Murphy came forward, scowling but not arguing.

'You're with me. We're covering Norton,' he said. *Because I don't want to let you out of my sight.*

He didn't say the last part, but that's what his brain was screaming at him.

He let Murphy pass and shouldered his C8, getting a nod from Foster. These guys were all attuned to each other. All moving in sync. And Church wasn't the only one who'd noticed something was amiss.

Foster tightened his grip on his weapon and pressed himself to the wall to cover their six.

Church and Murph lined up behind Norton, protecting him, and Church listened to him work, expecting the 'Charges set,' even before it came.

Norton moved backwards, spooling out the wire that

linked the detonator switch to the RDX explosive compound. It was designed to explode inwards, funnelling all blast force and heat in a specific direction.

'Going loud in ten,' Church called out, he and Murphy clearing the gate. Norton and Mitch moved away, pressing themselves to the wall.

'Five,' Church said, taking cover.

'Three. Two.'

He pointed at Norton.

He clicked the button, the blast immediate and intense. The shockwave rattled his bones, the whine in his ears deafening.

Church blinked a few times, waiting for his eyes to regain focus, and then stood, turning towards the gate, which was now lying ten feet inside the wall, smoking and warped.

'Move!' Church ordered, and they all swung from cover, slipping through the gap, moving in a wedge formation.

Church was at the tip, with Mitch and Foster at his shoulders, covering outwards at forty-five-degree angles. Murphy and Norton were a few steps behind, covering the flanks and rear as they made across the driveway towards the back door that Church had carried Fletcher out of the day before.

He felt the air ripple in the wake of the bullet first, then the sound of it zipping past his head second. There was a dim flash in the fog, and he knelt and brought the sight to his eye as the word left his mouth on reflex.

'Contact!' he called, firing back, putting a bullet into the spot where he'd seen the flash.

There was a moment of stillness, and then a wall of flashes erupted in front of them, bullets flying everywhere.

'Get to cover!' Foster roared, letting off a series of tight bursts.

They rushed forward towards the house, Foster and Norton on Church's left, laying down cover while they hit the back steps and climbed towards the door.

Church reached out and pulled on it.

Locked.

'Planting charge,' he barked, and they all backed up in unison, moving in one fluid pack like a murmuration of starlings, each feeding off one another.

Without him having to ask, Mitch was pushing a shape charge into his hand. He squeezed it against the door, the plastic explosive deforming to the jamb.

He could feel Mitch standing behind him, waiting for him to ask.

Church held up his hand, and Mitch pushed the timer-detonator into it.

They carried both types—manual and automatic. Church fixed it to the charge and set the timer for ten seconds.

'Charge set,' he called out.

Mitch patted him on the shoulder, and they moved, back to back, Church keeping his left hand raised, watching the second hand on his watch tick around.

Five seconds.

'Cover,' Church yelled, and the shooting stopped.

Everyone covered their heads.

The charge detonated, flinging the door open viciously.

'Breach!'

In unison, they funnelled up the steps and into the house, Church leading once more.

His eyes stung from the smoke and dust, but inside was clear, and the first breath of unclouded air was like the first breath he'd ever taken. He raked it in, coughed, and spat a mouthful of sand onto the marble tiles.

Zawadi's men scrambled to attention in the corridor, a handful of them taking cover in the doorways and behind the marble statuettes.

They unleashed fire, digging holes in the walls and floor.

'Sending stunny,' Foster shouted, popping the pin from a stun grenade and hurling it down the length of the corridor.

It bounced and skittered and then lit up. The mixture of magnesium and potassium perchlorate ignited, the flash blinding. It filled the corridor, the bang louder than the shape charge. The men at the other end ceased firing and clutched their heads. In close proximity, the concussive power and volume of the blast were enough to burst eardrums, disrupt sight. There'd be a short window before they recovered, and the guys knew that.

Church and Mitch plunged forward, each taking one of the men.

Church didn't see faces, just shapes. Centre mass

and headshots were all he was looking for. One in the chest, one in the skull.

Both men fell to the ground, and they waited for the others to form up. There'd be more men, but they were at Zawadi's office now.

Norton and Foster covered the rear, making sure their exit was clear. Mitch kept his eyes on the corridor, and Murphy, without being asked, made it clear he was going into Zawadi's office with Church.

He came to the door and met Church's eye. Church wasn't sure he liked what he saw.

Murphy was already pulling another stun grenade from its place, hooked on the front of his vest. He held it up and pulled the pin, keeping his fingers on the lever.

Church understood. They'd done this a hundred times.

Zawadi's door was locked but not fortified. It was solid, but enough force into the mechanism would break it.

Murph pinned himself to the frame, and Church wound up.

He took a deep breath, stepped into it, and launched his heel into the wood just below the handle. It splintered, and the door flew inwards. Church spun sideways out of the path as a line of bullets ripped through the opening and churned up the opposite wall.

Murphy hooked the grenade into the gap and turned away.

It detonated, and cries of shock echoed out.

Church and Mitch swept in low, counting the bodies.

Zawadi behind the desk, two other hostiles, one on either side.

They put them down first, leaving Zawadi alive.

'Hands, hands, hands!' Church yelled, he and Murphy splitting up so that if Zawadi tried anything, he couldn't get them both.

Zawadi was hunched forward, hands at his ears, and knowing he was done, slowly lifted them and straightened, squinting around.

He looked at his two guards, both dead, and then finally lifted his eyes to the two men in his office. A wry, furious smile crept across his lips. He was trembling with rage, leaning forward slowly until he set his hands on his desk. His gaze moved between Church and Murphy, oscillating between incredulous and murderous.

'This is how Blackthorn treats his friends?' Zawadi spat. 'I invited him into my home, we sat at my table, he ate my food, he looked me in the eye, and we made a deal.' His lips peeled back over his teeth as he finished speaking, and he bore them in an ugly grimace.

'Deal's off,' Murphy said, lining Zawadi up between the sights of his rifle.

'No,' Zawadi said suddenly, a grin mutating out of his snarl. He laughed a little to himself and then looked at Murphy. 'A man like Walter Blackthorn does not break deals. He just makes new ones.'

Church came forward a few inches, and Murphy cast him a quick glance, the apprehension in his face apparent.

'What do you mean?' Church asked.

Murphy hushed him and threatened to shoot Zawadi once more, but he didn't seem to care much about the gun pointed at his head.

He let out a low, sinister laugh. 'Whatever reason you think you're here doing this, I'm betting my life that you're wrong. Whatever excuse he gave for killing me, it only serves one purpose, and that is benefiting Walter Blackthorn.'

'We don't work for Walter Blackthorn,' Church replied, doing his best to hold his head up high.

Zawadi smiled, almost in pity at Church. 'If you believe that, then you're just as stupid as I was for trusting him in the first place.'

'Fuck this,' Murphy muttered, pulling the trigger before Zawadi could get another word out. The bullet struck him in the forehead, and he stood straight for a moment, his eyes staring blankly into space. Then he teetered and fell backwards, collapsing dead on the floor of his office.

Church felt an intense heat on the back of his neck, a desire to turn around and lay Murphy out for that. He knew that wasting any more time was only giving Zawadi's men more opportunity to find them, to lay siege to the house. But he wanted to know more, as much as he could. And Murphy had just extinguished all chance of that.

'Let's go,' Murphy said, turning away from the office, back towards the door.

'Wait,' Church urged him, seizing his arm. 'What do you know about Blackthorn?' Church demanded.

Murphy pulled his arm free roughly. 'The fuck's that supposed to mean?'

'You know something,' Church snapped. 'You, Cole, Reed, Boyd—Blackthorn's got your fucking ear, and if I didn't know any better, I'd say your fucking balls too.'

'Watch yourself,' Murphy warned him, squaring up to the big man. 'You wanna talk shit about me? About Cole? Your team? Whose side are you on?'

Church stood his ground, staring down into Murphy's bloodshot eyes.

'You know,' he growled, 'I was just asking myself the same goddamn question.'

TWENTY-FIVE

PRESENT DAY

Church wasn't a big fan of being frogmarched at gunpoint. But whatever conversation it was that this woman wanted to have, doing it outside the fence of the mine in the dead of night was not the right way to handle it.

When they reached their battered old Land Cruiser, they found it'd been hemmed in by a trio of ancient Isuzu Troopers, a car Church hadn't seen in years. During the walk, there were no words exchanged, and he was doing his best to work out who these people were and what the hell was going on.

The armed men looked official army—they were in red berets with black detailing, jungle camo, wielding AKMs, Russian-made modern AK-47s, complete with foregrips and enhanced optics. Church cast a glance back as they approached the vehicles, thinking. They weren't well-armed enough to be PMCs, and their gear was too new for an assembled militia like the one running the mine. Which left only one option: DR Congolese army.

So who was the woman? She spoke perfect English, but not without an accent.

Danish, maybe? Church guessed. His mind worked as they were ordered to climb into the back of one of the Troopers, and the woman told two of the soldiers to take the Land Cruiser and follow behind.

Church tried to snatch words as she spoke but couldn't put a finger on who she was or what her motivations were. She wasn't from here, but she was in charge, and she was armed. NATO, Interpol, maybe.

He said nothing, just followed orders, noting that they'd not been stripped of their weapons or even asked for their names as yet.

Which either meant this woman had no idea what the fuck she was doing, or she knew *exactly* what she was doing and who she was doing it with as well.

They pulled back onto the road and drove quickly back to town, pulling off the main drag and heading into what seemed like the industrial sector. There were scrapyards, car garages, and machine shops. All small outfits that kept the town going.

Church watched them go by in the moonlight until the convoy veered through a gate being held open by another soldier and came to a halt in front of an unmarked, metal-clad building that looked about as nondescript as buildings came.

The woman was in the lead car, and they were in the one at the back, and there seemed to be no expectation of them leaping out while they were in transit. Hell, they didn't even lock the doors.

Mitch cast Church a look that told him he was as confused as he was, and then they both climbed out, curiosity getting the better of them.

The woman in the white shirt approached as the soldier rattled the chain-link and wood-panel gate closed behind them.

Church and Mitch drew back slightly as she lifted her hand without warning and then realised she wasn't pointing a gun at them but rather offering a handshake.

'Now that we're safe,' she said, looking from one to the other, 'Julia Hallberg, Interpol.'

Church stepped forward and shook her hand and was surprised at how strong her grip was. She had to be no more than five feet and three inches tall, her features delicate and pointed, but despite that, and her surroundings, she exuded a capability, a confidence that was impressive.

'Solomon Church,' Church replied.

'Of?' she pressed.

'England?' he replied tentatively.

She looked from Church to Mitch and back, pulling her hand away. 'Wait a minute, you guys aren't…'

'Aren't what?'

She narrowed her eyes. 'So what the hell were you doing inside that mine?'

'That depends,' Mitch said, folding his arms. 'What did you see?'

She stared at them and then laughed. 'Oh, well… Uh…' She cleared her throat then. 'I'm sorry, I'm a little thrown here. I assumed—well, I don't know what I assumed, really. But…'

She seemed thrown by their lack of affiliation, and just like her, Church was now trying to gauge how to play this.

They were in tactical gear with rifles and sidearms, the two of them splattered with blood that clearly wasn't their own. It'd be difficult to argue they were here sight-seeing, especially as, if this Julia Hallberg knew where to find them in the dead of night, she was tracking them, or at least watching the mine in some meaningful way. She'd seen them break in, seen them come back out. Seen how they moved and operated. She'd know they weren't civilians. Hell, by now she probably knew how they got here, too.

So whether they were forthcoming about their true identities or not, she probably knew all she needed to.

So was there any point in hiding anything? They might be able to learn more if they played ball. And if she wanted to detain them, she could certainly have the army do so right here. So being coy was going to be a zero-sum game.

She approached them without a gun raised, asked if they knew Blackthorn—she made the assumption that they were working against him. And why would she do that without any prior knowledge of who they were?

And if she was watching the mine, then it was likely she was also watching Zawadi's compound, too. Which meant…

'You met Foster.'

Hallberg looked up at him but said nothing.

'You did, didn't you? Paul Foster. He went into Zawadi's compound three days ago and never came back out.' Church inspected her face for any kind of tell. 'And you let him, didn't you?'

She swallowed and lifted her chin resolutely.

Church scanned around the faces of the soldiers, their tight grips on their rifles, their stern expressions. 'You've got two dozen men here, I'd bet. Armed to the teeth. And you're looking to take Blackthorn down. Take his operation down. And you want to roll over that place, don't you? Find what you need. But you don't have the authority.'

Church's mind worked furiously. 'The government are getting too many kickbacks from Blackthorn, aren't they? They won't move against him unless his guilt is undeniable and they're being held to account by Interpol.'

Hallberg sighed. 'And the evidence of his involvement is inside that compound, and we can't get authorisation to go in until we have it. Yeah, that's about the sum of it.'

'But who did you think we were?' Church asked. 'Who did Foster say he was?'

'SAS,' Hallberg replied. 'Here on covert orders to complete a singleton mission to gather intelligence on

Blackthorn's operation at the behest of the powers that be.' She bit her lip, cursing herself silently. 'But I'm guessing that was a lie.'

'In part. We should talk inside,' Church said, gesturing to the building.

Hallberg nodded. Blackthorn as good as owned this town, and you never knew who was watching.

They headed through a large set of steel doors and into an open space. There was a mobile command tent set up in the middle of it and a generator chugging away against the wall. Cables ran from antennae and sat dishes affixed to the exterior wall and fed directly into the tent itself.

As Church and Mitch pushed through the flap, following Hallberg, they saw that it wasn't just where they were running their operation—it was where they were living, too.

'How long have you been here?' Church asked.

'Nearly ten weeks,' Hallberg replied, walking past a central length of desks topped with computers. They were dark currently, but the half-dozen bodies in the bunks at the far end of the tent told Church that this place was in full swing during the day.

Hallberg motioned them through into a private compartment where a table and chairs were set up and gestured for them to sit. 'Coffee?' she asked.

They both nodded, doubting sleep would come any time soon or easily.

Hallberg turned to the makeshift counter against the wall and lifted a pot from the drip filter machine, filling two paper cups and handing them to Church and Mitch without offering sugar or milk. 'Sorry, it's not Starbucks.'

Church put his hands around the cup and realised it wasn't even hot, let alone fresh. 'So what happened to Foster?' he asked.

'You don't beat around the bush, do you?' Hallberg took her seat.

'Time's short,' Church replied, thinking of Foster inside the compound with a set of jumpers around his testicles.

'So let's cut to it. Who are you, and why are you here? Because I'm starting to think that your friend Foster fed me a whole load of bullshit. So what's the real story?'

Mitch didn't seem sold on trusting this woman, but Church didn't think they really had a choice. 'We used to be SAS. Ten years ago, we were here on an op to gather intelligence on the warlord who was running the mine—General Kwame Zawadi. We arrived with Sir Walter Blackthorn, posing as his private security. He was here looking at the mining rights to the area with the hope of securing a supply chain of ethically sourced cobalt for the UK's newly burgeoning EV market. The intended outcome was to remove Zawadi from power and then work with the Congolese government to put infrastructure in place in Maroua that meant both the UK and the DRC would benefit from the arrangement, all brokered by Walter Blackthorn. They could set up a real, sanctioned mining operation with a guaranteed buyer for their raw material. The UK would front the set-up cost, and everyone wins.' Church held his hands up to signify how simple, how black and white that had been.

'But that didn't happen.' It wasn't even a question.

'No. After we successfully *removed* Zawadi from power, several members of our team turned on us at Blackthorn's orders. They tried to kill us because we wouldn't take the money. And they thought they'd succeeded. Instead of working with the DRC to lift Maroua up, he seized power in the vacuum and took direct control of the mine and Zawadi's compound, paying off who needed to be paid off to make it happen, and secured the cobalt supply for his own machinations.'

Hallberg listened intently. 'And the three of you who supposedly died—Foster, yourself, and your silent friend over here'—she looked at Mitch for a moment—'are now risen from the dead because Blackthorn's making a run for PM in the upcoming election.'

'Something like that.'

'But you don't have any affiliation with the SAS currently? Or the British Government?'

Church and Mitch shook their heads.

'And no one knows you're here?'

They shook their heads again.

'And this is unsanctioned and completely off the books?'

'We don't even have books,' Mitch said, his arms folded into a tight knot.

Hallberg let out a long breath. 'When we saw you heading into the mine, I guessed you had to be sent to find your friend, or finish what he started, at least.'

It sounded like she was hopeful of that fact. But there were still some puzzle pieces missing.

'So what's Interpol's stake in this? Blackthorn's a walking, talking bag of rotten shit,' Church said, 'but he's smart enough to keep his nose clean for the most part. What are you looking for here in Maroua? Specifically?'

If they hadn't been in the mine, then maybe they didn't know about the slavery. Or more likely, they did, but couldn't *prove* what they needed to.

She seemed cagey on it but knew she was backed into a corner. She didn't have a lot of support, and if she was here, ten weeks into the operation, with nothing to show for it, surely she didn't have a lot of runway left.

'We're an auxiliary unit in a multi-country investigation looking at a huge human trafficking network. The DRC is just one of the sources of the people—children, girls specifically—who are being smuggled into Europe and the UK. We've been tracking the network for months, and that trail led from businesses and properties owned and operated by shell corporations and proxies that I know are tied to Blackthorn—'

'But you can't prove it, I'm guessing,' Church said, judging from her tone.

She didn't answer that or dispute it.

'—and leads all the way here. We've been following boats and trucks, tailing drivers and brokers. And one of the trails brought us here. To Maroua. Blackthorn is not just forcing these people into slavery conditions and working them to death, he's stealing their children, their daughters, and he's selling them to the highest bidder.'

She choked a little on the last words. 'And what awaits these girls...' Her eyes shimmered a little. 'They wish they could have stayed at the mine.'

A fury burned hotter in Church than he'd felt in a long time. A deep and gnawing shame. He'd spent ten years with his head in the sand while this was going on, doing it to *protect* the people he loved, while Blackthorn hurt hundreds, thousands more.

Church leaned forward and rested his elbows on the table. 'What do you need us to do?' he asked, his voice cold.

'I want you to do what I can't,' she said. 'I want you to go into Blackthorn's compound, gather as much evidence as you can—something, *anything* tying Blackthorn to the mine, the trafficking ring, and bring it to me. We can't go in there. Not with the army. But two unaffiliated operatives? I can claim ignorance on that and keep Interpol's relationship with the Congolese government clean.'

Church and Mitch were silent for a moment, and then Church spoke.

'There's nothing about this that will be clean. If we go in there, people will die. Lots of people. Blackthorn's people.'

Hallberg stared right back at him. 'They're not people,' she muttered. 'You've seen what they're doing to the people at that mine. And if you saw what they were doing to these girls…'

'We'll do it,' Mitch said then. 'We'll do what you're asking. We'll get what you need, and we'll get Foster out. And then…' He drew a slow breath, and the next words from his mouth sent a shiver down Church's spine. 'We'll kill them all.'

TWENTY-SIX

TEN YEARS AGO

There was a knock at the door to Zawadi's office, and Church and Murphy looked up to see Mitch standing there. 'If you two are done canoodling, should we get the fuck out of here?'

Church and Murphy exchanged a glance and then stowed their argument. It wasn't the first time two team members had nearly come to blows in the middle of a mission, but there was a time for infighting—after they were home and safe. They made for the exit, knowing that their exfil was in one direction and one direction only.

Out the front door and through the front gate. That's where the Land Cruiser was, and that's where the road to Maroua stretched out.

They weren't set up for trekking through the jungle,

and they had no way of contacting exfil now. If they wanted to get home, it was through Zawadi's men.

They formed up in the corridor, and Church looked around, their fate still firmly in the driver's seat despite Murphy's marching orders.

'We move fast,' Church said. 'If it moves, kill it. It's weapons free.'

The guys nodded back at him, and Church looked at them once more, wondering if they'd all make it back— or hell, if they'd even make it to the vehicle.

'Let's go,' he said, turning and heading towards the door, running in the vanguard.

If there was one thing Church wasn't, it was the kind of man who asked his men to do something he wasn't prepared to do himself. If he was marching them into certain death, he'd be the first one to go.

The house was empty. It seemed like all of Zawadi's men had been called out to the tree line to lie in wait, save a few stragglers kept inside the walls to protect the general. But by now, they'd have realised their attackers had managed to get into the house, and they no doubt had the place surrounded.

Church slowed as he reached the front door and peeked through the window next to it.

The fog was still heavy, blotting out the sun, bathing the entire area in an eerie red twilight. But it was clearing somewhat, sinking to the ground little by little, and visibility was up to fifty feet. Dark shapes swam in the murk, weaving back and forth. Zawadi's men searched for cover, moving up a few feet at a time.

For a moment, Church thought the cloud was working against them—but then he realised the opposite was true. He looked around at his men.

'Smoke,' he said.

Mitch raised an eyebrow. 'You don't think we've got enough already?'

Church shook his head. 'Throw everything, and then we go quiet—right through the middle. No shots. Stay low. CQ only.' He had it, pulling his knife from his belt.

Everyone understood then. They could shoot their way out, sure, but there was no way to know how many men Zawadi had. And this way, they might just manage to do it without firing a single round.

They all dug into their packs and pulled out a few smoke grenades each, popping the pins ready on Church's go. He threw his elbow through the window and tossed the first grenade out.

It hissed and started spewing a pillow of white smoke into the air. It mingled with the dust, turning it yellow, providing enough of a screen that they could open the door and plunge into the fray once more.

Mitch and Foster rolled their first grenades out to the flanks and hurled their second ahead. Murphy and Norton pushed through the pack and followed suit—two wide, two ahead—leaving Church's final grenade in his hand.

He breathed out, visualising the distance between the gate and where he stood, then threw the thing. It arced into the air and disappeared, swallowed by the mist. A faint clack as it landed on the stone in the distance.

Church looked around at the men once more and motioned for them to stay low.

They moved off the path and onto the lawn to hide their footsteps, sweeping forward in a single-file line, rifles over their shoulders, knives out.

There was a cough and spluttering ahead, and Church slowed, holding his fist over his shoulder to signal the men to stop.

He went on alone, not making out any of the man's features until he was right on top of him.

The man's eyes widened, but Church was already inside his reach.

He raked the blade of his knife over the back of the man's fingers, forcing them off the trigger of his rifle. But before he could even call out, the tip of the knife found its home under his chin, the blade skewering his tongue and lancing up into his soft palate.

Before he could utter a sound, Church pushed it in deeper and guided the man backwards to the ground, laying him there on the grass before motioning the others forward.

He pulled the knife free and wiped it off on the guy's shirt as Mitch assumed the vanguard, and they moved like that, taking out two more of Zawadi's men until Church stepped over what he knew to be his final grenade.

By the time he reached the gate, Mitch and Murphy were already over. Foster was there, lifting them, and as

Norton stepped up into his grasp, he popped him upwards like he weighed nothing.

Foster nodded to Church as though signalling that this was the best course of action as well, that he was ready to help him over, and Church obliged, stepping up and finding his way to the top of the gate.

He straddled it, the metal rattling as he reached back down.

Bracing himself for Foster's climb, he took a few steps back, then came forward and jumped, grabbing Church by the arm, his boots scrabbling against the smooth steel until his other hand found the top of the gate and he pulled himself up.

The noise was something they couldn't avoid, and just as Foster managed to get himself over, the bullets started peppering the steel.

Sparks danced above them, the shouts of Zawadi's men echoing as they all made for the Land Cruiser.

Mitch aimed for the driver's seat, and though Murphy was right next to him, he didn't seem to want to sit in the passenger seat.

He lingered, letting Norton go by as Church and Foster caught up.

Church slowed, catching his eye, and before he could even ask, Murphy said, 'I'll cover the rear. Jump in the back, make sure we're not followed.'

It was a strange thing to say, a strange offer—and any other day, Church might have found it less suspicious. But today wasn't any other day.

His brain worked quickly. *Why would you want to*

sit in the back? he thought. *Why would you want everybody's backs turned to you?*

He could only think of one reason.

'No, you're right up front with Mitch,' Church ordered him. 'You're a good shot, and if they're blocking the road, I trust your aim.'

Murphy hovered for a second, as though trying to calculate whether refusing would jeopardise his fragile lie.

After a few seconds, he just nodded. 'Of course.' Then, with a twisted grin, he slapped Church on the shoulder and jumped into the passenger seat next to Mitch.

Foster, the only one still not in the car, looked over at Church and raised an eyebrow.

And though Church would have loved to tell him what he thought.

Now wasn't the time.

And if he was proved right, then he wouldn't need to say anything at all.

They bundled into the Land Cruiser, Norton slotting onto the very back seat and Church and Foster sliding into the rear. Church positioned himself behind Mitch so that he could see the side of Murphy's face, his unease growing with every passing second.

Mitch wasted no time putting the vehicle into reverse and backing in a circle. He swung them around so they were facing the exit and then floored it, all four wheels biting into the soft ground, forcing the car forward, snaking as it did, searching for traction on a surface that really didn't want to give any.

They bounced along at speed, Mitch checking the wing mirrors constantly, but there was no one behind them. Norton was swivelled around in the back, watching their tail, but while everyone else was searching for Zawadi's men, Murphy had his eyes strangely fixed ahead, vacant almost, licking his lips subconsciously, as though nervous for an entirely different reason.

They hammered forward in silence for a few minutes, and then Mitch slowed down, mercifully sparing Church's spine from the incessant jostling. Mitch let out a long breath, steadying himself, and then looked over his shoulder from the driver's seat.

'So you want to tell me what the fuck is going on? What was all that in Zawadi's office?' Mitch asked, hoping for an answer, but no one gave one.

Church certainly wasn't going to speak up, and Murphy clearly wasn't either, though Church was holding out a steadily waning hope that he might find a backbone—or at least a shred of honour. And yet, it didn't look like he was about to give in to his morality, despite how hard he was wrestling with it.

'Okay, nobody tell me shit then,' Mitch finished, twisting back towards the road. 'We're a few minutes out. I'm going to raise Cole on the radio—'

But he didn't get to finish.

It was then that Murphy struck, as though the name alone was enough to sway his decision.

He lunged for the wheel before Church could react and grabbed it, yanking down, turning the wheels violently. Church tried to reach out for him, but the sudden shift in direction and momentum threw him into the window, hard enough that his head cracked the glass.

The Land Cruiser's tyres dug into the ground and sent them veering off the side of the road into a ditch. The vehicle bounced, its front bumper gouging a hole in the earth before launching itself into the air, careening at an angle so violently that it nearly did a full barrel roll. It landed on its roof and pitched sideways into a violent tumble.

The windows and back windscreen blew out as the roof buckled under the weight. Church threw his hands towards the ceiling to brace himself. A yell of shock rang out behind him, and from the corner of his eye, he saw Norton ejected clean through the back window into the air. But then he was gone as the Land Cruiser rolled once, twice, three times before its front clipped the trunk of a tree and sent the whole thing spinning and sliding upside down into the undergrowth.

It came to rest there, steam spewing from the obliterated radiator.

Church tried to blink himself clear, only semi-conscious, feeling blood trickling from somewhere on his body—up his neck, over his chin. It was a strange sensation, and for a moment, he didn't quite understand what was happening. Then he realised he was upside down, his head and shoulders pressed against the buckled roof, his legs above him, wedged in the footwell.

He was trapped by his own weight, for a second immovable.

In front of him, Murphy swore and reached up, unfastening his seatbelt. It seemed like he was the only one who had it on, which was no surprise. He'd known what he was going to do the second Church had prevented him from sitting in the back seat and having a clear shot to execute them all.

This had been his plan, ill-thought-out as it was.

Murphy fell against the roof with a loud bang and swore again, crawling out of the passenger window on his hands and knees.

Church ran his tongue along his teeth to make sure they were all still in his head, then coughed a mixture of blood and dust onto the headrest of Mitch's seat in front of him.

'Mitch,' he called out. 'You dead?'

The man grumbled in response.

'Foster?'

But there was no answer to the second question.

Church pushed himself clear of the headliner an inch or two with great effort and managed to turn around. Foster was slumped almost entirely on the roof of the Land Cruiser, a gash to the top of his head weeping blood. Awkwardly, Church reached over and pressed his fingers to the man's neck, smearing his skin red. But even through the blood, he could feel a pulse.

It would take more than that to kill this bull.

But what about Norton? Where was he?

Church caught a glimpse of Murphy then, and he realised that was the least of his problems.

Murphy was already getting to his feet, trying his best to fumble for the pistol strapped to his thigh.

A cold fury seized Church then, and all of the pain in his body left him. He gritted his teeth so hard he thought they were going to crack and dragged himself free of the wreckage, crawling on his elbows and knees. He looked around, blinking, searching for cover, for some way to defend his team from what he knew would be Murphy's final assault.

He meant to kill them all.

He was the only one who was supposed to get back to Cole and Blackthorn.

But Church was damned if he'd let him.

He staggered into the corner of the Land Cruiser, guiding himself around it on the dented bumper until he was at the rear quarter and able to spy Murphy, still struggling to pull his weapon free and chamber a round. It looked like he had a dislocated shoulder.

He was trying, with difficulty, to use his thigh to rack the slide—but before Church could draw his own gun, Norton's voice cut through the thick African air.

'Murphy!' he yelled, lurching forward, all but dragging his left leg, his face slick with blood, his pistol raised. 'You motherfucker!'

He fired without warning.

The bullet hit Murphy in the chest, twisting him

away, his ballistic vest protecting his heart. He dropped to a knee, meaning Norton's second shot went over his head. On the way down, he managed to get that slide after all.

He lifted his gun quickly and fired back.

The first bullet hit Norton in the thigh, putting him on the ground. The second struck him in the shoulder, blowing through the strap of his vest. He collapsed and tried to kick himself towards the Land Cruiser.

Church didn't think—he just acted.

He charged into space, firing blindly over his elbow as he rushed towards Norton, only the thought of saving his brother in his mind.

He slid up to Norton and sank behind him, grabbing him by the arms, trying to heft him into a seated position to drag him to safety.

But before he even managed to get him halfway, another shot rang out.

This one struck Norton in the throat.

It ripped through his carotid artery, and a long spray of arterial blood soaked the ground to Church's right.

He gasped suddenly, staring up into Church's eyes, fingers clawing at his neck. Church's hand leapt there too, sandwiching Norton's between his own and the wound. But no matter how hard he pressed, the blood pumped over his knuckles, and Church knew it was futile.

He lifted his gaze to Murphy, expecting to see a sadistic grin on his face. Instead, he saw tears.

Murphy stood there, a broken and crooked man, his left arm hanging limply in the socket, his right raised and trembling. His eyes were as full and human as Church had ever seen. His mouth opened as though he wanted to say something, and Church could almost hear the apology—before Murphy pulled the trigger.

And even as he knew he was about to die, Church felt a flicker of gladness that doing something like this didn't come so easily.

But when the next shot rang out, it wasn't from Murphy's gun.

A plume of dust puffed up from Murphy's vest, and he jerked backwards. Another shot followed, then another, and Murphy, taking three to the body, lost his footing and fell.

But Mitch—now out of the vehicle—wasn't satisfied.

Not that Murphy was down. Not that he was subdued.

He marched forward, taking his pistol in both hands, and kept firing, emptying the entire magazine into the man he once called brother.

Shot after shot struck Murphy's chest, his shoulders, his neck, his head.

By the third bullet, he was dead. But Mitch didn't stop at three.

The slide kicked back. The magazine ran dry.

His finger clicked uselessly on the trigger, and only then did he stop, sagging to a knee.

Church watched as Mitch took a fistful of earth,

gripping it so tightly his knuckles turned white, and then let out a low, primal scream.

He hung his head.

Everything fell silent.

The only sound left was the dull, idling click of the Land Cruiser's ruined engine.

TWENTY-SEVEN

PRESENT DAY

THERE REALLY WAS no time to lose.

Church and Mitch downed their lukewarm coffees and started limbering up. It was almost four in the morning, and though this was the kind of op that needed planning, they now had support.

As they walked out of the briefing, Hallberg spoke quickly. 'We've got the latest satellite imaging as well as low fly-over drone footage. We don't know the layout inside, but—'

'That's fine,' Church said, striding quickly towards the exit. 'We've been inside before.'

'Right, yeah, okay,' Hallberg replied, uneasy suddenly. She was an intelligence officer. That's what Interpol did. They provided support to local police and armed forces. They didn't actually get their hands dirty. And it seemed like that fact was rearing its head now.

Hallberg wanted this done, but Mitch's proclamation was a little too real for her.

War was never pretty. And it was never good. No one ever won it. And it was easy to forget that when you stared at everything through a computer screen. Sending men to kill other men was a hard reality to escape.

Hallberg paused at the desks with the computers for a moment and grabbed up a tablet, tapping the screen and bringing it to life before she chased Church out of the building.

They reached their Land Cruiser, and Mitch headed for the driver's side. Church climbed into the passenger seat, and Hallberg appeared in the door.

'Was he serious?' she asked under her breath, eyeing Mitch. 'About what he said in there?'

Church didn't answer right away. 'I don't know,' he said. 'But we're probably going to have to shoot our way out. Whether it's all of them... that's up to them.' He tried to close the door, but she stopped him.

'They're fanatical,' Hallberg said. 'The guy running it, he's crazy. Keeps his men drunk, high, a constant parade of women going in and out. He's...'

'Like all of them,' Church grunted. 'We know the type, don't worry. They bleed red all the same, don't worry.'

'He's been in charge there for years. His men are loyal to him. They'll die for him.'

'That's what they all think until shit hits the fan,' Church replied. 'What's his name, this fearless leader of theirs?'

'Katenda,' Hallberg replied. 'He used to—'

'Run the mine for Zawadi, yeah. We know him.'

'You know him?'

'Well enough to make sure he catches a bullet before the sun comes up.'

She let out a rattled breath, shaken by this. By the idea of sending someone else in there to die like Foster. 'Here,' she said, pushing the tablet into his hands. 'This has the footage on it. There are a couple of entry points my guys identified. It should help.'

Church took the tablet and looked at the aerial shot of the compound. He could see it had been annotated, showing where guards were posted, where they patrolled, the gates, the doors to the building. She was right—it was helpful.

'When you make it out, meet us back here. And remember—'

'Evidence tying Blackthorn to Maroua.'

'Or he gets away.'

'He won't get away,' Church said gravely. 'Not this time.' He closed the door hard enough that she had to step out of the way. But her eyes never left his.

'Good luck,' she said as Mitch fired the engine to life. 'And... thanks.'

She lifted a hand as he backed away from the building and put them into a J-turn, heading for the gate. The same soldier as before pulled it open for them, and Church glimpsed Hallberg in the wing mirror with a single hand in the air.

He sat straight as they hit the road and leaned his head back against the headrest, slowing his breathing.

'You good?' Mitch asked.

'I'm good,' Church replied, closing his eyes.

'Here we go again.'

He let a little smile cross his face, hating how much he liked this, how much he'd missed it. 'Here we go again.'

As they drove, he thought about it—about how he was smiling. About how much he hated that fact. He'd spent a lot of nights over the last ten years thinking about his life, the choices he'd made, the dangers he'd put himself in knowingly, willingly. He hadn't ever intentionally altered the course of a mission to induce conflict. He'd never thrown the first stone. But he'd never shied away from a fight, never been disappointed when things did go sideways.

There was a four-letter diagnosis that followed them all, everyone in this life. One that was terrifying because it meant you were broken, that this wasn't how you were supposed to be. Church, like so many others, was addicted to that chaos. To the fight. He never wanted that email to come through. He never wanted to come back. But there was a little nagging voice at the back of his head, one he'd locked away in a box, that was screaming, every single day, for a reason to. To get back in the fight. And that frightened him most of all. That for all his days, he knew he'd be the one that ran towards the sound of gunfire, not away. That his life wasn't worth living unless he was risking it.

And with his rifle between his knees, jostling through the Congo jungle in the dead of night, aiming for a compound full of men who'd love nothing more than to capture and torture him within an inch of his life, he never felt more at peace—his mind quieter.

He could feel the slow drum of his pulse in his ears, low fifties. Steady as it had ever been.

When the momentum of the vehicle shifted and began to slow, Church opened his eyes, seeing the outer wall of Zawadi's compound ahead. The walls were just as he remembered, the steel gate just as inviting.

'What's the plan here?' Mitch asked, trundling forward, looking at it. 'This place is going to be even more of a fortress than it was last time.'

Church thought on that, mind churning through the possibilities. 'We could do what we did in Tripoli?'

Mitch blinked in the darkness. 'It didn't work then. Why would it work now?'

'Basra,' Church offered. 'Shock and awe.'

'With just the two of us and no covering fire?'

The gate crept closer. 'Fine. Ashgabat.'

Mitch didn't reply right away. 'Ashgabat could work.'

'It was either that or what we did in Karachi.'

'I got shot in Karachi,' Mitch replied, looking over.

'It's why it was going to be my last suggestion,' Church said, reaching behind the seat and pulling his pack into the front. He fished inside it and pulled out three smoke grenades and a suppressor for his pistol. He slung the pack behind him and started screwing the suppressor into place while Mitch did the same, reaching behind him and rummaging in his own pack. He didn't even need to look as he did it, just drove towards the gate like nothing was wrong, fixing the attachment into place with one hand, in the dark.

They closed in on the gate and slowed to a stop.

A camera watched them from the top of the wall, and all they could do was wait for it to open. They kept one hand on their pistols, the other on the levers to release the seat backs to flat. Just in case a firing squad was going to greet them.

There were voices beyond the steel, and they tensed.

It moved, and Church's grip tightened on the release lever. But the gate didn't slide back all the way—just a few feet, an opening large enough for two men to slip out, AK-47s raised and pointed right at them.

Two of Katenda's guys rushed out in front of the car, one of them in flip-flops and a vest, the other in jean shorts and a floral shirt. They both kept their rifles pinned on the car as they circled, barking something, their eyes wide. No doubt the bodies at the mine had been discovered by now, and the place was on high alert.

Mitch spoke first through the open window. 'Katenda, Katenda,' he called. 'Blackthorn sent us. Blackthorn. Blackthorn?'

The men paused for just a moment, faltering at the name of their lieutenant and at the name of their true master. And that was all they needed.

The guards glanced at each other, and the instant

their eyes left Church and Mitch, they pulled their pistols up and loosed two rounds through the open windows, catching the men centre mass.

Before they even stumbled, Church and Mitch's doors were open, and they each put two more into their skulls.

They crumpled in unison and hit the ground together, and only once they were lying still did Mitch breathe a sigh of relief and look at his brother. 'That went better than last time.'

'Don't get too excited just yet,' Church replied, grabbing the smoke grenades from the footwell and popping the pins. 'That was just step one.'

He wound up and launched the smoke grenades over the gate and into the compound, listening as more shouts echoed in the distance. The suppressors had a slight chance of masking the sound of the shots, but the camera didn't lie, and the two men at the gate were clearly not here to deliver pizza.

Which meant Katenda's men were lining up inside, taking defensive positions, ready to open fire on whoever came through the gate.

Once all three grenades were over, Church levelled his pistol once more and took care of the camera for good. It spat sparks into the distance, and Mitch stared at it.

'What's wrong?' Church asked as he pulled his pack and rifle from the car.

'I really thought we were all done with this shit,' he grumbled.

'You didn't miss it?'

'You did?' Mitch looked over at Church, waiting for an honest answer.

He wouldn't get one this side of sunrise.

Mitch took the silence as a suggestion to get on with it and went hunting at the roadside for a suitably sized rock.

On the other side of the gate, Katenda's men were beginning to form into loose lines. Eight of them had been scrambled from their posts and beds and had taken up a position behind the great stone fountain that Zawadi had installed.

They had their rifles rested on the edge of it, no clear direction or instruction to hold them in place, just a half-trained, half-drunk militia defending what they felt was theirs.

There was silence among them as they waited, unsure what to do other than sit with their fingers on their triggers, a wall of slow-moving fog in front of them obscuring their view of the gate.

There was no sound from their attackers, and beads of sweat clung to their brows, running into their eyes. They wiped them away with their knuckles, hearts pounding. No one had ever attacked before. No one was stupid enough to. The police were paid off, and everyone else knew better than to cross Katenda and his men. Which was what terrified them the most.

The rattle and grind of the gate being rolled back echoed through the smoke, and they all stiffened.

Then, an engine began to rev. It climbed and fell and then suddenly hit the limiter and stayed there.

The men were frozen, waiting for whatever came next. And then, suddenly, a vehicle exploded through the miasma—an SUV, snaking wildly forward, spraying stone and gravel from its wheels as it fought for grip.

They all fired at once. Eight muzzles lit up in a stream of automatic fire that coated the Land Cruiser in a blanket of sparks. The windscreen shattered as bullets tore through the seats and shredded them. But the car ploughed forward all the same, hitting the fountain, pitching upwards over the wall of the fountain, and spearing forward.

The men called out in shock and scattered as the Land Cruiser smashed through the central feature and obliterated it, sending water and rocks like shrapnel.

The front bumper dove forward, mowing down one of Katenda's men, and the whole car landed, bounced violently, and then grabbed traction, shooting forward straight into the bushes at the side of the house.

It hit the wall with an almighty crash, and steam exploded from the bonnet, the throttle still pinned wide open, the wheels trying their best to spin as they dug themselves into the ground.

The remainder of Katenda's men managed to get to their feet and crept towards the Land Cruiser, rifles raised, looking for their attackers. Dead, surely?

But when they reached the Land Cruiser and peeked inside, the cab was empty, a large rock wedged against the accelerator pedal. The first man understood and turned, opening his mouth to call out that it was a distraction. But before he could make a sound, a bullet struck him mid-chest and extinguished the cry before it even left his throat.

Another one came swiftly, followed by another and another.

Four men fell before they knew what was going on, and the others tried to scramble for cover.

But there wasn't any, and Church and Mitch, emerging from the fog in their flank positions, picked off the remaining three with ease, moving up on the house with their rifles tight to their shoulders.

'Clear,' Church called as he neared the front steps.

'Clear,' Mitch confirmed as he swooped around the other side of the fountain and linked up.

They didn't stop to chat and instead made their way up the steps, keeping to the sides of the staircase so they were harder to hit.

Church remembered these stairs, this door as he closed in on it. Huge and ornately engraved wood. Worth more than the annual income of ninety-nine per cent of the people living in Maroua.

Church paused at the door, nosing it open with the muzzle of his rifle.

They'd already taken down ten of Katenda's men, but who knew how many more were hidden inside?

Not many, Church hoped.

As he stepped into the cavernous entrance hall, the grand staircase wrapping upwards to a landing on his left, chandelier overhead, he remembered the layout from ten years ago. He didn't think he could ever forget. There was something in his brain—he could still map his way through every building, every compound, every place they'd hit over the last twenty years, across every country they'd been to.

He moved forward through the archway, he and Mitch ready to do a sweep of the ground floor. Room by room, they cleared it: the study, the dining room, moving along towards what had been Zawadi's office and towards the steel door that led to the basement. If Foster was anywhere, he'd be down there. But just like ten years ago, it was protected by an electronic lock and a keypad to which they definitely didn't have the combination.

Mitch pulled back out of Zawadi's old office and gave a nod that it was clear. There was no one else on the ground floor. It seemed like perhaps all of Katenda's men had been called outside to protect the place, but there was no sign of the big man himself. He hadn't gone to die with the rabble, and if he wasn't here, then that only left two options: either he'd locked himself away behind the steel door—in which case they'd have to get creative—or, hopefully, he was upstairs.

They moved back along the corridor until they reached the entrance hall once more, then turned right, heading up the stairs. At the top, the landing split to the right with another corridor leading to several bedrooms and bathrooms. They moved silently along, opening the doors one by one and clearing the rooms, silent and fast, fingers on triggers, ready to put down anybody they came across. But each room was empty. Some of the beds looked slept in, others not, but none of them screamed 'dictator'. None were fancy enough, palatial enough, which meant that the final door at the end of the corridor was the one their prize had to be hiding behind.

Mitch moved out in front and reached for the door, glancing back at Church. This kind of tight quarters was never fun to work in—no space to the side of the door to take cover, and if anyone was standing behind it with a gun, you were a sitting duck.

That thought had barely crossed Church's mind before the wood exploded in front of Mitch. The dull report of a 12-gauge reached Church's ears. Mitch was blown off his feet and sent flying backwards, landing on the polished tiles in front of Church. He didn't have time to look down at Mitch or wonder if he was dead. He could only react.

He launched forward and kicked the door in, sending it flying inwards so violently that it nearly came apart. Katenda was standing there in a red silk robe and a pair of underpants. Beyond him, on a huge four-poster bed, three women cowered under the covers, staring out. Church barely registered them in his periphery before he homed in on his target.

Katenda's eyes widened, and he tried to pump the action on the shotgun, ready to fire another round, but Church was quicker. He charged forward, rifle at low ready, and barely had to line up before he loosed a single shot that hit Katenda square in the right thigh. He buckled backwards and howled, nearly dropping the gun altogether, giving Church enough time to reach him before he could chamber another shot.

Church grabbed the still-smoking muzzle of the shotgun and drove it upwards, hard, straight into Katenda's face, his nose exploding under the polished black steel. Blood spurted across the floor, and Katenda did his best to wrestle the weapon out of Church's grip, but he was no match for the big man. With a violent yank, Church dragged him out into the corridor and sent him sprawling.

He landed on his knees and scuttled forward on three limbs, dragging his bloodied leg behind him, trying to get to his feet, bouncing from wall to wall, stepping over Mitch, who was now groaning and clutching his ballistic vest. The Kevlar had done its job, stopping the shot from peeling him apart.

Church ignored his brother for the moment, taking off after Katenda, glad that he hadn't tried to flee earlier, that his hubris had kept him in bed until the last second. So self-assured that he was untouchable in his castle, that no living man could harm him. But that was just it, wasn't it? Church was a ghost. He'd been dead for years.

With cold malice, he caught up to Katenda and grabbed him by the shoulder. Katenda turned, swinging the shotgun he still held as though to take Church's head off, but Church caught it before it came anywhere near him. A sudden reverberation of a shot rang out; the steel ball tore into the plaster over Church's right shoulder, showering him with dust. This time, he made sure

Katenda wouldn't get a third try and ripped the weapon from his hands, launching a fierce punch into his gut.

Katenda doubled over Church's fist and staggered backwards onto the landing, raising his hands—but not to fight, to beg. There was no mercy, not for him, not after what he'd done to Foster, to the people in that mine, to the people of Maroua. Church let his rifle drop on its sling, swinging under his arm. In one fluid motion, he pulled his knife from his belt, flicking the blade out. Katenda's eyes went to it, and his pleading grew more fervent. He stopped moving backwards, and for a second, Church thought he would drop to his knees.

But like the coward he was, Katenda lunged instead, driving his shoulder into Church's midriff, taking two steps forward. He was half-lame, though, and lacked conviction. Church was fuelled by something deeper—rage, guilt, the need for vengeance. Ten years of shame rose up in his throat as he reached across Katenda's body and twisted him upright so he was facing away. He marched him forward, driving the knife backwards into his shoulder just above the right lung. Katenda let out a pained cry, but it fell on deaf ears.

Without warning, still gripping the knife's handle, Church picked up Katenda's left leg, hoisting the man into the air, then dumped him over the railing of the banister. He fell a few feet before Church's knife stopped him, the blade pinned between his ribs. He hung there on that thin sliver of steel, stabbed into his flesh, his organs, his veins, hot blood spilling over Church's knuckles as Katenda's entire weight was suspended by the blade.

His cry of pain turned into guttural mewling. He spoke a language Church didn't understand, but Church knew he was begging. 'I'll do anything. I'll give you anything. Just let me live.' It was always the same.

'The code for the basement,' Church demanded. 'What is it?'

Katenda wailed, tears rolling down his face, but it didn't take him long to get control of his senses enough to cough up the four numbers that would let Church access the locked door. Satisfied with his performance, Church simply let go. Katenda fell, and for a moment, there was silence—then the snap of bone as he landed on the polished tiles some fifteen feet below. He folded up like an old deckchair and slumped forward, clutching his chest, blood pouring out.

There was a noise behind him, and Church twisted reflexively, seeing Mitch staggering towards him, wheezing, winded from the shot that had punched neat holes in the front of his vest. Church slowly lowered the knife and stepped forward, slipping his hand under Mitch's arm, supporting him, helping him towards the stairs.

'Yours or his?' Mitch asked, eyeing the blood covering Church's arm and leg.

'His,' Church said grimly, as they turned the corner and started down.

At the bottom, they reached Katenda's body. His right leg was still bleeding from the gunshot, his left twisted badly, an open fracture of the tibia sticking through his shin. He was facedown, clutching desperately at his shoulder, his ragged breathing telling Church he'd punctured a lung when he stabbed him. The man was sobbing under his breath as his free arm reached out towards the open door just six feet away.

'You going to put him out of his misery?' Mitch asked.

Church paused only a second to look down at him. 'No,' he said, helping Mitch over the blood trail. 'Not until I know he didn't lie about the code to the door.'

TWENTY-EIGHT

TEN YEARS AGO

By the time Church looked down again, Norton was already gone. His eyes were staring blankly past Church's head. And when he pulled his hand away, Norton's arm fell limply to his side.

The blood was still trickling from the wound in his neck, but there was no saving him.

'Mitch?' Church called out. 'Mitch?'

The man looked up, then turned his eyes to Murphy once more, shaking his head as though still in disbelief. He pushed himself to a weary stance and came over, muttering under his breath as he laid eyes on Norton's bullet-riddled body.

'Good God,' he said, touching his hand to his forehead, then dropping it to his heart and painting a cross over his collarbones.

He held out a hand to Church then, and he gladly

accepted it. There wasn't a single part of him that didn't hurt.

He got to his feet, Norton lolling onto his side, and they both stared down at him, wanting desperately to take his body, to do the right thing, to bring him home—but knowing that they couldn't.

As much as it hurt, they just had to leave him here.

'We've got to go,' Church said.

'Go where?' Mitch asked, looking around.

'Anywhere. We've just got to get out of this fucking place,' Church spat. 'This is Cole. This is Blackthorn. They did this. This was the plan all along.'

Mitch shook his head. 'No. I don't believe that. Not Cole.'

'You've got to fucking believe it,' Church said, taking Mitch by the shoulders and turning him towards Murphy. 'Otherwise, what the fuck do you think that was? This whole thing may have started as a mission to ghost Zawadi, but Blackthorn got his hooks into Cole and twisted him. They wanted to kill Fletcher because she knew who he really was. And I didn't want to believe it, but I do now.'

He pointed down at Norton. It was all the illustration he needed.

'I don't know how they manufactured the explosion, the ambush, but they did. I know it. We were never supposed to come back from this mission. Mitch... Cole tried to kill us.'

Mitch was still shaking his head, but mercifully,

Foster started groaning in the back seat, taking both of their attention.

They rushed over and dragged his hulking body through the broken window, laying him on his back. His eyes blinked separately, then seemed to regain a little focus.

He stared up at them.

'The fuck happened?' he asked.

'You farted,' Mitch said. 'I tried to ram us into a tree, put us out of our misery,' he added glibly.

It was strange how, even in times like this—even in the darkest moments—the knee-jerk reaction was to joke, to make light of it. A thin veil against the reality of their situation. Of their whole lives.

Against Norton's body lying there on the ground a few feet away.

Foster grunted, laughed, then winced, putting his hand to his head to shield his eyes from the onslaught of the sun.

'Did... Murph do this?' he asked. 'Or am I just concussed?'

'Can't it be both?' Church replied, offering his hand to Foster.

He took it and got to his feet, doubling forward with his hands on his knees. As he caught his breath, he looked around, spying Murphy's body—then Norton's.

'Fucking hell. We're going to kill somebody for this, right?' he asked, lifting a hand towards his fallen brothers.

'Oh yeah,' Church said. 'Somebody's going to fucking die. But I don't know if it's going to be today.'

He stood up and looked around, still aware that Zawadi's men could arrive at any moment. And though they were a few minutes out of town by road, they were still a long ruck to Maroua in this heat.

'So what are we fucking doing?' Mitch asked. 'We can't stand around here all day.'

'No, we can't,' Church admitted. 'We need to get out of town and out of the country.'

'With what equipment?' Mitch said. 'We've got no water, no rations, nothing that'll help us.'

Church weighed the odds.

It would be difficult—nigh on impossible. None of them spoke the local language, and they couldn't hike to the border.

'The hotel,' Church said. 'We've got to get back, get our gear, get a sat phone and call this in. Organise exfil. Then we get the hell out of Dodge.'

Mitch put his hands on his hips, lowering his head to try to catch Church's eye.

'Maybe you're the one that's concussed. If what you're saying is true and Cole has gone off the reservation, then I don't think he's going to be too happy to see us if we walk in the front door.'

'Maybe not,' Church replied. 'But I'm banking on him thinking Murphy accomplished the task, and he won't be expecting to see us at all.'

'That's your plan?' Mitch said. 'Catch him by surprise?'

'Unless you've got a better one?' Church asked.

The silence was all the answer he needed.

'Good. Then get your shit,' Church sighed, heading back towards the totalled Land Cruiser for his pack.

'It's a long march. And we're out of time.'

They were drenched with sweat by the time they reached the hotel. As bad as rucking through the jungle on its own was, after you'd just crawled out of a car wreck, it was a whole lot worse. Church's leg was half numb, a bolt of pain lancing from his heel into his left hip every time he put his foot down. The side of his neck and the top of his arm were cut from the glass from the windows of the car, and his headache was back with a vengeance. Just like Mitch and Foster, he was black and blue.

The first thing they did when they got a vehicle for an op was disable the airbags. If you needed to ram a gate or make a quick exit somewhere, any kind of impact could set them off. So it was better to disable them right out of the gate. The downside being that during a real crash, you didn't have them.

Mitch was rubbing his chest as he ran, wheezing a little. Church didn't know if it was cracked ribs, but he was keeping quiet about it despite the pain. He'd have bet Mitch would have a steering-wheel-shaped bruise when he took his shirt off.

But despite all that, they trudged forward, and a little under thirty minutes later, they reached the edge of town. They skirted it, keeping off the main road, and then cut in once they spied the hotel.

Some of the denizens of Maroua shot them surprised looks—bloodied, battered foreigners armed to the teeth running into the middle of town wasn't exactly low profile. But they didn't pay civilians any mind. Militants, Zawadi's guys, that's what they were keeping their heads on a swivel for. That and Cole.

But the coast seemed clear. Almost as though now that Zawadi was gone, a different sort of status quo had already been established. Church expected the town to be overrun with his men, but it was empty.

They stepped up into the air-conditioned interior of the hotel and found it empty. He risked a little sigh of relief. Maybe Cole and Blackthorn had already pulled out. Maybe they were alone here. Maybe—

'Church?'

A voice echoed from his right, and he turned to see Reed laid out on the couch in the lobby. The same one he'd been sitting on when Norton had wanted to stitch him up.

Rage flared in him, but he tempered it. He had to play this smart.

'Hey,' Church replied, taking a slow step towards him. 'Where's Cole?'

Reed couldn't hide his shock at seeing them. He looked past the three of them, nerves breaking across his face.

'Just the three of you? Norton?' he asked, hesitating a little. 'Murphy?'

'They didn't make it out of the compound,' Church replied. 'It's just us.'

'Oh,' Reed said, forcing a little grin and then realising it wasn't the right expression either. 'I, uh,' he began, wincing as he tried to pull himself upright. He grunted and managed it, then slowly got to his feet, clutching at the freshly dressed wound on his flank, just above his appendix.

'It's good to see you,' he said then. 'I'm glad you made it. Norton, Murph…'

'Yeah,' Church said gruffly, his fingers twitching above his thigh, above his pistol. 'Where's Cole?'

'Cole?' Reed said, looking at each of them. 'He's… around.'

Church could see his pulse quicken in his neck, the sweat under his jaw despite the coolness of the room.

Reed lifted his left hand then, pointing towards the stairs. 'If you head up—'

But Church didn't let him get any further. Like a gunslinger, he ripped the pistol from its holster on his leg and popped Reed in the thigh.

Mitch and Foster both flinched at the sudden noise, but Church didn't leave it at one and put two more into Reed's chest. He flew backwards onto the sofa, still wearing his vest, the Kevlar weave absorbing the impact but not dulling the pain.

He landed hard, gasping and dazed, and Church charged forward, swinging a vicious kick into his hand.

Reed had managed the pistol from his holster, but Church had been faster, had been expecting it. The weapon came free and spun through the air, landing on the other side of the room.

Reed coughed and raked in tiny breaths, winded.

Church didn't bother to say anything else. He took Reed by the collar of his vest and lifted him up. He met his eyes for a moment, seeing all the confirmation he needed, and then launched a brutal punch square into his face. He felt the man's nose explode under his knuckles and then dropped him back on the couch, unconscious.

Church turned back to Mitch and Foster.

'He was going for his gun,' he muttered, heading for the stairs.

They allowed him to pass wordlessly, not arguing, not saying any different.

Even though all three of them knew that it wasn't the case. He might have been thinking about it, but he hadn't made the move yet.

Church just didn't care.

And the only thing that had stopped him jamming the barrel of his pistol between Reed's teeth and pulling the trigger was the fact that when all was said and done, he wasn't Cole.

Church didn't betray his brothers.

He was a better man than that.

TWENTY-NINE

PRESENT DAY

Mitch gained strength with every step, and by the time they reached the basement door, he was standing on his own.

Church punched in the code and listened to the lock hum its approval. He didn't even bother to look back out at Katenda and was more than happy to let him try to crawl his way to freedom. He wouldn't get far.

Mitch groaned and held his stomach as they headed through and into the bare concrete corridor, the stairs at the end wrapping down into the earth.

'Can you shoot?' Church asked, casting a sideways glance at the way Mitch was cradling his rifle.

'You worry about yourself,' he grunted back. 'And next time, you're first through the door.'

Church didn't respond to that—the thought of a next time was both something that invoked dread and a guilty excitement in him. But there was no time to explore those feelings now. He pressed on, leading the charge into the bowels of Zawadi's house, following the stairs down as they doubled back on themselves, ending in a large open space the size of the entire footprint of the house above.

There were shelves on either side lined with food and fuel, as though the place was set up to endure some kind of extended siege. Lengths of plastic were draped from the ceiling, making makeshift compartments in the room, and as they pressed forward, spreading out to the walls, carefully pushing through each layer, they realised that this place wasn't set up to protect the denizens of the house, but rather to hold those they didn't want escaping.

There were cots lining the walls with eye bolts drilled into the concrete, chains hanging from them with manacles on the ends—long enough that whoever was unlucky enough to find themselves here would be able to lie down in some fashion.

They moved on to the next room, discovering much the same: enough cots for probably two dozen people, and by the smells of the buckets set in between them, it hadn't been long since they were used.

Church thought back to what Hallberg had said, that this was no longer just a mining operation, that it was the beginning of the trail leading into a devious and despicable human trafficking ring.

Was this what they were doing here? Was this what Katenda's men were doing on Blackthorn's behalf?

Were they snatching up families from Maroua—sending the fathers, mothers, and sons to the mine to dig, and then sending the girls here to endure a fate worse than death before they were boxed up and shipped elsewhere?

Church's lips twisted into an ugly grimace, and he picked up his pace. A shadow swam beyond the curtain, and he didn't even pause for consideration. Church lifted his rifle and pulled the trigger. A tiny hole appeared in the sheet, the length of plastic barely moving as the bullet punched through and found its target. The shape collapsed, and a thin spray of red mist landed on the translucent material.

There was no more sound, and Church knew they had to be at the end now. This was it. If Foster was down here, he'd be behind this curtain—if he was still alive, that was.

Church pushed his weapon into the gap at the side of the sheet and swept it back, stepping into the final compartment and freezing.

He laid eyes on Foster first: a bloodied pulp on a chair, duct-taped in place, his hands folded behind his back. His face had been rearranged terribly, both eyes swollen shut, his mouth hanging open, teeth missing, lips split, the colour of plums.

But he wasn't alone.

The last of Katenda's men stood behind him, a hand on Foster's forehead, exposing his throat, to which he had a vicious curved knife pressed.

Mitch came through on the other side, and they both

stepped into the middle of the compartment, over the body of the man Church had just shot, and met the torturer's eyes.

He was tall and thin, with a narrow jaw and wide head, his eyes wild and dark, but not afraid. It was clear from the first glance that this wasn't a man who felt things like normal people. His vocation was to hurt—to extract information—and, Church guessed, a whole lot more, considering the space he called an office.

'Another step,' the torturer said with a thick accent, pulling back Foster's head, pressing the knife into his skin hard enough to draw blood. 'I'll kill him.'

Church looked down at Foster. His eyes fluttered just a little. Church couldn't tell if there was any recognition there or if he was even conscious. Based on how many blows he'd taken to the skull, Church wouldn't be surprised if he was brain-damaged or worse.

Death might be the best thing for him.

Church looked over at Mitch as though to ask if he agreed, but before either could decide, Foster twisted his head suddenly, the knife biting into his neck, and sank what few teeth he had left into the torturer's wrist, pinning his hand in place, stopping him from slashing his carotid.

Church wasted no time, lifted his rifle, and fired, putting a bullet into the man's head, just under his right eye. He twisted to the floor, and Foster spat out his hand with as much disdain as he could muster.

He looked up at Church, only one eye semi-functional, and coughed.

'Took you long enough,' he growled.

'Had to shop around for cheap flights,' Church said back. 'You know how it is. Inflation and all that.'

Foster tried to form his mouth into a wry smile and failed. 'You going to cut me out of here?' he asked.

Mitch shrugged. 'Don't know. Kinda suits you, I think.'

Foster hung his head forward, and the smallest laugh escaped his lips.

Church and Mitch went together then and cut him free, taking his weight and lifting him out of the chair.

'Wait,' Foster said, turning his head and lifting what looked to be a broken finger towards the side of the space.

Church hadn't even noticed, but as he looked over, he saw a stained mattress in the corner, a camera on a tripod set up in front of it, a lead trailing to a small steel desk and a laptop.

Church didn't want to imagine what kind of movies they'd been making here, but he could guess well enough.

'I've seen them emailing,' Foster said. 'I don't know who, but…'

'Blackthorn?' Mitch questioned him.

He didn't have an answer.

Either way, Hallberg had said they needed intel, something linking this place to Blackthorn, and that was their best chance of getting it. They wouldn't leave evidence like that lying around upstairs. Down here in this vault was their best shot.

Church took Foster's enormous weight—the man was even bigger than he was—and Mitch went for the laptop, gathering it up and putting it into his bag.

He took the SD card out of the camera too, for good measure. If they could tie it to Blackthorn, the footage on it might be the extra nail in the coffin they needed. Anything and everything would help.

Blackthorn was slippery and would do all he could to wriggle free of this noose.

They gathered Foster up once more and headed for the door. Ascending the stairs back into Zawadi's now-empty mansion, they moved along until they found Katenda. Church was impressed—he'd made it almost to the threshold before giving out and was now lying dead just inside the door.

Foster turned his head as they passed, and a glob of blood and spittle landed on Katenda's body. Whether the liquid had just leaked from Foster's lips or he'd made a concerted effort to spit on him, Church didn't know. Either way, nothing made him happier than knowing he had died in pain.

Outside, the smoke had cleared, leaving only the bodies of Katenda's men and the wrecked Land Cruiser.

'You two made a mess,' Foster said, doing his best to look around.

'You know us,' Mitch replied.

They made it all the way to the bottom of the steps before the first shot rang out. The back gate to Zawadi's compound was now open, and across the walled-in courtyard, men were moving—disembarking from the bed of what looked like an old Toyota Hilux. Half a dozen of them, and another truck coming down the road. Reinforcements had been called in, probably by Katenda when he saw what was going on outside his house. And although they were too late to save their leader, they were still prepared to die for the cause.

Mitch unfastened himself from Foster and lifted his gun, laying down some covering fire as Church did his best to carry Foster onwards. Church didn't think they'd broken Foster's legs, but it looked like they'd driven knives or nails behind his kneecaps. Maybe they'd popped his toes with a hammer. No matter who was doing the torturing, it was always the same. Men like that were universally cruel and always ended up doing the same horrid shit.

Mitch was firing off tight bursts towards the Hilux, doing his best to pin them down, but the men were spreading out, and Mitch, Foster, and Church were fully exposed. The covering fire was good for keeping the enemy suppressed, but they moved forward with little sense of self-preservation, firing incessantly and wildly in Church's direction. And the closer they got, the likelier they were to land a shot.

'We could be in trouble here,' Mitch called, ejecting his first spent magazine and grabbing a second from his belt, strafing to keep pace with Church and Foster. He only had one more—then his sidearm. And holding Foster, Church had little hope of helping. He had to make a choice: either carry his brother forward or shoot back, but not both.

They made as much progress as they could, but Katenda's men were coming thick and fast, with a third Hilux now roaring into the compound. Foster was doing his best to shove Church away, to sacrifice himself, but there was no way they'd come this far just to let him die now.

'Put a gun in my hand. I'll cover you,' Foster demanded.

'You can't fucking see,' Church forced out, hauling his immense bulk forward.

'There's no need for you two to die. Not for me. I made my choice—'

'Shut the fuck up, would you?' Church said, squeezing him tighter so he'd quit trying to let himself fall down. Foster relented and did his best to get his legs under him.

'If you really want to help—just run.'

'You run when you've got ten broken toes,' Foster shot back.

He was right to be angry. And he was right to want to sacrifice himself. It was a long way to the gate, and without an escape vehicle or anything resembling an exfil plan, they stood little hope. Fighting their way through two dozen of Katenda's soldiers with limited ammo, no cover, and no positional advantage—this was a lost cause. They had no vehicle either and no chance of making it through Katenda's men to one of their trucks. Like Zawadi, he had a fleet of sports cars on his driveway, but who knew where the keys were—and even if they got them, none of those cars had back seats or the ground clearance to handle these roads.

They were too far from the house now to fall back and take up a position there, which meant this was the end of the line. For all they'd accomplished, it looked like they'd die right here, where it all started. In Maroua.

Lights flared ahead of them through the front gate, and Church knew it was over. They were about to get pinned in from both sides with nowhere to run. He dug his sidearm out of its holster with his left hand and pushed it into Foster's chest. Foster reached for it with his maimed hand, doing his best to slot a barely functioning index finger through the trigger guard.

'Looks like you're going to get your wish,' Church said, hauling his rifle up to attention with his left hand. It waved around in his grip, heavy and unwieldy, but if they were going to die, if this was the end... they'd go down fighting.

But it wasn't a battered pickup full of troops that screamed through the gate. It was a trio of old Isuzu Troopers, and in the light of Zawadi's courtyard, Church glimpsed the red berets of the army through the windscreen. They hammered in and swerved in front of Church and Mitch, creating a barricade—the two lead cars forming up bumper to bumper as a wall while the third swung around and pulled a sharp handbrake turn so it was facing the gate once more.

The front passenger door opened, and Hallberg

leaned out, beckoning them over frantically. 'Quick,' she said. 'Get in!'

They needed no further invitation. And as the Congolese army disembarked and started fighting back against Katenda's men, Church and Mitch shoved Foster into the back seat and climbed in after him, cramming onto the bench. The door wasn't even closed before the driver threw the car into first gear again and sped off, tearing through the front gate into the night.

Behind them, the sounds of gunfire rose and echoed in the thick African air, the first dim streaks of dawn setting the sky on fire in front of them.

THIRTY

TEN YEARS AGO

Church made it to the stairs and looked back.

Foster was walking after him, but Mitch was standing there, staring at Reed's limp body.

'Mitch,' he called out.

But Mitch didn't move.

Church nodded for Foster to go on to his room, get his stuff together, and then he went back for Mitch.

He put a hand on his shoulder, and Mitch jolted.

'This isn't the time to lose your shit,' Church whispered. 'I need you, Mitchy. One more push. We gotta get out of here.'

'I just can't…' Mitch started. 'Cole?' He turned to Church, his eyes wide and vacant.

'I know,' Church said. 'I know. And I hope I'm wrong. I really do,' he said, knowing he wasn't. 'But we can't risk it. If you stay, and I'm right…'

Mitch reached up and put his hand on Church's, squeezing.

They didn't need to say anything else.

Church pulled Mitch away, and they all climbed together. Where the others were, Church didn't know, but he also didn't care to find out. If they could be out the door with their kit by the time Reed came around—if he didn't bleed out from his leg first—then it would make their lives a whole lot easier.

But as Church gathered up his things, linked up with Mitch and Foster at the stairs, and started down, it wasn't to be.

They reached the landing of the first floor before they heard the voices. Hushed and hurried, but clear as a bell.

Church held up his hand, and the trio slowed, staying back behind the corner to the last flight.

The voices fell away below them, and Church could see Cole standing there, finger to his lips, quieting Boyd and Reed wordlessly, eyes turned towards the stairs.

Church slipped his pistol from its holster and held firm, hoping they wouldn't have to shoot their way out —but knowing they would.

'Church?' Cole called out, his voice soft and warm, as though calling up to a friend. 'That you, buddy?'

Church felt his blood rise.

'Come on, don't give me the cold shoulder here... I can explain everything.' The quiet but unmistakable click of the slide of a pistol being pulled back cut through the still air. 'Just come down here, and we can talk about this, alright? You've got the wrong end of the stick. And Reed'll even forgive you for shooting him. He promises.'

Church steeled himself.

'But I won't forgive you for ordering Murphy to shoot us. He killed Norton. Would have killed me if Mitch hadn't put him down.'

There was silence for a second.

'I don't know anything about that,' Cole lied. 'Come on, you're going to make me yell up the stairs to you like this? Let's deal with this like adults, shall we?'

'I wish I could trust you,' Church replied, the truth stark in his words. 'I do. But I can't. And I don't. And I know the second I stick my head out, you'll put a new hole in it.'

'Is that what you think of me, Sol?'

'That's the problem, Cole,' Church said coldly. 'I don't think anything of you anymore.'

He could almost hear the steam coming out of Cole's ears.

'This isn't right,' Mitch muttered next to Church.

Church turned his head to say that he agreed, but there was nothing they could do. Before he could say anything at all, though, Mitch was already around him, stepping into the stairwell.

Church almost lunged after him, stopping himself just shy of the corner.

Mitch was on the top step, hands at his sides, tense and stiff, as though waiting for a bullet to come. But one didn't.

'At least one of you has sense,' Cole said with an audible sigh. 'Come down here, Mitch.'

'Don't do it,' Church urged him, voice low enough that Cole wouldn't hear.

'Come on, Mitch,' Cole said again.

'Don't you *fucking* move,' Church growled.

'What's wrong?' Cole laughed. 'Don't you trust me?'

There was a change in the air, and Church knew it was going to happen before it did.

Silence fell like a curtain, and Mitch's hands locked into fists. He twisted like he was trying to jump out of the way, but before he could, a bullet hit him mid-chest.

He stepped back, the sound of the shot reverberating up the stairs an instant later.

Mitch staggered, a second shot clipping the top of his left arm.

Church watched as he dived back towards cover, three more bullets digging into the wall behind where he'd been standing.

Church and Foster seized him by the wrists and dragged him back behind the corner, panting and winded from the first shot, bleeding from the shoulder from the second.

They sat him against the wall and checked him over. He was clutching at his arm, the blood running steadily but not too heavy. Church peeled away his hand and checked the wound—just a graze, thankfully. Though the round lodged in his ballistic vest, right above his aorta, put more credence to Cole's previous claim that he could shoot the eye out of a field mouse if he wanted to.

'What the fuck was that?' Church asked him, not waiting for Mitch to catch his breath.

The man took hold of his shoulder once more and squeezed. 'Needed to see for myself,' he squeezed out through gritted teeth. 'Needed to see it in Cole's eyes.'

'Satisfied now?' Church practically snapped back.

Mitch nodded slowly. 'Yeah, that's kind of hard to argue with. So what now…' He trailed off, picking his head up to listen.

Church did the same. Cole had stopped his speech, but that didn't mean he wasn't doing something.

There was a clinking of glass, like bottles being moved.

Church, Mitch, and Foster all remained still, listening, wondering what he was up to now.

'You know,' Cole's voice echoed from below as the clinking continued, 'this isn't what I wanted. Not at all.' It almost sounded like he believed himself. 'I wish you could have seen your way to get on board. But that shit with Fletcher…' He laughed a little, and the sound of tearing fabric reached their ears. 'Once you crossed me on that, I knew. I knew it was already over.'

There was sloshing now, and Church's brain worked furiously to put the puzzle pieces together.

'I knew there was no coming back. But still… for it to end like this? That's the biggest shame of all.'

Before the sound of the match being struck even rang out, Church knew.

He gripped Mitch by the vest and hauled him to his feet, shoving him towards the stairs up before the first flaming bottle arced through the opening and smashed on the landing.

The spirit went everywhere, the lit rag setting it all ablaze. While not as flammable as diesel or petrol, anything over fifty percent alcohol content still burned surprisingly well. And that's what Cole had been looking for. Something strong. Something flammable.

A second Molotov cocktail exploded on the back wall, and flames licked the ceiling. There wasn't anything in the way of fire-retardant construction here, and the cheap polyester carpets, the plastic wallpaper—it all went up instantly, blackening and melting as the fire spread. Thick curls of acrid smoke coated the ceiling and threatened to choke them all then and there, and they threw their arms to their faces for protection.

The stairwell down was the only way out of the building, and for the next five seconds, they had a chance to make it—run through the fire and onto the ground floor.

But if they did, they'd be executed.

If they stayed here, though, they'd burn alive.

As that realization seemed to settle in for all three of them, they looked at each other. No one saying a word.

No one needing to.

This was the end, and the only thing they could do now was choose how they went out.

THIRTY-ONE

PRESENT DAY

FOSTER NEEDED A HOSPITAL, but there wasn't one.

He groaned and winced in the back as they made tracks for the airfield. Church hadn't considered the ramifications of what they'd done, but he suspected they'd be far-reaching now. Without Katenda running this place or paying those whose palms needed greasing, what would happen to Maroua?

The gunfire was still audible as they streaked through town, people now stepping out onto the streets and looking toward the noise.

'The army will do what they can,' Hallberg said, as though reading their minds in the silence. 'They'll keep peace here as long as they can, and hopefully, without the head of the snake, they'll be able to find some kind of peace.'

'You mean Katenda or Blackthorn?' Church asked gruffly.

She looked back at him but said nothing.

The driver veered off the main street and headed for the dirt runway they'd touched down on the day previous, tearing toward the open back of a dual prop.

The Trooper skidded to a halt behind it, and Church could see that in the narrow cargo bay, there was a gurney, an IV stand, and a tall guy with curly brown hair and glasses in a pair of cargo pants and a polo shirt.

'Thank God for Doctors Without Borders,' Hallberg said. 'We found him in the next village over. Looks like Foster got lucky.'

'Does he look lucky?' Church replied dryly, staring up at the kid. He was in his late twenties and lifted a hand nervously.

Hallberg climbed out, not wanting to answer that one either, and greeted the doc, an American by his accent. Church and Mitch helped Foster from the car and carried him up, laying him on the gurney, where the doc started assessing him, muttering expletives under his breath at the clear and widespread damage to his body.

Foster lay still, breathing through what must have been an immense amount of pain as the doctor poked and prodded, bearing it like the bull he was.

'Plane's going to Nairobi,' Hallberg said as the engines sputtered to life and the props started spooling up. She turned back to Church. 'I've arranged for an Interpol team to meet you on the tarmac when you land, get Foster to a hospital, and then debrief him!' she called, her voice rising. 'Have you got anything else for me?' The hope was apparent in her tone even over the wind rush.

Mitch hesitated before lowering his pack and handing over the laptop and the hard drive from the mine, albeit a bit reluctantly. Church understood. If they could get this back to the UK, to Fletcher, they could go through it, go public with everything.

But what Hallberg was doing trumped that. The investigation into the mine, the trafficking—it was bigger than just Blackthorn. And they needed to do what they could to help.

'If you find what you need,' Church yelled, shielding his eyes from the wind, 'you'll arrest Blackthorn?'

She hesitated, screwing up her eyes, her black hair flapping around her head. 'We'll build the case,' she said. 'Fast as we can. But it's part of a broader investigation. That's not my decision!'

'That sounds like a cop-out!' Mitch shouted.

'It's the reality!' Hallberg shouted back. 'I know it's not the answer you want, but once we pass this along, it's out of my hands!'

'How long?' Church asked. 'Until he pays?'

She just shook her head. 'I don't know! But you've made a real difference here! Saved lives. You should be proud!' She reached out and squeezed Church's arm. 'Thank you! I've got to get back, call my supervisor, but

Interpol in Nairobi will make sure you get home. You've got my word.'

She released Church's arm and reached inside her jacket, pulling out a card and handing it to him. 'If you need anything, call me!'

Church took the number and watched as Hallberg headed down the ramp, pausing to look back up at him from the bottom. 'Thank you for this. The world needs guys like you—whether it wants to admit it or not!'

And with that, she climbed back into the SUV, and it backed away. Above Church, the light changed from green to red, signalling that the cargo ramp was coming up.

It raised under their feet and enveloped them into the belly of the plane.

Church pocketed the card and held up his hands, glowing red in the light, still soaked with Katenda's blood.

Mitch was seething next to him. 'Part of a larger investigation,' he spat. 'Can you believe that? They're not even going after Blackthorn.'

Church's hands curled into fists. 'It doesn't matter,' he muttered, closing his eyes. 'Because we *are*. It won't matter whether Interpol comes for him in a week, a month, or even a year,' he said coldly. 'Because he'll already be dead.'

They touched down in Nairobi in the late morning, and a trio of unmarked police vehicles surrounded them, along with an ambulance. The doc on the plane had sedated Foster, and he was loaded into the ambulance, limp and unconscious, whisked away, flanked by two of the unmarked cars stocked with Kenyan police and Interpol officers.

One car remained, and a middle-aged man, tall and blonde, greeted Church and Mitch, not asking about the blood, the weapons, or anything else. 'I've been asked to take you wherever you need to go,' he said, his Dutch accent clear.

Mitch and Church looked at each other before answering.

'Home,' Church said.

'But maybe after a shower?' Mitch interjected.

The man smiled briefly at them. 'I'll arrange a flight for you. When do you want to take off?'

'Yesterday,' Church said, striding past him and toward the waiting car. 'The sooner we're back, the better.'

The next hours passed in a blur. An airport hotel. A hot shower. A phone call that a plane was waiting. Boarding. Take-off. Sleep.

The sun was down by the time they landed, the smell of wet, cold British air a welcome reprive from the heat of Africa. Church couldn't remember how much he'd drunk or eaten in the last few days, but it was not enough. His hands were wrinkled and leathery, the inside of his mouth chalk, gums raw from the corners of his teeth. Dehydration had set in.

Mitch drove them back to the farm while Church chugged bottles of water in the passenger seat, cleaning his weapons and reloading them, just in case Cole had decided to stake out the farm.

But all was quiet as they approached through the woods. They parked the car where they left it and rucked the last few miles, moving silently, approaching from the high side of the farm. Mitch slowed as they approached the treeline, and they both took to a knee, staring down at the rubble of his farmhouse. He looked at it sombrely but didn't say anything.

They both took out their binoculars and scanned the area thoroughly, and only once they were satisfied that the place was empty did Mitch dig out the sat phone and dial the number.

He had called Nanna before they'd set off from Nairobi to give her an update and said that he'd be in touch when they were back.

And now they were.

Church was fidgeting as the line connected. He listened to Mitch tell them to take the door, the tunnel to the shepherd's cottage nestled in the trees a few yards behind them.

When he hung up, Church let out a shaky breath.

'Of all the shit we just did, *this* makes you nervous?' Mitch asked, eyeing him.

He swallowed the lump in his throat. 'Just tired,' he lied. But Mitch was right, he was nervous. When he was alone, when he was in a fight, there was no one else. His world was small, and his actions had no consequences. If he lost his life, then it was everything he'd done catching up with him. Time to pay the piper. But seeing

Nanna, the girls, Fletcher even—it made it real. Too real. His actions, his decisions, had weight. Had fallout.

When he thought they were dead, he'd walked headlong into gunfire without concern for his own life. Wishing, even, for it to be over. For that release.

He was more than happy to have them back—he was changed by it—but it didn't come without its costs. His world had just got a whole lot bigger, and of everything he had faced, was facing, and would face, that scared him the most. The weight of the lives of others on his shoulders once more, a burden he'd not missed.

It was a few minutes before there was a loud clang and Church stood up, stepping through the undergrowth towards the dilapidated stone cottage being reclaimed by the forest. Ivy was growing up the side, the roof had half collapsed, and one of the walls was down where a tree had fallen through it. Anyone who looked at it would think nothing of the place, which was why it was perfect for the other end of Mitch's escape tunnel.

Mitch pointed Church to the centre of the room where an old, soaked piece of wood, rotten through, was lying across the middle of what had been the living room. It was moving slightly, and Church wasted no time pulling it out of the way. A featureless slab of steel stared up at him, one end lifting an inch or so before flapping back down.

He dug his fingers under it and hefted it upwards, revealing Nanna on a ladder. She shielded her eyes from the sun and then squinted up at Church. 'Jesus, you look like hell.'

'You want me to put the lid back down?'

She grinned at him and offered her hand. 'You going to help me out of this hole or not?'

Church lifted her clear of the tunnel and then pulled the girls up too. They were ruddy-faced, unwashed for a few days, and looked completely miserable. No phones, no internet access, nothing. In any other circumstance, Church would have said that kind of detox would have been a good thing, but they looked like they'd bite his face off for the chance to swipe or scroll.

Neither of them said a word to him as they stepped clear of the tunnel, staring around at the trees like they'd never seen them before.

Fletcher was last, and she took Church's hand, holding on tightly as he pulled her from the hole.

She got to her feet and dusted off her legs, almost falling back into the hatch. Church caught her by the arm and moved her clear of it.

'Thanks,' she said, offering a weak smile. 'Haven't really moved in a few days, feeling a little unsteady.'

'I get it,' Church replied, kicking the hatch closed with a bang.

The six of them stood there in the ruin of the cottage, none of them seeming to know what to do next.

Church had an idea, but it wasn't something that he wanted Nanna and the girls to hear. Mitch gleaned that and beckoned them towards him. 'Come on, we shouldn't hang around too long. There's a car in the woods. Not far.'

'How far?' Lowri asked, pouting.

'Just a little way,' he lied with a smile.

The girls grumbled and set off, and Nanna followed, pausing to get a look at the farmhouse. The smoke had now cleared, but the place was just a mountain of stone and charred wood.

'Fucking hell,' she muttered, staring down at it. 'Mitch, your house…'

'It can be rebuilt,' he said, almost sounding like he believed it. 'Come on. We should move.' He called Nanna over and gave a nod to Church. Fletcher lagged behind, imperative to what happened next.

She held on, waiting until Mitch and the girls were out of earshot, and then turned to Church, folding her arms. 'Seeing as you're alive, I'm guessing it went well?'

He started after Mitch slowly. It was a walk to the car. 'That's a relative term,' Church replied.

She stopped him, taking his elbow, determined to look in his eyes while she heard it. 'What happened? What was it like there?'

'The same. Worse,' he admitted, staring at her. He was surprised by how much she'd changed from the woman he met ten years ago. Being back there, he remembered her as she was—young and naïve, impetuous and determined. She'd lost that youthful shine, but she was still as beautiful as he'd thought when he first saw her on that runway outside Maroua. 'The mine's gotten much bigger. Katenda, Zawadi's lieutenant, was in charge of the whole thing now.'

'You questioned him?'

'I killed him.'

She took a little step back but kept her grip on his elbow, as though he'd run away again if she let go. 'What aren't you telling me?'

'We had a run-in with someone there... Interpol. They're investigating an international trafficking ring, and it led them to Maroua. Blackthorn's not just shipping cobalt out of the DRC anymore. He's smuggling people too. Girls.'

Fletcher's lip trembled a little, and she clamped her teeth together. 'Proof?'

'What I saw. What Mitch saw.'

'Anything tying Blackthorn to it?' she asked, looking at him desperately.

'I don't know. We pulled some hard drives, a laptop, but Interpol took it to form part of their investigation.'

Her hand fell from his arm now, and he missed its warmth instantly. It seemed like he didn't have any human contact unless it was his knuckles against someone's face.

'So they're not going to arrest him? Not go public with any of it?' she asked, the incredulity clear in her face.

'The officer we spoke to said her hands were tied. It wasn't her decision.'

Fletcher's eyes fell to the ground, and she shook her head. 'So what the hell are we going to do? We can't get a story out there without any proof. He's just going to keep doing what he's doing. He'll be prime minister.'

'No, he won't,' Church replied. 'I refuse to let that happen.'

'What other choice do we have?'

'We kill him.'

'And he'll die a hero,' Fletcher said.

'Better than having him walk around as one,' Church replied.

'There is another option,' Fletcher said slowly.

'What is it?'

'That depends. How much are you willing to give for this?'

'Anything.'

'Everything?' she asked, looking at him once more. 'We can do it—we can get a story out there, get it picked up.'

'What will it take?' Church asked, steeling himself for the answer.

'Your life.'

'I gave my life for this years ago,' Church said.

'That's just it. You don't need to give your life,' Fletcher replied. 'You need to take it back.'

THIRTY-TWO

TEN YEARS AGO

THE FIRE ROARED.

It ate at the floor, the walls, the ceiling, mutating and growing with every second, swallowing the stairs and the landing.

'Solomon.'

Cole's voice drifted through the flames.

'You can't win, Solomon. You can't survive this. Run while you can—I'll make it quick.'

'Tempting, but I think we'll go with door number two: fuck you,' Church called back, shielding himself from the fire. Mitch and Foster began edging up the stairs, the only way they could go. Higher into the building.

Cole laughed. A long, deep, cold laugh. 'It's fire, Church. Fire. To live in fire is a sinful thing, didn't your daddy ever teach you that?'

Church gritted his teeth, motioning Mitch and Foster up. He paused on the step and hung his head, hearing Cole's words.

'It's a good thing we're not the good guys after all, then, isn't it?' he called back. He stifled a cough and headed up, anything else Cole said eaten by the crackle and hiss of the fire.

Up, up, up they went. Second, third, fourth floor. They got to the top and slowed, sputtering on the smoke, their air quickly turning toxic up here too as the fire spread. The whole building was going to be in flames soon.

'Don't suppose this place has got a fire escape?' Foster grunted hopefully, looking around.

'No,' Mitch replied. 'Didn't see one when we did the recce.'

'So we're just burning to death then,' Foster said dryly, unholstering his pistol. 'Interest either of you gents in a quick and semi-painless death instead?' He held the gun up. 'I'll do you if you do me.'

Mitch's brow crumpled. 'I don't think that's how that works.'

'Quiet,' Church ordered, coughing on the smoke. He squinted through the building haze and headed towards the end of the hall, past where Blackthorn's room was. He hadn't seen head nor tail of the rat, but Church figured Cole had him stashed somewhere safe.

But Church wasn't aiming for Blackthorn's room.

There was one final door at the end of the hallway. It

was unmarked, but Church had been in Blackthorn's room, knew it butted up to the wall, which meant...

He didn't waste time, didn't bother with the handle, just put his foot through the door, splintering the wood and sending it flying inwards.

Beyond was a small concrete box, just breeze blocks and a ladder leading up towards a metal hatch.

Church looked back at the men, and Foster promptly holstered his pistol and came forward.

Mitch glanced back down the stairs, still clutching his grazed shoulder, his sleeve now red with blood, and followed.

Church went up first, shouldering open the hatch, and emerged into unrelenting sunshine. He screwed his eyes closed, climbing onto the gravel-covered roof of the hotel, and realised how tired he was, how dehydrated. The air inside had been air-conditioned but thick with smoke. Here, it was clean but hot and oppressive. He wasn't sure which he liked less.

He helped Foster out and then pulled Mitch free, a column of smoke rising around him as he climbed clear.

His knee-jerk reaction was to close the hatch, but he knew it was better to leave it open. The thickening smoke would be a good measure of how close the flames were. How long they had. But even now, it was impenetrable and black, the fire surging through the first, second, maybe even the third floor.

He was under no illusions that they had any time at all—a minute, maybe two, before the roof started catching, before it began to weaken. And as much as Church didn't want to burn to death, he definitely didn't want to plunge into an inferno if the rafters gave in. Which meant they needed to find a way down. And fast.

Mitch and Foster spread out to the edges of the building, checking the sides and back. They didn't need to check the front; they knew what was on that side, and if Cole, Reed and Boyd had vacated the ground floor by now, they might be watching the building go up. And Church definitely didn't want to get spotted. If they had any chance of getting off the roof alive, he didn't want to go right back into the stand-off they'd just escaped.

Church's side was a bust. Sixty feet straight down to a concrete roof.

Foster came back from the other end, shaking his head.

Mitch was standing at the back, staring over the edge, but he wasn't cheering, so Church didn't think it was a good option, whatever it was.

'Mitchy, you got something?' he asked, jogging over. He knew he was imagining it, but it felt like the stones were growing hot under his feet already.

'Nothing good,' he replied, putting his hands on his hips.

Church and Foster arrived in unison and stared down.

At first, Church didn't see anything, but then he spotted what Mitch was looking at.

'You're kidding,' he muttered.

'I don't see much of another choice, unless…' He

looked over to the open roof hatch, the smoke now coming out in a solid stream.

'It might be less painful,' Church admitted. 'Couple of deep lungfuls…'

'That how you want to go out?'

'I don't want to go out at all,' Church said, looking back at Mitch's plan.

Two storeys below, there was a cylindrical metal structure about six feet across. A sheet of corrugated metal, rusted and speckled with holes, had been fashioned into a rough conical lid. A small metal pipe ran from the side of it down into the building below.

This was their only option.

A water tower.

And there was no way to even know if it had anything in it.

'When was the last time it rained?' Church asked.

Neither Mitch nor Foster replied to that.

'Threading a needle,' Foster said instead. 'Best case scenario, you hit the middle of it, bust through the lid and land in five feet of water.'

'Worst case, you hit the side and cut yourself in two.'

Foster growled his frustration. 'Fuck it,' he said, taking a step back. 'Move.'

Mitch looked at him, then at Church, as though pleading with him to stop Foster from killing himself.

And Church obliged. 'No,' he said, stepping in front of the man and holding his hand up. 'It's too dangerous.'

'Someone has to,' Foster said back, trying to push him out of the way.

'I know,' Church replied. 'And it's going to be me.'

He looked at his two brothers and smiled, taking them both by the backs of their necks, pulling them in so their heads knocked together gently. He held them there, squeezing them for a few seconds. The last time he thought he ever would.

'I'm the reason you're in this mess—I pulled you into it with Fletcher. I'm the one who's going to get you out.'

'Or kill yourself trying,' Mitch scoffed.

Church grinned. 'Or kill myself trying.' He let them go and nodded to them both. 'It's been an honour, gents,' he said, taking his pack off his shoulder and slinging it off the roof.

He tried not to pay attention to the long fall before it landed next to the water tower. From this height, if there was no water, he'd shatter his legs. Probably his spine. He just hoped he'd have use of his arms if he did—the ability to lift his pistol.

Church steadied himself with a deep breath and squinted up into the cloudless sky.

The sun beat down, hot on his skin, and he thought of all the terrible places he'd been, all the terrible things he'd done.

'Not the good guys,' he muttered to himself.

And then he turned his eyes to the ledge, to the twelve feet across and thirty feet down to the water tower.

THE EXILE

To the almost certainty of his death.

And had to wonder if this was right—if it was just. If this was to be his end. Or if there was a road that stretched out ahead. Some greater plan for him.

He couldn't know that.

And he didn't.

All he could do was hope.

And with that in his mind—he jumped.

THIRTY-THREE

PRESENT DAY

'MY NAME IS SOLOMON CHURCH. I am a former SAS trooper, and I've conducted missions all over the world in service of King and country.' Church took a deep breath. 'Ten years ago, myself and a small team were deployed to the Democratic Republic of Congo to investigate claims that a warlord was exploiting locals to mine for cobalt, which was being used in batteries supplied to the UK for EVs and other industrial applications. We travelled there with Sir Walter Blackthorn, the man now running for Prime Minister, with the aim of negotiating better conditions and pay for those working in the mine.' Church looked up at the camera. 'During the course of that mission, Blackthorn schemed with several members of my team to conspire against the interests of the Crown for his own benefit. After removing the warlord responsible for the mine, Blackthorn installed himself as de facto leader and paid our brothers-in-arms to kill everyone who stood against the plot.' Church felt his blood rise, thinking about it. 'We should have died that day, but we didn't. And now, having been back to the DRC, I can confirm that these atrocities are not only still going on—they are worse than ever.' Church wanted to leap from his chair and scream it into the lens. 'Walter Blackthorn is a major part of not only a large-scale modern slavery operation operating in the DRC, but he is also trafficking young girls out of the country and into Europe. Into the UK. I ask you now—do not bury your heads in the sand. He is an evil man, and if you allow him to be your Prime Minister—if you allow him to walk free for another day—your country, your friends, your family, and the world will pay a heavy price. Do not let that happen. I failed in my duty to this country ten years ago to stop him, and I hope you won't make the same mistake.'

The little red light blinked off, and Church settled into the chair, exhausted. Twenty-mile ruck over the Brecon Beacons in the pissing rain with a fifteen-kilo pack? Any day of the week. Five takes reading cue cards to camera? Kill me now.

Mitch put the final card down and re-ordered the pack, giving him a quick thumbs-up.

He squinted in the spotlight they'd rigged, trying to make out Fletcher's expression behind the tripod. She didn't look happy.

'One more,' she said, watching it back on the little screen on the back of the camera.

'It's good enough,' Church grunted. 'We've been at this for hours.'

'You look like a homeless person,' she retorted. 'If you just let me—'

'No. I told you no make-up,' Church snapped. 'And I look like shit because we've just crawled out of the guts of Africa.' He stood from the chair and stretched his back, looking around the slightly shabby Holiday Inn room they'd rented for their Scorsese moment. 'I didn't mess that one up, so it's good enough. You wanted me to do this, it's done. You get that out alongside Mitch's photos from Maroua and your article, and it'll be enough—maybe not to have him arrested, but it'll be enough to derail his run at Downing Street, and hopefully enough to send him scurrying.' He stepped forward out of the light so Fletcher knew that it wasn't up for debate, and cut the air with his hand. 'We go to phase two. Now.'

'Music to my ears,' Mitch said, dropping the cards.

'You can get it done?' Church confirmed, stopping next to Fletcher and looking her in the eye.

She swallowed, then nodded. 'No promises, but…'

'Just get it out there. You said you had contacts. Use them. Call in every favour you have. We're not going to get two shots at this.'

She let out a rattled breath. 'Okay. What are you going to do?'

Church looked at Mitch. 'We're going to get ready. If nothing else, this will be a fight.'

Night fell, and the story broke. A few independent

outlets at first, some social media buzz. But then indie journalists started getting wind, and before midnight, it was splashed across the major outlets. They resisted often enough when things weren't to their benefit, but the story was going so big so fast, they had to grab the coattails or face the questions of why they didn't run it.

Fletcher had called in every favour she had, and before Big Ben even called the new day over Westminster, people were screaming for Blackthorn's head. Which was exactly what Church had hoped for.

Cole, Boyd, and Reed rolled up to his front door in Mayfair before the frenzy started, the police already redoubling their patrols in the area.

They brought Blackthorn out, still doughy but with more hair now than he had ten years ago, thanks to his trip to Singapore six years ago to get a transplant.

His fake locks danced as he trotted down his steps, covering his face with a signet-ring-clad hand to stop the long-range paparazzi from snapping his shamed expression.

They bundled him into the back of a blacked-out G-Wagon and raced away into the darkness, streaking through red lights and past speed cameras, desperate to be out of the city and away.

Blackthorn owned a country home in the Surrey Hills. A quaint little eight-bedroom summer getaway spot nestled in an acreage, away from the prying eyes of reporters.

They approached the electric gates at speed and opened them remotely, zipping through without braking,

Reed in the driver's seat and Cole next to him with his C8 Carbine rifle sitting upright between his knees.

His eyes roved the grounds as they tore up the driveway towards the house. An assault would be coming, he knew that. Church had announced his resurrection to the world and named Blackthorn in the process. Their photographs and names had been shared in the articles flying around, and the whole world was putting them under a microscope.

A deep, burning hatred festered in the pit of his stomach. He knew that he couldn't be angry with Church after what he'd done to him. But he was anyway. And now they needed to prepare for what came next. Coming here wasn't just about taking Blackthorn out of the media's reach—it was also about digging in, taking a defensive position that they could hold.

Church would be alone, or maybe with Mitch. Blackthorn had news from Maroua that Foster had been all kinds of fucked up. Not mission-capable. But two other men had assaulted Katenda's compound, and they had to be Church and Mitch.

And now, they'd be coming again. There was no way that they'd settle for scuppering Blackthorn's political ambitions. After this, they'd be out for blood.

The house was dark as they pulled into the driveway. It was a large tarmacked space in front of a Georgian-inspired house. Blackthorn had all but demolished the original structure and rebuilt it in his image. A mix of traditional and modern—a good metaphor for his political stances, too. Though he could posture about the mix of conservatism and liberalism all he liked, the reality was that he'd taken a piece of history with this house and, in his hubris, shat all over it.

But the new security system, the cameras, the motion sensors, the safe room in Blackthorn's office—all welcome additions at a time like this. Because as good as Cole was, he'd be a fool to think that Church wasn't a formidable combatant.

Blackthorn tried to open the door before the engine even cut out. But Boyd stopped him.

'Wait,' Cole said, glancing at Blackthorn in the rear-view. He never particularly liked the man. The opposite, in fact. But he paid well, and when you were in for a penny… 'Let us do a quick sweep first.'

Blackthorn paled a little in the darkness of the vehicle. 'Make it quick,' he spat. 'I need a drink.'

'You can get fucking plastered once we make sure you're safe,' Cole replied, giving Reed a nod to get out as well.

Boyd stayed put as the two men climbed from the vehicle and pulled back the bolts on their weapons, chambering a round, making them fire-ready. They headed up the stairs to the front door quickly, both distinctly aware that there were plenty of places to fire a long gun from in the treeline. But Blackthorn would be target number one, and he was safe in the car behind an inch of bulletproof glass. That's why Boyd was in there with him. Any sign of trouble, and he'd jump in the driver's seat and get Blackthorn out of there.

But nothing moved or made a sound, and they got to

the front door, punching in the code to open it. The lock clicked, and they stepped inside, the burglar alarm beeping to signal it was active.

Cole didn't let his guard down as he disarmed it, opening the cabinet next to it and pulling out a ballistic vest. He tossed it to Reed to take back to Blackthorn in the car, then pulled out a pair of infrared binoculars.

He signalled for Reed to get Blackthorn, knowing that the house was buttoned up tighter than a duck's arse. There was no way someone could get in without tripping the system. The house was secure.

As Reed went down to the car, Cole stayed on the top step, scanning the treeline for anything resembling warmth. A few birds nestled in the trees. What looked to be a mouse or rabbit skulking in the bushes. No bodies. Good. They were ahead of them.

He nodded to Reed, and he got Blackthorn out, pushing the vest over his head without asking and despite his protests. As he was escorted towards the house, Cole started flicking lights. Vaulted entry hallway with chandelier. Corridor to the kitchen. Living room one. Living room two. Study. Dining room. The whole place came to life—polished marble and stone, everything shimmering and shining like a fucking Christmas tree. A thousand blind corners, and as many hiding spots.

Cole had wanted to take him elsewhere, to a safe house or at least somewhere more defensible. But no, Blackthorn had insisted on this place.

He came up the stairs looking less than impressed

and lifted his hands at Cole. 'You happy now? Can I get a fucking drink?'

'Knock yourself out,' Cole growled, glowering at him as he passed.

Blackthorn shook his head dismissively and breezed past, heading for the study.

Reed and Boyd formed up in front of him—Reed bald and thin-lipped, Boyd brutish and square-headed.

'Sweep the house. Every room. Under every bed, in every cupboard, in—'

The first shot rang out, muted and dulled by the suppressor, but clear as a bell to him.

In the shine of the light from the house, the G-Wagon sagged sideways, the hiss of air escaping the oversized tyres audible through the still-open door. Another shot made the back drop, then another, and another popped the remaining two, and in seconds the vehicle was undriveable, sitting on the rims.

Cole's hand shot out, reaching for the lights, but before he got there, they died. Every light, all at once. The power to the house cut.

He froze, standing in the dark.

'What the fuck is this?' Blackthorn called from the study. 'What happened to the fucking lights?'

Cole drew a deep breath and looked at his men. 'Check all the doors, windows. Make sure this place is buttoned up. Tight,' he demanded, poking Boyd in the chest. 'I'm taking Blackthorn to the safe room.'

'I'll call it in,' Reed said, reaching for his phone. 'Get some backup out here.'

'No point,' Cole said, looking around the darkened hallway, just the smallest hint of a tremor in his voice. 'It'll be over by the time they get here—one way or another.'

Church and Mitch watched the house and had been for the last several hours.

They'd banked on Blackthorn coming here, bet everything on it. And they'd gotten lucky. They were at opposite sides of the property and had taken coordinated shots to put their vehicle out of commission. They might have taken a shot at Blackthorn while they were whisking him into the house, but Reed and Boyd had covered him well. Their training was unignorable.

And now Church watched Cole give the orders, and the men split up, taking a wing of the house each to do their sweep. The one advantage they had was that they knew how Cole worked, how he thought and how he strategised. But they were outmanned, and the men inside that house were no pushovers.

Church pulled back from his position in the window of the top floor and held up his phone. He'd watched Cole check the treeline for them on the video feed, and he hadn't seen them because they weren't there. They were already inside. And that was their head start: that Cole would have them focusing on the outside of the property, on ingress points first.

But they were already inside, and it hadn't been all that difficult. Like everyone else, Blackthorn was beholden to planning laws, and the plans he'd submitted for his house were public record. That was step one. Step two was getting the name of the security company he'd used and getting to them—finding the right person to pressure into risking their job to give away the information they needed to get inside without setting off the alarms.

The company's LinkedIn was the first stop, and finding someone in that roster who disliked the idea of Blackthorn getting to the PM's office, combined with what was breaking across every screen in the country, wasn't much of a challenge.

And then they were inside, tapped into Blackthorn's own security system. And with the alarm rearmed, Cole was none the wiser and was looking for them to hit from outside. The car was the final touch—four well-placed shots would have Cole searching distant cover for them. When in reality, it was Church and Mitch from either end of the house.

Church moved softly through the bedroom, stepping slow to keep the noise of his steps low. 'Mitch,' he whispered into the comm in his ear. 'Moving downstairs. I've got Cole herding Blackthorn to the saferoom in the master bedroom. Reed and Boyd are securing the ground floor. Wait until Blackthorn is stashed, and then seek and destroy.'

'Wilco.'

'Maintain radio silence,' Church said, pausing at the top of the stairs. 'Out.'

There was nothing more. Mitch knew his mandate.

Boyd. Church was to take Reed. Cole was going for the bedroom with Blackthorn, and they could make sure of that fact. Church watched him take Blackthorn in there and head to the back wall, to the walk-in wardrobe. He entered and hit the keypad, opening the saferoom and slipping inside. Cole stood sentry, rifle raised and trained on the bedroom door. And that's where he'd remain, like the good lapdog he was.

Church moved down, watching as Boyd swept towards the back door, the sunroom and pool, and Reed went the other way, towards the side terrace and statue garden. That's where he'd get him.

Church headed down the main staircase, giving the master bedroom a wide berth, and reached the ground floor. Mitch was just ahead of him and gave him a nod before plunging into the dining room and disappearing after Boyd.

Church steeled himself. The battle rifle was upstairs against the windowsill. This was too close quarters for a big gun like that. The suppressed pistol on his thigh was a much better option for room clearance. And it was why it was in his hand, leading the way towards Reed. The man was two rooms ahead of him, currently drawing the curtains across the French doors leading onto the terrace. By the time Church came up behind him, he'd be headed down the narrow staircase towards the lower floor and the statue garden beyond it, separated from the outdoor pool by the tennis court. The thought of Blackthorn playing tennis almost made

Church smile. But now, in the midst of trying to murder a former brother, he didn't feel much like doing it.

He slipped into the hallway leading onto the terrace, just the light of the moon spilling through the windows and the crack of the drawn curtain to guide him, and stalked Reed down the stairs.

The man was halfway down and moving slow, but with each footstep, the wood creaked. There was no way that Church would be able to get close to him without him knowing. And despite it all, he was above shooting Reed in the back. Or, at least, if it wasn't his honour preventing him from doing it, it was the need for Reed to know it was him. To look the man in the eyes as he made him pay for his betrayal.

But shooting him in the back of the leg? That he could live with.

He reached the top of the stairs and lined it up. Reed was moving carefully below him, rifle against his shoulder, covering the door ahead of him.

Church's hand was steady on the gun, but his finger wouldn't do it. Not like this. It was too clean, almost. Too good for him. A quick shot to the leg, double-tap to the skull.

No. Not for Reed, that rat.

He needed to know that he was bested. Or at least, Church wanted him to know that.

Fuck it.

He put his foot on the top step and Reed froze.

Now a smile crossed Church's lips, and he leapt

forward, throwing his right knee out and sailing through the darkness towards Reed.

He twisted at the sound and almost made it around before Church landed on him, knee square to the chest, blowing him off his feet.

Reed flew backwards and hit the wall behind him, stunned for a moment.

Church got his footing and drove forward, shoulder into his gut, the wind leaving him in a sharp, squeezed groan.

He stood before Reed, allowing the recognition to set in. 'Brother,' he muttered, pulling his pistol into position and blowing out Reed's right knee.

He called out with what little air he had in his body and did his best to lift his rifle.

Church caught it and twisted, listening to his index finger break, trapped in the trigger guard.

Reed was about to swing with his left fist but stopped when the cold steel of Church's muzzle kissed the soft patch of flesh under his chin.

'That's it,' Church said. 'Don't fucking move.'

'Solomon,' Reed said, looking back at him. 'It's good to see you.' His words were laboured. He grinned a little. 'I had a feeling you weren't dead.'

'Not for a lack of trying,' Church growled back, twisting the pistol.

The muzzle bit, and Reed winced just a little. 'So, what? You just going to execute me?'

'That's the idea.'

'I know things,' Reed said back. 'Things you can use.'

'Maybe,' Church replied. 'But I don't give a fuck. I just wanted to look you in the eyes before I killed you.'

And then he pulled the trigger, and the back of Reed's skull exploded, a bloody splatter arcing up the wall.

Church let Reed collapse in front of him as tiny shards of bone peeled themselves off the plaster and fell to the floor around him.

He stepped back from the man and looked down at him for another second, hoping that the suppressor, combined with it being pressed against the skin when the trigger was pulled, would be enough to keep the sound from reaching Boyd.

Now he had to hope that Mitch would be able to dispense with him too.

He had to trust that. Had to trust Mitch. And after all this time of being alone, trusting anyone was a hard thing to do. Was harder than he remembered. Harder than he realised.

Church shook those thoughts from his head. He had to focus on the mission here.

Had to focus on Cole.

On Blackthorn.

And with that fury, he found focus. And started back up the stairs towards his captain, his friend, his brother. The best and worst man he'd ever know.

THIRTY-FOUR

PRESENT DAY

'Reed is down,' Church whispered as he started back up the stairs towards his next target.

Mitch didn't respond, and Church guessed that meant he was still in the hunt, still about to kill Boyd and not the other way around. There was a fair chance Mitch had been bested, that he was dead and Boyd was already headed up towards Cole, but Church couldn't think like that. He'd deal with it if that eventuality arose, but not before he made his way back towards the main staircase, pistol raised, ears pricking for any sound of hurried footsteps. If Boyd had come out on top, he'd be running to Cole, but Church heard nothing. The house was quiet. Mitch was smart and would have the drop on him, and Church had faith he could get it done.

He mounted the stairs and took them slowly, sticking to the outside of the treads next to the wall to limit the noise and the chance of the wood creaking under his bulk. When he got to the upper corridor, he moved along it, closing his eyes briefly to recall the layout: where the master bedroom was and where the panic room lay inside it.

He pulled his phone out then and skipped through the security cameras, checking Blackthorn's bedroom to see Cole standing in front of the door, carbine in his hand. Church slowed as he approached, knowing that he'd never get inside before Cole pulled the trigger. No, he had to handle this differently than he did with Reed. He eased up to the frame and hugged the wall, readying himself, lifting his phone to make sure he knew exactly where Cole was.

'Building secure,' he called out, muffling his voice a little, hoping Cole would buy it.

Cole flinched and pulled up his rifle, staring at the door just to Church's left. He stayed quiet for a second and then, without warning, put half a dozen shots through the wood and into the corridor. Church screwed up his eyes as the bullets tore past him and into the wall opposite.

'Solomon, you out there?' Cole called. 'Or were you stupid enough to be standing behind the door?'

Church smiled a little to himself. 'I was hoping you'd forgotten what my voice sounded like.'

'Never could,' Cole replied. 'Still rattles round in my head every time I close my eyes.'

'Haunted by the ghosts of your past?' Church asked, resting his head against the wall, steadying himself.

'I've got plenty of regrets,' Cole answered, keeping his rifle tight against his shoulder, sights trained on the door.

'And is trying to kill me one of them? Or is it failing to do so that's keeping you up at night?'

'Can't it be both?' Cole laughed. 'You know there's still time... time to come over, time to make the right decision.'

'You'd still take me in after I just repainted Blackthorn's downstairs corridor with Reed's brains?'

Church watched as Cole tightened his grip a little on his rifle but didn't let the words get the best of him. 'That's the job,' he said. 'They knew what they signed up for. If they didn't want to die, they should've been sharper.'

'Ever the pragmatist,' Church said, reaching to his belt and easing a stun grenade out of the little pouch there. He very slowly removed the pin, making sure it didn't make any noise, and stared down at it in his grasp. 'You could just hand Blackthorn over,' Church said.

'Hand him over?' Cole laughed. 'He's locked himself in the panic room and there's nothing I can do to get in there. Which means if you've got any sense, you'll hand *yourself* over. I promise I'll make it quick, and I'll even leave Hannah and the girls out of it.'

Church let out a long, slow breath. 'Nah, you wouldn't,' he said. 'Because you know if you killed me, she'd come for you one way or another, and you'd be forced to do it. I know what you're like, Cole. You're a cold bastard, and you'd go in there, dead of night, and execute all three of them in their beds before they even knew I was dead. And you know what? You'd think you were doing them a favour while you did it, which is why I'm not going to make anything easy for you.'

Church stepped from the wall and tossed the stun grenade into the room. It landed, bounced once, and then detonated, the flash blinding. An instant later, Church was through the door, almost throwing it off its hinges as he charged into the room. Cole leapt backwards, shielding his eyes from the dazzling light with one hand, pulling the trigger with the other. A stream of bullets carved a deep line through the floor, wall and ceiling, filling the room with plaster dust, but Church was already past the line of fire and charging towards Cole, his pistol up and ready to resign him to the same fate as Reed.

But Cole was fast—just as fast as Church remembered—and reacted almost instinctively, throwing out his hand and blocking the rising gun, keeping it pointed right at his gut, his hand seizing Church's from the air like the strike of a viper.

Church changed tack, pulled the trigger three times, putting three rounds into Cole's ballistic vest, sending him staggering backwards with a pained grunt.

If he wasn't holding on to Church, he would have lost his footing—but he was, and Church stopped him from going over. He bared his teeth, spittle flecking onto Church's face as he tried to bring the carbine up once more, tried to cut Church's head off with it.

Church grabbed it with his other hand, fist around the muzzle, and Cole—squinting through the stars he was still no doubt seeing—pulled the trigger and held it, letting out a long stream of bullets that cooked the barrel in seconds, searing Church's flesh. He called out in pain, holding on desperately until he heard the click of the mechanism on an empty chamber, and then launched his head forward hard, forehead connecting with Cole's nose. It exploded, and blood poured down over his lips, soaking the pair of them.

But he wasn't done yet. Nowhere close. Cole dropped the gun in his right hand and sent a vicious hook into Church's ribs, making him spasm. Church keeled sideways and took a step back, tossing Cole's red-hot gun behind him. He protected his body but was too slow to react as Cole swiped across between them and stunned his wrist, forcing his hand open and sending his pistol flying under the bed.

Cole brought the back of his hand upwards in a vicious chop aimed at Church's throat, and it was all he could do to shove himself away from his former captain or be struck. There was space between them now, and they formed up, circling one another, hands up.

'You've gotten slow,' Cole spat, blood dripping onto Blackthorn's cream carpet.

'And you've gotten old,' Church replied, inspecting the deep lines on his captain's face. He'd aged more than the ten years since Maroua. 'All the shit Blackthorn's made you do weighing on your conscience?'

'You're not looking so good yourself,' Cole replied.

'Aren't we past this? Wouldn't you rather be raising a glass with me than raising your fists?'

'No, I've been waiting to punch you in the fucking face for ten years,' Church said. 'I'm not going to waste the opportunity now.'

He rushed forward, anticipating the knife before it flashed from the back of Cole's belt. He remembered where he kept it, and he also remembered how he struck —low and fast, the thrust aimed right for the gut to make it hurt, just like he always had. Church stepped in with his left foot and parried the blow with his forearm, feeling the bite of the blade into his skin as Cole tried to react. He spun past Cole's arm, stepping around, and drove his right elbow backwards into the side of Cole's head, the reverberation sending a bolt of lightning down his arm.

Cole staggered sideways and tried to keep his feet, but the blow was savage, and Church was already on him. He seized Cole's hand from the air and twisted it towards him, shoving the knife into the space inside Cole's right hip, just below his ballistic vest. Cole's hand opened, and he pulled it away, still dazed, but the scream that rose from his throat told Church the pain had registered.

Church took Cole by the neck now, his biceps squeezing against Cole's throat, locking him into a rear naked choke. He felt Cole's windpipe close and watched as his arms began to flail. Church wheeled him around, pulling him backwards so his heels caught on the carpet, then forced him down into a seated position, kneeling behind him, threatening to break his neck unless he yielded.

The only hope Cole had was to rip the knife from his hip, but if he did, the blood would come shooting out. There was no good place to get stabbed, but inside the hip was particularly bad, with plenty of major arteries and veins that delivered blood to and from the legs. They found a protected home inside the pelvis, and Cole's own knife was in there doing who knew what kinds of damage.

'Do it... do it,' Cole urged Church, squeezing the words out past Church's arm. 'Just fucking do it.'

'Bring Blackthorn out,' Church called.

Cole tried to laugh, but the sound was strangled. 'I wasn't lying. He's locked in that panic room, and there's no getting him out. You can kill me or let me live, but you're never getting to Blackthorn, and there are fifty guys on the way here right now to make sure that you never will.'

He tried to laugh a little more, and Church tightened his grip further, listening as the sound was extinguished.

'I wasn't talking to you,' Church said, looking up at the panic room in front of them. They were both staring in through the open door to the walk-in wardrobe—the door a solid steel slab at the back, completely impenetrable from outside. But the little red light above the door suddenly blinked green, and it swung open.

Cole tried to jerk, not understanding what was going on, but knowing he was beaten. Church held fast, held strong, and both of them knew he could snap Cole's neck at any time he pleased. He was just choosing not to.

Blackthorn appeared in the gap, furious and drawn, and stepped into the bedroom.

'What are you doing?' Cole managed, but Blackthorn didn't reply.

'Hands,' came a voice from behind him, and Blackthorn slowly lifted them next to his head. As he stepped into the bedroom, he revealed Anastasia Fletcher standing behind him, a pistol levelled at the back of his skull.

Cole squirmed, not understanding how, but knowing there was nothing he could do.

'This is for Africa, for Norton, for everything,' Church whispered in Cole's ear, and then he reached down to his hip, yanked the knife free with a spurt of blood, and drove it in between Cole's collarbones and twisted. Blood gushed from Cole's mouth, and Church let him go. He fell backwards, reaching meekly to his neck, touching at the grip of his combat knife but not daring to pull it free. He stared up at Church, his mouth filling with blood, and Church stared back down, watching it bubble over and run down his cheeks, feeling nothing as the life drained from Cole's eyes and he fell still for good.

Church turned his attention to Blackthorn then, who barely even glanced down at the head of his security.

'That show for me?' Blackthorn asked dryly.

'No, that one was just for me,' Church replied, beckoning Fletcher forward. She walked in a circle around

Blackthorn and handed the gun over to Church, who kept it steady, aimed right between Blackthorn's eyes.

'Can I put my hands down now?' Blackthorn asked, not waiting for an answer before dropping them with a tired sigh. He appraised the pair of them and pursed his lips. 'I suppose asking *"how much?"* is a little redundant.'

'A little,' Church said.

There was a creak outside the room then and Church glanced over his shoulder, watching as Mitch appeared in the doorway, his face bruised, and entered the room. Mitch gave Church a nod, looking down at Cole, then turned his attention to Blackthorn, standing at Church's shoulder.

'You know you'll never get away with this,' Blackthorn said. 'You know who I am. You know who my friends are. Killing me would be the most moronic thing you could ever do.'

'That's what they all say,' Church said coolly. 'And it never helped any of the others.'

Blackthorn bristled a little and puffed out his chest. 'Just let me go now, and I'll forget all about this. Forget all about you. But I'm only making that offer once.'

'Do we look that stupid?' Church asked.

'You really want me to answer that?' Blackthorn replied.

Church smirked a little.

'You know if you pull that trigger, your lives will be a living hell. You'll never stop looking over your shoulder. You'll never stop being hunted,' Blackthorn hissed.

'That's a price I'm willing to pay,' Church said. 'It's a price I've always been willing to pay.'

He glanced at Fletcher, and she looked back at him.

'I don't want to see this, do I?' she asked quietly.

'Not if you want something resembling deniability afterwards,' Church said back.

She glanced at Blackthorn a final time, her emotionless eyes lingering on her former employer, then laid a hand on Church's shoulder, squeezed as though approving his actions, and walked out the door.

Blackthorn let out a low laugh. 'Jesus Christ, you've really deluded yourselves into thinking you're the good guys, haven't you? That what you're doing here is right, that some kind of justice is being served by your hand?'

'No,' Church said, looking at Mitch. 'I accepted a long time ago that we're not the good guys. Never have been. But we're just going to have to live with that.'

And then, without another second's hesitation, he put Blackthorn's head between the sights and pulled the trigger.

EPILOGUE

PRESENT DAY

CHURCH STEPPED out of Blackthorn's mansion and down onto his driveway, a great weight lifted off him. He felt light for the first time in years.

The air was cool in his lungs, the night still full on them. Church glanced down at his watch, saw it was barely two AM yet. They'd be able to slip out and away before the sun came up. And by the time anyone came around to check, the bodies here would be long cold. What happened after didn't matter much. Not to Church at least. What happened to the country, to the world? That mattered. And Church was proud to know he had a hand in it. It didn't erase his past failings, but it was a start to make up for them.

Fletcher was standing in the darkness next to the G-Wagon they'd brought Blackthorn in. She was leaning against the wing, arms folded, dark bags carved under her eyes.

'Is it done?' she asked, not veiling the look of disgust on her face.

Church offered a nod, trying to read her expression. When it broke into a wry smile, he knew the disgust was for Blackthorn himself, not what they'd done here tonight.

She seemed to notice the wound on his arm then and came forward, pulling it up to get a better look at it. But it was dark, and Church didn't want to be here any longer than he needed to. He could tend to it later. And would.

'What happens now?' Fletcher asked, trying to tilt it towards the light over Blackthorn's porch.

'Now?' Church asked. He hadn't thought about it. Hadn't thought he'd survive the night. Or at least, he hadn't been betting on it. 'Now, I guess… we dig our heels in— *You* dig your heels in,' he corrected himself. 'You make sure this story doesn't get buried, that they don't spin it to make Blackthorn look like a martyr, that the powers that be, the ones who knew who he was and want to protect the empire of suffering and evil that he built, don't turn this around. Don't make his death some tragedy to be mourned. You make sure the world knows exactly who he was.'

Church pulled his arm towards his body, pulling Fletcher with it. She looked up at him.

'Don't let them forget.'

She swallowed and nodded slowly.

Mitch stepped down onto the driveway behind them, groaning and sighing. He was nursing his right leg, walking stiffly.

'You good?' Church asked.

He waved Church off. 'Yeah, just getting too old for this shit.' He held up the keys to the G-Wagon that he'd liberated from Cole's body and jangled them softly. 'Ready to get out of here?'

'Where will you go?' Fletcher asked him, finally releasing Church's arm when she realised she was still holding it. She cleared her throat, focusing on Mitch instead.

'Home,' Mitch said. 'To what's left of it, I suppose.' He sighed and screwed up his face.

'What's going to happen to it?'

'I'll rebuild it,' he said without hesitation. 'There's nothing else to do.' He looked at Church and Fletcher then. 'Many hands make light work, though.'

She laughed. 'Yeah, I've got my mandate: I've got to make sure the whole world knows what a piece of shit Blackthorn was. I'd consider my hands pretty full. Solomon, though…'

Church looked at her and then at Mitch.

'What do you say, Church?' Mitch asked. 'Or is that dingy cave on the Scottish coast calling your name?'

'It's a cottage, actually,' Church replied. 'And I could definitely spare some time to put your house back together. It's the least I could do.' He let out a long breath. 'And anyway, it might be better if I stick around a while. Stay closer to Nanna, make sure I'm on hand if there's any blowback from this, if anyone comes after us.'

'Once the house is done,' Mitch said, 'you could always fix up the old shepherd's hut at the edge of the forest.'

Church restrained a smile. Mitch had said that almost too quickly, betraying himself. He'd been cooped up out there alone for too long. Church had seen it when Nanna and the kids were around—Mitch liked having people there. He was lonely.

'Yeah,' Church said. 'Could do.'

'Well, if there's anything I can do to help…' Fletcher said, putting her hands on her hips. 'Anything that doesn't involve manual labour, of course.'

Church thought on that for a second. 'Yeah, actually, there is something you can do,' he said, looking around Blackthorn's empty driveway. 'You can find out what the hell Cole did with my fucking car.'

EPILOGUE II

FIVE MONTHS LATER...

Church was asleep when his phone rang.

When it did, he still leapt to attention. He wasn't used to owning a phone yet, let alone having it ring. And when it did, it only meant something was wrong. Four people and four people alone had his number: Nanna, Mitch, Foster, and Fletcher.

And if any of them were calling, it was serious.

Reflexively, he snatched the loaded pistol off the nightstand next to his bed and jumped out. His bare feet slapped against the cold flagstones of the shepherd's hut. The house was silent, the final few yellow coals in the log burner casting a dim light across the living room.

He ran to the window next to the door and pushed the curtain aside an inch, looking out into the darkness. What time it was, he wasn't sure, but the first flecks of dawn were creeping into the sky in the east. Nothing moved outside the hut, and slowly, he left the window and crossed back to his phone, vibrating on the bedside table. He picked it up, the old flip phone displaying the number on the blue-and-black screen.

He didn't recognise it.

His heart beat a little harder as he thumbed the top half of the device up and held it to his ear, not saying anything.

For a few seconds, there was silence, and then a familiar voice rang in his ear.

'You're a hard man to find, Solomon Church.'

At first, he didn't reply. He considered hanging up, breaking the phone in two and tossing it in the log burner. But it was someone he'd thought about, someone he'd wondered if he'd ever see again. Someone he wasn't completely unhappy to hear from. Though how she found him, and his number, he didn't know.

'Julie Hallberg,' Church replied softly.

'You remember my voice,' she said, her smile audible on the line.

'Hard to forget. There's also not that many people that think I owe them something,' Church said, easing himself down onto the bed and placing the pistol on the mattress next to him.

'Is that what I think?' Hallberg replied. 'You owe me something?'

'I'm guessing you're not calling in the dead of night for the *other reason* women call men in the middle of the night. You want something, but I don't think it's that.'

She chuckled a little. 'You know what, you're right—you do owe me. You went on TV and dragged Walter Blackthorn's name through the mud. You know what that did to our investigation? How many rats scurried back into their holes when they knew that Blackthorn's end of their operation had been exposed?'

'I suspect it fucked it. A bit, at least,' Church replied.

'You suspect right,' Hallberg said. 'You did fuck my investigation. Set it back *months*. Years, maybe.'

'So that's why you're calling,' Church said, licking his lip. The air was cool on his shoulders, the room cold now save for the meagre heat coming out of the hearth. 'You've got a problem that needs solving, like your problem in Maroua, one wrapped up in red tape. One you can't solve yourself.'

'And like you said,' Hallberg sighed. 'You owe me.'

Church narrowed his eyes in the dark, thinking. Extrapolating. 'You said rats have scurried into holes. Blackthorn's associates. You want me to drag these guys back into the light for Interpol to snap up? No,' Church said, realising instead what it was she was after. 'You want me to draw them out, don't you? You want to set the hook with me as the bait—these guys are going to want to hit back for what we did to Blackthorn, and I'm the perfect reason for them to make a move. And then Interpol moves in and grabs them.'

'You're perceptive,' Hallberg chuckled, 'I'll give

you that. But you're wrong about one thing. I don't want your help putting these guys in cuffs, Church. I want you to do what you do best.'

There was a pause, and even before the words came out of her mouth, Church knew what she was going to say.

'I want you to kill them.'

Church closed his eyes.

'You there?' Hallberg asked.

Church's hand settled on the grip of his gun and tightened. 'I've got just one question.'

'What's that?' Hallberg asked.

Church smiled in the darkness. 'When do we start?'

AUTHOR'S NOTE

Hello!

If this is the first book of mine that you're reading, then thank you so much for giving it a chance, and welcome. If it is indeed the first of my books you're reading, then you won't know that I finish them all off with an author's note.

It's such an inward experience, writing a book. You sit alone in a room for a couple of hundred hours, imagining all these things and then writing them down. You create these characters, these places in your head, and you spend so long on them that they become real—a whole world laid out inside the mind. And I think it's such a special thing to sit down and read a book and take that journey into what is essentially the writer's imagination. I love the idea that you've been on this adventure with me in some fashion. And now, here we are!

AUTHOR'S NOTE

For the last couple of hundred pages, you've had Church's voice echoing through the pages—or if you've listened on audio, it's been Scott Fleming's!—and now, you get a little of mine... or Scott's. Anyway...

I've written lots of books: romance, fantasy, science fiction, dystopian, historical... and, most recently, crime thrillers with the Jamie Johansson series. And now I'm writing military thrillers. Why the jump? Honestly, I've always wanted to. I've always had a deep fascination with the military—from the structure to the equipment, to the mindset and the brotherhood of it. I love war movies, I grew up reading Chris Ryan and Andy McNab, and I've always just deeply admired the men who put their lives on the line in the pursuit of something greater. Whether it's stopping evil men from doing bad things, protecting those who can't protect themselves, or simply operating by a code of morality that we all have and wish we could do more to appease... The pull of stories about modern heroes is as timeless as the pull of stories about the likes of Achilles or Hercules.

History is studded with men who fought back against evil, and when I began writing the Jamie series, I chose a female lead because I believed that the time of strong male heroes might have been fading. That we were in this sort of post-masculine world where tough guys who operated by their own compass and made the bad guys pay in blood were some kind of relic of the past, best left there.

And I'll admit—I was wrong. There's a lot I could

talk about when it comes to Solomon Church—a million reasons I made him how he is. But just know that, at its core, I wanted to add to the canon of stories with a character who's everything I wish I could be. Someone who did the things I wished I could do if the moment came. Someone stronger, braver, and more capable than me. But he's not a superhero, either. He's flawed, filled with regrets, carrying the weight of his mistakes and missteps. He's human. But he's willing to fight. And that's what matters.

I don't know. A lot of the time, I look around this world and see so much wrong with it. War, violence, and poverty in every corner. It can seem like there's little hope left. The worst people rule everything—politics, business, life. We're in a time that lacks heroes. And though I certainly don't want this series to be a political statement of any kind (don't worry!), I don't think it could exist without being in that zeitgeist. Without skirting prevalent issues.

The story of *The Exile* is fictional—there was no secret SAS mission to the DRC (that I know of, at least!) to secure cobalt mines for our EV supply chain and prevent China from monopolising. And yet, the EVs that run on our roads do use cobalt slave-mined from the Congo and DRC in batteries built in China. And we do have those in seats of political power who ignore humanitarian crises all around the world to ensure that our country is hitting its 'Net Zero' targets and such.

On Thursday, 30th November 2023, Lord Alton of Liverpool brought it up in the House of Lords, asking the government what action they'd take to support efforts to end the use of child labour from 'artisanal cobalt mining' in the DRC, urging them to exclude batteries resulting from slavery from the global supply chain. You can find this on the UK Parliament website under the title *Child Labour and Artisanal Cobalt Mining in the DRC, Volume 834*.

Walk Free, the non-profit that tracks modern slavery, says that the DRC has a 94/100 vulnerability score and that 407,000 (4.5 people per 1,000) live in modern slavery today (at the time of writing this). This doesn't include the number of children recruited into armed conflicts, though. In 2021, the DRC government identified that both adults and children were in forced labour in the cobalt mining sector, as well as being forced to mine for gold, tin, tantalum, and tungsten ore. And in 2019, a lawsuit was filed against global tech companies, seeking damages for the forced labour of children in cobalt mines in the DRC. Walk Free also notes the commercial sexual exploitation and trafficking of the people of the DRC. This is all available on the Walk Free website.

Amnesty International published an article in September 2023 entitled *Democratic Republic of the Congo: Industrial mining of cobalt and copper for rechargeable batteries is leading to grievous human rights abuses*. NPR published an article in February of the same year entitled *How 'modern-day slavery' in the Congo powers the rechargeable battery economy*. The Guardian, in November of 2021, wrote the article *'Like slave and master': DRC miners toil for 30p an hour to fuel electric cars.* And the list goes on.

As I said, this isn't a political book, and these stories are just that: stories. But I do want to draw from reality. I want the stories to hit hard, and I want to tap into this sense of justice we all have—the one we all want to see prevail. Normal people like us don't have that much power, not much ability to move the needle. We can vote, we can protest, we can go online and say how much we disagree, but what does that accomplish these days?

I think heroes like Solomon Church are important. They give us hope—that there are those out there who stand up for what's right, no matter the cost. Those who have nothing to lose and still want to give it for the things that matter. I wish I were as brave as Solomon Church—but I've got a family to provide for, responsibilities that keep me within the great machine. I think there's a part of all of us that longs to be outside of it, our own swords when the scales of our modern world don't seem to weigh up right.

I had more fun writing this book than any other in a long time. But it was also not easy learning about the things that made it more real. Every time I delve into subjects that make good fodder for these kinds of stories, I find myself feeling more and more hopeless. But it reminds me that heroes aren't gone. And they're needed now more than ever. I hope that Church gives you a little hope—that there's a modern counterpart out there, doing the right thing regardless of the cost. And I believe there is. I know there is.

In preparation for this book, I read a lot, and I listened a lot. Getting Church 'right,' in a sense, was important to me. I wanted him to be a rich and real character, reflective of the kind of person he might be in the real world. I listened to podcast after podcast with SAS soldiers, Navy SEALs, Green Berets, Army Rangers, and Force Recon …

Guys like Christian Craighead, the SAS soldier who was in Nairobi when the DusitD2 complex was attacked by Harakat al-Shabaab al-Mujahideen and went in without orders or backup to rescue the civilians. He killed several of the attackers himself and saved countless civilian lives. Shawn Ryan has had so many of these heroes on his show: John McFee, Tim Kennedy, Nick Irving, Chris Fettes, Tom Spooner, Nick Lavery, Kris Paronto, Rob O'Neill, Leif Babin … These are the men who inspired a character like Church. They're tough, they're focused, they're unstoppable forces. But they're also men of substance. They're family men—men who believe there is a right and wrong and are willing to be the person who steps between villain and bystander. I wanted Church to be like this—to be loyal, to be honourable, to be a good man. But to be a man who grapples with what that means every second of every day.

I was under the illusion that somehow we needed to trade old for new—guys like Solomon Church for women like Jamie Johansson. That this was the more inspiring route. But I think there's so much evil in the world that there's more than enough space for the old guard and the new guard to stand shoulder to shoulder.

And I hope you do, too.

Anyway—that's probably way more than my two pence for this one. I just wanted you to have some insight into what went into this book, into this story, and into Solomon Church. More than anything, I just hope you had fun between these pages and that you're interested in sticking around for the next one!

It's called *The Fury*, and it's a story of rage and revenge. We'll delve more into Church's past, his career, and the weight of his decisions, and we'll see what happens when one of his worst comes back to haunt him.

Thanks for reading. See you in the next Author's Note!

All the best,
    Morgan Greene

THANKS FOR READING

Reviews are the best way to support authors you like. They help other readers discover new writers, and they tell Amazon that books are worth reading! Just leaving a rating or a few words is immensely helpful to indie authors like myself, so if you enjoyed *The Exile,* please consider leaving me a rating or review when you have a second.

And if you'd like to reach out to me to let me know what you thought of this book, please do! I respond to all reader emails and messages when I can and I love hearing from you.

To stay up to date with all things Solomon Church and Morgan Greene, find me on Facebook as Morgan Greene Author, or head to my website: *morgangreene.co.uk*

SOLOMON CHURCH WILL RETURN

Almost two decades ago, a clandestine mission into Eastern Europe turned bloody. People died on both sides—not all of them soldiers. The truth was buried, the guilty walked free. But now, a deadly foe has risen from the ashes and he's hunting those who took his life from him.

He lost everything. And now he wants to watch the world burn.

Can Solomon Church find this ghost before he claims even more lives?

The Fury is out in 2025. Secure your copy today.

Made in the USA
Monee, IL
18 July 2025